ARTHUR REX

A Legendary Novel *by*
THOMAS BERGER

"FOR A THOUSAND YEARS THE ARTHURIAN LEGENDS HAVE ENDURED UNDIMINISHED . . . IN THIS TRIUMPHANT COMIC REAFFIRMATION BY THOMAS BERGER, THEY WILL CONTINUE TO ENTHRALL READERS . . . SPLENDID . . . SPEAK[S] ELOQUENTLY TO A MODERN AUDIENCE."
—*The Washington Post Book World*

"CHARM, INSIGHT, AND HUMOR . . . BERGER COULD MAKE US BELIEVE ANYTHING."
—*The Philadelphia Inquirer*

"A STUNNING TALENT . . . A REFRESHING EXPERIENCE . . . ONE OF THOSE RARE TOMES THAT THE READER HATES TO SEE DRAW TO A CLOSE."
—Associated Press

"A BAWDY CHARM . . . A FEEL FOR THE MEDIEVAL FLAVOR OF THE LANGUAGE AND LIFE-STYLE."
—UPI

"SUCCEEDS—AND SUCCEEDS SPLENDIDLY . . . A UNIQUE RENDITION."
—*The Houston Post*

Novels by

THOMAS BERGER

ARTHUR REX

THOMAS BERGER

A DELL BOOK

*TO MICHAEL
AND ARLETTE HAYES*

Published by
Dell Publishing Co., Inc.
1 Dag Hammarskjold Plaza
New York, New York 10017

A portion of Book IX originally appeared in *Playboy* magazine.

Dell ® TM 681510, Dell Publishing Co., Inc.

ISBN: 0-440-10362-2

Reprinted by arrangement with
Delacorte Press/Seymour Lawrence
Printed in the United States of America

First Dell printing—November 1980

The Rubrics of the Content of the Books

BOOK I

*Of Uther Pendragon and the fair Ygraine; and
how Arthur was born.*

Now Uther Pendragon, King of all Britain, conceived an
inordinate passion for the fair Ygraine, duchess of Cornwall, and having otherwise no access to her, he proceeded
to wage war upon her husband, Gorlois the duke.

Thereupon Gorlois closed his wife into the lofty castle
of Tintagel, high upon an eminence of adamant, and himself took refuge in another strong fortress called Terrabil,
which Uther Pendragon put under siege with a mighty
host of men, but nevertheless could not penetrate.

And unable to achieve his purpose the king fell ill with
rage against the duke as well as with love for the fair
Ygraine, and he lay endlessly on a couch in his silken pavilion, before which was mounted a golden device fashioned in the likeness of the great dragon from which he
took his surname (and which had appeared as a fire in the
sky over Winchester when he assumed the crown).

To Uther now came one of his barons, the dotard Sir
Ulfin of Rescraddeck, saying, "Sire, when you are ill, all
Britain ails."

"Even a dragon," said the king, "can be felled by love."

"But love," said old Ulfin, "can not be taken by sword
and lance."

"Yet the favorable conditions for love can be so established," said Uther Pendragon. "Could I take Terrabil, I should put Gorlois to death. The fair Ygraine, widowed and undefended, then must needs accept my suit."

"Alas, Sire, while we are fruitlessly occupied here upon the plain before Terrabil," said Ulfin, "the Angles and Saxons are regrouping their forces in the east, augmented by new hosts from barbarous Germany."

And Uther Pendragon fell back groaning. "Ulfin," said he, "I can not do without this woman. Unless I may have her, I can not rise from this couch, I shall sicken further and I shall die, and Britain shall die with me, and this beautiful land, which my forebear Brute, the grandson of Aeneas, conquered from the giants who then ruled it, will fall to the German toads and become a vile place named Angland."

And Ulfin nodded his old white head. "It is apparent to me, Sire, that this love which holds you in thrall, you who might on demand have any other woman in the realm but this one, is due to a spell worked upon you by some sprite or fiend evoked by one of your enemies—perhaps by another female whom you have spurned. Now, my counsel is that you consult Merlin, than whom no one is a greater authority on the powers of the unseen."

"A spell so powerful," the king agreed, "that it hath closed my mind to the obvious. Merlin, of course! If he could by magic transport from Ireland and erect in a circle at Stonehenge the monoliths that an entire army could not budge, he can get for me one damned little wench." But here he blanched and seized his beard. "I am overwrought, Ulfin. The fair Ygraine is for me the only woman in the world, and I shall die unless I can have her." He closed his eyes and his thick black beard did fall slack upon his mighty chest.

Now having taken leave of his sovereign, old Ulfin found him two knights and charged them to discover Merlin and fetch him hither with all haste, and these knights set out for Wales. After a journey of many days they found themselves deep in an enchanted forest at a spring called Alaban, and on the branch of a tree which hung over this spring sat a large raven whose body was so glossy black as to show blue reflections in the sunlight that filtered through the foliage.

And both the knights and the horses, being sore thirsty, drank from the crystal water of the spring (into which one could see forever because there was no bottom) and by the time they had soaked their parched throats the men had been transformed into green frogs and the horses into spotted hounds.

Now in despair and confusion the knights clambered with webbed feet from the steel armor which had fallen around them as they diminished in size, and the horses howled in dismay.

"None may drink of my waters without my leave," said a voice, and looking aloft the frogs saw it was the raven that spake.

Then the glossy black bird flapped his wings twice and before their bulging eyes he was transformed into a man with a long white beard and wearing the raiment of a wizard, which is to say a long gown and a tall hat in the shape of a cone, both dark as the sky at midnight with here and there twinkling stars and a horned moon. And the next instant Merlin (for it was he) caused both knights and horses to return to their proper forms, and only then did he laugh most merrily.

"Forgive me," said he, "for my magician's japery. Surely it did no harm."

Then the knights informed him that he was required by the king, and he revealed that through his arts he had long known the summons would come and should be at Uther Pendragon's side in an instant, and so he was. But the knights were constrained to return as they had come, and as it happened they were never seen again, and it was supposed they had been destroyed by monsters.

Now when Merlin materialized in the king's pavilion Uther Pendragon said to him, "Merlin, I have all the grief in the world, being ruler of all the civilized portion of it.

A spell or charm hath been put upon me in which I love to the point of madness the one woman I am denied. Either get for me the woman or relieve me of the spell, and thou shalt be granted any good that is within my power."

"Sire," said Merlin, "your distress is at an end. You shall lie with the fair Ygraine this night, and you shall have pleasure to the limits of your capacity, which a thousand women can certify is formidable as befits a mighty king."

"Thou undercounteth me somewhat, Merlin, unless thy computation refers only to the previous twelvemonth," said Uther Pendragon, rising from the couch. But then he peered suspiciously at his wizard, saying, "Methinks thou wilt ask a king's ransom for making this arrangement. Thy sovereign is not Croesus."

"What I shall ask, Sire," said Merlin, "is nothing which you now possess, no gold, gems, land, castles, nor serfs. The material is of no value to me, I who traffic in the ethereal." Saying which he moved his wand and for a moment the pavilion was thronged with airy spirits who danced on fox fire. But with another gesture Merlin caused them to vanish as quickly, and then he spake as follows.

"By your exertions this night you will beget upon the fair Ygraine a male child. This child is what I ask you to grant me."

Now though he had heard pleasantly Merlin's listing of the rewards which he would never ask for, the king was not quick to assent to the positive demand.

"A son? *My* son? Though having no interest in my gold, Merlin, surely thou art extravagant with my blood. My heir and successor? The next king of Britain? For what purpose, pray? To apprentice him in the black art of nigromancy?" Uther did scowl. "A British king kills many, but it would be unnatural for him to speak with the dead."

"Even so long ago as the reign of your predecessor," said Merlin, "the unfortunate Vortigern, who introduced the treacherous Anglish and the vile Saxons into this land to help him fight the barbarous Picts and savage Scots (and soon found the Germans at his own throat), I did prophesy the coming one day of a great king, the greatest king of all that was and would ever be amongst humankind."

"Indeed thou didst do," said Uther Pendragon, plucking from the little tree of stag horns next the couch his crown and placing it upon his head. "I have reigned now for twelve years."

"Truly," said Merlin, who was also a diplomatist, "only from the loins of such a mighty king could come the one who would realize my prophecy."

"I see," said Uther Pendragon, who could not long have ruled his realm were he a mere vassal to his own vanity. "Well, no man can escape what hath been foretold. If I am to be father to the greatest, and not the greatest in mine own self, then so be it."

"Therefore," said Merlin, "the time is at hand for the conception of that future king, whom you will beget on the fair Ygraine. And even as it is I who will make possible your begetting of him, so must it be I who will prepare him in the time of his nonage for the high office to come."

"I grant that which thou wouldst have," said Uther Pendragon. "But my pleasure in thinking on his future achievements is stained with the awareness that I must necessarily be dead before they come about—for I warn thee, Merlin, that I shall, unlike my forebear Lear, not while I live relinquish my crown to my offspring, be he another Alexander or Caesar."

"Far greater than either," said Merlin, and this statement caused a shadow to cross through Uther Pendragon's eye with the swiftness of a swallow darting over a battlement. Therefore the wizard was quick to distract the king with the nearer prospect of lust satisfied. "But now, as to the business with the fair Ygraine, through my craft I shall change you into the very likeness of her husband, the duke of Cornwall, and in such guise, while Gorlois stays besieged here at Terrabil, you shall go to Tintagel, be admitted to that castle as its proper lord and into the chaste Ygraine's bed as her rightful master."

Now this plan did bring a glint to Uther's eye, and he went to pick at his great nose even as it began to diminish in length and fatten at the lobes to become that, in image, of Gorlois. So did his height dwindle, the massive tun of his chest lose half its capacity, his legs bow, and his arms wither, for the duke of Cornwall was not a comely peer though married to a beautiful woman as is often the case.

And had not Merlin soon remembered to transform the king's robes into a perfect representation of Gorlois's clothing, the figure before him would have been ludicrous, with the crown supported only by the little ears like unto a squirrel's and the ermine piled high around his feet.

"God's body!" cried Uther Pendragon in a foul oath, staring at his altered visage in a looking-glass, "what an ugly toad is Gorlois and now, perforce, am I as well!" Then suddenly a terrible grimace did ugly his features further, and he grasped himself at the privy parts. But soon his brow cleared and he did grunt in an amazement that began as pleasurable but was shortly colored with wry reflection. "Either thou hast allowed me to retain mine own virility, Merlin, or" (and here he frowned in a certain envy) "there is substantial reason why the fair Ygraine hath ever been a loyal wife."

But Merlin diplomatically assured his sovereign that the former was rather the case, though in fact he had transformed him into the duke of Cornwall in every wise.

Thereupon old Ulfin was summoned, and Merlin changed him in a trice into the image of Sir Jordan, Gorlois's loyal retainer, and then Merlin transformed the day into the night, for the king was impatient to set out for Tintagel. But before they started for Cornwall, Uther Pendragon sent old Ulfin out of earshot and he spake privily to Merlin. And his voice was now that of Gorlois and of a thin and reedy quality foreign to his natural throat, the usual sounds from which were as of the drums of war (and when in his normal person he sought to whisper, the silken walls of his pavilion would tremble as in a tempest).

But as the duke he could scarce be heard until the magician came to his very stirrup.

"I have me the peculiarity," said the king in this weak voice, "with a woman I have long desired, to tup her so often with the tool of the mind that when it comes to close buttocks my actual meat will not stand. It is as if a malignant spell hath been put upon it."

"'Tis but the shock of reality (which always hath a touch of squalor) as opposed to the perfection of the fancied," said Merlin. "But be you now at ease, Sire. I myself shall accompany you in the guise of Sir Bertel, another of the duke's close retinue, and be assured you will be a stranger to this trouble, against which I can provide counterspells."

Then having taken on the mirror-image of Sir Bertel, a very fat knight with a mustache like unto the horns of an ox, Merlin was bored with the prospect of a journey of some leagues, and therefore he transported himself, the king, and old Ulfin instantly, through magical means, to the great ironbound gate of lofty Tintagel on its eminence overlooking the seat which was so far below that the surf could not be heard in its furious dash against the base of the precipice.

"Ho!" cried Sir Ulfin at the lancet window of the porter's lodge, within which all was dark, and "Ho!" thrice again, and then finally a feeble light did flicker within and at last a guttering taper was thrust into the window, the which served only to illuminate the turnip-nose of him who held it.

"Who stands without? And to what purpose? Speak, else I shall call the guard and loose the mastiffs."

"His Grace the duke of Cornwall!" cried old Ulfin.

And the candle did disappear and soon the huge bolts that secured the gate did squeak and groan and the ponderous counterweights were lowered and the great gate did lift.

"Your Grace," said the porter, bowing with his torch of pitch and tow.

Now Uther Pendragon was occupied with his lascivious anticipations, and he stared aloft among the many towers as if to identify that which would contain the fair Ygraine. But Merlin, in the guise of Sir Bertel, spake.

"Doth the main gate of Tintagel go unwatched except by thee, sleeping, in time of war?"

"Sir my lord Bertel," said the porter, " 'twas not this unworthy creature who made that arrangement but rather Her Grace, who did send the guard to bed and me as well, and the mastiffs would seem ailing or sopped, for they lie quiet in the kennels." The porter shook his head in the torchlight. "Indeed, had you not been the duke and his retinue, but rather the warlike Uther and his host, I fear Tintagel would have been easily overwhelmed and Her Grace most vilely mishandled by that most goatish of monarchs."

"Insolent knave," said Merlin. "Dost criticize the duchess of Cornwall? Thou shalt be whipped." But his false anger served to conceal his true amusement, and to himself he said, *that cunning baggage!* For not even Merlin, with all his arts, could divine the ways of women. And then he did wonder how she could have known the king would come this night, and he learned from the porter subsequently that these orders had been in effect since the duke had left Tintagel to be besieged in Terrabil at the very outset of the war, now a fortnight in progress.

But Uther Pendragon meanwhile did not await for the arrival of the grooms to dismount but rather flung his reins to old Ulfin, leaped afoot, and with lustful impatience hastened through the courtyard and hurled open the portal of the keep, which was unlocked and unguarded as well, and penetrating the darkness of the great entry hall, so lost himself, making a clangor amidst the shields hung upon the walls there.

"Ho!" cried the king. "A light! A light!" And at length

a steward appeared in nightdress, carrying a dripping candle and rubbing his sleepy eyes with his knuckles.

"Your Grace!" cried he in amazement, freeing Uther Pendragon from entanglement in the straps of a shield. "We were told by Her Grace that Your Grace had been slain in the war with the king and to expect your return nevermore."

Now Uther Pendragon was most pleased to hear this, but he nevertheless remembered to serve his imposture, and he said gruffly as he could in the duke's thin voice, "No more of thy prattle. Where is thy lady?"

"Surely in her bedchamber, Your Grace," said the steward, and he bowed, spattering tallow on the stones of the floor. "She hath not gone elsewhere since your departure."

"Give me that light," said the king, "and begone." But no sooner had the steward obeyed this order and gone away than Uther Pendragon realized that he knew not the route to the fair Ygraine's bedchamber, and he feared that he might spend the night in a vain search through the vast corridors of lofty Tintagel.

But meanwhile Merlin had come in from the courtyard, and he now undertook to guide the king to the private quarters of the duchess of Cornwall, the situation of which he knew exactly though never having been in this castle before. And soon this pair, monarch and wizard, in the guises of duke and knight, arrived before an arch framing a door upholstered in red silk onto which a golden dragon had been worked in cunning appliqué.

Now Uther Pendragon could not forbear from swearing vilely, "God's blood! The traitorous Gorlois doth privily usurp my device. I'll have his ugly head for that—after having swyved his beautiful wife."

But Merlin spake in a whisper. "Methinks that is the work of the fair Ygraine and unbeknown to the duke, whose head she doth expect you will have already taken. But soft now, Sire. She waits within." And the magician went to turn the handle of the door, but the king delayed him with a statement of great intensity.

"Thou hast done thy service, Merlin, and may retire."

"But was it not you yourself, Sire, who applied to me for aid? Think on your habitual peculiarity arising from passionate anticipation."

"Wouldst climb into bed along with me?" asked the king. "Art thou unnatural in this as in thine other modes of life?"

"As you wish, Sire. I shall await without until you need my craft," said Merlin.

"I command that thou go away altogether!" said Uther Pendragon. "I assure thee that having seen my dragon upon this very door I shall never know my old peculiarity once I am within." So saying he threw the door handle and plunged into the chamber beyond.

Now this proved to be but an anteroom, and he did hurl himself through it emerging in a chamber of which the walls were hung with silken tapestries, these illuminated by a fire which cast its glow as well on a bed upon which lay, under a robe of white fur, the most beautiful woman in Christendom, the fair Ygraine, her hair flowing down the velvet pillow like unto streams of molten gold.

And she had been in a slumber, but the clamor of Uther Pendragon's arrival (he whose stride was unruly by reason of his concupiscence conjoined with the duke's borrowed shanks, to which he was not yet used to walking with) caused her blue eyes to open and display their sapphire stars.

But recognizing her husband's mean figure she did corrupt her beauty with a grimace and say in ill-humor, "Gorlois! How in heaven's name—" But seeing him begin to divest himself of his clothing she left off the expression of disagreeable amazement at his return alive, and she hastened to inform him of the sickness that had claimed her on his departure this fortnight, which surely was the pestilence, association with which would kill him quickly as it was killing her by degrees.

Saying the which she swathed herself tightly within the white robe, making an impenetrable mummy-wrapping like unto those of the kings of Egypt who when living bed their own sisters and have skins as black as night.

But if the king heard these exceptions to his purpose he gave no answer, being occupied, damnably, with the to him foreign fastenings of the duke's garb, which did defy his fingers, and soon in frenzy he abandoned all restraint and tore himself altogether naked, dropping the tatters where they fell, and then he vaulted onto the bed, discovered the fair Ygraine within the white robe as lackeys unroll a carpet, and then he closed with her alabaster body as a ram doth address an ewe.

Now the fire had dwindled to powdery ash before Uther Pendragon did unjoin himself, though now much against the will of the fair Ygraine, but as after much killing even a king must rest, so in love, and he did stretch his limbs and cool himself and clear his throat and then, thrusting his tongue into the cavern of his cheek, he spake as follows.

"My dear Ygraine, I confess to thee that I am greatly relieved to find that thou hast been faithful to me—for no appetite that had been fed within the last fortnight could yet be so keen as thine."

"Methinks," said the fair Ygraine, "that absence hath also done thee a world of good, my dear Gorlois."

And Uther Pendragon grimaced sternly to repress his gloat, and elevating himself upon one of the duke's sharp elbows he said, "I never liked the gleam in the king's eye which fell upon thee at the Easter festival at London."

"The king, my lord?" asked the fair Ygraine, a faint flush introducing itself into her snowy forehead.

"The mighty and most puissant Uther of the Lion's Head," said himself. "Terror of the Paynims, Defender of the Faith, King of all Britain—"

"And most luxurious man, by reputation," said the fair Ygraine. "Thief of Maidenheads, Ravisher of Chastity, Scepterer of Subjects—"

"Be thou not too severe upon thy sovereign," said Uther, "whom we call Sire with respect to his divinely appointed role as father of his people. In submitting to him, a woman doth serve God."

"*Thy* wife as well, Gorlois?" asked the fair Ygraine with a peculiar flare of flawless nostril and stare of starry eye.

"Naturally!" roared Uther Pendragon, for an instant forgetting he was in the guise of the duke, and then with the quick wit which in combination with his keen sword had made him king, he said, "*Naturally* I should not assent to mine own cuckolding, not even by my king, to whom in all else I am a loyal vassal. But there are extraordinary situations of great extremity, enterprises of moment, pitch, pith—"

"In thine hot desire thou hast acquired a stammer," said Ygraine in chiding affection, and she did cordially place her long white fingers upon the summit of his belly, which was the duke's and as pale of wispy hair as the king's own was black and bristly as the back of a boar.

"Prithee, one moment more," said Uther Pendragon though he stirred at once. "Didst thou not enjoy the king's look upon thee? Didst thou not sip from the cup he sent around to thee at table? Didst never nibble at the dainties he took from his own plate for thee? These were marks of high favor, my girl!" And transported by remembrance, he reached across and slapped the smooth globe of her damask bottom.

"My lord," cried the fair Ygraine, recoiling. "Thou liest with the duchess of Cornwall, not with the great gross wench of the cook's."

"And by God I am the king!" roared Uther Pendragon. "That is, the *duke*, of course, the loyal vassal of the king. . . . I was merely putting myself in his place for a moment. With his eyes I seemed to see an answering light in thine own, there at Easter table. Methinks I saw good reason why when thine husband detected as much—that is, when *I* did—he led thee away from the festival without asking the king's leave, making the great insult which occasioned this war."

"One could not very well spit upon a titbit offered by a

king," said the fair Ygraine, soothing with her white hand her now rubicund ham. "One could not very well scowl into the smiling face of one's sovereign, though his ultimate purpose were base lechery."

"This was then but courtesy?"

"No more than," said Ygraine. "But as much as I could manage, what with the utter revulsion inspired in me by that great hairy brute of a king."

Now Uther Pendragon, who had continued to stir from the effect of her soft touch, did wither instantaneously and he would surely, if called upon to perform, have suffered from the old peculiarity to which he had made Merlin privy.

But as it happened at the next moment a thunderous knocking was heard upon the door of the antechamber and calling, "Sire, Sire!" someone continued to knock.

And the king leapt from the bed, saying, " 'Tis a courtier, with an impedimented speech, crying 'Fire!' Remain where thou art, in safety, whilst I go to see what burns."

And he strode into the anteroom in his gross nakedness, flung open the outer door, and seeing old Ulfin, with a torch and no longer in the guise of Sir Jordan, he gave him a great wink and said, in false annoyance, "Villain, how dare you knock me up?"

And Ulfin said, "Sire, the duke of Cornwall is dead."

"Is he now?" said Uther Pendragon.

"Having received an intelligence that you had left the field, Gorlois issued forth from Terrabil leading a host, the which, after a most bloody passage at arms, were defeated by your forces, Gorlois himself being among the fallen. Fleet courtiers have brought these news, and his head as well, which"—and here Ulfin did show his yellow old tusks in mirth—"is the spit and image of that which you do currently wear upon your shoulders, Majesty."

"Indeed," said Uther Pendragon in distaste. "Go thou and bring Merlin to transform me into my proper person."

"Sire," said Merlin, materializing from the shadows beyond Ulfin's light. And in the next instant the king felt himself swell and widen, and warm with his own pelt of black hair on head, cheeks, ears, nose, chest, reins, and even shoulder-caps and small-of-back. And only then did he know modesty, concealing his massy groin behind two hands, saying, "Death to him who looketh upon his king's nakedness."

And Merlin and Ulfin did go away, and Uther Pendragon returned to the bedchamber, expecting the fair Ygraine to demonstrate her astonishment, but seeing rather that she did not.

"My dragon!" she cried instead, and uncovered herself from the white robe, and it was not until a long time later that Uther Pendragon was able to satisfy his curiosity as to her lack of wonder at his appearance as himself.

And when that time came, along with the first light of morning, he asked, "Didst thou know me from the first though in the mean form of thine husband?"

"I do not pretend to know how thou camest by that guise," replied the fair Ygraine. "But I did not recognize the manner as that of the late duke. . . . Forgive me, I beg of thee, for failing to show more complaisance at the Easter feast, but Gorlois was a jealous man—though craving more for page-boys for his bed than me, but such is often the case."

"O vile man!" cried Uther Pendragon. "Nothing is more loathsome than the crime of sodomy. This is evidence that he treacherously leagued himself in secret with the Saxons, for 'tis a notorious German practice. I shall have his head mounted atop Lud's Gate at London for the populace to jeer at. But enough of this unnatural felon. Thou art now queen of Britain, or shall be when the archbishop of Canterbury solemnizes this arrangement."

Now, in his happiness the king forgot altogether that Merlin had told him of the child he would plant this night, and next morning he and the fair Ygraine, accompanied by a great host (for all of the knights of the late Gorlois now swore fealty to Uther), traveled to London, a journey of many days which brought about the devastation of countless villages along the route, though they were friendly and British, owing to the need of such a vast army for food. Nor was a maidenhead spared above the age of eleven, though none was, for once, taken by Uther Pendragon, who was most satiated with the fair Ygraine.

And arriving at his capital city Uther Pendragon was good as his word. Having mounted Gorlois's head atop Lud's Gate, with the legend TRAITOR AND SOD beneath the ragged neck, he forthwith had the old archbishop summoned from Canterbury to marry him to the fair Ygraine and crown her as his queen.

Now, as was his wont, the archbishop used this occasion to speak at length on the necessity to wage war upon the remaining pagans on the British island and to deplore any mercy that might be shown towards them as an heretical practice that might well bring the pope's excommunication of the offenders. Uther Pendragon thereafter went northwards with a vast host for to exterminate the savage Picts and the barbarous Scots, who were threatening to come across Hadrian's Wall and do the same to the Britons.

Thus the king was away when the fair Ygraine began to thicken at her white belly and grow more abundant of pap and to acquire addictions such as cutlet of griffin and roc's eggs.

But finally the day came when the queen was delivered of her child, by many of physicians and attendants, all of whom were afterwards put to death because they had seen the royal nether parts uncovered, and the babe was put into the hands of a wet nurse, who would also be disposed of when her job was done, along with her own infant and whichever other children had fed from the milk now being used to nourish a future king.

But Merlin materialized at this moment, just as the nurse had bared her dug, the which to offer to the tiny gasping lips, and he seized the child and saying, "I claim my prize," he vanished as quickly as he had come.

And the fair Ygraine, and all those present, did wonder at this strange event, but none would question the ways of

BOOK II

*How Uther Pendragon died; and how Arthur took
the sword from the stone; and of the challenge to
King Arthur by the Irish Ryons.*

Now Merlin had no facilities for caring for a babe, and
therefore he took the infant Arthur to a remote part of
Wales, to the abode of Sir Hector, the which was if not
mean then modest, for this good knight was an honest
man who had not profited by his service to the king except
in honor.

And Merlin found Sir Hector at the kennels, where he
threw offal from a basin to his slavering hounds.

Nor was Sir Hector amazed to see in such a homely
place the white-bearded wizard carrying a naked pink infant, for in that day men of worship did not question the
unlikely. "My lord," said this honest knight, "I am at your
service."

"Sir Hector," said Merlin, "I believe your wife is in
milk currently. I hold here a child which seeketh nourishment and beyond that a good British upbringing for the
next fifteen years, after which period has elapsed he will
go on from you towards the achievement of a special purpose. Are you willing to provide this without question?"

"On mine honor as Briton and as knight," Sir Hector
did instantly reply.

"You are a worthy knight," said Merlin. "One day you

will know the value of your service and be well re-warded."

But Sir Hector did frown as he pitched the remainder of what was in the basin to his dogs. "I do nothing for love of pelf," he said stoutly.

"Or love of self?" asked Merlin with his unique sense of irony, quite foreign to the mortals of that straightforward time, and the question was as obscure to Hector as if it had been put in the language of the Danskers. "Well then," the magician continued more soberly, "you are the foster-father of this child, and I ask you to raise him as though he were the proper issue of your own loins."

Now Sir Hector would have taken the babe from Merlin, but his hands were foul from the bloody offal, and being no rude Saxon who would wipe his fingers on his breech he said, "I shall summon my old woman, who will attend to this matter."

But saying, " 'Tis done," Merlin made the infant to vanish from the kennel yard and to reappear within the cottage, indeed within the very arms of Hector's wife, a-sucking at her left pap whilst her own infant son, Kay, was feeding from the right, and she did start, so that little Kay was dislodged from the nipple and did mewl. But Hector's wife, who had only just been delivered of her first-born, was much pleased to have its apparent twin, with hair as fair as Kay's was dark, and therefore she did not wonder long at its appearance for fear it might be an illusion worked on her by some sprite or fiend of the sort that preyed on Welshwomen and as such be made to vanish as quickly as it had come should she question its reality.

Thus when Hector came in to eat his midday meal she said nothing of this strange event, but in silence served him up his leeks and potatoes.

"A wizard," said Hector, "appeared to me at the kennels carrying a naked babe, the which he asked me to nourish and to bring up to young manhood. But, saying that, he vanished, himself and child as well. I tell thee, Olwen, I take this as a portent, with the hollow thunder we have lately heard in the mountains and at which the hair on my hounds' backs doth rise and my horse doth seek to cover his dung like unto a cat, and near the lake is the spoor of a wyvern of a kind hitherto unknown in Wales. Indeed we may be at the advent of a most monstrous epoch, as foretold by Merlin." He dropped his knife, with a great piece of leek on it, and uttered an uncharacteristically blasphemous oath. " 'Swounds! The very wizard who appeared to me was Merlin himself!"

And he plucked up his knife and chewed the leek. "I tell thee, Olwen, this is passing strange."

That good woman, saying nought, left the room, shortly to return with the new babe in her arms.

"Would this be it?" she asked.

"Or another very like," said Sir Hector, spearing up a boiled potato.

" 'Tis a pretty fool," said Olwen, rocking the wee infant in her arms. "I expect that if we are to rear it for Merlin, he hath provided or will furnish the means for this, for being an honest knight thou art poor and with now still another mouth to feed."

"Do not speak of that which is beyond thine understanding, old woman," said Sir Hector, who himself was seven-and-fifty while his wife was eighteen, but such was the routine style of address in bucolic Wales.

Therefore Arthur was not reared in luxury, but ate good Welsh leeks throughout his childhood, with only the odd sausage and that largely of meal and not meat, and his garb was the coarse stuffs woven by his foster-mother on her loom. Of footgear he had nothing in summer but rawhide soles secured to his ankles with thongs; in the cruel Welsh winters strips of old blanketing were wrapped up to the knee. His bed was a pallet, the straw of which was home to multitudinous bugs in all seasons, and in cold weather he was constrained to share the palliasse with the hounds, who had a great fondness for him whereas they

did spurn his foster-brother Kay, who at an early age acquired a disdainful manner that was at odds with his gifts
at that time, the which were not of note in any wise, while
Arthur was easily excellent at all he essayed. At riding,
archery, spear-play, and swordsmanship his proficiency
was exceeded only by his modesty and magnanimity, for
he would defer to Kay and often would misrepresent the
results of their contests in favor of his brother.

As when after shooting their arrows at a mark he would
examine the target, saving Kay the displeasure of wading
through the mud, and announce that his brother had as
usual been more accurate than he (though his own arrow
had split the center of the stave while Kay's had caught in
the bark at the periphery: which Kay could see quite
clearly, and therefore he did despise Arthur for pretending
to be worse when he was better).

And oftentimes at table, when Olwen, who Arthur assumed was his natural mother, gave him a larger portion
of food than she served to Kay (which she did regularly if
for no other reason than that Arthur ate robustly of whatever was offered, whereas Kay did toy with his plate and
curl his lip; and if Sir Hector saw this he would cuff him
to the floor, for that good knight lived by manly British
principles), Arthur might well try surreptitiously to exchange his greater quantity with the lesser plate of Kay,
thus earning his brother's despite once again, for leeks
were an abomination to Kay, who was in that, as in much
else, an unusual Briton and more suited by nature to the
menus of Rome, of which he had not yet had experience.

And the brothers therefore had no special affinity, Arthur having (though he did believe Hector and Olwen to
be his natural parents) an essential sense of his own superiority of mind, heart, and body, not only to Kay but to
all others; while Kay thought of Arthur as being all in all
a bore, but in no case did he hate him, for Kay himself
did not at that time aspire to be a warrior and indeed
would never have picked up sword or lance had Hector

been capable of envisioning another career for his sons than that of knight.

Now during Arthur's childhood Merlin did not appear in that part of Wales though he spent much time at the spring of Alaban, which was not far distant, refining his conception of the Golden Reign to come. On the occasions when a human being came into his vicinity, which were rare, because the spring was deep within an enchanted wood and could never be found except by accident, the magician would take on the guise of some beast or tree so as not to be disturbed by pointless conversation. But if a dragon came there to drink, Merlin would transform it into a timorous scampering little newt.

Now Uther Pendragon fought many wars against the Picts and the Scots and invaders from other countries, the Irish, the Danes, the Frisians, and the Angles and Saxons, and the Romans did attempt from time to time to take back the realm they had relinquished owing to their continental troubles with the Vandals, Huns, Goths, and Visigoths. And soon did Rome itself fall to the barbarians. And when there was no war available on his own ground, Uther went across the British Channel and assaulted the Normans, the Burgundians, the Flemings, and those various savage tribes which lived along the Rhine. He killed many men and took many maidenheads wherever he went and was considered the greatest king of his time.

Yet as the years went by he fell into a melancholy owing to his realization that the time of his reign was inevitably growing shorter, for no man could escape the tyranny of the tides, the phases of the moon, and the relentless seasons. And he came to find a sameness in his battles, for there was a limit to the ways in which he could ride his charger and swing his sword, and he had plunged so many spears into so many bodies and swiped off so many heads, that these experiences, once so gratifying, had become tedious. And so with females, of whom the wise man saith, *Turn them upside down, they do look much the same,* and the vile crime of sodomy was never to his taste, therefore when a pander once brought him a perfumed dancer from Egypt, and he removed its veils and found it a boy, he sent it away for emasculation and put the procurer to death.

And whenever Uther Pendragon was away from Britain, a conspiracy was formed by his rivals, who were usually related to him by blood (some being his own bastards), to seize power in that land, and because the king would take along with him the greater part of the British fighting men, the traitors must needs ally themselves with the Anglo-Saxon Germans, and soon this alien and felonious people would establish themselves in the southeastern portions of his country, and Uther was constrained to fight for reentry.

Now having become queen, the fair Ygraine had no further aspirations except to Heaven, and she would closet herself with the archbishop of Canterbury to pursue religious matters such as the social hierarchy of the celestial kingdom and where she should be seated at God's table on feast days, whether nearer to or farther from Him than the queen of Ireland, whom she considered her principal competitor. But when the old prelate in affixing around her swanlike neck a devotional medal did lower his yellowed claws within her bodice to tweak her proud breasts, the fair Ygraine dismissed him from her presence and subsequently studied in succession many another faith, the doctrines of Zoroaster from a Persian merchant of carpets, Judaism from an armorer (for the Jews had made that profession their own), and the worship of Druids, which is to say, for trees; and many more, as well; but finding them all wanting in some wise, she did settle on the religion of gluttony, in which one eats God in every bite, and she ate so much that her legs could not support her body, and she was carried about the palace on a litter borne by eight large footmen.

So passed fifteen years from the time of Arthur's birth, which neither the king nor the queen could remember with clarity, as they could scarcely remember the time when either had last seen the other, for when Uther Pendragon was in Britain he stayed mostly in the castle at Winchester, where he kept his dogs and horses in the great hall and himself bedded down on a pallet near them, for he had come to prefer the association with dumb beasts to that of men, while the stout Ygraine remained at London, now seldom leaving her chamber, where on a great bed she lay like unto a mounded white pudding with her eyes small as two currants.

Now by this time few but old Ulfin, who was now ninety-six years of age, dared to approach King Uther, for the king was thought to have gone off in his reason, forsaking his kingly duties to share mutton bones with his dogs and doing himself the mucking out of the stable he had made of the hall, though not often enough, for piles of steaming dung were everywhere and reeking pools where his animals had staled.

And during this time the barbarians increased their inroads into the realm, and soon the cities and villages under British sovereignty were islands in an Anglish sea, except for remote Wales and also Cornwall, in which Gorlois's successor Mark held sway and took unto himself the new title of king, which you can be sure Uther Pendragon, if his old self, would never have suffered him to do.

When finally the Anglish forces were nearing Winchester itself, old Ulfin holding his nose went unto Uther Pendragon and spake as follows.

"Sire," said he to the king, who lay upon straw before the disused fireplace large enough to roast three beeves at once for the banquets of yore.

Now the king recognized him with difficulty through reddened eyes and the unkempt beard which, not having been trimmed in many months, all but covered his visage. "Ah, is it thee, old Ulfin? Look thou there, at the sorrel!" He pointed to a snorting stallion that did at the moment lift its forequarters to mount a complaisant mare. "Once such cockstands were routine to me," said Uther Pendragon, directing Ulfin's gaze to rest upon the horse's stout tool, then he fell into a desolation, saying, "Alas, no more. Ulfin, I am ill."

"Ill, Sire?" asked the aged Ulfin.

"The corruption hath reached my brain, I fear," said Uther Pendragon. "I can fasten my mind to nought."

"Alas," said Ulfin, "the Angles and the Saxons are at our gates with a great host and can not long be withstood by our forces unless the men are inspired."

And at this Uther Pendragon did attempt to rise, for his British heart had not lost its valor, but his limbs were too feeble to sustain him. Therefore he commanded Sir Ulfin to fetch a litter and bearers for it, and it came and he was placed upon it and he was carried without the walls at the head of his army, where upon the plain before Winchester he did battle with the Saxons and he defeated them soundly. For though himself too weak to swing a sword, from his litter in a voice that was still mighty he urged his host on in such words as these.

"Cut down the shit-eaters and carve their rotten bellies out and wind their stinking guts around their necks and drive staves up their dirty arseholes. Rip off their ballocks and shove them down their muzzles," and so on in language of the greatest eloquence for its effect on the British warrior. And great carnage was made. But the effort proved to be the last such ever made by Uther Pendragon, for when he was carried into the castle once more he knew he was dying, and he did call old Ulfin to him and say as much.

Said Ulfin, "Shall I fetch the bishop of Winchester, for to perform the last rites so that you will be in the proper state to be received in Heaven?"

Uther Pendragon swore a terrible oath, the which the ancient knight took as evidence that the malady had indeed polluted the royal brain, and the king then roared, "I'd sooner burn in Hell than admit that bloody bugger! Fetch me Merlin."

But Ulfin did not have to go far, for Merlin appeared in an instant and came to the litter.

"Merlin," said Uther Pendragon, "thou dost find me dying. Nor can thine arts restore me now. But I seem suddenly, if dimly, to recall that I begat a child upon the then fair Ygraine many years ago, the which thou didst take away at birth. Dost yet have it someplace?"

"Indeed, Sire," said Merlin. "I know where he is kept."

" 'He,' " said Uther. "Then 'tis a male, Merlin?"

"Male," said Merlin, "and hale."

"Doth he, Merlin, display the attributes of a future king?" asked Uther.

"Those of a very great one," said the magician.

"Then," said Uther Pendragon, "I expect we had better find someone we can trust to establish a regency until this boy comes of age, who must now be five or six years old."

"He is fifteen, Sire," said Merlin.

"Damn me!" swore the king. "Can that be true?"

"Time, Sire, hath the speed of a diving falcon," said Merlin. "Arthur is tall and strong and already could unseat with his lance any knight now in this realm."

"Arthur's the name, is it?" asked Uther, still wondering at the age of his son. Then suddenly frowning he asked, "He is not a vile sodomite?"

"Certainly not," said Merlin. "He hath been reared in hardy Wales, far from the effeminacy of cities."

And though dying the king roared with coarse laughter. "Then he already doth tup fat ewes, Merlin. I too was reared rustically."

But Merlin was humorless as to the carnal appetites, being himself a stranger to them. "Assuredly, Sire," said he, "Arthur is pure in that regard and in all others."

"Then he's no son of mine," said Uther in disgust. "Nor, methinks, a suitable king for the robust British." And he made a feeble effort to rise from the litter. "Perhaps I shall not die now and leave my country a trunk without a head." But he lacked in the strength for further movement and he fell back groaning most bitterly. "There is no man who doth not lust for something," said he. "If not for females, then for his own kind. 'Tis the prime func-

tion of a man to use his prick, and a king is the quin-
tessence of manliness and a model to the masculine orders
beneath him. Swyving one's own sisters, as do the monarchs of bawdy Egypt, though a most unnatural practice,
is not so heinous a crime as having at a boy. O cruel destiny, that a sod should succeed me!"

"Forgive me, Sire," said Merlin, "but it has been or-
dained by another Power than yours or mine." (At which
old Ulfin, who stood near by, piously crossed himself.)
"And therefore 'tis no shame for you to hear, nor disrespect for me to utter, that yours is a primitive philosophy.
Superior to the unrestrained barbarism of the Anglish, and
the Picts and the Scots, it is itself savage *sub specie aeternitatis.*"

"Damn thy Roman parlance," said Uther Pendragon.
"Thou speakest like some prating prelate, Merlin. I had
thought better of thee."

Merlin said, "Your conception of monarchy was like
unto that of a child: action is all. Though you had some
simple sense of Britain as a land you must preserve and
defend, you were lacking altogether in the capacity to ele-
vate this to a noble idea. That which should distinguish a
king from another man is neither sword nor virile member, but rather a moral superiority."

"Once again a term for which I could find no meaning,"
said Uther Pendragon, "even were I disposed to search for
one. I shall die happily now, Merlin, to escape thy jabber,
which is no doubt in the jargon of alchemy or another of
thy recondite pursuits."

"Sire," said Old Ulfin, "neither do I understand this
fully, yet methinks Merlin hath some method apart from
his magic. Men grow old, even as you and I, and God suffers no one to live forever. Yet Britain continues, being
beyond human mortality. But merely to repeat is not to
continue. A successor who is but your image, great model
though it be—"

"Shut thine ancient meat-trap!" ordered Uther Pendragon, for he had no patience with prating even though he was not long for the world.

"Be assured, Sire," said Merlin, "that the best of your own qualities will be remembered, your hardihood, your courage—"

"My figure on a horse," said the king. "I rode well, methinks. I do not apologize for a certain quality of coarseness when afoot. I am no Roman fop. I do despise perfumes and baths. What my dogs won't have, neither will I. Steel armor is my wardrobe. I do not mince about in velvets. . . ." Here he did wince and grasp the hair on both his cheeks. "Ah, Merlin, methinks Death is disemboweling me as I once eviscerated Saxons. And is it night, then? Or only in mine head? Godsfuck, I do not like this dying!" And he uttered more hideous blasphemies to the degree that old Ulfin fell to his ancient knees and crossed himself multitudinously. Then using his sword as brace he rose to his feet and despite the king's expressed wish never to see the bishop of Winchester, staggered off in search of that divine, whom however he could not immediately find, for that man of God was off selling indulgences in the provinces, having no trustworthy pardoners in his employ at that time.

Now when the violence of his convulsion had ceased, Uther Pendragon said to his wizard, "Though I have defended the Faith from Scotland to the Alpine mountains, I should not be astonished to find the gate of Heaven closed against me, for kings are capricious in their ways, and I shall there be but a vassal to the most puissant monarch of all. If this doth indeed prove to be the case, wouldst thou, Merlin, recommend me in Hell? For I do believe thou hast some connection there through thy father."

But before Merlin could respond to this plea, Uther Pendragon gave up the ghost, and when this happened his dogs did howl most mournfully and his horses did neigh and stamp. But when word reached his barons, they emerged from the places where they had taken cowardly refuge against the Saxons and fell to quarreling bitterly amongst themselves as to the succession, for they knew not of Arthur's existence, all persons who had attended his birth having been put to death and, in the night after the day on which his father had died, his mother, the stout Ygraine, was suffocated by food lodging in her windpipe, for she had supped most gluttonously.

Then Merlin went to the archbishop of Canterbury (for though the wizard was not himself a Christian, he did believe that faith furnished a shape to the amorphous existence of men and an oriflamme to follow that did not so quickly tatter as those of mortal reigns), and he began to reveal his plan to that resourceful prelate.

"My lord," said Merlin, "I require your license to mount, in the yard of St. Paul's, at London, a block of stone—"

"Never," said the aged archbishop. "That is church property, Merlin, and it would be a great heresy to perform there a druidical ceremony." He drew from his sleeve a silken kerchief and honked into it like unto a goose. "Unless, of course, thou art willing to share thy collection to the measure of three-quarters." Anticipating an objection, he clapped both hands to his miter. "God love you, wizard, at such a place you have ready to hand a host of Christians who will gather for any entertainment, to stare openmouthed at a conjuror or dancing blackamoor. Thine one-quarter of the gain therefore will exceed the sum thou wouldst collect elsewhere. Therefore we urge thee not to be Hebraic in this negotation."

"Pray hear me out, my lord," said Merlin, secretly and mischievously changing the liquid in the archbishop's flagon from wine to water (for that churchman, a notorious toper, sat drinking in his chambers). "In this block of stone shall be embedded a sword, the which cannot be removed except by the next king of Britain."

"Aha." The archbishop nodded and squinted his eyes to demonstrate his quick understanding. "The sword surely will have an hole drilled through it, but cunningly concealed amongst an elaborate decoration of engraving.

The stone shall have a matching passage, the which, when the sword is in place, will oppose precisely the hole in the blade. Through the both, stone and sword, a bolt will be inserted secretly, to be maintained through the trials of those who would be unsuitable as king, but stealthily withdrawn when our favored candidate mounts the stage."

And he rubbed his old chin, making a rasping noise, for his barber, who was occupied with bleeding a trull, who was ill of a disorder of Venus in the stews that abutted the walls of St. Paul's, had not yet had opportunity to shave him that morning.

"We do like thy plan, Merlin," said Canterbury at length. " 'Twould calm the barons' quarrels, seeming as it would a heavenly edict. The sword must needs be replaced by another, without an hole, as soon as it is pulled forth. We must get hold of some rogue who is skilled at sleight of hand."

He gulped at his flagon and soon pulled a face. "Our steward hath been at our cellar and doth seek to water away evidence of his thefts. We'll have him racked and pulled apart at the nuts." Then he found himself and said, "That is, we shall chide him. God love the man."

And not wishing to bring punishment to some poor seneschal, Merlin changed the water to wine again, and spake as follows to correct the prelate's misapprehension as to the sword and stone.

"Nay, my lord, this will require no secret stays or latches. A solid cube of adamant hath been discovered in a fastness of Wales. Within this cube, sunken to the guard, is a sword with an handle of finely wrought gold encrusted with rare gems. At the base of the adamantine block, in a gold lettering of such radiance that it is like unto flame, is this legend: 'Whoso pulleth this sword out from this stone is the only rightful king of Britain.' "

"Merlin, Merlin," said the archbishop, "and I thought thou wert shrewd! These miracles are a penny an hundred. God knows we have had enough experience at them!" He hastily quaffed from his flagon. "That is, in ex-

posing them, of course, as vile blasphemies and burning
their perpetrators." He did add the wrinkles of wonder to
those of age, and stared at his wine that now tasted no
longer as water. He coughed and said, "We feel the onset
of an ague, and must call this audience to a close."

"My lord," said Merlin, "I assure you that this is no
charlatanry. The sword is sealed within the rock as if the
stone when molten had flowed around it and hardened.
You may inspect it with your own eyes and fingers."

Now the man of God knew Merlin of old, as being the
least likely to be gulled as anyone within the realm, and
though the archbishop officially deprecated Merlin's powers as rubbish, he privately respected, nay, feared the
wizard to the degree that he never wished to make of him
an enemy, for he put no credence whatever in Christian
miracles.

Therefore he now said, "Well, Merlin, as thou knowest,
the Church is no temporal institution. Caesar will do as
Caesar would do, as we say. Nor shall we stand in the way
of youthful enterprise, my lad." The archbishop at this
time was an hundred and four years old, whereas Merlin
was but the age of a century. "Go then fetch thy bloody
great rock and we shall inspect it."

"It stands already in the yard," said Merlin. And the
prelate rose and walked with an unsteady gait, owing to
age and wine, to the window and leaning, his miter against
a mullion, looked down and said, "We'll be buggered if it's
not! Thou art a cunning wight, Merlin. *Fait accompli*, as
we say in the Latin of the liturgy."

And he clapped his hands and he called for his chair,
and four robust lackeys brought it, and the archbishop sat
down and was carried from his palace into the yard of the
adjoining cathedral, where the stone stood with its protruding sword-handle.

"Our eyes are not so sharp as of old, Merlin," said the
prelate. "Do thou read the legend for us." And Merlin,
who was aware that the churchman was not literate in
British or any other tongue, performed as requested, read-

ing aloud the words that had not changed since his quotation of them earlier.

"Aha," said the archbishop. "If, as though believest, this is genuine, then 'tis passing strange, *weird* if thou wilt permit me that Saxon word meaning fateful or according to destiny. God knows we need a new sovereign in this realm, and that late lecher and his fat drab had no issue."

"Very good, my lord," said Merlin. "And in that conviction I did summon the barons, who are even now arriving."

For indeed the peers of Britain had begun to collect in the yard, and some bluffly and some with diffidence, each eventually mounted the wooden stage Merlin had caused to be erected and seizing the sword each endeavored to pull the blade from its adamantine imprisonment, but all without success.

"With that rum lot at hand," said the archbishop, "we had better to warn the beadles to guard the relics and other precious objects." And he forthwith had himself carried off into the cathedral.

Now all day the barons came and tried to remove the sword, yet by vespers it was still in place. And when darkness fell Merlin himself stood sentry at the stone till dawn, and thus he inhibited several attempts of the nobility, and one by the jades from the adjacent stews, to pry away and purloin the gems in the sword-handle.

Meanwhile Sir Hector and his sons Sir Kay (who had been knighted at the previous Allhallowsmas) and Arthur, approaching London on their journey from Wales that had consumed six weeks, had stopped for the night at Hammersmith, at an inn that offered bed and breakfast for twopence each, an outrageous price, but this was to be expected in the balieues of the capital: so said the honest Hector.

Now Sir Hector, and the newly knighted Kay as well, had a purpose for to compete in the annual tournament held at London at Christmas, which was two days hence. But when they had arisen next morning and eaten their porridge and were riding on the Great West Road towards London, Kay did discover that his scabbbard swung empty at his side, sans sword. Yet he would have kept the loss a secret, for though no coward he did relish not the jousts, which seemed to him a foolish employment for a man of his superior tastes, had not his father noticed the lack soon enough.

And Sir Hector did reproach his son, saying, "A knight should lose his sword only when he loses his life as well."

"Arthur," said Kay, "negligent boy! Thou didst not replace my blade after polishing it. Thou art a careless fellow. A good job I yet have my shield." For since Kay's knighting he had used his foster-brother as squire, in which role Arthur served with good-humored obsequiousness, thereby annoying Kay more than had he been lazy and impudent like a normal brother.

And now though the failure had not been his own Arthur accepted the blame and did ask Kay's pardon, which Kay granted soon owing to his sudden memory that during the night before he had thrown the sword at a wall within which a rat was gnawing and disturbing his sleep, and he had not remembered to retrieve it in the morning.

But Sir Hector was most vexed, saying, "Arthur, thy fecklessness is a shame. Being honest knights we are too poor to buy another sword, and without one Kay cannot compete in the tourney."

And so they had traveled by afternoon to the City, where while they were stopped at an horse-trough to water their steeds Arthur saw in a near-by churchyard a block of stone with a sword-handle protruding from it, and because the weapon had seemingly been abandoned by its owner (the barons having gone away in frustration), he went to the stone block and drew out the sword as easily as if it been stuck into a cheese and he returned and presented it to Kay.

But Kay drew back, saying, "Do not add theft to thy misdeeds, Arthur." And Sir Hector, who had never seen where the sword had been obtained, chided him as well.

Therefore Arthur conducted them to the stone, where Sir Kay read the legend written in gold on the stone, which Arthur in his haste had ignored.

Then Kay raised the sword above his head, and he cried, "I am therefore king of Britain."

But Sir Hector ordered him to replace the blade in the stone, and Kay mounted the stage and so did. "Pull it out then," said Hector, and Kay tried amain and could not move it whatever.

"Now, Arthur," said his foster-father, and Arthur did ascend the stage, grasp the jeweled handle, and draw forth the sword as easily as if from water.

"Sire," said Sir Hector falling to his knees, and Sir Kay then followed suit.

"Why do my father and my brother kneel to such a varlet as I?" asked Arthur.

"You are the king," Sir Hector said.

"But how might that be," asked Arthur, in affection reverting to the names of his early childhood, "when thou art my Da and Kay is my Bruz?"

"Your Majesty," said Sir Hector, "I was never your old dad nor was Kay your proper brother. Merlin brought you unto me when you were a babe, and promised that one day you would go from me to the achievement of a great purpose, which this is obviously."

Then Arthur came down from the stage and with the tip of the sword he did touch the shoulders of each of them, then commanded both to rise as his loyal vassals.

And Sir Hector said, "Sire, shall you love me yet though king?"

"We assure thee of our dearest affection," said King Arthur, "and in proof we would grant thee a boon."

"I wish nought for mine own self," said Hector. "For I am an honest knight who did never profit from service to my king. But for my son Sir Kay I ask this: that you make him seneschal of your court."

Now Kay did wonder at this request, which it would not have occurred to him to make for himself. But when

King Arthur with the most gracious condescension granted
Hector's plea, saying, "We shall do, and never whilst we
and he live shall another man have that office," Sir Kay
did reflect that in this service he would have the steward-
ship of the royal wine cellars and control the composition
of the regal menus, and thus he could pursue the interests
for which he had early shown a preference (if then, in remote Wales, in only a negative fashion, finding the diet
obnoxious on which he was raised).

"Sire," said he now, "I do thank you, and now I ask
your leave to go to the palace and arrange for your *déjeu-
ner,* which will be sumptuous in the degree to which your
breakfast was mean."

But King Arthur frowned. "Cold beef and pickes will
do nicely for the midday meal," said he. "As king we shall
eat no tarted-up dishes. Sumptuousness has caused the ruin
of the Roman Empire. On boiled meat we shall expel the
gluttonous Anglish-Saxon pagans and make our island a
British bastion."

Then he pointed toward the east wall of the churchyard. "And speaking of tarts, from the stage next the stone
we saw what looked very like a dreadful stews just there,
beyond the wall, and a queue awaiting entrance to it of
peers of this realm, as well as divers monks and friars."

Now at this point Merlin materialized from behind the
stone, which was large enough to have hid him naturally,
and the king was therefore not amazed.

"Indeed, Sire," said the wizard, "it is called the Nunnery
of St. Paul's and its strumpet residents, the Archbishop's
Sisters."

"Go and have it burned," commanded King Arthur.
"And send those unfortunate trollops to a proper convent.
As to that queue, and whoever is within the bordel,
feeding his beastly appetite—O scandalous baron, O
unchaste monk!—have all put in close arrest and delivered
to the Tower, there to be scourged."

And recognizing that this was the zeal of youth conjoined with a novel sense of power (but the lad was a real

king, for only such could have identified at long range a brothel, another ensample of which he could never have seen living in bucolic Wales), Merlin cast a spell upon King Arthur, in which he seemed to see smoke and flames arising from the stews, and therefore he was satisfied.

Now the king next demanded that the archbishop of Canterbury be brought to him, and Merlin fetched from the cathedral that aged prelate, who as always was carried upon his ornate chair by the robust bearers.

But seeing young Arthur the archbishop did snort, and ask, "Merlin, hast thou become a pander? A king? This is but a beardless varlet, and by the look of his soft cheek, a Nan-boy."

And Sir Hector did gasp, and seeing him the prelate said, "And this clown his father, come to sell him at London. Well, 'tis not mine own pleasure, but many of my bishops could not say as much."

Then to Merlin, King Arthur said, "Have this toad quartered, then burned. Then have his bishops flayed alive."

"Sire," said Merlin, "I would speak with you alone, as so often I spake with your father, in the privacy which befits the graveness of the theme."

Therefore the young king drew aside with the old magician, saying, "Methinks I know thee, but as if in a dream."

"I am Merlin," said the same, "and we were companions in your infancy. . . . Now, as to the Church, it is a very complicated business. Certes, its leaders are caitiffs, and what you have commanded is not nearly such condign punishment as they deserve. Yet as an institution Christianity doth provide a containment for the mob as the banks of a stream a channel for the water, and as a faith it doth meet the universal requirement of men for that which is beyond the evident, the which is often vile. And the Nazarene, by taking upon himself the guilt for all human pollution, hath proved the most cunning god of the many to which mortals have resorted."

"Merlin," said King Arthur, "in thy special situation

thou hast special privileges, but blasphemy (which is to be expected from the son of an imp) is never one of them. I shall be a Christian king because Christ was Our Saviour, and not because of expediency, political or spiritual. Loving and fearing God, I shall display no device but His Cross, and around me I shall gather, at a circular table at which no seat is more favored than the next, a body of knights as devout as they are brave. Our purpose shall be solely to serve the Right, by destroying the Wrong. There shall be no material magnificence, no personal aggrandizements, and no wars except in defense. Indeed, we shall offer our hand even unto all paynims, who will have nought to fear from us unless they reply with the sword, in which case we shall serve as God's instrument and strike them down.

"Our brotherhood shall be as chaste as it is pious. Concupiscence, gluttony, vanity, covetousness, envy, and sloth we do proscribe utterly, and those who practice these sins, unless in innocent ignorance, are our sworn enemies."

"Your list," said Merlin, "is wanting only in Anger, perhaps because you are, yourself, angry at this moment. I do counsel you to remember the four cardinal virtues, for not even a Christian king can rule long on the seven negations. *Prudence, justice, temperance,* and *fortitude.* Three of these, omitting justice, should be applied in this matter of the Church, which you distinguish (correctly, perhaps, though I am not the one to speak with authority of this) from the Faith. Mountebank, charlatan, rogue that he is, Canterbury yet controlleth that institution in Britain. If he is deposed at this time by you, you will run afoul of the pope, who is notably jealous in this regard. Then, too, the archbishop might well transfer his fealty to the detestable Saxons and serve Masses for their barbarous deity Wotan."

Now the young king did scowl. " 'Tis true, Merlin, that I am yet a novice at ruling, but must I accept thy cynicism? Is it not a poor beginning?"

" 'Tis rather a rich one, methinks," said Merlin, "if at the outset you see power clearly."

"Then what wouldst have us do with this filthy old man?" asked King Arthur.

"Have him crown you," said Merlin, and while Arthur waxed incredulous the wizard continued in this wise. "And with all ceremony and, despite your distaste for display, much pomp. When seated firmly on the throne you may do as you wish, but first you would be wise to do what others expect. Precedent may be mostly rubbish, but timorous mankind looks with less fear on that which is oft repeated, even if evil, than on the new, even if good."

"One thing we know as a kingly principle," said Arthur, "and that is that no monarch may hesitate for long. We shall therefore accept thy counsel, Merlin, for we know of thy powers, which have ever been at the service of the British throne."

"You will never regret this decision," said Merlin. "Subsequent to your coronation I shall cause the pope to receive intelligences to the effect that Canterbury does connive secretly to break away from Rome and establish his own British Church. Be assured that the old caitiff will soon be excommunicate."

And this was all done as Merlin promised. Arthur was crowned with great magnificence, and all the peers and all the commons swore fealty to him. And within the twelve-month a papal messenger came with the archbishop's excommunication, and Merlin spirited away the ex-prelate and dropped him over Hadrian's Wall, amongst the pagan Picts, whom he expected him to corrupt, thereby weakening some enemies of Britain without resort to violence.

But before that happened, King Arthur was constrained to fight two wars, the first of which was against an alliance of the very barons who had earlier sworn fealty to him at London, but then reaching the remote counties began to see as suspect the manner by which he gained the crown: which is to say, not by the traditional means of war, or at least murder, bur rather by sleight of hand, and joining together in a mighty host they did attack him.

And at the head of his loyal forces, the which were not mounted knights but rather common kerns who fought afoot, and brandishing the sword from the stone, he did defeat these traitors soundly. But once the war was over he took no revenge against the defeated.

Now King Arthur's second war was fought against the Angles and the Saxons, who did spurn his hand of friendship, and therefore he drave them from Britain and into the Channel, where those he had not killed by spear and sword perished by water, either by drowning or by the aquatic monsters who there abound and who cause the tempests for which those straits are notable.

Then King Arthur did remove his main seat from London, which had been a Roman town and yet possessed many souvenirs of that time, including ingenious systems of conduits to bring water into the buildings and even to warm it. And such decadent conveniences were believed by the king to weaken the British spirit (especially in the public baths, which encouraged the vile crime of sodomy), and therefore he took his court to Caerleon-upon-Usk, in Wales.

Then Arthur called Merlin unto him, saying, "Killing so many traitors and Anglish savages hath dulled our sword. The Jewish armorers have had to sharpen it so often as to grind the blade into little more than a bodkin. We know now it was thou who arranged for us to take it from the stone: and we ask thee now to furnish us with another sword, for King Ryons, who is sovereign lord of Ireland, hath sent us the most villainous and lewdest message that ever one king hath sent another, to this effect: that he would have us do homage to him by flaying off our beard and presenting it to him so that he might trim his mantle with it."

"Sire, you are yet too young to have grown a beard," said Merlin.

"That is beside the point, Merlin," King Arthur said,

ruefully rubbing his bare chin. "We can not accept this insult. Ryons saith furthermore that if we do not furnish him with the hair of our chin, he will cross over to Britain and lay waste the land and burn and slay and never leave till he takes the beard by cutting off our head which bears it."

"Then," said Merlin, "let us go to the Lady of the Lake." And he conducted King Arthur to a lake of which the water was still as glass until suddenly, as they watched, an arm clothed in white samite rose above the surface of it and holding in its hand a sword.

Now Merlin found upon the bank a punt and into it the king and he did enter, and Merlin poled it to the middle of the lake, of which the water was shallow until they reached the arm, and then there was no bottom that could be seen.

"This is thy Lady of the Lake?" asked King Arthur. "Doth she breathe water, Merlin? Doth she kneel amongst the fishes?"

"Take you the sword from the hand, Sire, and ask no more, for of any mysterious thing it can be said that to explain it is to degenerate it of all power."

Yet Arthur did still hesitate, saying, "Did not the greatest sage amongst the Greeks say that the unexamined life was not worth living?"

"Indeed he did," said Merlin, "but soon afterwards he was constrained to drink poison. Therefore perhaps he was not the wisest man in Athens but the greatest fool. Pray you take this sword, which is hight Excalibur. With it you will be invincible till the end of your days."

"Which," said King Arthur, "is to say nothing more than that a man liveth till he dies. The end of our days might well be the end of this very day, for example. Dost mean rather that with the aid of this sword we shall live longer than without it?"

"Indeed," said Merlin with wryness, "I mean just that, Sire. I am a wizard and not a logician, as you are a king

and not a philosopher. Any effort to compound these of-
fices is inadvisable. Pray take the sword."

So Arthur shrugged and bracing himself with a foot on
either side of the punt, did lean and grasp the cross-
handles of the sword, for the white hand clutched the hilt
firmly, and his movement caused the boat to swing away
behind him, so that he found himself arched over sheer
water, and he did cry out in a certain vexation.

Then Merlin poled the punt around so that the king regained his balance, and Arthur plucked forth the sword
from the hand, and the hand sank slowly into the water, in
the which, though it was clear as air, nought could be seen
except the rippling lights in its crystalline depths that
seemed to extend to infinity.

"A stout weapon," said Arthur, weighing the sword in
his hands, and then hurling it into the air, where it spun,
pommel over point, for several revolutions too rapid to
count, he seized the hilt from amidst the whirling brilliance
of its descent to the boat.

Now Merlin did gasp, and say, "Surely you are deft,
Sire, but I would that you performed no more legerdemain
with Excalibur." And from out of a secret place in his
robe he drew a scarf of such fine and weightless weave
that in comparison to it a cobweb would seem opaque and
gossamer leaden, and asking the king to extend the blade
horizontally, Merlin threw the scarf into the air above,
and it floated downwards more softly than dissipating
steam, and when it touched the edge of Excalibur it was
parted in twain.

And then Merlin poled the punt to the shore, where
stood an adamantine boulder large as three oxen, the
which had served a giant in his game of bowls, making a
sound that men an hundred leagues away believed thunder, and the magician asked the king to strike it with the
sword. And Arthur did so, with one blow dividing the
great rock as though it were a Caerphilly cheese.

"Now see the edge," said Merlin. And Arthur lifted the
sword and saw the keenness burning like fire from hilt to

point, the blade unflawed by the adamant. "Now," said Merlin, "read the legend engraved around the flange below the pommel."

And King Arthur did so. " 'When thou art done with me, return me whence I came.' " The king pondered on this for a moment and then he put Excalibur into the empty scabbbard on his belt. "No doubt thou art wise, Merlin," said he. "A king should not be too skeptical. Yet dost admit that he can not afford to be naïve? Is there a scale so fine that 'twill gauge the moral differences which are oft so delicate?"

"There is none ready to hand," said Merlin. "Each king must fashion his own, and determine for himself where pride becomes mere vanity, where apparent generosity is real meanness, where justice is not held in equilibrium but is overweighted towards spite or cowardice."

"Give us thy mind in this matter of the Irish King Ryons," asked Arthur, "for it is new to us to be mocked, though we are already much blooded in direct and honest battle."

"No one," said Merlin, "exceeds the Hibernians in bravery, but they do take delight in derisive wit. What they can do by the word, they save doing by the sword. This is their only economy. But do not believe King Ryons' boast to be empty. He will have your head if you permit him to take it."

Then Arthur touched the hilt of Excalibur. "Now, Merlin," said he, "if with this sword we are indeed invincible, would it not be unjust to do battle against a man armed with only a conventional weapon?"

"Not when it is he who seeks you out!" said Merlin with vehemence. "*You* do not yearn to decorate *your* mantle with *his* beard. 'Tis never justice, but rather sentimentality, to deal mildly with intruders. Magnanimity is properly shown only to the defeated. As to Ryons, you require only that he let you alone."

"Methinks," said the young Arthur, "that merely to be a British king doth attract envy."

52   *Thomas Berger*

And so they returned to the castle, and King Arthur sent to King Ryons an envoy with a message to the effect that he would never give him his beard nor allow him to take it without great resistance, and that if he tried to take it by force he would certainly fail and lose his own head into the bargain.

Now when King Ryons received this message he believed it a great impudence and he waxed wroth and did assemble a mighty host, with the which he embarked in a fleet of many ships and crossed the Irish Sea and, invading Wales, did arrive before Caerleon, where he drew up his army in array.

"Well, Merlin," said King Arthur looking from the castle onto the vast field of lances and pennons that extended to the distant horizon, "Ryons was not dissuaded from his emprise, and here he has come to meet his death."

"In furnishing which to him you must not feel regretful," said Merlin. "The old Greek Stoics accepted passively the imposition of a greater power than their own, and that was wisdom in their situation. But a puissant king must be as stoical, and as wise, in exerting such power as he possesses—when such exertion is necessary."

So King Arthur girt himself with Excalibur and taking up his lance Ron, he mounted his horse Aubagu, and ordering the drawbridge lowered, he proceeded at a deliberate walk to where King Ryons sat on his caparisoned charger before the vast army.

And coming to his adversary Arthur said, "You are Ireland, my lord?"

"Varlet, I am indeed," said Ryons, who was an huge man with a great ginger-colored beard which projected from the opened visor of his helm, and his great horse was half again as tall as Aubagu. "Go and tell thy king I am come to take his head and, having that, his lands as well."

"We," Arthur said quietly, "are the king of all Britain."

Ryons did stare at him awhile, and then he said in wonder, "Thou art but an infant. I came to beard a man." He shrugged within his armor, making his breastplate creak on its straps. "Well, boy, give me thy fealty and I shall do thee no harm."

"To you," said Arthur, "we extend the same offer, my lord. But had you stayed where you belong, we should not have asked even that. Of your own volition you came here as invader: you shall leave as vassal or corse."

Now King Ryons ground his teeth in ire. "Insolent boy! I have overwhelmed seven kings, and in homage to me they did flay their beards and give them me. Dost think a beardless varlet might defy me and keep his head? Defend thyself!"

Saying the which he threw closed his visor and pricking his steed galloped to a distance across the field, turned, and with lowered lance charged upon King Arthur. Therefore Arthur closed his own helm and gave the spur to Aubagu.

When the two kings met it was with a sound like unto a clap of thunder, for each lance met the opposing shield simultaneously, and both shields split from top to bottom and fell away in parts and the two lances broke in twain as well. But King Ryons was so distracted by his fury that he turned and charged again, though armed with but the stump of lance.

Now King Arthur drew Excalibur and when Ryons reached him, he leaned from his saddle and inserting the point of his sword between the greave on Ryons' leg and the horse's belly he did cut apart the leather that supported the stirrup, and Ireland's foot in the heavy steel boot thereupon dropped free. And so was his center of balance altered drastically, and he fell out of the saddle and onto the ground.

Then King Arthur dismounted and raising his visor spake to the Irish king as follows. "You have done what valor would demand. Now leave our country with impunity." And he offered his hand in aid of Ryons' effort to rise from the earth, no easy achievement when suited in hinged steel.

But Ryons struck the hand away and, with much heaving and squeaking, he climbed onto his two feet and drew his sword. Then he spake to Arthur, at first incomprehensibly within the visor, but then lifting it he said, "By accident I have been unhorsed, but 'tis no inconvenience, for I should have had to be anyway afoot when I cut off thy head. Thou hast a final opportunity to submit to me a vassal. Therefore kneel now, and live hereafter."

"My lord Ireland," said Arthur, "in justice we must warn you that with our sword Excalibur we are invincible. 'Tis a magical weapon, given us by the Lady of the Lake, and it can cut lace or iron with equal ease. To use it against a mortal man armed with a conventional weapon would defy the principles of chivalry—unless he were warned against it, as you are now."

"Chivalry, boy? What shitful rubbish is that?" asked Ryons, weighing the flat of his own great blade in his huge hands.

"A code for, a mode of, knightly behavior, in which justice is conditioned by generosity, valor shaped by courtesy," said King Arthur. "The vulgar advantage is declined. Dignity is preserved, even in a foe."

"And is that all?" asked Ryons mockingly.

And Arthur saw fit to add, "Graciousness is sought."

But King Ryons did guffaw in derision. "Thou art not only a boy, thou art a pompous ass of a boy! Hadst thou taken orders, thou shouldst already have been made bishop." He raised the sword. "Now, boy, were I 'chivalrous,' I should not take advantage of a beardless varlet, I who have vanquished many powerful monarchs, giants, and fearsome beasts, I who by force of arms won my crown amongst the ferocious Irish, the most awesome warriors on the face of the earth, each worth ten Britons and twenty Saxons. But as it is, I am a king and not a bloody prating little preacher. Thy Lady of the Lake is a whore, and her sword will soon make my toothpick. Defend thyself!"

And King Ryons thereupon lifted overhead his sword,

which was five feet long as he himself was seven feet tall, and then he brought it down in a two-handed cleaving of the air and with sufficient force to split an anvil.

But before the blade could reach him, Arthur stepped aside, making as he did so a horizontal stroke with Excalibur, so quick and deft that it was scarcely visible to the front ranks of the Hibernian host, and from the battlements of Caerleon, where his own forces were watching, it could not be seen at all.

Now Ryons' blade penetrated the earth, at a slant, for half its length, and as Ireland braced himself to pull it forth, King Arthur returned Excalibur to its scabbard and did mount Aubagu.

At this Ryons opened his helm and called out, "Poltroon! Dost flee?"

Looking down upon him, but not so far, owing to the great height of the Irish king, Arthur said, "Shake your head, my lord."

And Ryons did so, though more in puzzlement than to comply with the request, and his helmeted head did tumble off his neck and over his shoulder and plunge to the ground, where it rolled almost to the forefeet of Aubagu, who shied from it. And through the open visor Ryons' face could be seen, the eyes and mouth frozen open in amazement. Meanwhile the huge body still stood erect and from the severed neck sprayed a fountain of blood which descended on the armor and enmantled it like unto a crimson cloak.

Then from the battlements of Caerleon sounded a mighty roar of exultation, and from the Irish host a vast groan of despair. Then all of Ryons' army dismounted and fell upon their knees, and King Arthur went before them and addressed them as follows.

"Hibernians, ye have seen the necessary failure that will attend any invasion of Britain. Arise and go now, home across the Irish Sea, and no harm will come to ye."

At which the Irishmen, all ten thousand of them as one,

swore fealty to him and arose and went away as commanded.

But Arthur returned to the castle and he was melancholy of humor when he spoke with his wizard.

"Tell us, Merlin," said he, "why do we feel no sense of triumph in this?"

And Merlin answered, "Well, is not triumph a childish feeling, Sire? Perhaps though you are still young in years you have already become old in authority."

"Then," said King Arthur, "the feelings which lift the heart must be alien to a king? There can be no joy in it, no exultation? Nought but duty?" He pondered on this matter. "We have learnt that our father was more or less a barbarian. But did he not have it better?"

"But," said Merlin, "the era has changed."

"If the truth be known," said King Arthur, "we did admire the late Ryons for his ebullience, nay his very effrontery. He did wear his crown with a certain zest. Whereas we are afraid that he was right about us: we do tend towards pomposity. But we are young and yet beardless, and with Excalibur we are invincible in battle. How to be righteous without being sanctimonious we see as our problem."

"If I may be so bold," said Merlin, "it is not required for your dignity that you habitually use the first-person plural when referring to yourself. That you are the king and whatever you say is said by a sovereign and not a mere man is self-evident."

"Yet," said Arthur, "I am a man for all that. I must eat, sleep, and use the close-stool. What subjects look for in a king, methinks, are not reminders of their own baseness but rather that which is elevated above it. And speaking for myself, after a reign of two years, I must say that what a new king requireth is a constant reassurance of his own kingliness, especially if he hath yet to celebrate his eighteenth birthday and with no beard to frame his face. When I say 'we,' therefore, I am addressing myself foremost."

"Not even with my powers," said Merlin, "can I provide you with a real beard, for only Nature can create hair. But I can place upon your chin the illusion of a beard, the which will serve your purpose until you can grow a real one."

"But, Merlin," asked King Arthur, "would this not be dissembling? If I am a true king, how might I wear a false beard?"

" 'Twould not be false," said Merlin sighing. "Magic, Sire, is that to which reason cannot be applied." He cleared his throat. " 'Tis another realm of being. A fish cannot converse with a bird, because each inhabits another medium, yet they both exist and in so doing share the universe. So with magic and reality."

"Which fish?" asked King Arthur. "And which bird?"

"Neither," said Merlin. "Both are real, but air and water are magical."

And now King Arthur frowned and said, "How so?"

"They have no individuality," said Merlin, "one drop of water, one breath of air being like every other of their kind. They have no duration, which is to say no beginning and no end, for if water leaveth here, it goeth there: so with air. The general amounts of both in all the world do never change. Finally, by application of fire, water changeth into air, to which if cold is brought, air changeth again into water."

"This," said King Arthur, "is alchemy, Merlin, and beyond my province. I must deal with men. Already I have learned that they come in all variations. To do perfect justice to them they must be dealt with individually. But a king hath not sufficient time to treat fully with every idiosyncrasy of each of his subjects, not to mention those persons who come from abroad to invade his realm, like Ryons, whose spirit I nonetheless admired."

"But only," said Merlin, "after you killed him."

"Perhaps unjustly," said Arthur, "with an invincible sword."

"Without it you had been a boy of seventeen, and he

seven feet high," Merlin told his king. "But would you not nevertheless have faced him?"

"Certes," said King Arthur, as if in wonderment at the question. "Doth a king have such a choice?"

"Well, some might," said Merlin, "but you do never. Therefore you must not refuse the help of my magic, which at its most powerful could not misrepresent your character."

And so did Arthur acquire a luxuriant golden beard, on loan so to speak from Nature until it was natural for him to grow his own. And having this, and Excalibur, he needed for his rule a Round Table, knights with which to furnish it, and the most beautiful woman in the world for his queen.

BOOK III

How King Arthur had converse with a lady, and
who she was.

Then eleven kings from the north came into Britain for to
attack King Arthur, and he fought the third war of his
reign, the which lasted for three years.

Now during a respite between battles, his enemies having been repulsed in Wales and gone to the neighboring
kingdom of Cameliard for to besiege King Leodegrance, a
loyal ally of Britain by reason of his old friendship with
Uther Pendragon, a beautiful lady came to Caerleon to
seek asylum there. And little did King Arthur know that
she was the wife of King Lot of the Orkneys, for she
represented herself only as a woman in distress, though
her secret purpose was to do harm.

Now Merlin's powers were defied by women (unless
they had already, as with Arthur's mother the fair
Ygraine, determined independently of him to follow a
course that happened to serve his wishes), and therefore
he could be of no service to King Arthur in this case. And
King Arthur believed this lady's account of how her castle
had been overwhelmed by the hosts from the north, her
husband its lord and all his men killed, and all resident females but herself ravished most foully, she alone escaping
through a hidden postern in the wall.

And King Arthur was now twenty years of age, but he

as yet had had no experience of females, and though when dealing with men he had put aside the pomposity that had been noted by Ryons just prior to that king's losing his head, he returned to its use now, for this lady had long chestnut-colored hair of high gloss and an ivory neck that was bared to the division of her thrusting bosom, and her robe of pale-green velvet was as a second skin on a body of luxuriant health, which would not suggest that her castle had been so long under siege that she did suffer famine.

And she knelt rather more closely to the throne than even courtesy would require in a subject, and Arthur found that this proximity disturbed him strangely.

"We grant thy petition for asylum," said he.

"And my castle, Sire?" asked the lady. "Shall I ever see it again?" Now the tears did well from her comely eyes green as emeralds, her snowy breast heaved in anguish, and she seemed to offer to swoon, so that Arthur rose and taking her hands brought her to her feet.

"Lady," said he, "we are engaged in a war of some magnitude, and we have only just repulsed the enemy host. Soon we must needs meet them again, and though our cause is righteous and they are condemned by God to eventual defeat, the strife will first be violent. We can not therefore promise thee in meticulous particularity when we might retake thy castle." And here King Arthur extended his arms in a gesture of hospitality. "Meanwhile, Caerleon is thine."

But the lady mistakenly saw his gesture as rather an invitation to embrace and she fell against his bosom with her own. And from this movement King Arthur recoiled, stepping backwards, and the edge of the throne did meet the hinge of his knees, and he sat down, the lady descending into his lap.

As it happened he was unattended at this time, the lady having asked for a private audience with him, owing to the shame it would be for a noblewoman of her high degree to relate her distress in the presence of lower or-

ders. Therefore Arthur had to deal with this unprecedented event on his own. Now, had the lady in sitting in
his lap acted by volition it would have been lese majesty
but there was great reason to assume that she had rather
lost her balance, a loss to which he himself by retreating
had contributed.

Whilst he pondered on how to deal with this matter as a
king, the warmth and weight of the lady's body did arouse
him virilely, and though as a Christian he knew these sensations as detestable, the principles of courtesy inhibited
him from dislodging her abruptly, and before he could do
so with polite deliberation, she had further chafed his loins
by adjusting her situation, clinging to him around the neck,
his beard (which was now real) falling into the devision
between her breasts, for her bodice gaped open. Her moist
lips were thus brought to the proximity of his ear.

"But are we indeed safe in Caerleon, Sire?" she asked,
her breaths tingling at his temple. "Do your forces guard
all the walls, and in what number? And are there secret
posterns through which the furtive enemy might insinuate
himself? Tunnels, cellars, underground galleries, hidden
stairways? For this is a cunning foe."

Then she sprang from his lap of a sudden and did color
prettily, saying, "Ah, I am but a defenseless widow."

Now King Arthur coughed to remove an obstruction
from his throat, and he rose from the throne. "Thou hast,"
said he, "a military turn of mind, to be commended in a
woman. But not to worry, for Caerleon is well defended at
all points. And such secret entrances as are here and there
tucked into its walls are secured by massive bolts, the
which, unless opened from within, are impregnable. And
who amongst my people would throw the bolts? Treason is
unknown in the simple, loyal philosophy of the British
folk."

"A spy, Sire?" asked the lady.

"None such could gain admittance," said King Arthur.
"In these times the drawbridge is kept raised and both
portcullises lowered. Only we ourselves may order them

dropped or lifted as the case might be, as indeed we did lately on thy weeping arrival."

"Forgive me please my fears," said the lady. "But mine own castle was similarly protected, and yet it was soon taken, by means of a mine dug beneath the eastern wall, through the which the enemy did burrow into the cellars like unto a swarm of rats. Pray let me accompany you upon a tour of Caerleon and point out such places as would be accessible to clandestine entry."

Now King Arthur was much taken with this lady who thought like a soldier while armored only in green velvet and helmeted in silken hair the color of the hide of his favorite horse but with another scent, as he had ascertained while she sat upon his lap.

"Very well," said he, "let us make such an inspection."

Now he was about to call his retinue for to provide escort, but he decided that it would be pleasant to be alone with this lady for the tour, which would have small practical value, for Caerleon was impregnable.

Therefore he took one of the burning torches from its bracket on the wall and hurling aside a great tapestry of Arras he thereby discovered a little doorway giving onto a spiral staircase that connected the throne room with the lower regions of the castle.

"Ah," said the lady, "this is just such a privy passage as might be employed by a regicide, Sire, unless it is well guarded at the inferior extremity."

"As it is not," said the king. "For 'twould not then be privy, as thou must needs admit." He was in a jolly mood, for this tour seemed to him a lark. His torch however stank of burning pitch and alas he could no longer smell the lady's scent. "Now," said he, beginning on the downwards spiral, "mind thy step. Yet never worry if thou dost slip, for thou shalt be contained by the walls enclosing this helix and thy tumble would not be precipitate. In any case I shall be not far below."

"Your speech, Sire, is sufficient unto your majesty," said the lady. "I shall linger behind a turning or two, for to evade besmirchment by your fuliginous torch." For a draught came from below, and the enclosed staircase performed as a chimney for the smoke from King Arthur's light.

Therefore she waited as he wound around beneath, until the playing of the flame on the gray stones of the wall was the dimmest shimmer, and then she raised her robe and took from her garter a bodkin with a long slender blade furnished with a point keen as a needle.

"Dost descend?" King Arthur asked hollowly from below.

"I do," said the lady, holding the dagger sinistrally against a fold of skirt as with her dexter hand she followed the curve of the wall and felt with her dainty feet the stone treads, of which she used the broadest portion, at the maximum of their centrifugation, and the masons had laid them with such marvelous exactitude that each conformed to the rule of all, so that having found the pace, one could misstep only willfully, unless the constant revolution ever downwards agitated the humors causing vertigo.

The which, in the case of this lady, came to happen, owing to the rapidity with which King Arthur with boyish vigor made his own descent and her need to reach him and stab him before he arrived at the bottom of the stair.

Therefore in dizziness she halted now, hearing Arthur go onwards, and she could not call him back because he would come face forwards, with the torch, and therefore when she had recovered sufficiently to continue she first returned the dagger into her garter.

Meanwhile King Arthur reached the bottom of the stairway, where he found and pressed the stone which caused a section of the wall, secretly hinged, to open as a door, and there he waited for the lady to join him. Which she did eventually, and she was yet giddy, all the more so when reaching the level place, as when coming upon land after a voyage one feels the waves surging under him more strenuously than when at sea.

And it did seem as if she might well swoon. Therefore

King Arthur gave to her his arm, into which she put one hand and then the next, and finally her bosom. And the king was aroused once more, for he had not played at mammets since being a baby, and he had no memory of that time. He was now sensible of a desire to tear away the bodice of this lady's dress and make free with her paps. But he resisted this inordinate impulse, for nothing would seem more at odds with the principles of courtesy than to misuse a woman under one's protection.

Therefore thrusting his torch ahead he led her through the doorway into the cellars, where there was a great chill of dampness and the odor of mold, and beyond the reach of the light the noise of scurrying could be heard.

Now the lady did shiver and cling more urgently to him, saying, " 'Tis a Stygian place."

"And labyrinthine," said King Arthur, "and continuing so throughout. These walls are constructed of great blocks of adamant, the which will cause to bend or break any tool of metal that is presented to their surface. And the doors are double-bound iron and give onto the moat."

"Yet," asked the lady, "could not such a door, however stout, be finally breached? With levers or other cunning implements, or by means of instruments with edges of diamond, to which no metal is invulnerable? Or with corrosive fluids which can devour any substance?"

King Arthur marveled that she was conversant in these matters, as well as being so womanly in her great beauty.

"Perhaps," said he. "But no enemy would be suffered to come so close to the base of the exterior walls, or even if that were to happen, he would not be allowed to remain there sufficiently long to achieve his foul purpose."

"Ah," said the lady, "I ask you to forgive me for my timorousness. I am but a helpless female, and I am cold here, dressed as I am in nothing but this velvet robe and stockings of the finest tissue, so that my limbs feel quite naked." And once more she quivered against him. "But you have satisfied me that my fears are needless. Shall we return as we came? And then perhaps you will give me leave to go to some private, quiet place and rest upon a silken bed, warming myself under soft furs."

"There is a shorter route," said King Arthur, for they had by now made several turnings in the subterranean corridor, "and we are just near it, but shouldst thou not first want to see the stores, the great sacks of grain, the sides of mutton, the massive cheeses, and the barrels of onions?"

"With all respect, I think not," said the lady. "I am most monstrously cold."

"And the wines, which are the pride of Sir Kay my seneschal," continued King Arthur. "We were, he and I, raised as brothers, and on a diet of little more than leeks, oat-cakes, and Welsh spring water, and these, with a bit of well-done beef, are yet adequate for mine own nourishment. But Kay hath developed Roman tastes, laying in casks of Falernian from Campania, Samian vintages, and even Rhenish from the lands of the Saxons, late our enemies, subdued only after the most bloody strife. But I can not deny to this dear chap his amusements. He was most awfully disappointed when he could not withdraw the sword from the stone and so become king. His budget is extravagant, but we do not lack in treasure."

"Treasure, Sire?" asked the lady, stirring on his arm.

"All manner of it," said Arthur. "Quite more than I do know what to do with."

"This lode then," asked the lady, "is maintained in the castle?"

"We have in fact reached the very portal of the treasury," said Arthur, illuminating with his torch a door much banded and multitudinously studded in bronze.

"Now," said the lady, "may I assume that a troop of soldiers is stationed within? For this is just such a place as would attract any invaders who did penetrate Caerleon, scoff though you might at the possibility."

"It is guarded by one dwarf, no more no less," King Arthur said smiling. "Come let us rouse him, for he is a droll little fellow." He took his arm from the lady's and thumped his hand upon the door crying, "Ho, there!"

At length a voice of high pitch came in answer: "Which rogue doth disturb me?"

King Arthur laughed merrily. " 'Tis a peevish minuscule man," said he to the lady, and to the door he cried, "The king!"

There came the sound of bolts being withdrawn and at length the door opened sufficiently so that a small face could be seen, and it was at the height from the floor of a normal man at kneel.

"With a wench," said the dwarf disagreeably, and the lady did gasp at this impudence, but King Arthur made a jolly laugh, saying, "Thou shouldst be whipped were there enough of thee to meet the lash."

The dwarf groaned rolling his tiny eyes, as if too often had he heard the same witticism, and he asked in ill-humor, "What want you of me?" and he opened the door no farther.

"To see my treasury," said King Arthur.

"Why?" asked the dwarf. "Do you think it has been pinched?"

"Sire," asked the lady in amazement, "shall you suffer such insolence?"

"That which in a person of full size would be lese majesty," said the king, "in a dwarf is another matter, according to royal British tradition, as it has been transmitted to me through my ninety predecessors to the throne, the first of them being the Trojan Brute who routed the resident giants and founded Britain. 'Tis no dishonor to be chaffed by a dwarf, a jester, jackanapes, or the like, because they have no claim to a general responsibility. This tiny man's peculiar duty is to protect the treasury, and that he does exceeding well."

"Well, either come in or go away," the dwarf said now in almost a snarl. "The draught is chilling my tea."

And he withdrew from the entrance and King Arthur and the lady went into the chamber, the which was furnished with a pallet of straw, a table, a chair, an hanging lamp, and a fireplace in which a skillet sizzled on a grate over live coals. All of these were of half the size as such familiar objects usually possessed, and the ceiling was so low that the lady could scarcely stand erect, while King Arthur must needs bend considerably were he not to scrape the crown from his head.

"Is this not amusing, to see these miniature things?" asked the king, going in his crouch to the fireplace to inspect the frying pan. "Ah," said he to the dwarf, "do I see a pair of good British bangers bubbling in the grease? . . . Look," said he to the lady, "even his sausages are of an appropriate size."

And she looked and indeed saw two little cylinders of meat the size of the smallest normal finger to the second joint.

The dwarf pushed rudely between them and speared up his sausages with a tiny fork, put them onto a plate, put the plate onto his table, and then taking a steaming kettle from the hob, poured hot water into a teapot.

"This is indeed diverting," said the lady, "but I see no treasure."

"Whilst thou eateth thy tea," King Arthur said to the dwarf, "we shall just take a peek at the treasure."

In silence the tiny man swirled the warming-water in the pot. Then he said, "Well, go and do it."

"But only thou canst open the vault," said King Arthur.

"Can this be true?" asked the lady.

"Certes," Arthur said, "treasure is ever entrusted to the care of a dwarf, by tradition. Once again, methinks, the matter of relative size comes into play. Dimensions are destiny. For what could a miniature man do with wealth? He could scarcely use it to mount a rebellion against the full-sized, for who would follow him? There are no large number of dwarfs extant at any time, being monsters of Nature."

Meanwhile the dwarf, preparing his tea, did scowl at his sausages. "You've thrown me off the proper sequence," said he bitterly. "I should have left these bangers in the skillet, to be eaten piping hot just when my first cup was ready. And I haven't even been able to toast my muffin!" Suddenly he threw the contents of his plate into the fire and stamped furiously to his pallet and hurled it away, thereby discovering an iron ring on the floor, the which he clasped and raised, bringing a trap-door along with it. "There's the bleeding lode then," he cried angrily.

Before going to look down through the hole thus revealed, the lady did say to King Arthur that she found it remarkable that only the dwarf could lift such a door, which had no locks and was only of the thickness of ordinary boards.

"Singular," said the king and provided no further explanation, and she went and looked into the opening and saw gold and gems in a great heap the summit of which was so close that she could have knelt and with two hands gathered sufficient of it to buy a kingdom.

Now the dwarf had meanwhile found a pail with a rope attached, the which he carried to the hole in the floor and then lowered thereinto. And he spake as follows: "I expect that bloody Kay hath been buying more sack or them black fish eggs from the Russkies and stinking rotten cheeses from Cammyburt, which nobody won't eat, you yourself least of all, Arthur, and damn me if I know why you let him. And you never brought no woman down here before, and I can't answer for the consequences."

And he continued to grumble while fetching up the pail, which when it came into view was brimming over with golden coins and glittering jewels, some of which fell out and clattered on the floor, a fat emerald bouncing near the lady, who unobtrusively covered it with the instep of her slipper.

"It's a bit of a bore," said Arthur, "as is any surfeit, and I should long since have dispensed it to the needy, but for Merlin's opinion that it causes less mischief here in the vault, for justice is a very uncertain thing when treasure is to be distributed to those who have not won it by force, for what then shall be the criterion? Need, alone? But one-man has made himself poor by wenching or wagering, and with new funds he will only return to the trulls or games. The next, an honest wretch, will be the envy, and thus the hatred, of his fellows if he profits more than they. Thus if, by having a greater need than they, he asks more in alms, he incurs their envious anger; if he asks less, they despise him. It hath been said by a sage that each man should have two guards posted upon him, but then who would watch the guards?" Arthur sighed. "Such are the matters that occupy the head that wears the crown. On the one hand, the rascal many; on the other, the peerage, who I fear are a lot of rogues, greedy, lascivious, and treacherous."

Here the dwarf snorted impatiently, and he lowered the pail to the floor. "If you have got all day, I have not," he said.

Now King Arthur said to the lady, "Choose a bauble for thyself."

"Surely," said she, "you are jesting."

"Nay," said King Arthur, "I am in earnest. Thou art needy, who lately lost thy lord and castle. There can be no doubt that relieving such distress doth serve the ends of justice. Take a winking sapphire or crystalline diamond, a carbuncle red as blood—"

"Or the greenie she has got her hoof on," said the dwarf.

Now the lady said, as she uncovered the emerald, "Ah, I did never know 'twas there." And she colored, not in shame but rather from hatred for the dwarf, whom she determined to have put to death when the castle was hers. Then she bent and fetched up the gem, saying, "A pretty thing it is," holding it so that the light did flash verdantly through it. But then all at once she pitched the emerald into the vault below the floor, and she said proudly, "I am distressed but not destitute, Sire. I never did come here to beg for alms."

And King Arthur was without experience in dealing with noblewomen, and he believed that he had insulted her. "I intended no offense," said he. " 'Twas to be but a souvenir. . . . But come, let us leave this place, for I see thou art trembling once again, for this little fire is enough only to heat a little man."

Then in ill-humor the dwarf emptied the contents of the pail through the hole in the floor and kicked the trap-door shut. "If a woman don't take one jewel," said he, "then it's that she doth want two. Methinks your dad, being a whoremaster, did understand females better than you, Arthur. Now go along and let me drink my cold tea in peace."

Therefore Arthur and the lady went out of the treasury, and the lady said, "Yet he seems an exceptionally foul dwarf to endure even if only for the tradition."

"Alas," said the king, "he speaketh justly of my father, who by all report was a notoriously lecherous man."

"But your father was surely a king?" asked the lady, for that Uther Pendragon had sired Arthur was as yet unknown to all but Merlin, who had arranged for the sword in the stone so as to give the succession the aspect of being a faëry thing, the which with to awe the Britons.

"I never knew him," said Arthur. He was now concerned that the lady would think the father's luxuriousness had been bequeathed to the son, and therefore he kept a distance from her, carrying the torch which he had reclaimed from a bracket outside the door of the treasury. And indeed he hastened so rapidly ahead that once again the lady had no opportunity to take the dagger from her garter, and soon he turned into another staircase than that which they had descended, and climbing it they reached a large chamber with bare stone walls and a cold fireplace.

"These then shall be thine apartments," said King Arthur to the lady, who was quite breathless from toiling up the stair. "The proper entrance is the door just there, which leads to the waiting-rooms where thy women will attend thee soon as I can have them collected from amongst the wives of my men. We are unused to having ladies in residence at Caerleon, and these will doubtless not be the handmaidens to whom you are accustomed, for which my apology: but I have been fighting wars almost incessantly since putting on the crown, and therefore my court hath remained rude."

The lady looked about for a place to sit as she caught her breath, but she saw no couch or chair, for indeed the chamber was barren.

"Forgive me, Sire," she asked, "but where shall I take my repose?"

"Of course!" cried King Arthur, holding his torch, the which now burned low but no less smoky, into a shadowy corner to which the light from the little window-slits did not reach. There was a large box there, and he threw back its lid. "I roll up in these robes," said he.

"These then are your own apartments?" asked the lady in wonderment. "The royal bedchamber?"

"Simple," said the king, "clean, and without rats, and it has lovely fresh air."

"There are no panes in these windows, methinks," said the lady, going to look out, but she could not see much, for the slits were but wide as her hand and the embrasures were too deep to allow access to the openings.

"I am kept healthy by the good Welsh wind," said Arthur. "Agues, rheums, catarrhs, these all come from stale air. Kay, for example, when we were boys was ever ill with the maladies that come from sleeping in a warm room. He would shut his window in winter! Well, he being the elder, I could not justly quarrel with him, and therefore I went often out to the open kennels and slept with the hounds." The pleasant memory brought a smile to King Arthur's face, but then he did knit his brow.

"Methinks, however," said he, "that thou art not happy with this chamber, at least in its current condition. I shall have the lackeys fetch in a couch and such other furniture as thou wouldst require, and cover the walls with silk hangings, for though I have known no ladies previously, I have been told they like costly stuffs."

"Perhaps we might meanwhile have a fire," said the lady, enwrapping herself in her two arms.

Then King Arthur flung his torch into some charred wood that awaited in the fireplace, and shortly there was a blaze. "Now," said he, "I shall go to arrange for the new furnishings." And he went out through the anterooms.

Now as soon as he was gone the lady descended again to the cellars, found one of the iron doors giving onto the moat, threw back its several bolts, and making a great effort, for it was heavy and had rusty hinges, she swung it open slightly and peered without. Some small distance beneath rose the waters of the moat, on which not far away was afloat a swan, the which on seeing the lady did swim to her, for she had taught him to do this, having raised the bird from a cygnet.

And from her sleeve she took a silken handkerchief, and this she flung to the swan, who caught it in his beak and swam away. Then the lady returned to the bedchamber, where soon the lackeys began to come in with many furnishings: couch, chests, tables, and candlesticks, and wall-hangings of fine samite, blankets of velvet and fur, and pillows stuffed with down. And next a glazier came and heating his pot of lead in the fire covered the windows with glass. And evening had come when the work was done.

Meanwhile the swan had swum around the moat to the place where a churl in a boat was cleaning the surface of the water of the green scum that formed there, as well as other rubbish and filth found afloating, for though Kay the seneschal had established strict rules against befouling this water, with stern punishments for the offenders (even unto flaying alive for the dropping therein of excrements), yet the kitchen workers were wont to throw their refuse into the moat and charwomen to empty slops out of the windows, and there was often a noisome stench from the water that rose high as the battlements.

So this boor was at work with a long-handled dipper of wood, which when filled he emptied into a barrel in his boat, and the swan swam past him dropping the kerchief, which before it could sink he grasped up on the end of his implement. Now this kerchief was cunningly knotted so as to indicate at which place the iron door had been left ajar to admit, after dark, an armed party from the army of the Orkneys, who were secretly waiting in the forest near Caerleon for a message from this lady their queen, and the churl in the boat was one of her knights in disguise, who had murdered the poor fellow who did this job usually.

So the knight now rowed the boat to the embankment and hastened to fetch his party.

Meanwhile, whilst the apartments were being made suitable for the lady, King Arthur sent to her an invitation to sup with him, and she accepted this, but she was disappointed to find that the meal would be served in a private room rather than in the great hall with all of his men, where she could have caused some disorder, swooning at table perhaps, to distract them while her force penetrated the castle.

And so many servants were present at the private meal that she could not poison Arthur with the venom concealed in a hinged compartment of her ring. Now, in the circumstances the lady had little appetite for food, but being anxious she did partake of the wines in great quantity, for Sir Kay had provided the best vintages from his cellar, and he came himself to pour, after sniffing the stopper and tasting a splash in the little silver cup which hung in a chain about his neck, and inspecting each flask for sediment. But King Arthur did take only a polite sip of each wine, whereas he swallowed great draughts of water from the well beneath the keep, a liquid that was stained amber-colored from subterranean salts.

Soon from the effects of impatience and drink the lady did feel beside herself, and she asked the king's leave to retire to her bedchamber, the furnishing and decoration of which she trusted had been by now concluded. But her secret purpose was to steal down the stair to the cellars and meet her men there and lead them to the king to murder him. Then when this foul crime had been committed, they would go throughout the castle and kill all of Arthur's men in their beds and then sack the treasury.

But King Arthur rose in gracious condescension, saying he would himself conduct her thither, there to determine whether all that was necessary for her comfort had been laid on. And there was nothing that the lady could do but suffer this hospitality.

Therefore they went to those apartments, and now in the anterooms were a number of goodwives who had come to attend her, and they rose from their sewing to curtsy in a rustic fashion, for they had never been trained for this service, and they were dressed rudely in homespun stuffs and did smell of greasy kitchens and pissy nappies. And the lady did despise Caerleon and long to see the last of it.

And in the bedchamer itself, which earlier had been more chilly than the outdoors, a great fire had burned for some hours and the stone walls were covered with hangings, the door to the cellars now being concealed as well. But the lady believed she could simply cut away the silk with her dagger when the time came.

King Arthur however disabused her of this belief. "To allay thy lingering fears of enemy invasion," said he, "though they be needless, I ordered the glazier to seal with his molten lead the bolts on that door to the lower reaches. Thou canst now sleep in peace, in these invulnerable and most remote apartments of impregnable Caerleon."

Smiling he inspected the new glass in the windows, and when he turned to wish the lady a good night she had taken the green robe from her white body and was standing with her arms extended towards him. And her nakedness was wondrous to him, for he had never before seen a woman except fully attired, and while the breasts could be imagined the belly was indeed unique.

However the display did not arouse him to the degree that he had been stirred by his earlier random contacts with her clothed flesh, for a true king is habituated to spectacle, whereas he is seldom touched.

Therefore he did not now approach the lady, saying instead, "Ah, thou art no longer cold."

"Indeed, Sire," said she, "I am burning."

"Alas," said King Arthur, "the window glass is now fixed. I warned thee of the danger of stale atmospheres." He picked up a stool and went to the embrasure. "Nothing for it but to smash it out." And he raised the stool to do so.

"Hold you, Sire!" cried the lady. "I speak not of the air but rather of my blood, which hath been heated by your Samian vintages, as my brain is clouded. For an instant I did believe you were my own dear lord. I remember now that he is dead, and I am quite alone and defenseless and at your pleasure. You could ravish me with impunity." Weeping she did recline upon the silken couch and cover her face with her hands, leaving all else exposed.

Now King Arthur did lower the stool and come to her, for to aid ladies in distress was ever the duty of the chivalrous. "Thou hast the word of the king," he said, "that thou shalt never be molested in Caerleon! There is no greater evil than to misuse a woman under one's protection. Now pray dry thy tears." And from his sleeve he drew a fine kerchief and gave it her, except that for a reason he could not understand he retained one end whilst she took the other and drew it towards her, but she was looking fixedly into his eyes and he was unused to this, for a king is seldom stared at unless by an enemy of equal rank like unto the late Ryons of Ireland.

And though King Arthur possessed a most puissant strength for which that of a woman could be no match, the lady did pull him inexorably down onto the couch, for he could not loosen his grasp on the kerchief until he lay beside her. Thus he realized he was in the power of some spell against which it was useless to struggle.

Now the lady's dagger lay concealed within the green robe which she had dropped to the floor beside the couch, and as if fearfully avoiding King Arthur's attempt to embrace her, the which in fact he had not made, she shrank away to the far edge of the couch, from where she could with trailing hand find and grasp the keen bodkin, with a purpose to plunge it into the king's back when he mounted her.

But this lady was unaware that Arthur being innocent of women had not even yet formulated such an intention. Instead, still lying supine and yet fully attired in ermine-trimmed robe and with his crown so secure upon his head that the fur pillow behind his neck did not push it askew, he stared upon the ceiling, saying, " 'Tis time I took a queen. Thou art available, being a widow. Thou art comely and gracious, and thy company is pleasing to me. But art thou of sufficient rank?"

Now the lady had already found the dagger in a fold of the discarded robe and she was thinking that if he did not soon roll upon her she might stab him in the chest as he lay. But she was now so struck by the burden of King Arthur's speech that she dropped the weapon, which fortunately made no noise falling into the velvet of the robe, and in a trice she had put away her previous plan. The possibility of becoming the queen of Britain was more attractive to her than remaining the consort of the king of the remote Orkneys. And if she were not a widow she might soon enough arrange to be one, using the dagger on her husband rather than on King Arthur.

Therefore she moved so that her naked breasts were in touch with the manly chest of the king, and her hot breath was upon his mouth and her white belly did writhe upon him, and she said, "My mother was a queen."

Now, though Arthur had not previously known a woman, he soon discovered how to close with one, in the which procedure the lady lent much aid.

Meanwhile, in the cellars below, the armed party from the enemy host had gained clandestine entrance through the door giving onto the moat. Being greedy men they looked immediately for the treasury, with an idea of sacking it first and going only afterwards to kill the sleeping population of Caerleon and raze the castle. And from this plan to its refinement was the work of a moment: having emptied the treasure vaults they would flee straightway with the spoils, and you can be sure, never to return to the army of the Orkneys, for unlike the honest Britons, but like many Picts, Scots, Irishmen, and all the Saxon lot of Germany, these men thought nothing of betraying their own cause.

Thus they sought and soon found the door behind which the dwarf slept over the treasure vault, and they knocked him up, for after supping on a bowl of barley soup he had gone to bed on his pallet. And when with even more bad humor than usual he opened the door and peeped out, these men, all great stout fellows armed cap-à-pie, burst within, the foremost seizing the dwarf by his neck with a purpose to wring it like that of a goose.

But the little neck swelled and burst from the grasp, becoming a serpentine throat covered with golden scales, surmounted by a great dragon's head with red eyes and enormous fangs and a snout from which came two bursts of flame which burned the knight from the Orkneys into a cinder, and then the tail swung around collecting the entire party and they were likewise consumed by flame. When this was done the fearsome beast transformed himself into a dwarf once again, who swept up the ashes with a little besom and dustpan and deposited them in the fireplace.

For these rogues had forgotten that by tradition a dragon guards all royal lodes.

Now King Arthur lay sleeping when the lady woke up next morning. And he had removed his crown the night before and placed it onto the floor beside the bed, yet its impress remained in his golden hair. And he was the most handsome man in the world, and the most powerful king. But owing to inexperience he was not the best lover with whom the lady had performed the act of darkness (for she was much practiced in venery, having inherited a luxurious nature from her mother), but she believed that she could soon guide the king towards great proficiency in the art or sport, and also as his queen have access to the most robust of his knights.

Next she began happily to think of the treasure lode of which she would soon be mistress, and only then did she remember the party of Orkneymen who had presumably penetrated the cellars the night before. But if they had done their job they would long since have reached this bedchamber, having murdered the entire complement of Caerleon. Therefore she supposed that they had proved a lot of cowards and had fled without making an attempt at entry, or getting in had been despatched by Arthur's men so easily that no one had bothered to awake the king to report it. Whichever, the matter could be dismissed now that she would become queen of Britain, and she leant across King Arthur and awakened him with a kiss.

For a moment he was startled, having never woken to look upon a woman on the next pillow, but then he smiled and said gently, "Lady, lady . . ."

"Now that we are betrothed," said the lady, "thou shouldst know my name is Margawse."

"A beautiful name," said King Arthur in a murmur, being not fully awake. "And a queenly one as well." Having yawned comfortably, he then said, "Didst not tell me thy mother was a queen?"

"The fair Ygraine," said Margawse, "she who wedded the predecessor Uther Pendragon and therefore wore the crown of Britain that you will place upon mine own head."

Now Arthur opened his eyes fully and asked, "Then King Uther was thy father?"

"Nay," Margawse did cry. "Mine own father was Gorlois duke of Cornwall, and felonious Uther did take away from him my mother and bring about his death!" And her eyes glared in hatred. "Alas that Uther Pendragon died without issue, leaving none of his blood on whom to take revenge." But then she made her face soft and said, "But all of this is of no concern to thee, Arthur, for thou didst come from nowhere to take the sword from the stone. Thou art free of these feuds."

Then Arthur retrieved his crown from the floor and his robe as well, and he dressed himself discreetly with his back turned to his half-sister, saying, "In truth, a British king is never free to do his will. He is captive of many laws, ordinances, traditions, customs, and moreover, prophecies. And these last can not be defied, for they are forecastings of what must necessarily happen in the future. And as it happens, Merlin tells me it is written that my queen shall be a golden-haired virgin."

And Margawse seized the dagger from amidst her clothes on the floor and sprang at King Arthur with a purpose to kill him, for in shame he still kept his back to her, but at that moment a knocking came at the door of the chamber, and he went to answer, ignorant of the attack made upon him that was now carried no further.

Then the king went into the next room, where a messenger waited who had come from the castle of Leodegrance of Cameliard now under siege, with the news that unless succor could be provided, the castle would soon fall to the enemy host, for the stores had been exhausted and the well was discovered to have been poisoned by a spy or traitor.

Now Arthur was greatly relieved to be called away from the matter of his half-sister Margawse, which was a shameful thing though he had been ignorant of his relation to her and had committed the vile sin of incest unknowingly unlike the pagan kings and queens of Egypt with whom it was customary.

Therefore to the messenger, a young squire who was fearful he might be punished were his news unwelcome, Arthur said, "Go to the stables and get thyself a fresh mount. With mine host I shall ride towards Cameliard within the hour, there to relieve my ally King Leodegrance."

And when King Arthur left Caerleon at the head of his forces, Margawse his half-sister also went away but by another route. By her husband King Lot she was mother of Gawaine (who would in time to come achieve great renown as a knight and lover of maids), the noble Gaheris, the valiant Gareth, and Agravaine (who would be Launcelot's enemy).

And from Arthur's seed she was at this very moment conceiving Mordred, from whom would come much evil, as much indeed as any son has ever brought against any father.

BOOK IV

How King Arthur took a wife and acquired the
Round Table.

Now King Arthur with his host fell upon the forces that
besieged Cameliard, who numbered three times as many as
his own and were led by King Rience of North Wales, for
his ally King Lot had returned to the Orkneys after the
failure of Queen Margawse to conquer Caerleon by
treachery.

And having begun their attack after matins, by sext Arthur and his men had won the field, for they were Christians whereas Rience's host were paynims though not so
heathen as the Angles and the Saxons, for their faith was
druidical which is to say the worship of trees, and not
shameful Teutonic idols like unto Thor and his hammer.

When this had been done and the remnant of Rience's
host had fled in disarray, King Leodegrance had the drawbridge lowered and King Arthur entered the castle of
Cameliard, where the two kings embraced.

"My dear Arthur," said King Leodegrance, "I have
heard of your prowess, but what you have done here this
morning exceeds all expectation. You have delivered
Cameliard, and as a warrior I have not seen your like
since the death of my old friend Uther Pendragon. But after such a victory Uther and his men would now be swal-
lowing all the drink they could find here, molesting all the

women, and looting the treasury, so that the difference between ally and enemy might dwindle to the thickness of a mouse's whisker."

"So have I heard," said King Arthur, pleased to allow his paternity to remain unknown.

"Whereas," said Leodegrance, "do I not see your entire host on their knees at prayers?"

"Indeed you do," said Arthur.

"Well then," said King Leodegrance, "I am at a loss as to what to give you in reward."

"We British," said King Arthur, "fight for no gain save in honor."

"That is unique in mine experience," said the old king of Cameliard. "And whether such practice can be consonant with a long reign remains to be proved. Yet no doubt 'tis noble. But, my dear friend, permit me by the license of my gray hairs to say that honor can not properly be gained by depriving another man of his own. Namely, I should be shamed were I not allowed to reward my deliverer. But after this long siege my cupboards are bare and my coffers empty, and there is no land in tiny Cameliard that I might give away. Alas, I can not even invite you to feast with me now, for there is nothing to eat in the castle."

"My lord," said Arthur, "permit me if you will in these circumstances to feed you, for my seneschal has come along in the rear guard, with stores and cooks. If he might use your kitchens and banquet hall, we shall have our feast."

And when the meal had been prepared under the direction of Sir Kay, who had brought along from Caerleon all that was necessary, the two kings were seated together at an immense round table that filled the great hall which was a quarter of a league broad and the same distance in length. And as this table was the most vastest that he had ever seen, King Arthur inquired into the provenance of it.

"Was a wheel from a giant's cart," said King Leodegrance. "See there in the middle the hole for the axle, where the servants stand currently, carving the joint."

"So they are," said Arthur. "I had supposed they were kneeling on the top."

"Is a solid disk, you know," said Leodegrance, smiting the wood with his several rings. "A cross-section of one great oak, perhaps but a sapling in the olden time. The world has gone smaller throughout its history. The Colossus at Rhodes is said to be but the statue of a typical Greek of the time of its construction." The older king guffawed. "And if one could believe him whom you have succeeded, mine old chum Uther Pendragon, the River Thames came into being from the piss of one great dragon." Leodegrance laughed again. "Perhaps himself, for 'a would void vast quantities of urine when drinking!"

And Arthur reflected that he had never heard ought of his father and did not offend his own taste.

"And unlike most drunkards," the older king went on, "Uther was a prodigious swyver as well. I have known him to deflower a maiden for every bottle, when in his prime, and in the course of a week he would drink up half one's cellar. He sorely taxed the resources of little Cameliard."

"Well, then," said King Arthur, concealing his grimace in his beard, "the special value of this table methinks is that there's neither head nor foot to it. At Caerleon we have no table as yet for the reason that I have never wished to cause envy amongst my men over these matters of precedence in sitting at meat. A circle can never be put to the hierarchical uses of a rectangle, turning each corner of which is, in a sense, a moral event: he at the head is exalted; he at the foot, debased. 'Tis rubbish, but 'tis believed."

"But many years have passed since we last entertained a British king," said Leodegrance, "and meanwhile my villeins have produced a new supply of maids. I shall have a selection of these wenches sent to your chambers, for of course you will be my guest for the night." For King Leodegrance had never himself been a great lecher, but he was of the sort of men who are pleased to feed the luxuriousness of their friends.

"My lord," said King Arthur, "I never heard tell of a cart the which did not have at least two wheels."

"Indeed," said Leodegrance, who had quaffed more than a little of the Rhenish wine brought by Kay, "and a maid hath two tits and two cheeks of her bum."

"Therefore," said King Arthur, "there might well be another giant's wheel in Cameliard, the which I might take back to Caerleon for to make mine own table?"

King Leodegrance took the flagon away from his purple-stained mustaches and beard and uttered a vile blasphemy. "By God," he cried, "that's the very thing. You will take this very table, my lord young Arthur of Britain, as reward for delivering Cameliard from the foe."

"Yet it is enormous," said King Arthur.

"Will never go through a door," said the old king. "I'll have the bloody roof pulled off, then, and winches brought into play. Once outside, it can be put upon its edge and rolled unto Wales."

"Let me first have a word with Merlin, who transported Stonehenge from Ireland to Salisbury Plain without human labor," said King Arthur. "But in speaking of the enormity of this table I think rather of the number of knights needed to fill its places, an hundred or more by the look of it. Whereas I have in my service only old Sir Hector, who has in fact returned to his bucolic cottage and his hounds, and Sir Kay my seneschal. My army as you see consists of simple kerns. I have mine own self engaged all mounted enemies."

"I did marvel, watching from the battlements this morning," said King Leodegrance. "Never have I seen such bravery against such odds."

"My lord," said King Arthur, "with Excalibur I am invincible. Therefore bravery is not to be considered. I go to war only to defend Britain or such an ally as yourself. It is necessary to subdue enemies, but I get no satisfaction from the fighting itself, as I am told did Uther Pendragon. Indeed, war to me seemeth but a brutish enterprise."

"So hath it ever seemed to me, as well," said Leodegrance. "But with a kingdom small as mine, situated as it is on the route which must needs be taken by any force going to assault another, one necessarily prefers peace. Yet in my dreams I have often enjoyed putting thousands to a sword like Excalibur! Methinks it is natural in every man of noble birth to seek supremacy to the limits of the conditions imposed upon him by God." These thoughts did seem to sober him to a degree, and he cleaned his face on his sleeve.

Now two small varlets took the large salver which had been piled high with beef at the axle-hole of the great wheel, and bending placed it upon the stones of the floor and then pushing it before them they did proceed to the outside crawling on their knees beneath the table top.

"My goodness, that will never do," said Sir Kay, who had come with another flask of Rhenish to replenish King Leodegrance's flagon. "Be cold as a jelly when it gets here." Therefore he had brought into the hall a cart, and into it he had them put braziers of live coals and over the coals kettles filled with water, and on top of these a great trencher holding an entire side of beef, the which was thus kept warm by steam, and so it was brought to the two kings.

Leodegrance did praise Kay highly for inventing this trolley, not having ate hot meat since he had owned the round table, and he fell to with great appetite.

King Arthur however ate little, for he was much occupied with thoughts of how to use the table in the pursuance of chivalric ideals. He now understood that he had been led to it by the same destiny which guided him in all things, that indeed it was for the sake of this table that he had been directed to deliver Cameliard from its foes, for it was otherwise an inconsequential place with a king who had no vision.

"Now, Arthur," said King Leodegrance, soon giving his

empty plate to Sir Kay to fill again with meat, "I can provide you with an hundred knights to fill much of your table, leaving places but for fifty more which you might find on your own, say by means of a tournament."

"And where, my lord, will your knights come from?" asked King Arthur, for he had seen no other person but Leodegrance since entering Cameliard, and the two kings sate alone at the vast table, and he believed that all defenders had perished from famine during the siege.

"They are mine own," said Leodegrance, "and went away some time since, and for that reason I was ill defended."

"Then these are a pack of poltroons!" King Arthur cried indignantly.

"Not at all," said the older king. "They went upon a quest, you see." And Sir Kay returned to him his plate, heaped, and he did attack it with vigor.

"Sire," said Sir Kay to King Arthur, "your meat is going cold though I have been at some pains to serve it hot."

"Forgive me, my dear Kay," said Arthur and he obediently chewed a piece to please his former brother, though in this effort he was usually unsuccessful, as now, for Kay did sigh disdainfully while looking at the vaultings of the hall.

"Indeed the quest for the Sangreal," said Leodegrance.

"This is some fearsome beast?" asked King Arthur.

"I had supposed you a Christian," said Leodegrance. "And you know not of the Holy Grail?"

And Arthur was ashamed, saying, "I was reared piously, my lord, but in a rustic place, remote from learned men. I am ignorant of much."

"Well then," said King Leodegrance, "the Grail is a mysterious thing of which little can be precisely told, except that it is holy and was associated with Our Blessed Lord Jesus Christ."

" 'Tis not a splinter from the True Cross?" King Arthur asked suspiciously. "Or a thorn from a Savior's crown, the blood scarcely dry? Or a patch torn from St. Veronica's handkerchief? For all these and more were sold every day by the charlatans at London."

"Nay, none of those," said Leodegrance. "The Sangreal is rather a vessel, though its precise nature is as yet unknown, for the reason that it has not been seen within living memory. But if it be a platter or a dish, then it was served to Our Lord at His Last Supper; or if a cup, then He drank His wine from it. Or, again, His blood was caught in it dripping from His body hanging upon the Cross, or—"

"Methinks it is strange that an hundred knights are questing for that which they do not even know the look of," said King Arthur, who had begun to suspect that he was being guyed.

"The very mystery of it is a lure," King Leodegrance said. "And it is the kind of thing that will be recognized when it is seen. If one has never traveled to Afric one has never seen an ocean of sand, yet one would know the desert when one reached it. As to the Grail, whatever its nature, it was brought to the British island by Joseph a rich Jew of Arimathaea to whom the Romans gave Christ's body, and who forsaking his wealth became Christian and came to Glastonbury, where he stuck his staff into the earth and it took flower, and the tree still grows there today."

"No doubt this quest is commendable," said Arthur, "but my purpose in assembling a company of knights would be to right proximate wrongs. Therefore I should want my men at hand."

"The Sangreal," said King Leodegrance, "is peculiar in that it can not be seen except by him who is perfectly pure and without sin altogether."

"My lord," said Arthur, "is this not then a blasphemous idea? For as we know, only Our Savior was perfectly sinless."

"Indeed," said Leodegrance smiling wryly. "Therefore my knights will return presently from this impossible quest, and you may have them along with this round table.

For," said he falling again to his meat, "I am an old man and have grown tired of these sieges. Thus I do swear fealty to you and become your vassal, incorporating Cameliard into Britain, and you must protect me henceforward."

And Arthur did marvel at the old king's cleverness, for if he accepted him as liege-subject he must needs take responsibility for him or violate the principles by which power could be exercised honorably, nay, even practically, for privilege is founded on duty, and if the horse carries the man, the animal is fed before the rider himself doth eat. Thus in certain respects the first comes last, and the greatest king is the loneliest.

"Further," said Leodegrance, "if I gave you this castle along with the table, 'twould not be necessary to remove it to Caerleon."

"And where, my lord, might you go?" asked King Arthur.

"If I might have me a chamber in some remote tower," said Leodegrance. "But were it not that I have a daughter to look after, I should take me to a monastery, Arthur. At my age 'tis time I became pious. For some years I have yearned to put away my crown, having got too old for to feel the satisfactions of sovereignty. And I am ill. I shall pay dearly in my guts for eating and drinking so abundantly as I am doing here. Most of my teeth have gone, and my belly wars with anything but gruel. I should long since have abdicated my throne had I a son to succeed me, but Lear's experience was a lesson to us all in the horrors of female regiment."

"This daughter, my lord," asked King Arthur, "doth she have hair of gold?"

And Leodegrance shrugged. "One might call her yellow-headed, though the years have dulled the brightness of youth."

"Is she then very old?"

"The late queen could calculate better than I," said the old king. "But I should need more fingers than I have when counting Guinevere's years. She's thirteen if a day, perhaps even more. She was such a pretty fool as a child. She has spots now," said he grimacing. "Be assured I shall never allow her to vex you."

After the meal King Arthur retired to the royal apartments which Leodegrance insisted he must occupy as liege-lord of Cameliard, and though he had little concern for such things he was aware that these rooms were much more attractive and comfortable than his own at Caerleon even after they had been redecorated for his half-sister Margawse, who of course he had not identified as being such until he had bedded her, alas! For it was a great sin. Though not, he believed, so great as if he had known a priori of this relationship, which he could not have done without questioning her previously to performing the carnal act, which firstly he had not known he would do, and secondly would have been a gross violation of the laws of hospitality, for a stranger must be offered unconditional welcome when under one's roof.

Now Arthur regretted that the deliverance of Cameliard had taken so little time, for there was this to be said of battle: it was the best distraction from the matters of conscience that puzzle the will, and once again, as on every recent night, he slept fitfully. And he did dream as follows: that he sate upon a golden throne and was tied to the arms of it with golden chains, so that he could not move from it, and the throne was mounted not on legs but on wheels, like unto the invalids' chairs for the cripples that take the medicinal waters at Bath, and he was on a height from which the inclined ground led to a pool of water, and even as he looked at this water and saw it boiling with all manner of serpents, the wheels on his throne began to roll down the incline towards this loathsome end, and he was powerless to halt them. . . .

And he was awakened by Merlin, who carried neither lanthorn nor taper but rather a globe of clear glass large as an orange, with a fiery glow within it which cast a brighter light than had ever been seen.

"Merlin, art thou in my dream?" asked the king.

"You are not dreaming now, Sire," said Merlin. "Though I am always something of an apparition."

And King Arthur did chide him. "I have seen little of thee lately in any form."

Then Merlin spoke sternly. "You are no longer a boy, and it would not be proper for me to attend you constantly, extricating you from every difficulty, for then I should be the king, and you the retainer."

And King Arthur was ashamed, murmuring, "Perhaps thou shouldst be present to tell me that truth from time to time."

And Merlin said more gently, "A king hath at least as many failures of nerve as a commoner, and a great king hath many more, for greatness consists not in having no weaknesses, which is impossible, but rather in using them as strengths."

"If there is sense in what thou sayest," said King Arthur, "it doth elude me. But perhaps I must confess to thee, Merlin, as in fact I have done to no other, not even my confessor, and with that failure compounding the sin, that I have committed the beastly sin of incest, than which there is none more foul unless it be the incestuous sodomy which the Angles and Saxons are said to commit with their sons." And he told Merlin of his bedding with his half-sister Margawse.

"Well," said the wizard when King Arthur had done, "what are crimes to this religion of Jesus of Nazareth are of indifference to Nature, Sire, and though I expect you shall find me blasphemous, let me say that Nature was here first and will be here last. Beyond that, you were in innocent ignorance of your blood-tie to this woman, though it might be said, in a philosophy unknown to you, that you found her peculiarly attractive owing to her resemblance to your mother, which would then make it finally a form of love which killed Narcissus, as indeed is all incest ultimately, as well as homophile sodomy for that matter."

"Again thou speakest too cryptically for me," said King Arthur. "And with a suggestion of the fiendish, which is no doubt due to thy demoniac paternity—but then, for that very same reason, because thou art without the scheme of normal things, I can confide in thee. I fear I have brought down a curse upon myself by performing (however unknowingly) this unspeakable act, the which shall ruin me one day."

"As undoubtedly it will," said Merlin, weighing his mysterious light in his hand. And King Arthur shrank away in despair. "But, Sire, the curse which shall ruin you eventually is the selfsame which ruins all men, irrespective of their actions good or evil, and that is Time, which is the issue of an incestuous act performed by God on reality."

"There is this to be said of the metaphysic, Merlin," said King Arthur. "Whenever it is not totally obscure, it is altogether immoral. And it is astonishing to me to hear thee, an atheistical demi-demon, speak of God."

Merlin smiled, and in the radiance of his light he looked more angelic than devilish. "It is finally only the fiend who doth truly worship God, as the felon adores the hangman, for the one is defined by the other. But enough of this materialism. Do consider my light, which draws its power by abstraction." He gestured with his globe.

Now in spite of himself Arthur was cheered by the alchemical foolishness. "Well, Merlin," he said, "never have I seen such a collection of glowworms. This is no magic. Undoubtedly there was also some practical explanation of the disembodied arm which rose clutching Excalibur from the lake: a lever, a pulley, a wire. With age and experience of kingship I am no longer so credulous. Yet I understand the value of such illusions for the people, who require the legendary."

"True enough," said Merlin, "but to believe in themselves kings need it even more, and therefore they must be able to distinguish genuine magic from false. The secrets of the Lady of the Lake are her own. I can not divine the doings of women, real or faëry. But as to this lamp, it is indeed magical, abstracting its energy as it does from the very air, which though it is invisible to the human eye can be seen by the penetrating vision to be a throngèd fluid in which particles swim, the which, knocking together, make a force. Thus if one walk across a fur, then touch a sword, a spark would leap from finger to steel. In this globe I have imprisoned a quantity of such sparks, the which I gathered by a certain means. You see, I have explained this thoroughly as to the essentials, yet it remaineth a mystery."

But King Arthur had got bored before Merlin completed his statement on the light and anyway suspected that the wizard spoke with some persiflage at his expense, which he must needs permit, for Merlin's devotion to him and to Britain could never be doubted.

"My friend," said King Arthur, "I have done an evil thing by reason of my lasciviousness, the which I fear I have helplessly inherited from my father, for apparently Pendragon blood is thicker than the pure Welsh spring water of my foster-parent Sir Hector, a chaste and honest knight. And if I was once so inordinate, then I might well be again if I were in the presence of a woman."

"Sire," said Merlin, "not all women are your kinsfolks."

"Yet," said Arthur, "who might tell, with all the seed my father did broadcast?"

"But," Merlin said, "Uther Pendragon did bed in the main the female issue of churls or defeated paynims, generally virgins of very tender age, as is so often the taste of kings. Except with your mother, the fair Ygraine, his spirits were not wont to rise for women who approached him in rank. And in that case, it was a thing of destiny, the same destiny that in its further workings brought to you your half-sister Margawse, from which encounter there will doubtless be more consequences which you will be unable to alter."

"Then I am fundamentally a slave, I whom you call the most glorious king of all?" said Arthur.

"No man is free who needeth air to breathe," said Merlin.

"Nevertheless," said King Arthur, "I believe I must get married. Now, King Leodegrance hath a daughter who would seem suitable, being of appropriate age. Also, he is now my vassal and hath expressed a wish that I take this castle as mine own, along with the round table in the great hall, for which I have a special purpose, and his hundred knights as well, who are off currently on a quest, but from which they will soon return unsatisfied, owing to its peculiar nature. However, I do not think this quest, being of a religious type, frivolous. And questing is furthermore always the proper pursuit for a knight: the sedentary grow fat and lecherous."

"Have you seen this princess?" asked Merlin. "And doth she please you?"

"I have never," said Arthur. "The point is that this Guinevere is at hand here in Cameliard, and the round table as well, and, when they return, the hundred knights. She is therefore recommended by convenience. Also, she is accustomed to living in this castle, which, if I decided to make it the principal seat of my court, would therefore not need to be redecorated for my queen. Whereas Caerleon is very rude." But the truth was that Caerleon was unpleasant to him because of memories of Margawse.

"Sire," said Merlin, "would it not be reasonable, if you are marrying so as to be protected from illicit desire, to determine first whether the woman you shall marry be licitly desirable to you?"

"Aha," said Arthur. "Nay, there thou speakest again with a fiend's disregard for the moral law, Merlin. I shall be prohibited by my vows of marriage from traffic with any other woman, whomever I do wed: her identity being irrelevant."

"True," said Merlin, "I know little of woman, but even so methinks there be none who exist without a sense of self, and all the more so when a party to a marriage of convenience rather than in the connection called love, for pride is to be considered."

"Pride is a sin," said King Arthur, "and never to be considered in a Christian queen. We might assume that this princess hath been reared to be pious, for though Leodegrance, being an old friend of my father's, is surely no better than he should be, he can be relied upon to bring up a daughter properly, sequestering her once she has reached womanhood. Therefore she can not, having known no man, be vain."

"I have noticed before now this Christian confusion of pride with vanity," said Merlin, "which is perhaps due to the first adherents of that faith having been slaves. And with the passing of the old Greeks, the distinction between both and *hubris*, a much more noble concept, hath been forgotten." He brought his globe of light to his white-haired face and gazed profoundly into its glow. "I can," he said, "see no woman."

"It may be," said King Arthur, "that thy nigromancy is no longer as puissant as it was once, Merlin. Producing Excalibur was one thing, marriage is another. Perhaps I must rely on reason now."

Now on the morrow King Arthur went to King Leodegrance, who was lying on a bed groaning.

"My lord," said Leodegrance, "forgive me for not rising. But as I foresaw I have me an ache in my guts from eating too much of your beef, as well as a heavy head from your wine."

"My lord Leodegrance," said Arthur, "I shall accept your offer of the round table, the hundred knights, and the land of Cameliard with this castle, the which I shall make my principal seat. And now I ask of you another boon: the hand of your daughter in marriage."

And King Leodegrance pulled a face of amazement. "Guinevere?" Then he did belch and rub his belly.

"She is I believe available?"

"I expect so," said the older king, pursing his lips. "But to be queen of Britain might require sterner stuff. This is a girl, my friend, who doth dream incessantly by daylight, though until a year or so ago was lively as a child could be. But melancholy was concomitant with the onset of her courses, and spots as well. I am afraid that she hath turned quite plain of both face and mind."

"These news do not discourage me," said King Arthur. "For what I seek in a queen, as I admire it most in a woman, is modesty above all."

And Leodegrance pulled back his lips to suck his teeth. "Modest she is certainly, and hath good reason so to be."

"Then might I have her for a wife?" asked Arthur.

The old king did writhe upon his bed. "I tell you, my lord, my bowels are most unhappy with what my palate did so enjoy. In one's dotage one pays the debts incurred in one's youth. There was a time when I was as great a trencherman as old Uther, though at venery he did never have a match."

Then suddenly King Arthur knew a great apprehension. "My lord," he asked, "the late King Uther Pendragon my predecessor, whom I never knew, was he your guest at Cameliard when your late queen was yet living?"

"The late queen," said Leodegrance, smiling in spite of his distress, "did have a great aversion to him, by reason of his stench. For Uther did rarely bathe within a twelve-month, and disdained all scents as being appropriate only to vile sodomites." Wincing the old king produced a laugh. "One learned to keep upwind of Uther Pendragon."

But King Arthur was relieved to hear this, for the reason that then Guinevere was not likely to be another of his half-sisters.

"My lord," said he, "I await your answer."

"Oh," said King Leodegrance, "well of course you may marry Guinevere if in spite of what I have said you persist in this aim. Will be a great honor for me, and a greater one for her, for whom else would have her?"

And after groaning again and complaining of his sore guts, he clapped his hands and a page appeared, and he told this varlet to fetch the princess to him.

Now Arthur was overcome with shyness and said he would go away until these news had been imparted to Leodegrance's daughter, and so he went a-falconing.

Meanwhile the varlet returned without Princess Guinevere, saying she was in the aviary contemplating the peafowl and did refuse to budge from it, and Leodegrance did have him whipped for failing in his task, and at length though ever more ill the old king arose from his bed and himself went to find this chit, for actually he was quite keen on getting her married before his death, which he believed imminent.

But when he entered the aviary, causing a commotion of feathers, she was no longer there, and he succeeded only in befouling his slippers on the abundant droppings that covered the floor, and he ordered that the churls who had neglected to muck out the great cage be punished by the loss of one hand each, but rather the left than the right, for he was a merciful monarch and not a cruel paynim. But nonetheless he knew that owing to his mildness Cameliard had long been in decay, for as a horse would not gallop unless feeling the spur, neither would a lackey labor earnestly without the threat of pain.

Now whilst Leodegrance did wander feebly throughout the castle looking for his only daughter, King Arthur was in the meadow without the walls watching his tercel dive through the sky to plunge its talons into prey, of which his retainers relieved it though often with difficulty, for this raptor was not well trained in relinquishment.

And it happened that though it was a gray day and the heavens of a color like unto dull pewter, Arthur did become aware of a golden radiance coming from one of the towers of the castle, and he looked towards it, but it was so bright that he could not distinguish its course, and he decided that it was again Merlin with some cunning alchemical device.

But when he turned to look at the still quivering body of the canary, which had been torn from the claws of his tercel and brought for his inspection, it was transformed into a fish, and Merlin thereupon made himself appear, chuckling at the amazement of the lackey, who did drop it upon the grass, where it flopped and gasped, and he crossed himself wonderingly.

"Thou hast left thy magical light upon the tower," said King Arthur, "and it has grown considerably brighter, but methinks the better use of it were at night."

" 'Tis no glow of mine," said Merlin, squinting at the heights of the castle. Then turning away and producing from the folds of his robe a square of clear glass, and next a lighted candle, he held the flame so that its soot did obscure the glass, and when it was well blackened he placed it before his eyes and stared again at the tower.

" 'Tis a woman," he said, "or a girl merely."

"Give it me," said King Arthur, and he took the smokened glass and looking through it he saw the most beautiful maiden in the world. And a great wonder arose in him, for she could never be Princess Guinevere, who was plain and had spots.

"Alas, Merlin," said he, "that thy powers can not apply to women, for I would fain know the identity of that maiden, who now goeth within the tower, yet her shimmer remains behind." But next he groaned and said, "Alas, too, that I am pledged to marry the plain Guinevere, for I know that I shall want yon maid all the years of my life."

Meanwhile, within the castle King Leodegrance had returned to his bed feeling very seedy, and now that he was done looking for her, Guinevere came to him.

"Father," said she, "there is a beastly knight who is hawking in the meadow, and I would have him put to death."

"Ah, Guinevere," said Leodegrance, "I did search for thee everywhere, feckless child."

"Or stretched upon the rack or broken on the wheel," said Guinevere, "for his detestable peregrine hath murdered my dear canary, the which I had taken for an airing upon the balcony."

"Enough of thy prattle, chuck," said Leodegrance. "I

have managed to get for thee a husband, indeed the most noble to be found on this island." He took his hand from his belly and raised it in triumph. "Thou shalt be queen to Arthur of Britain, and as dowry I must provide no more than the round table, my company of knights, and the land of Cameliard, from all of which I have long wanted to be rid."

"But," said Princess Guinevere, "I do not wish to be married never, Father, and I do not care to be queen of Britain, wherever that may be, for it has an ugly name as if it were a land of toads." And she made more complaints, to the which Leodegrance did not listen carefully, believing it mere maidenly rubbish.

Therefore he soon ordered her to be still and hie her to her chambers before Arthur returned, for she did have a slatternly appearance.

"Have thy women wash thine hair and dress thee in thy best robe. And for another, I would that thou coverest the spots with powder," said Leodegrance. "For I do not know whether Arthur hath yet given his binding pledge to wed thee, and certes he might change his intent were he to see thee as thou art currently, with jam-smears on thy skirt and canary-droppings on thy sleeves. But then, poor wretch, thou hast not since early childhood had a mother to tend thee, and what could I, a man, do in this regard?"

"How tiresome!" Guinevere cried petulantly. "Well, if I do this, then thou must punish that cruel knight, tearing away his fingernails with hot pincers, flaying him alive, or quartering him with four stallions."

Then she went away for to return to her tower, but passing through a corridor she met face to face with the very knight whose tercel had murdered her gentle bird who would sit upon her finger and sing sweetly to her. And never had she hated a man more.

But King Arthur, for it was he, once again saw the glorious radiance when he looked at her, the which was too much for his eyes, and therefore he averted his head while bowing and saying, "My lady, your servant."

"Felon!" cried Guinevere. "Thy lady shall be the Iron Maiden, and she will embrace you with spikes."

"Gladly shall I submit to torture if it please you," said King Arthur. "I am promised to another, but I love you more than life itself." And to his vision she was all golden and white except for the celestial sapphires of her eyes, and never did he see what Leodegrance noticed in his daughter, and the truth was somewhere between: for there was some jam on her robe, but not much, and she had fair hair which could be distinguished from pure gold but was clean enough, though needing a brush, and her features were comely but not yet, owing to her youth, as well defined as they would come to be. Finally she had but one small spot on her cheek, the others being blemishes from candle-soot, for after pinching out a wick she was wont to sit in the darkness and ponder on bird songs and the scent of flowers and sunsets seen across waters. But when she fell asleep she would dream of a knight with hair and beard of very dark hue and brooding eyes of the deepest brown.

Whereas he who had murdered her canary was fair as she herself, and with bluer eyes, and she could not abide blond men, for she believed them shallow and unfeeling.

"Thou shalt go to my father the king," she commanded now, "and receive thy just deserts."

"Then you are sister to Princess Guinevere," said Arthur, "to whom I am affianced?"

"Alas," cried Guinevere, "I am herself." And she wept bitterly.

And that was how King Arthur met his queen, whom he did love faithfully all his life long.

BOOK V

*Of Sir Gawaine and King Pellinore; and how
Merlin was assotted with the Lady of the Lake.*

Now King Leodegrance did soon die, as he suspected he
would, and the period of mourning lasted one year. And
then King Arthur was wed to Guinevere at London in St.
Paul's, by the new archbishop of Canterbury, who was a
pious man and not the corrupt lecher of old, who had
been deposed, and to the great ceremony came all the
barons and all the knights in the kingdom, and they swore
fealty to Arthur. And emissaries from the Angles and the
Saxons and Jutes and Danes and Picts and Scots and the
Irish came as well and made pacts of renewed friendship
with the Britons, for they had no hope of overwhelming
them so long as Arthur was king.

And after the wedding Arthur and his queen returned to
Cameliard, where he would make his principal court,
owing to the presence of the Round Table there, though he
kept many other castles as well, such as at London, Caerleon, Winchester, and Weston-super-Mare. And he did
change the name of Cameliard to Camelot, so as to make
it his own. And finally all the hundred of Leodegrance's
knights returned from their quest for the Holy Grail, without any of them, as the old king had foreseen, having seen
a glimpse of it.

Now the Round Table had seats for a hundred and

fifty, and King Arthur did call for a great tournament to be held at Easter, the winners at which would fill the remaining fifty places. By Good Friday the colored pavilions had been erected around the castle as far as the eye could see and the shields that hung outside them numbered into the thousands and bore every device in the realm and also some from France and Sicily and Byzantium, and there were knights with black faces from Afric and brown-skinned knights from Ind, and Turks with curved swords and turbans, Etruscans with horsehair helms, and Vandals and Mongols and Goths and Huns, and also Saracens who worshiped Tervagant and Apollon.

And though mountebanks and charlatans, along with trulls, had been forbidden to come, many of all of these were there nonetheless and did much commerce, though if they were caught they were cast into dungeons and punished sorely.

But before telling of the events of this tournament, the greatest that was ever held, it should be said (without violating the privacy of a marriage, the which is a Christian sacrament) that though Guinevere did not remain forever bitter against King Arthur by reason of his killing of her canary (and when he learned of this loss he furnished her with another bird and furthermore would never go hawking again), she did not ever have for him as great a love as that he bore for her, for unlike him she did not desire what she safely possessed but rather yearned always for that which she did not have, for God did not make all of us in the selfsame mold as to particulars even if *sub specie aeternitatis* we be fashioned in His image.

However, she was not unfriendly to King Arthur, and in addition she did respect him greatly as a king, than which there was none more just nor gallant nor noble, and she believed that his purpose, to fight Evil, was a good thing. And after she became queen, she also became in truth the most beautiful woman in the world, the which he had thought her to be when but a girl with jam on her robe and tangled hair. And though she was but fifteen when married and crowned, she soon thereafter became as if of an indeterminate age, fully matured yet youthful, at which she was to remain for the succeeding half century, so that her image on the gold coins that were struck was for a very long time an excellent likeness, whilst that of King Arthur, on the obverse, was soon to seem young.

And it was not obnoxious to her to have an hundred deferent knights to whom she was their lady, whose honor they were sworn to protect with their lives, and the thousand competitors at the tournament did each come before her and kneel in homage, even unto the paynims, and then again en masse, and they were the bravest and most comely knights in the world.

Therefore she was not unhappy, and as to ecstasy, she did not believe it was possible of attainment outside of dreams, for it would be wrong to think of Guinevere as having a willful attraction to wickedness.

So all the knights went to Mass on Easter morning, with the exception of the ones who were pagan, who danced howling around their beastly idols, and then the tourney began, with a great melee in which all set upon all, and soon there was much breaking of lances and unhorsing of men, and many stallions were wounded or killed and some heads were broken and many knights were maimed, though none was slain except by accident.

Now by noon the knights still in the field numbered only one in ten of the original assemblage, so that the winners of the contests between each pair of these would furnish the fifty knights for the Round Table, and these individual matches then began.

And the first knight who despatched his opponent was a fine tall man, who when he came to kneel before King Arthur and Queen Guinevere, and removed his helm, had a head of ginger hair and sparkling eyes of an aquamarine color.

"What is thy name?" asked Arthur, raising Excalibur.

"Gawaine, Uncle," answered the knight.

"I am truly thy relation?" King Arthur asked in wonder.

"My mother," said Gawaine, "is Margawse, wife of King Lot of the Orkneys, daughter of Ygraine of Cornwall."

Then Arthur did touch him quickly on both shoulders, saying, "Rise, Sir Gawaine, as knight of the Round Table."

And when Gawaine had risen and gone away, Guinevere said, "You never knew of this nephew, methinks?"

"No, I did not," said King Arthur, "as I never knew my mother Ygraine nor my father Uther Pendragon." And then for the first time ever he told her of his upbringing and of all else about himself except for the episode with Margawse.

"Perhaps you have more sisters," said Guinevere, "and brothers as well." For she was quite unaware that for him this subject was unhappy.

And another knight then unhorsed his opponent and they had at each other on foot and with a great blow he chopped off the other's sword just beneath the hilt and put his own blade to the slits in the other knight's visor, commanding him to yield. And he did, and this young man came to the silken canopy under which sate King Arthur and his queen.

"Thy name?" asked Arthur.

The knight answered, "Agravaine, Uncle." And he was a stout young man with a neck thick as an oak, and did in no wise resemble Gawaine.

"Thy father," asked King Arthur, "is a brother to me?"

"Nay, Uncle," said Agravaine. "Your sister is my mother, the fair Margawse."

And this same thing happened for the third time, when Gaheris defeated his rival and knelt to be knighted. And Gaheris was a sinewy youth and of the middle size, and he was a brother of Gawaine and Agravaine.

"These young men," said Guinevere, "especially Gawaine, are not greatly younger than you. Therefore their mother must be considerably older."

" 'Tis strange," said Arthur stiffly. "I had believed I was

quite alone in the world." Then suddenly he thought he would do best to learn which other relatives he did have, and therefore he sent a page to find Sir Gawaine and fetch him to him.

But the varlet returned at length alone, and having some news he seemed ashamed to relate before the queen, he requested a private audience with King Arthur.

But saying, "We keep no secrets from the queen" (though we know there was however one), King Arthur commanded this page to speak openly.

"Well then, Sire," said the varlet, "Sir Gawaine directed me to say that he was in chapel, at prayers."

Now King Arthur could not abide foolishness and therefore he said, "Why couldst thou not have told me this immediately?"

But Queen Guinevere spake as follows. "For the reason that it is not the truth, and this good boy did not wish to speak falsity to his king. Is that not so, my boy?"

And the page did color and say bowing, "Indeed, my lady."

"Then what is the truth?" sternly demanded King Arthur.

The color of the young page did deepen. "Sire," said he, "Sir Gawaine doth lie with a maid."

Now Guinevere did simper in mirth at these news, but Arthur frowned darkly. "Such roguery," said he, "would be scandalous in whomever, but Gawaine is first knight of the Table."

"Tell me, boy," asked Guinevere, "doth the maid make protestations?"

The varlet now turned almost purple in shame, for secretly he did have fantasies of himself in intimate congress with the queen, and this was vilely wicked, but he could not bear to mention it in confession and therefore he did suffer boils upon his forehead. But he took a breath now and answered as best he could.

"Far from it, my lady." And then he showed his teeth

from ear to ear, as though in a smile, but actually it was confusion.

"Enough!" cried King Arthur, and he sent the varlet away. To Guinevere he said, "If Gawaine, of the blood royal—indeed, of mind own blood—be a vile lecher, then what hope can there be for the Round Table?"

"My lord," said Guinevere, "I am aware that this table is more to you than the great disk of oak which hath been a routine sight to me all the days of my life, and indeed it was rather a bore to feast at, as a child, though amusing to run about on when the hall was empty and roll one's ball for one's puppy dog to chase. And then," said she, "when King Uther was a guest—" But here she broke off, remembering he was Arthur's father.

"No doubt," said King Arthur groaning, "you are about to speak of seeing wenches cavort there. O how wicked that you as a child should have to witness such!"

"Well then," said Guinevere, "I was never forced to be present. Indeed, I had long been sent away to bed, but would steal back in girlish curiosity and stay in a place of concealment. . . . But look you, Arthur, the way of a man with a maid, is it not according to Nature?"

Now her speech did amaze the king, who if he had not known her as the embodiment of virtue might have thought it devilish.

"But, my dear lady," said he, "is it not Nature that the Christian Faith, through its instrument the Round Table, must correct? Is not Nature cruel and unjust? Doth Nature not bring famine?"

"Not to the squirrel," said Guinevere.

"Pestilence and war?"

"Never the latter," said Queen Guinevere, "for the beasts do not wage it, and they kill but to eat, and Merlin doth tell me that the plague is itself made up of minuscule animals, too small to be seen with the human eye, who art grievously hungry and eat men through their blood."

"Perhaps Merlin hath served his purpose," said Arthur. "His druidical alchemy hath ever verged on the blasphemous. It is God Himself who sendeth the plague as deservèd punishment to mortals, and He doth never work in miniature. You should remember that Merlin's father was an imp."

But now Sir Gawaine did finally come before his uncle the king, and his countenance was flushed to almost the color of his ginger hair.

"Thou art rubicund and breathless, Nephew," said Arthur severely.

"When my sovereign, and uncle, summons one, I come in all haste," said Gawaine.

"Art thou aware of St. Paul's adjuration?" Arthur said. "Best is for a man to live entirely without women, but if he is incapable of such purity, then he should take him a wife."

"Methinks, Uncle, that the sainted Paul was not a knight but rather a tonsured clerk. Swinging a sword doth warm the humors," said Sir Gawaine, and he wore a fetching smile, the same which made him so charming to many women, and not even King Arthur could long stay angry with him.

And King Arthur now reflected again on his own trespass with Margawse, who was not only his half-sister but must be nearly forty years of age, and he remembered that his kinship with her, and thus with Gawaine, was through his mother and not Uther Pendragon.

"But what I summoned thee here for," he said more kindly, "was to ask as to the extent of thy family. Here thou art, with thy brothers Agravaine and Gaheris. Are there even more at home?"

"Another boy of ten years," said Gawaine, "who is Gareth, and finally an infant delivered of my mother but a twelvemonth ago, and remarkably so, for she was thought to be beyond the age of childbearing."

Now Arthur did count silently and find that but twelve moons had waxed and waned since the visit of Margawse to Caerleon.

"Suddenly, Uncle, you seem saddened. Well, my father

King Lot was indeed your recent foe, but he is now at peace with you, and that my brothers and I have come to join the company of the Round Table assures our own fealty."

"My newest nephew," said King Arthur, "his name is what?"

"Mordred," said Gawaine.

And King Arthur did shudder in wonder that a new life could so sound like old death.

"And dost have," he then asked, "more aunts and more uncles?"

"Aunts to the number of two," answered Sir Gawaine. "Your sisters Elaine, who is married to King Nentres of Garlot, and Morgan la Fey, who lately left school at a nunnery to marry King Uriens of the land of Gore."

Now during this colloquy between Arthur and his nephew another knight had defeated his opponent in no more time than it took him to fewter his lance and charge, for there was none better in the entire world except one man, and this adversary was not he, and therefore he was lifted clear out of the saddle in the heavy armor and flung, as if a mere doll, over the hindquarters of the horse. And when he lay upon the earth he was quiet and did not rise.

So the winner removed his own helm and he came to King Arthur to be made a knight of the Round Table, and he was a handsome man with chestnut hair and mustaches and very sad eyes.

Now whilst he waited for King Arthur to recognize him, who was yet occupied with Sir Gawaine, Queen Guinevere seeing his melancholy expression spake as follows.

"Why art thou so *triste*, fair knight, thou who hast such great prowess at arms?" And she did smile upon him, and she was beautiful in her white robe trimmed with ermine and her gold crown shone not so brightly as her hair beneath. For to be addressed by her would bring joy to the most lugubrious of men, and she understood this without vanity.

But this knight remained sorrowful, and he said, "Forgive me, lady, so hath God been pleased to make my nature, and my name is even Tristram."

"Hath thine experience," asked Guinevere, "authenticated thy name?"

"Well, my lady, it hath never been happy," said Tristram.

"I would hear thy tale of woe," Guinevere said, for there was a depth in this knight, the which she had not yet detected in any of the men who were then at Camelot, and she was pleased by the melodious quality of his voice, as well as by the unusual rhythms in which he spoke the British tongue. "Thou art not a native of this island, methinks?"

But then King Arthur observing the new knight was called to his duty and turned from Sir Gawaine.

"I am Tristram of Lyonesse," said the same.

" 'Tis in France?" asked King Arthur. "And what brings thee to Britain?"

"He doth have a sad story," said Guinevere, who like all married women relished more the hearing of male sorrows than of victories, and she had little interest in Gawaine and his conquests of maids and could therefore regard him with amused tolerance.

But for his own part Arthur had little patience with melancholy, all the more when it was French, the which (though he knew little of that country beyond the hearsay of travelers) he suspected of being perfumed, like the Gallic sauces used to mask inferior meat.

Therefore, he said, "Men can look for joy in Heaven. At the Round Table we think only of duty." And then remembering Sir Gawaine, he asked, "Art thou married?"

"Sire," said Tristram, "I am an exile, alone in all the world."

"Then thou has found a community," said King Arthur. "Now I must attend to the tournament, the which I see hath stopped, for a knight is lying upon the field and will not get up." And he said to Gawaine, who was yet stand-

ing near by, "He is breathing, but methinks his brains
have been addled."

"Alas," said Sir Tristram, "I never meant to hurt him."

"Thou hast done this?" asked Sir Gawaine skeptically,
for in talking with Arthur he had not seen Tristram's contest, and already he was jealous of the Frenchman, by reason of Guinevere's interest in him, for Gawaine in general
desired all the women in the world, though he would have
been shocked to think of a particular lust for his queen
and aunt.

Now King Arthur too doubted the prowess of Tristram,
not having watched the match, and he said, "Good Tristram, forgive me, but I was distracted and did not watch
thy bout. Be good enough to joust with another opponent,
pray. This first one would seem to be quite ill."

And Guinevere did secretly despise these men for their
vanity and spite, though it was not her place to say ought
to this masculine matter.

"Surely, Sire," said Tristram, whose sadness was somewhat relieved by the prospect of another passage at arms,
for he was the greatest knight then in Britain, and he felt
best when practicing his métier. So he mounted himself
again and he charged the new adversary, and he did the
same to him, as he had done to the former, with the difference that when this knight came a cropper he fell so
that he broke his neck altogether and so died.

Now when Tristram knew this he was sadder than ever.
And Sir Gawaine was more jealous, and he determined
that one day he and Tristram must face each other and
determine which was the better. And in this Gawaine was
a fool, for there were to be four knights greater than he,
of whom Tristram was one, and none of them ever fought
for vanity.

But seeing Tristram's prowess King Arthur did love him
for it, and he said to him, "Thou shalt be the foremost of
my knights, and therefore thou must put thy sadness away,
for it is a gladsome thing to fight evil."

"Sire, I shall try to be merrier," said Sir Tristram, but it was his nature to be doleful.

Now the tourney continued all the day, but only one more match will be spoken of here, which is to say, that of Sir Kay, who was not obliged to compete, for that he was already Arthur's seneschal. But Kay was never admired by the other knights, owing to the peevishness of his temperament for he did have a low opinion of the taste of others, thinking them loutish at table and generally deficient in courtliness, and he was wont to employ sarcastic speech, the which in return caused slurs to be made against his manliness, for a sharp tongue amongst the British was considered to be a womanly organ. Therefore Kay, who did not lack in courage, believed he must prove his virility upon the field, and he appeared at the lists in a hauberk of fine silver mail, made by the most cunning of Jewish armorers, and he rode a handsome white Spanish stallion and carried a damascened lance which he had purchased from a turbaned Arab with a face dark as walnut. For Kay did ever have the best furniture for whatever he undertook.

But alas for him, he drew as his opponent Bors of Ganis, who was a very great knight indeed, with whom even Sir Tristram would have had an arduous contest, and therefore Kay was soon thrown.

Then Bors dismounted and with the first blow of his sword he took away the crown of Kay's helmet and along with it the topmost hair of his head, so that his naked skull could be seen. Nevertheless Sir Kay gallantly persisted, and Bors with each stroke cut away more of his armor until he stood in little more than smallclothes, and there was much laughter from those who watched this.

Finally Bors with a mighty blow severed the blade of Kay's sword just below the handle and presenting his own sword to Kay's unprotected neck, he said, "For God's love, Kay, shalt thou yield?"

But Sir Kay said, "Never."

" 'Tis no dishonor in it, man," said Bors. "One must win and one must lose."

"But I yet stand upon my feet," said Kay.

Therefore in exasperation Bors flung his sword from him, removed his gauntlet from his fist, and he struck Sir Kay (whose entire helm had been cut away) on the point of the chin, so that the stubborn seneschal fell to the ground.

"Nay," said the recumbent Sir Kay with great disdain, "for you did not fell me with a weapon. You are an unchivalrous fellow and you can not claim to the name of knight."

But at this point King Arthur stopped the match and declared Bors the victor, saying, "Now, Kay, what wouldst thou prove further? Thou art gallant, and though combat will never be that at which thou canst demonstrate thy greatest strength, thou art proficient enough at it to hold thine own with all but the finest. Thou art good, whereas Bors is excellent."

And Sir Kay arose, and though in singlet and hose he yet possessed a certain dignity, for you can be sure that these garments were well-cut and of the finest linens and silks, and even after fighting his hair (except where it had been sliced away) and beard were still as if newly brushed.

"Sire," said he, "as I believe you know of old, I have no patience with that which is less than perfection, in myself as well as others."

"Well, Kay," said Arthur, "no man is equally good at every emprise. Methinks this fine knight"—and here he indicated Sir Bors—"might not know his way about thy wine cellars. My counsel to thee, dear foster-brother, is, insofar as it be possible without corrupting thy standards, to consider the wisdom of the Stoics in some matters."

Then Arthur turned to Sir Bors. "I would be hard put," said he, "to say which amongst my knights thus far be the greatest on the field. Nor"—and he looked sternly at Gawaine, who he knew was accessible to envy—"will I tolerate any contest among them to determine this, except at legal tourneys, which we shall now and again hold for sport. But I should say that all together never has there been such a company of valiant men upon the face of the earth, not in Rome and not in Sparta."

"With all respect, Sire," said Sir Bors, "may I say that a greater knight than any here present doth live currently at a remote monkery."

"Indeed?" asked Arthur in wonder. "And might we expect him one day to come to the Round Table? For evil is active, and can not be destroyed by a cloistered virtue."

"On your command I shall go to him as your emissary," said Bors, "for he is mine own cousin, Launcelot of the Lake."

"This name," said Queen Guinevere, "doth fall trippingly from the tongue, Sir Bors. Is he a fair knight or dark?"

"Dark, my lady, with swart hair and beard, and greatly strong. He hath no equal in all the world with lance or sword. Yet he is of a pacific temperament, unless exceedingly provoked."

Now in the aggregate these were the qualities of the knight which Guinevere had seen only in her dreams, and she had a great love for him already, so much so that she dreaded nothing more than his incarnation, for Guinevere was already a very wise woman who sensed that dreams might better stay unrealized, being the yeast that doth cause the bread of life ever to rise, the green that keeps the flower vital, for life is a sequence from present into past, and not even God can alter the latter.

Therefore said she to King Arthur, " 'Tis perhaps not the proper matter for my womanly concern, but shall you not, by result of this tournament, have a surfeit of worthy knights?"

"*Worthy*, certes," said King Arthur, "and with Gawaine and Bors, great. With Sir Tristram, very nearly the greatest, by my judgment. But the greatest is yet to come, and I must have him. Perhaps he is Launcelot."

"My lord," said Guinevere, "(and again I beg your pardon for my interference), but I do reflect on what you lately told Sir Kay, whose quest for perfection is sometimes frustrated."

"But Kay," said Arthur, "is properly a seneschal and as such, the best of his kind. I am a king. As we well know, absolute perfection is found only in Heaven. But if 'tis gallant to seek it as a vassal, it is obligatory to seek it as a king. We know, at the outset, if even the Christ Himself did die as man, that we shall necessarily and ultimately fail. But we can fail gloriously, and glory doth come only from a quest for that which is impossible of attainment."

King Arthur fell silent, and he wondered at his own speech, for never before had he identified, even to himself, his guiding principles. And that was what a woman was for: so that a man was led to know himself.

For her part Guinevere did both at once admire him and believe him a fool withal, as a woman doth for whom she feels attachment but not passion, whereas her feeling for a lover is compounded with hatred and fear.

Therefore King Arthur sent Sir Bors to find his cousin Launcelot. Then he did assemble at the Round Table his company, and he found they numbered two less than an hundred fifty, for twice both opponents in a contest had been disabled or killed by accident. And if Launcelot was to fill one of the empty seats, then who would fill the other?

So Arthur sent for Merlin and asked him this question. And the wizard pointed to the chair at King Arthur's right hand, the which was currently occupied by a knight named Pellinore, who just as Merlin's finger was directed at him, rose hastily from his seat, crying that his bum was afire, and though no smoke could be seen he dashed a goblet of wine on his robe at the point where his rump was situated.

"That seat," said Merlin, "is called the Siege Perilous, and no man may sit there with impunity but one, the Perfect Knight, who will one day come to take his place."

"This will not be Launcelot?" asked Arthur.

"Nay," said Merlin. "Yet without Launcelot, he cannot be."

"I shall not try to penetrate thy riddle," said King Arthur. "But tell me this: where might I seek this knight?"

"You may not," said Merlin, "for these reasons: firstly, he doth not yet exist. Secondly, he will never be accessible to a search. Finally, never be impatient for his appearance, for when he cometh to complete the perfect circle, the Round Table, the company of knights, the matter of Britain, and chivalry itself will be at an end."

And King Arthur turned from him to the knight who had singed his fundament by sitting in the Siege Perilous.

"Sir Pellinore," said he, "prithee take this chair at my left."

"Thank you, my lord," said Pellinore. "And may I say that though I am now a knight of the Round Table, I am myself a king as well."

"Of some land beyond the seas?" asked Arthur.

"Nay," said King Pellinore, "rather, of a country not so far from here, very near Wales, actually. But one day I left my court to pursue the Questing Beast, the which I have followed many months, and I became lost and could not find my way back to mine own land. And then I came upon your tournament."

"One may mislay an entire country?" asked King Arthur, who was amazed. "This Beast would seem a heathen thing, Pellinore. No doubt you were in the grip of some powerful spell, which you will gain immunity from by becoming a better Christian. We shall find your country for you, my dear cousin! Meanwhile, welcome to the Round Table, at which you, as a fellow king, were quite right to choose the seat nearest me."

And Pellinore remained the only knight whom King Arthur addressed in the formal person, for all kings, who are appointed by God, are social equals even when lost, deposed, or even when enemies, and in return Pellinore called Arthur not "Sire" but rather "my lord" and sometimes even "Arthur," a name which Queen Guinevere, being but a woman and not a ruler but rather a consort, did seldom say.

Now hardly had King Pellinore deposited his hams upon the new siege when a snow-white hart burst into the great hall, pursued closely by a brachet quite as white, and then behind the bitch came thirty pairs of hounds black as night, and then the lot ran about the Round Table, the dogs baying and slavering, the stag leaping, and after they had encircled the table thrice, they did run out. And hard upon that, a beautiful lady rode in upon a white palfrey.

"Sire," cried she to King Arthur, "I would that you retrieve for me that brachet, for 'tis mine own bitch, and a wicked knight deprived me of it."

And the next moment, a huge knight in black armor galloped into the hall on an enormous horse, and reaching the lady he did seize her and lift her from the palfrey and then he wheeled and rode out of the castle.

'Well," said King Arthur, "this is a wondrous thing, but I am happy it is done, for I can not long endure a screeching woman."

And King Pellinore said, " 'Tis a redundancy when one bitch owneth another."

But Merlin, who had remained there, said to Arthur, "This episode, Sire, is not to be dismissed so lightly, for it is the first quest of the knights of the Round Table, and methinks King Pellinore is to have a role in it."

But Pellinore did grimace saying, "I lost my kingdom hopelessly pursuing the Questing Beast. Once bitten, et cetera. Besides, I have not ate my meat, and am sufficiently hungry to fall to an entire baron of beef."

But Gawaine hearing this, and already envious of Pellinore for gaining the seat next Arthur, when he, a nephew of the king's own blood, must sit away from him (and therefore Arthur's wish to allay envy by having a round and not a rectangular table was defied), he did purpose to go upon this quest himself and thereby gain great honor for himself and deny it to Pellinore.

But when Gawaine rose and announced his purpose, the king, who was determined to allow no intestine rivalry except on the jousting-field, said, "Thou, Gawaine, shalt seek the white hart." And turning to Pellinore he said, "Be a good chap, Pellinore, and pursue the knight with the lady."

Now Gawaine did sulk, for he had enjoyed an anticipatory vision of killing the knight and making lascivious use of the grateful lady (to whom furthermore he would be entitled by the old laws of courtesy). And King Arthur was well aware of this, which is why he gave Gawaine that part of the quest that concerned the stag. For Gawaine was not as yet so great in soul as he would become. Yet he lost no time in caparisoning himself in full armor and riding in pursuit of the white hart, the which he tracked by means of its hoofprints and also its fumets, which were pure white like unto those of a bird, and after many leagues this trail led to a castle.

Seeing nobody at the gate nor in the yard, Gawaine dismounted and entered this castle on foot, and no sooner had he got inside than a knight did rush at him with a naked sword, and he was hard put to defend his life. But at last he smote the knight to the floor, and he unlaced his helm, and putting his sword at the unprotected neck, he asked him to yield.

"Yield I do," said the other, "and I beg your mercy as knight and nobleman."

"That you may have," said Gawaine, and he allowed the knight to rise.

But no sooner had this happened than the knight proved himself a deceitful man and a violator of the laws of courtesy, for he picked up his fallen sword once more and again he rushed at Gawaine. But Sir Gawaine struck him down once more and removing his helm altogether he swore he would cut off his head.

Now the knight made great moan and begged so piteously for his life to be spared that Gawaine relented and gave him mercy. And then the knight arose, and once again did he attack Sir Gawaine.

Therefore Gawaine felled the treacherous man for the third time, and he said to him, "Felon, prepare to die." And he lifted his sword high, with great contempt owing to the shrieks which he then heard and believed to come from the knight who at the prospect of death had turned womanly. For Gawaine did not realize that it was indeed a lady who screamed, and now she came from behind him and she hurled herself upon the body of the knight, at just the same moment that the sword was swiftly descending to cut off the knight's head, and instead it cut off her own.

Looking upon this terrible thing that had been done by misadventure, Sir Gawaine was as if a man of stone, he who had been so great a lover of women, and the bright-red blood flowed around his boots.

Now the other knight rose from the floor and lifting up the headless body of the lady spoke as follows. "Sir Gawaine, you have done a passing foul deed in killing this damsel. All ladies are under the protection of the knights of the Round Table at all times and everywhere, whoever they may be and even when they seem wicked."

And Sir Gawaine knew the greatest shame.

"Now," said the knight, "for no quest is without purpose, henceforth you will be the pre-eminent protector of ladies amongst the company of the Table and their especial champion. Any knight must defend any lady who comes to him for succor. *You* must have it as your principal purpose to seek out distressed female persons and offer them your aid."

Now Sir Gawaine, though still knowing great dole, thought that his punishment, if such it were, was not so heavy as it might have been, for since being a very young child he had ever been a great womanizer and not only for narrow matters of venery: he was much pleased by female company from little maids to aged crones, whereas he was much uneasy, owing to feelings of rivalry, in the exclusive fellowship of men, for while he was never the very greatest knight, and though his superiors in prowess Launcelot and Tristram were to have single loves more famous than his (because adulterous, for Fame doth love Shame), Sir Gawaine would know women better than all the other knights together, for ladies are generally fond of those who admire them, and it is rather other men, owing to envy, who condemn lechers, and not women.

Therefore Sir Gawaine's part of this quest was finished, and he returned to King Arthur's court. And when he had gone from the castle where he had accidentally chopped off the lady's head the knight put her body down, and she took up her head from the floor and placed it upon her neck. For she was not a human woman but rather the Lady of the Lake.

"Now," said she to the knight, who was one of the men whom she held in thrall and used as retainers, "let us go to deal with King Pellinore." For it had been the Lady of the Lake and this knight who had created the scene at court, with the white hart and the false kidnapping.

Meanwhile, what had happened with Pellinore was this: though reluctant to go upon a new quest, when he did once begin one he soon grew fanatical on it, as he had been when following the Questing Beast, losing his country thereby. So now, when some leagues away from Camelot he came upon a damsel a-sitting beside a well, with a wounded, bleeding knight lying in her arms, King Pellinore saluted her but continued on his way to look for the lady who had been carried out of Arthur's court by the huge knight in black armor, for so only had he been charged to do.

And the damsel by the well cried out piteously, "Help me for the sake of Jesus Christ!" But King Pellinore, though he was a good man, would not suffer to be distracted when upon a quest, and thus he rode onwards, and in a little while the wounded man died in the damsel's arms, and in grief over this she slew herself with his sword.

But Pellinore knew nought of this unhappy event, for he had gone out of that valley and into the next, where he saw a silken pavilion in a meadow, and before it was the very knight who had come into the court of King Arthur and stolen the lady away by force.

Now riding up to him King Pellinore said, "Sir knight, I am charged to find the lady you took away and to return her to King Arthur. This is my quest, and it took me from my meat, which I would fain not have left. Therefore be sure that nothing will keep me from completing this quest but my death."

"My lord," said the knight, who was large as a tree and his armor was black as night, "know you that this lady is my property and there is no means to have her while I do live." Then he lowered his visor, mounted his huge horse, fewtered his lance, and King Pellinore did the same, and drawing apart the length of the meadow, they did charge upon each other.

Now in the shock of their meeting, which was so violent that the wind made by it did almost blow down the pavilion, both lances splintered against both shields, and the other knight was thrown from his steed. Therefore Pellinore dismounted, so as not to have the uncourteous advantage even though this was a fight to the death, and he drew his sword.

But the other knight jeered at him for this foolishness, saying, "Had you remained mounted, you might have lived longer." For he towered above King Pellinore, and his sword itself was five foot long.

"Sir knight," said King Pellinore, "there is but one manner in which a quest must be pursued, and that is according to the right principles, which do not admit alteration."

"Then die of excess courtesy," said the knight.

"And far better it will be than to live ignobly," said King Pellinore.

Then the knight raised his great sword in two hands high over his head, but before he could bring it down Pellinore smote him across the waist, cutting him through the belly, and next he gave him such a stroke upon the helmet that it parted down to the nasal, as did the head within it, the which was sliced as if it were a melon, and when King Pellinore took his blade away, the knight's brains did spew out of both parts of his cleft skull.

Then having cleansed his sword on the grass Pellinore did enter the pavilion, where he found the lady lying upon a satin couch, and she was stark naked and passing fair, with long red hair and green eyes, and she did greet him lovingly, with provocation of body, saying, "Take me, for you have won me."

"Nay," said King Pellinore, "my quest doth not permit me such a thing. I am charged to deliver you to King Arthur, and nothing more."

Therefore the lady rose and clothed herself. "Thou art a good knight," said she, "and have performed well. Yet thou art not perfect."

And on the journey back to Camelot, Pellinore pondered on this strange statement, which he did not understand, for he had done exactly what he had been commanded to do by his liege lord King Arthur, than which no knight could do more. And so they came unto the Round Table, where Arthur yet sate and with all the company including Sir Gawaine, who was downcast.

"King Arthur!" said the lady. "Know you I have lately tested two of your foremost knights."

"Then tell me, lady," said Arthur, "what is thy judgment of their performance. Did they do well or ill?"

"Both well and ill," said the lady. "Mostly well, but with a certain failure, the which in each case was significant."

Now King Arthur was some vexed, for he did not take to this lady, whom he believed too proud, and seeing both Gawaine and Pellinore still living, he knew that their quests had been achieved. "Lady," said he, "I hope thou art not being too fine in these matters, or over-nice. For obviously thou hast been delivered, else thou wouldst not be here."

"Well, Arthur," said the lady, "I do not speak lightly. Know you that I am the Lady of the Lake." And at this,

King Arthur and all his company did gasp in amazement.

"The same, then, who gave me Excalibur?" asked King Arthur, and then he knew shame. "I had supposed that a trick of Merlin's," said he.

"Know you then," said the lady, "that some things are not mere wizardry, and that a king must always allow for what I must call the possibility of the impossible, the existence of that which can never be explained to mortals, who foolishly distinguish between that which they can touch and that which they dream."

But King Pellinore's guts were rumbling with hunger, and now he looked for his plate of meat, which Sir Kay had removed, and therefore he was peevish.

"Well, lady," he said, "if you are impalpable spirit, I am a man, and damn me if I know for what you took me away from my meal, when I did as well as I could only to be told it wasn't as good as it should have been."

"Well," to him said the Lady of the Lake, "thy failure was a grave one. And thou shalt remember it all the days of thy life. The weeping damsel holding the wounded knight was thine own daughter, whom thou hadst not seen since thou didst undertake to follow the Questing Beast. The knight who bled into her lap was to have wedded her. Because thou wouldst not stop to aid them, he died and thy daughter slew herself."

And King Pellinore sobbed into his hands. "Yet," said he, raising his wet face, "what could I have done? I was upon a quest, charged by King Arthur in the name of the Round Table."

"No quest," said the Lady of the Lake, "should be conducted blindly, for ills and evils abound. To have a purpose is good, but to be so intent upon it as to see only its end is folly. Never to be distracted is ultimately to serve nothing but Vanity."

"Lady," said King Pellinore, with a certain bitterness, "me-think this is a cruel lesson, the which might have been kindlier taught."

"To a churl, perhaps," said the lady. "But thou art a

knight of the Round Table, who with thy fellows would set a precedent over the past and make an example to the future. He who is noblest becomes so by rising above pain."

Now Merlin had begun to dote on the Lady of the Lake, for her powers far exceeded his own, though that she was beautiful meant nothing to him, for he was incapable of carnal desire.

But the same was never true of Sir Gawaine, who now recognized her as the lady whom he believed he had beheaded by accident, and not only was he relieved to see her standing hale, but seeing her red tresses falling against her white neck, he knew a quickening of the reins, for it had been some hours since he had had a game abed.

"Lady," said he, "no doubt there was a moral to the adventure in which I was involved, the sorry initial results of which I am happy to see were not permanent. But should we not pursue the meaning of this mystery in private?"

"Lascivious boy," said the lady sternly, "'tis time thou didst go beyond thy simple philosophy of groins."

And to be so chided before the entire company of knights, Sir Gawaine was abashed, but he was also defiant. "But," said he, "if you were not killed by me, wherein lies the lesson I should learn? And what of mine obligation to be the peculiar defender of ladies?"

"The latter thou hast ever been," said the Lady of the Lake, and then she smiled, for Sir Gawaine had charm even for such as she (and as there is much boy in any lecher, there is some mother even in faëry women). "But thou art lacking in generosity to men. The knight whom thou didst fell yielded to thee. Yet thou wouldst have cut off his head had I not intervened."

Now Gawaine protested. "Twice earlier he yielded. Then, when I spared him, twice he rose and attacked me again. Surely there is some limit to mercy towards the deceitful."

"Nay," said the Lady of the Lake, "there is no limit to mercy, and the treacherous need it most of all."

"Then," asked Sir Gawaine, "these yieldings and forgivings should have continued *ad infinitum*?"

"Until," said the lady, "thou slewest him standing."

Now old Merlin did thrill with admiration for this lady, and her divine command of ruth, and he wished to impress her by some means. Therefore he said to King Arthur, "Methinks I must needs go away, now that you have your Round Table, its complement of knights (except for those who will come), and your queen."

And in truth King Arthur was somewhat weary of the old magician and his devilry, but nonetheless he professed polite regret and asked whether Merlin would remain away for long.

Now in his state of assotment with the Lady of the Lake, Merlin did boast, "Know you, King Arthur, that the matter of Britain is but one of the many irons I have in the fire. There are a myriad stars in the sky, and there is an universe in a drop of water. The air you breathe is not an emptiness, but a fluid in which swim minuscule particles, the which if made to collide together in a certain way could explode all of Camelot."

But the Lady of the Lake did grimace at him, saying, "What rot you talk, old man."

"My lady," said Merlin, "if you would accompany me to my alchemical laboratory I might show you these wonders."

"I am bored," said the lady, "by the physical application of reason. I am interested only in that which is mythical. Thou, Merlin, art incapable of making a true miracle. Thou hast never lifted a great weight except by levers, the which thou hast concealed from men's eyes by putting them under hypnotic spell. And all of thy tricks have been such legerdemain, for when human wits are befuddled Time seems to stop, gravity is suspended, and matter is transparent. But a charlatan can so perform at a fair: and all mortals yearn to be gulled."

Now her scorn did pique old Merlin, but deliciously, and he said, "Lady, if you will come with me I shall show you marvels not so easily dismissed, clear diamonds I have made from swart coal, and pearls from grains of sand. And a glass through which I can look into the body of a man and sees his bones and entrails, and a black box, the which I call a camera obscura, with which I can take me, upon an emulsion, a likeness of anything in Nature, like unto a picture painted of it."

"These are but childish sports with matter," said the Lady of the Lake, "but art thou capable of transforming Envy, Vanity, and Spite into the virtues of Self-Respect, Generosity, and Patience?" But then she sighed and said, "However, I shall come with thee, for the time for thy departure is at hand."

And the Lady of the Lake and Merlin then left the court, and King Arthur was not sorry to see them go; and as for King Pellinore, he was resentful at first as is any man who must recognize his own flaw as having been correctly identified, and he wondered why, if the results of Gawaine's failing had proved not to be permanent, his own daughter's death must be real and not an illusion: for his mistake had been mere neglect, which was to say passive, whereas Gawaine's, being one of action, would seem much worse: and thus Pellinore was yet the victim of confusion.

But Sir Gawaine did ponder on what the Lady of the Lake had told him, and he determined to be a better knight in future, for 'twas true that he had been wont to see other men only as rivals and therefore he had no male friends.

Now Merlin and the Lady of the Lake reached the Enchanted Forest, where they came upon the weird well of Alaban, where Uther Pendragon's couriers had found the wizard many years before, and he had gone to the king on their summons, and had begun the thing that led to this moment.

"Now, lady," he said, "you shall see what no other, male nor female, hath ever seen nor even heard of, for I confess that I love you with all mine heart." And he went to a great stone near by, the which he lifted with the tip of his littlest finger, discovering thereunder a flight of stone steps which led down into the ground.

But the Lady of the Lake shook her head and said, "Merlin, thy stone is made of parchment, is it not? And painted to resemble granite? Were it not for its hinges, concealed beneath, the wind would carry it away."

"Well," said Merlin, "there are more cunning things below." And he went down the stair, and he touched the wall there and a radiant light appeared, the which revealed a vast subterranean chamber, where there were many strange engines and countless vessels of glass containing corrosive fluids, and it smelled of brimstone.

"This sulphurous odor," said Merlin, "is the alchemist's and not the Devil's, though to be sure my father was an imp."

"Thy father," said the Lady of the Lake, "was a mendicant friar, and he did get thy mother, a milkmaid, with child, which became thee. As a boy thou wert assailed by cries of 'Bastard!' And couldst not fight the whole world, poor fellow. Therefore, thy wits being keen, thou didst decide to live by them, and not by the sword—or the begging bowl."

Old Merlin sank to a seat upon a bench on which alongside him an alembic boiled. "Then King Pellinore spake right," said he sadly. "You are needlessly cruel."

"It is but the truth," said the lady, "which is oft harsh. But what I know will never go farther than this chamber, Merlin, for I do not despise thee (except insofar as thou wouldst pretend to supernatural powers). Thou hast made much more of thyself than could be expected. And thou hast provided great aid to King Arthur in his gallant experiment to make noble that which hath ever been mean. But now thy time hath come to leave him, for in the irony that so characterizes human affairs, it is thee who art the realist, while he will go ever further into the legendary."

Now Merlin had recovered from his hurt pride and he doted on the Lady of the Lake more than ever. Therefore he sought again to fascinate her with his inventions: a box from which light played through a hole and cast images upon a white sheet affixed against a wall; a large horn, erected upon an engine which moved in a circular fashion, which did emit music; and two cups of tin, joined by a waxed cord, the which when pulled taut would conduct words spoken into one cup to the ear against which the other was held close.

And the lady examined these things politely, without showing disdain, but yet they seemed to her like unto battledores and shuttlecocks, for the entertainment of small boys.

"Thou art comfortable here," said she finally, "in thy cave of alchemy. Therefore here thou shalt remain and never come out again."

"That I should do happily," said the old magician, "were you to stay with me, for to speak truly, now that Arthur hath all the furniture required to reign well, he would seem to need me no longer. And knowing you, I have learned to appreciate women at long last. With my practical cunning and your supernatural powers, lady, there is nothing that we could not manage."

"Nay, old man," said the Lady of the Lake, "thou canst not so confine the feminine principle, though 'tis quite masculine so to try." Yet she was not so unfeeling as the libelous scribes would oft depict her in time to come, and she did promise to visit Merlin sometimes. And this she hath done throughout the centuries, for she is immortal, and as to Merlin, though he has no fiendish blood, he is long-lived through his lack of traffic with other humanity, for all men would live forever if they were not, as the Stagirite hath said, social animals.

BOOK VI

*How Sir Tristram fought with the Morholt; and
how he met La Belle Isold.*

Now the time came when King Arthur decided to send Sir
Tristram as emissary to King Mark of Cornwall, to determine why it was that Mark had not sent him evidences of
fealty, for the Cornish lands were traditionally part of
Britain, and Mark's predecessor Gorlois had styled himself
but a duke, and he was, as we have seen, a vassal of Uther
Pendragon's (and former husband of Arthur's mother the
fair Ygraine, as well as father to Arthur's half-sisters Margawse, Morgan la Fey, and Elaine).

So Tristram did undertake this mission and he left
Camelot. But he had not gone many leagues when he
heard an halloo come from behind him, and he therefore
stopped and turned, and he saw a knight putting his lance
in the rest, for to begin a charge upon him. Now being a
great master in the art of arms, Tristram held his own
horse stock-still, for this was not a tournament but a matter in which lives might well be in the balance, and when
his adversary reached him, Sir Tristram deflected the
other's lance with his own, and in the momentum of the
charge, the other lost his grasp upon the weapon and it
fell between the two horses. Therefore the other knight
wheeled and drew his sword.

Now retaining his own lance Tristram had the advantage, but while he considered whether the principles of courtesy would call for his discarding it, so that the fight could continue with like weapons betweens equals in chivalry, the other knight chopped his lance in twain. Therefore Sir Tristram hurled the broken shaft away and he drew his own sword, and for a long time both knights occupied themselves each with hacking at the shield of the other. And Sir Tristram found his adversary was indeed a mighty man and as formidable as himself with the sword if not even more so, but at last his own horse did trip in a hole in the ground, and he fell to the earth.

Now the other knight did dismount as well, and Tristram saw that he was a man of great honor. And so they fought afoot, and the fight that had begun in midmorning continued till the sun had begun to fall in the western sky, and both men were weary and sore from much buffeting, and here and there each had hacked pieces of armor from the other, and their shields were cracked and splintered.

But finally Sir Tristram put all his remaining force into a mighty blow, the which would surely have cut through the crown of his opponent's helmet and the skull as well, had not the other smote him in the side at the same moment, though happily with the flat of the blade, so causing his own sword to turn and also strike with the flat. Even so, its power was such as to knock the other knight to the earth, where he lay senseless.

Now Tristram unlaced and removed the helm of the fallen man, and he saw that he had fought all the day with Sir Gawaine.

Now when Gawaine awakened, Sir Tristram said to him, "My lord, I never knew it was you. And for your part, I can not but think that you mistook me for another. How terrible that we companions of the Round Table should smite each other!"

But Gawaine replied full of shame, "Sir Tristram, alas! It was no mistake that I attacked you, for I was well aware of your identity. I confess I did so in a mean exercise of envy, for which I humbly beg your forgiveness.

Now, not only have you proved that your prowess at arms exceeds mine own, but your gracious assumption that I fought you through error is further evidence of your nobility, whereas I am ignobled in every regard."

And he did rise and take up his sword, with the intent to break it upon a rock and so degrade himself, but Sir Tristram stayed his arm.

"My friend," said he with the greatest feeling, "firstly, thou art the most worthiest knight I have ever striven with. Look how mine armor is hacked and dented, and I fear thy final blow hath come near to splintering my ribs though it was given with only the flat of the blade. And as to nobility, when I was thrown from mine horse, thou might have stayed on thine and had the advantage, but thou didst not, else the issue would surely have been reversed. The difference between us was a thing of chance. Now let us join our hands and swear in fellowship that never will we fight each other again, but be sweet friends always."

And Sir Gawaine did grasp his hand and swear this, for he now understood that in a knight of the Round Table valor was ever to be conjoined with generosity, and so he conquered his envy.

Then they did wish each other to go with God, and Sir Gawaine went back towards Camelot whilst Sir Tristram resumed his journey to Cornwall, and when after many days he reached Tintagel, in his battered armor and carrying no lance, he was seized by King Mark's discourteous guards and cast into a dungeon.

Now he might have stayed forever in that evil cell, where the walls were wet and his only company were the rats who came to share the stale bread sometimes thrust in to him, had not the warder come within that dungeon once, bringing him a basin of water and a towel and commanding him to wash. And Sir Tristram did this gladly, for he had not been able to bathe since leaving Camelot.

Now so soon as he had dried himself, the warder, who was a detestable sodomite (and Tristram was a handsome knight), did purpose to perform with him a vicious crime against Nature, but Tristram seizing his neck did break it quickly and made egress from the cell wearing only his shirt, for the warder had torn away his hose. And though he was now clean, his hair was uncombed and his beard unkempt, and therefore as he went through the castle looking for King Mark he was thought to be a madman by those who saw him, amongst them more than a few ladies, and he was avoided by all as if a wild creature.

Now in an antechamber to the throne room he came upon a musician a-carrying a lyre, the which Sir Tristram seized from him and covered his privy parts with it, for they were naked below his shirt, and so he entered the court.

And King Mark was sitting on his throne, and he said, "Ho, comest to sing in thy shirt, insolent rogue!" And he commanded his retainers to administer a severe birching to the impudent fellow and then to hurl him from the battlements.

But Sir Tristram begged the king to hear his tale, and Mark relented.

"But," said the king, "thou must do it in song, for 'tis my time of day to be amused musically."

"Very well, then," said Tristram, and then he began to play the lyre, which he had learned to do when a boy, and he sang what follows in a marveolus voice, for he had such a gift and was the finest singer of all the knights of the Round Table.

"Now," he sang, "I was born in a land across La Manche, which is to say the British Channel, to a great king and a fair queen, and scarcely had I been born when a lady who did illicitly love my father the king enchanted him and locked him into a castle and then did poison my mother the queen."

Now King Mark made a great scowl, and he stopped the song, saying, "Unless thou dost soon become more amusing, I shall have thee whipped after all."

And Tristram continued in this wise: "The wicked lady

then did marry my father and become queen of the land, and once when I was a child she did give me a cup to drink of, but by error my father the king drank from it instead, and he fell dead, for it contained venom."

By this time King Mark had heard quite enough, and he said, "What this lady could not manage, I shall do here." And he directed his attendants to fetch a flagon full of vitriol and to pour it down the throat of him who sang such a lugubrious song.

But Sir Tristram continued to sing undaunted, "And therefore I fled that kingdom of Lyonesse—"

But at the sound of this name King Mark cried to his retainers to hold, and to Tristram he said, "Lyonesse, in France?" And then, because Sir Tristram was already singing of his rearing (which was conducted by the faithful Gorvenal, his father's loyal old vassal, in a remote forest), the king asked, "What was thy mother's name?"

And Tristram stopped singing at last and said, "Elizabeth, God rest her soul."

"My dear nephew!" cried King Mark. "For she was mine own dear sister." And with great joy and every evidence of affection he did welcome Sir Tristram to his court.

That evening a great banquet was held at Tintagel, with Tristram now properly attired in the finest clothing as befitted his station, and he was seated next his uncle the king. Now, the reason wherefore King Mark had not wanted to hear a sad song was that he had grievous trouble of his own and, contrary to the opinion of old wives, misery doth not always seek like company.

"My boy," he said to his nephew, "I am very sorry to hear of my sister's death, but that was now long ago and in another country. I am myself tormented currently. Cornwall is a small land, too small to hold its own without swearing fealty to one or another of the great tyrants on either side of it: Anguish of Ireland or Uther Pendragon of Britain, both of whom are monarchs most brutal. Uther for example murdered my predecessor Gorlois, so as to take his wife to swyve. Therefore I threw my lot in with Anguish, but the Irish king doth demand I pay an extravagant tribute to him each year, always in the amount of three hundred: three hundred pounds of gold, of diamonds, emeralds, rubies, or whichever precious gem. But in recent years he hath tired of treasure and asked instead for three hundred creatures, dwarfs, colored men, or young Cornish boys. And for this current year, this vicious king hath demanded three hundred virgins. Now, if I fail to provide these he will send to Cornwall a giant who will ravish my land."

"Uncle," said Sir Tristram, "firstly, Uther Pendragon is dead and the sovereign lord of Britain is now Arthur, who is the finest king in the history of the world. Indeed he hath sent me as emissary to you, for I am a knight of the Round Table, a fellowship of men devoted to bringing about the triumph of virtue. Swear fealty to him and you need pay no tribute to any tyrant. For his part, he will furnish you aid against such enemies as the Irish king."

"These are good news," said King Mark. "Therefore go to Arthur and tell him I am willingly his vassal and that I ask him to send me an host with which to deal with this Hibernian giant."

"Well," said Sir Tristram, "I shall alone fight this giant."

"Nephew," said Mark, "thou singest and playest the harp very well indeed, and thou art a comely young man. But this giant, who is hight the Morholt, stands so high as an oak. The very sight of him, with his great black beard, yellow tusks, and purple mouth opened wide as a cave, roaring with obscene mirth at the prospect of wreaking mayhem, is enough to send a battalion of the bravest knights to flee like unto a pack of curs from a whirling cudgel."

"Nonetheless," said Sir Tristram, "I am your nephew and a knight of the Round Table. It would be unseemly to send for further aid in view of these mine affiliations. I shall fight the Morholt."

King Mark saw that Tristram's heart was fixed upon

this purpose and that he could not deter him without causing shame for both of them. Therefore, though he privately expected to lose this nephew so soon after finding him, he gave Tristram permission to represent Cornwall in single combat against the Morholt, the dread champion of Ireland.

And so couriers were sent across the Irish Sea with this advice, and when they returned, many weeks later (during which intervening time Tristram sang and played the harp for the lords and ladies of the court, thus making many enemies, for the lords already did envy his relationship with the king), these messengers brought the reply of the Morholt to this challenge, which was as follows: "To Piss-tram, the so-called knight. If thou hast the heart for it, meet me upon the islet of St. Samson's, where I shall kill thee and by evening the gulls shall sup on thy brains."

Now incensed by this vile insult, King Mark would have put to death the poor couriers who had fetched it, though they were his own men, but Sir Tristram said, "Nay, Uncle, that is the practice of the primitive and brutal past, to blame the news on him who brings it. We are chivalrous now." And he did reward these messengers with gold for returning promptly.

Now King Mark lost whatever little hope he had had that his nephew would overcome the giant, for he believed Tristram to be womanish.

And he said, "I have me a plan. On the day before the fight is to take place, I shall send a company of knights to conceal themselves in the trees on that islet. When thou goest to face the Morholt, my men will attack him from behind, driving a score of spears into his back, while others hamstring him with swords and axes. Whilst he is so being weakened, thou canst deliver to him the *coup de grâce*, a thrust into his great stones. The Morholt will die only if his genitals are ruined, for he is a notorious satyr, and the living creatures in each tribute of three hundred have been used by him for unnatural sexual purposes."

"Uncle," said Sir Tristram, "know you that a knight of the Round Table fights fairly."

"But what can be unfair against a loathsome monstrosity?" asked King Mark. "When he hath killed thee he will ravish our three hundred maids with his great tool! That is, if I can find so many maidenheads still extant in Cornwall."

But Sir Tristram continued to refuse utterly this unjust aid, and therefore Mark determined privately to furnish it all the same. And he sent one hundred of his best knights to the islet of St. Samson's, which proved to be not far from the Irish shore, for the Morholt was a disdainful and arrogant giant too lazy to travel far for his victims, and because the sea of Ireland is ever a body of rough waters, this entire company of Cornishmen were sick on the voyage and arrived green-faced and puking.

And the islet was but half a league square and flat as a table and sans trees, so that these knights could not blend with the forest, and the Morholt came across from the shore in a sailboat which he impelled by the mighty gusts of air from his own lips, more powerful than the breezes that blew, so that the boat did race across the sea. Then he anchored it in nine feet of water and waded to land, the waves reaching only to his belt, and seeing this the Cornish knights, sick and fearful, did leap into the sea and perish.

Meanwhile Sir Tristram was sailing alone in a little boat, and when the islet came into sight he thought he saw a castle standing in the middle of it, but then as he drew closer he saw it was rather the Morholt, who stood six yards high and carried a ten-foot shield and was armed with a sword twice as long as Tristram was tall. Yet Sir Tristram was not frightened, for he knew the issue of all battles is in God's hands, who having given each of us a life hath the right to take it away when He wills, and in any event will take it sometime, whether today or tomorrow, and a knight can but live what he hath of it with courage. And Sir Tristram's life, having been unhappy, was not so great a treasure to its owner.

Therefore when he had disembarked from his boat he stove in its bottom with his sword and he shoved it from the sand into the water, where it sank.

Now the Morholt watched this with amazement and then he said, in his great voice the breath from which raised the dust from the ground between him and Tristram, "Little man, why dost ruin thy boat?"

And Tristram did grimace from the stink of the Morholt's breath, which was foul with a corruption which made sweet the odors of rotten cheese and the foist of dogs, and a gull flying through it fell stone dead onto the beach.

"Because," said Sir Tristram, "there will be but one of us who will leave this isle."

"O impudent dwarf," cried the Morholt in rage, and he raised his great sword and swung it with all his force, but Tristram was so far beneath him that the blade cut only the air above his helmet, and when the sword passed over him, he ran close in to the giant's legs and he hacked them both off at the knees, reducing the Morholt in height by two yards.

Yet the Irish giant did not fall but rather standing sturdily on the stumps of his great thighs, like unto two great stone columns, he struck at Tristram again, and now his blow was lower and it took away the crest of Tristram's helmet though did not quite reach unto the skull.

Then Tristram using all his force smote the Morholt through the waist, cutting off his lower portions altogether, and the huge trunk fell heavily onto the ground yet stayed upright and was as tall as Sir Tristram though three times as broad, and the Morholt was no nearer to dying, for (contrary to King Mark's belief) he was immortal except if his head was lost. But his blood did flow vastly and cover the entire islet, the sand of which is colored red to this day, and he did wax wroth at the loss of his lower body, for he set great store in his privy parts, with which he had misused myriads of men, women, children, and even animals, and indeed he knew no other pleasure.

Therefore swearing dreadful oaths and spewing his loathsome breath onto Sir Tristram, who was slipping on the slimy blood thick as treacle, he struck at him and now he wounded Tristram grievously in the left side, and he would have done worse had not, at his current height, his sword been too long to swing with accuracy.

But notwithstanding this terrible hurt, which was near mortal, Sir Tristram then hacked the Morholt's head off, but the neck being of solid bone, this job took more than one stroke, and a great piece of steel was broken from the blade of Sir Tristram's sword and remained in the neck of the Morholt.

Now the giant's head rolled along the beach and was soon a great ball of bloody sand, and then it went into the water, where it was washed off, discovering a face so hideous that a school of passing fish were struck dead by its sight and floated white bellies upwards.

But Sir Tristram was very near death himself, and when he cast off in the Morholt's boat for to return to Cornwall, he did soon swoon from his hurt, and the winds instead carried him to the Irish shore near by, where he was beached and lay as if dead for three days, and worms did grow upon his wound and the great birds that feed on dead things did perch upon the gunwales and watch his body hungrily.

But at last some fisherfolk came there and determined, by probing him with sticks, that he was yet quick though almost dead, and so they transported him to the best surgeon in Ireland, who happened to be the daughter of the king, and her name was La Belle Isold. And now that Guinevere was married, Isold was the most beautiful maiden in the world, with hair black as sable, skin white and soft as swan's-down, and eyes blue as the ocean under the morning sky.

Now when Isold bathed the forehead of Sir Tristram with the fragrant water of Cologne, he opened his eyes

and believed he had died and gone to Heaven, where he
lay in the lap of the Mother of God (for which blasphemous misapprehension he can be forgiven, owing to his
near-morbidity at this time).

"My lord," said La Belle Isold to him, "you are most
sorely wounded, but methinks I can cure you, for you look
to be a man of great worship." And she cleaned his wound
and anointed it with a wax into which quicksilver and gold
had been mixed with balsam and the droppings of uni-
corns, which were not noisome but sweet and had great
curative properties, and her own tears fell into this paste
and made it even more efficacious, for she did weep over
the hurt of this gentle, brave, and handsome knight, with
whom she fell in love on the instant.

Now though Sir Tristram began to wend towards good
health from the moment in which he first gazed into the
face of La Belle Isold, he did not recover in full for many
weeks, for the Morholt's fell sword had hacked in him an
hole the which could have contained two fists joined, and
of his vital spirits he had lost so much that he could
scarcely do more than flex his smallest finger. Therefore
holding his head in her lap La Belle Isold fed him broths,
and she bathed his face with scented oils and dried him
with the costliest silk stuffs, and when he had got some
better she brought her lyre and sang sweetly to him, for
she had a fine Hibernian voice.

And all this while Sir Tristram was falling in love with
her, so that he was in no hurry to recover, and when he
grew strong enough he joined his own fine voice to hers,
and together they sang so beautifully that the nightingales
would fly to perch upon the window sill and listen in silent
admiration.

Now one day a boastful, cowardly rogue walking along
the shore did by accident find the great head of the Morholt, which being too ugly even for sea monsters to eat,
had washed onto the beach on the tides, and it was yet
whole, with the piece of Tristram's sword stuck into the
bone of the neck.

And supposing that the death of such a fearsome giant would be greeted happily at the Irish court, and that he would gain much worship as the killer of it, this poltroon got himself a cart pulled by an ox and with great labor put the head into it, the which it filled entirely, and he hauled it to the court of King Anguish.

But when the Irish king saw what had been brought, he ordered the braggart to be racked and then quartered, for the Morholt was his own dear brother and he made much grief over the head, not only for that he was related to him, but also the king did not now have a means to subdue Cornwall. And La Belle Isold also grieved piteously, for the Morholt had been her favorite uncle, who swung her twenty feet in the air when she was a child and he gave her sweetmeats and trinkets (and little did she know that he had stolen them from persons he had murdered! for 'tis natural that children think well of those who give them presents).

Now King Anguish found the fragment of sword embedded in his dead brother's neck and he promised a great reward for the man who would find the blade it matched, for he much wanted to get revenge on the owner thereof, and his knights therefore looked high and low but could not find it because the sword was all the while in the scabbard hanging in the chamber where La Belle Isold was nursing Sir Tristram. And you can be sure that Tristram never told her who he was nor why he happened to be in Ireland, and he called himself Tramtrist, a wandering minstrel who had been set upon by robbers.

Then finally Tristram was completely well, and he knew his duty was to return to Cornwall and tell his uncle what had passed in regard to the Morholt. So he must needs bring to an end the first happiness he had ever enjoyed in his sad life long. Therefore, because he could not bear to say good-by to Isold his beloved, he stole away by night; and so as not to make a noise while stealing through the antechamber where she slept on her chaste bed, he left be-

hind his armor and his sword as well, and secretly he went
to the shore and took a boat and embarked upon the sea.

Now when La Belle Isold discovered next morning he
was gone, she wept piteously and took his armor for to
embrace it, and when kissing his scabbard she held it so
that the sword did slip out as far as the notch in the blade,
seeing the which she took the sword in wonder to her father the king, who fitted into it exactly the piece of steel
taken from the neck of the Morholt.

And King Anguish swore a great oath of anger, and La
Belle Isold thereupon came to hate Sir Tristram as violently as she had loved him earlier. "Would that I had
anointed his wound with vitriol!" she cried, and then she
wept in rage.

Meanwhile, Sir Tristram having caught a breeze was
well on his way to Cornwall, and when he arrived at Tintagel and told King Mark that he should have no further
Irish worry, there was a great celebration, but Tristram
himself was again very sad.

And at this banquet his uncle the king spoke to Tristram
as follows. "Dear Nephew, thou art a knight of greatest
worship. But art thou aware that in this world a person of
prowess doth attract much envy? My barons, for example,
do bear thee no good will for delivering them from the
terror of the Morholt, whom they were too fearful to face.
Instead they now brood over the matter of the succession
after my death, and worry that thou shalt inherit the
crown."

Now Sir Tristram, being the generous great knight that
he was, did not suspect that his uncle the king was also envious of him and worried that he, as now the man of most
worship in Cornwall, might well intend to usurp the
throne, for King Mark took seriously only matters of
power as concerns men, and lust with women.

Therefore Tristram said, "This is a most regrettable misapprehension. Did I seek a throne I should go home to Lyonesse and win back my rightful crown, most feloniously
taken from my father."

But neither did King Mark want to be deprived of Tristram's services, for he did trust none of his barons and he believed, now that the Morholt was disposed of, that they might well turn on him: for this was a land where men were deceitful and the women loose. Thus he said to his nephew, "Abide here awhile, pray. When mine affairs are fully in order, we shall together mount an expeditionary force and attack Lyonesse. Meanwhile I must make my reign secure."

"Your protection and surety are in King Arthur," said Sir Tristram. "On the morrow I shall leave for Camelot, there to deliver to Arthur your pledge of fealty."

But secretly King Mark intended to delay such expression as long as he could, forever if possible, and meanwhile to assemble an army and contrive to get Tristram to lead it in a war of conquest against Britain. For if the truth were known, Mark despised Arthur for what he had heard of him to the good, and he respected only tyrants, and furthermore he lusted for Guinevere, having heard she was the most beautiful queen in the world.

So now he did play for time, saying, "Well, there is no need for undue haste. For one, it is obvious that with Ireland out of the picture, I must needs be vassal to Britain. . . . Though indeed it is galling so to submit to anybody now that thou, mine own nephew, art at my side. With thy departure for Cornwall, Arthur's best champion became his nephew Gawaine, whom thou hast defeated in a passage at arms."

But Tristram had confessed this with reluctance, when his uncle had pressed him on the relative merits of the knights of the Round Table, and Mark's subtle appeal to his vanity went for nought, for he had little. Now Tristram said uneasily, "Know you that we fought only by accident, Uncle, and that the issue was but a thing of chance. In another contest I might well be defeated by the gallant Gawaine, whom I admire greatly." And in his noble innocence Sir Tristram added, "There is no hierarchy of worthiness amongst our company of the Round Table, and superlatives should be reserved for use only when speaking of God."

"I have heard," said King Mark, "that Gawaine is a notable whoremaster and that his greatest exploits are twixt the sheets and not upon the field."

"O base calumniators who have told you that!" said Sir Tristram. "He is rather the defender and protector of all womankind."

"Go to," said Mark, and then he asked, "Tell me again, Nephew, whether Queen Guinevere be the most beautiful woman in the world."

And thinking sadly of Isold, Tristram said, "The most beautiful *queen,* Uncle."

"I gather thou art making some distinction," said King Mark. "There is then some commoner who hath greater beauty?"

So Tristram found he must needs tell him of La Belle Isold, but never did he mention his great love for her.

"Ah, then," said Mark when he had heard this, "she is both maid and princess and therefore would be quite suitable to be my queen. For now that I no longer pay the ruinous tribute to Ireland I can afford a splendid wedding, and every king should have a consort by his side to furnish stability to his throne." He did not mention that he yearned for a son of his own blood, to whom to pass on the crown when he himself died, for as much as did his barons he enviously resented Sir Tristram's claim and did in no wise believe his nephew's disclaimer, for men who love power find incredible another's professed lack of interest in it, and take it rather for a cunning ruse.

Now Tristram did gasp at his uncle's speech, but King Mark thought this was because he believed the idea politically outlandish. Therefore he explained himself. "Perhaps it seems foolish to thee that I should apply to King Anguish for the hand of his daughter, I who but lately was his vassal and now, having killed his champion, do represent myself as his equal. Ah, Nephew, thou dost not understand the nature of kings! Be assured that he will be pleased.

Having lost his brother the Morholt, he gaineth a son-in-law. Having failed to move me by force, he will hope to do so, more subtly, by love, for a piece of Ireland will sleep in Cornwall's bed."

Sir Tristram's blood did go cold at this figure of speech. That La Belle Isold should use the same sheets as his uncle, who was a dotard of seventy years of age, was a terrible thing to envision. However, having witnessed the rage and hatred in which King Anguish ordered the search for the sword that had killed his giant brother, Tristram could not believe he would give his daughter to the enemy who had commissioned the killer. But he did not argue the point with his uncle at this moment.

But next King Mark said, "Now, Nephew, thou art again the very man I need for to send to Ireland once more."

And Sir Tristram did go all numb with amazement and dread.

"Thou shalt apply to King Anguish," said Mark, "acting as mine agent, for the hand of his daughter La Belle Isold, to be joined with mine in marriage."

"Uncle," said Sir Tristram, "you can not suppose that Ireland will smile upon me, who beheaded his brother, the knowledge of which act he will now be privy to, for I did leave behind my sword with its telltale notch."

"Nephew," said King Mark, "I understand these matters far better than thee. Thou shalt be as successful in this errand as thou wert in the warlike emprise. Now, when thou hast ate thy meat, which is growing cold, I would that thou leave forthwith for Ireland."

And Tristram did groan horribly within though not audibly without, nor did he oppose the wishes of his uncle the king, for a knight is ever obedient to his sovereign and elder relatives, on pain of introducing impious chaos into the human condition, which has been given order by God. Therefore, though he was so sad as to make it seem he had thus far lived a life of bliss, he finished his mutton chop and pease pudding and then he went to the shore and taking the boat in which he had lately crossed the Irish Sea, he embarked.

And though he would have welcomed stormy seas, the which might have stove in his craft and drowned him, fate provided waters still as any pond on a warm summer afternoon and a strong but not unruly wind, and he was unhappily not long in reaching the Hibernian coast.

But when he reached the Irish court and was admitted to the presence of King Anguish, that monarch recognizing him directed that he be held prostrate before him so that he might strike off his head. And though Sir Tristram was happy with the prospect of death, he felt obliged at least to announce the message he had been given by his uncle to deliver.

"Your Majesty," said he, "I have come as emissary of King Mark of Cornwall, who asketh the hand of your daughter La Belle Isold in marriage."

"Unhand that knight," King Anguish did command his retainers. "Now, Sir Tristram, is this proposal for a *matrimonium ad morganaticum*, or doth old Mark offer to make Isold a proper queen with all rank, titles, fiefs, and entailments, succession to which would pass to the children of such an union, in the usual order?"

"Certes, the latter," said Tristram.

"Then I do accept," said Anguish joyfully, "and now, my dear boy, let us celebrate this arrangement with food and drink." And so saying he did embrace Tristram and lead him to the banquet hall.

Now Tristram was sadder than ever, and as for La Belle Isold she did weep in hatred and rage against both him and King Mark when her father informed her she must go to Cornwall forthwith and be married.

"Father," said she, "would that you were rather sending me to my death."

But King Anguish believed this to be but girlish foolishness, and he had no time for her, having to arrange for as mean a dowry as he could get King Mark to accept, whom he knew as a lustful man, and he believed therefore that a royal Irish maidenhead would count with him as treasure beyond gold.

But Isold was attended by her loyal gentlewoman Brangwain, who had served her since she was a child and who loved her greatly, and actually it was Brangwain who brewed the potions and philters on which Isold had established her reputation as a physician, and which had healed Sir Tristram of his dreadful wound. And this Brangwain did love Sir Tristram with a great passion, but secretly, for she was plain and not of his rank and could therefore enjoy his love only through bringing him and her lady together, as would be proper for a faithful waiting-woman, and then she could steal some token from him and place it between her breasts, and in the morning see his impress upon the sheets where he had lain all the night with her gracious mistress.

Therefore when Isold, quite out of her wits with furious sorrow, came to her and asked for a poison with which to end her life so that she would not have to endure the shame of being escorted by Tristram to marry King Mark, the two men she hated most in all the world (and the former even more than the latter), Brangwain agreed to do this, on the condition that Isold would never swallow it until they were upon the sea, and also that Sir Tristram be induced to drink of the same potion.

"Yes," said La Belle Isold, "thou hast a finer cunning than mine, dear Brangwain. This will be a good revenge, for the ship will come to port bearing not only the corse of the intended bride, but that of nephew and finest knight as well."

So Brangwain went to brew the decoction, but instead of using adder's venom, crocodile tears, and the poisonous sweat of the toad, she rather put into the cucurbit a mandrake root, which shrieked when it was pulled from the ground and screamed when boiled, the ginger which turns Oriental peoples yellow with concupiscence, powdered pearls in which the aphrodisiac humors of the wanton mollusc collect, and the spunk of the unicorn, and from these arose a steam into the nose of the alembic and then turned into drops a clear fluid, the which fell until they filled a little silver flask with a distillation not of Death but rather of the most ardent and enduring Love.

And putting a stopper therein she gave this flask to La Belle Isold.

Now King Anguish was obliged to furnish Sir Tristram with a fine ship for the voyage to Cornwall, and this he did, but the dowry with which he filled the hold was only real gold and silver at the tops of the chests, being underneath cheap tinware of Irish tinkers, for he counted on King Mark to be so assotted with Isold that he would plunge his hands into her robe rather than deeply into the supposed treasure.

Now when they had put to sea Sir Tristram did continue to avoid the fair Isold, as he had done while at the castle of King Anguish, for though the Irish monarch had displayed great pleasure with the marriage arrangement, Tristram could hardly suppose that Isold would be happy, for he had observed that she was of a passionate temperament. Therefore he stayed in a close cabin below decks and owing to the roughness of the waters he suffered seasickness as well as his habitual sadness.

And because his absence made it difficult for Isold to poison him discreetly, she sent the loyal Brangwain to fetch him onto the open deck, where she sat in the sea air under a flapping silk canopy, and she was so beautiful that many flying fishes with gaping mouths leaped out of the water and soared across the boat so as to see her with their slimy bulging eyes.

Therefore Brangwain finding Sir Tristram said to him, "Gentle knight, my lady desires your company." And her voice was very sweet, for she adored him.

"Can this be true?" asked Tristram woefully. "For methinks she bears me no love."

"Women are changeable, *varium et mutabile semper femina*, so saith the honey-tongued Maro," said Brangwain, for she was literate in the Roman tongue, having been schooled by the nuns who with the monks of Ireland were the only classicists there. "And soon you will be her relative-in-law. She hath lost an uncle to gain a nephew."

Sir Tristram had never thought of this relationship as such, and now he was amazed. And he permitted Brangwain to conduct him to La Belle Isold.

"Greeting to you, sir knight," said Isold, who trembled with the effort to be gracious, for she hated him so much.

Seeing her shudder Sir Tristram said, "Lady, you are cold in this sea wind." And he removed his cloak, the which he presented to her to wrap about her shoulders.

But she drew away from it as if it were a filthy thing. "On the contrary," said she. "I am too warm and I am fearfully thirsty. Brangwain, bring some wine."

"Quite right," said Sir Tristram, his breath steaming, "indeed, it is the hottest afternoon I have known upon the Irish Sea."

And though about to poison him, La Belle Isold could not forbear from contradicting him as well, in sheer bloody-mindedness. "And fetch a fur robe as well, dear Brangwain, for I am chilled to the bone."

Her contrariness made no impression on Sir Tristram, for looking at her white skin and blue eyes and black hair in which there were red flashed even on a gray day, he loved her so ardently and hopelessly that he wished he could drink poison while she sipped wine.

Therefore when Brangwain brought the flask and poured from it two goblets of what Isold thought was venom and Tristram believed Rhenish, and which was neither, Isold raised the vessel to her red lips, but Sir Tristram dallied staring sadly astern into the foaming wake. And when La Belle Isold lowered her empty goblet, he had not yet tasted of his.

And she did cry out ardently, which caused him to put down his goblet altogether, for he did think her in pain, and he asked what he could do to relieve her.

"Kiss me, embrace me, devour me, mine own sweet love!" she cried in a voice which thrilled Tristram but also frightened him more, he the bravest of knights who could vanquish giants but he felt helpless with a woman in a transport of emotion. Therefore he seized his own goblet and drained it in one gulp, for to acquire courage from its spirituous liquors, and hardly had he swallowed when the amorous ethers enveloped his heart, and if he had already loved Isold so much that he wished to die for want of her, that passion was nothing to what he felt now.

Indeed in the violence of the emotion which they shared, mere fleshly contact would not have sufficed, therefore they did not join together except for one burning kiss, and then they sent Brangwain to fetch both their lyres, upon which they played a duet and sang together, making music so sweet that the fearsome serpents rose from the bottom of the sea to float and listen with eyes soft as lambs', and the melody calmed the previously truculent waters and the warm sun dissipated the gray clouds.

And so making this music they crossed to Cornwall as if in a dream. But when they arrived at Tintagel and were received by King Mark, it was as though waking on a rainy morning after a nightmare.

"Uncle," said Sir Tristram to the king, "having discharged my duties to you, I must needs now return to King Arthur and the Round Table."

"Well," said Mark, "thou must certainly remain for my wedding, dear Nephew, which without thy services would not be taking place! How can I thank thee enough?" And he drew Tristram aside and spake privately, with glee. "This Irish is a damned comely piece, my boy!" And in the heat of his foul lust he swore several other abominable oaths. "Would that old Uther Pendragon were still among the quick, to know I had me this fair chick to pluck. For I was one of his barons of old, and ofttimes we were constrained to watch him at his venereal sports with young virgins, but never did he enjoy such white flesh."

And Tristram was impatient to leave his presence, lest he be at once a regicide and an uncle-murderer. However, what the king commanded could not be denied, and therefore poor Tristram was compelled to stay at Tintagel for the nuptials.

"And by God," Mark said blasphemously, "thou art a faithful and honest knight, Nephew!" And he dug Sir Tristram in the belly with a forefinger. "For anyone else would have corrupted the virtue of this gorgeous princess when alone with her upon the sea." But secretly he believed Tristram was effeminate for not having done this, or perhaps had been made an eunuch by the point of a lance in some tournament, which happened to many knights despite the codpiece of steel.

So Tristram's previous sadness seemed like hilarity when compared with his present state, and pretending to be ill Isold remained in her chambers and wept steadily all through the day and night during the time in which the wedding was being prepared, which was some weeks, for King Mark desired that all the regnant monarchs of the world come to watch him being married, and invitations were sent far as Ind to the heathen kings there and also to the black-faced sovereigns of Afric, whose teeth were made of diamonds. But most of all, Mark wanted King Arthur to see him take a bride he believed more beautiful than Guinevere, for he did envy Arthur and bear him no good will.

However, this wish of King Mark's was not to be satisfied, for God doth confound the spiteful, and King Arthur would not come to Cornwall before he received Mark's pledge of fealty, which was not forthcoming, for King Mark was more arrogant than ever now that he was to take a queen. And it was only because of his nephew Sir Tristram, a knight of the Round Table, that Mark was not destroyed by King Arthur at this time.

Therefore La Belle Isold and the fair Guinevere were never to be compared side by side, but the latter was the greater beauty because her hair was of the color of gold, the most precious substance on earth, for which all men search and many die.

Now this wedding was one of great splendor, and many

of the invited kings did come from all over the earth, those from Ind on elephants and the Africans wore crowns of multicolored feathers and almost nothing else, their privy parts hanging in a little bag, at the size of which the ladies did gasp.

And King Mark enjoyed the expectation of bedding with La Belle Isold at long last, and sitting beside her at the marriage feast he did grope importunately at her under the table.

Therefore she found an excuse to leave him briefly, and she went to the loyal Brangwain, saying, "Surely now thou shalt brew for me a poison, the which I might drink before I must share the bed with that foul old man."

"My lady," said Brangwain, "I shall do something far the better. I shall distill a potion for King Mark to drink, the which will cause him to fall dead asleep and stay so till morn, yet dream to the effect that he hath had you all the night."

"Good my Brangwain!" said Isold, and she returned joyfully to the table and not only found it possible to endure the king's pawing but whispered in his ear certain aphrodisiacal sentiments, thereby distracting him while Brangwain introduced her potion into his wine.

After he had drunk this he could no longer contain himself, and he took Isold into his bedchamber there and then, where he tore off his robe discovering his fat old belly and withered legs and plunged into bed. But no sooner had he done so than he fell fast asleep.

Then Isold took up her lyre and went upon the balcony outside and sang sweetly to the night air, and Tristram, who was wandering disconsolately in the garden below, tearing his hands intentionally on the roses so as to assuage the worse pain in his heart, heard this song and, assuming it was for King Mark, he drew his dagger and though suicide was a terrible sin that would cause him to suffer in Hell throughout eternity, he preferred that to the torment he felt now, and he was about to plunge the blade into his heart when Brangwain found him.

"Sir Tristram," said the loyal Brangwain, "my lady would speak with you."

So he sheathed his poniard and went below the balcony, from which Isold stretched her white hand at him and said, "My love."

"My love!" cried he in return.

"Come to me," said La Belle Isold, and therefore he did climb on the vines and join her, though his hands were all sore from the thorns of the roses. Then she told him of the potion which Brangwain had administered to the king, and she showed him his uncle's sleeping body on the bed. "Now lift him from the bed and put him upon the floor," said she. "And then we, thou and I, shall celebrate our marriage."

"O impious thought," said Sir Tristram. "Knowest thou not that adultery is a crime?"

"I would burn in Hell for thee," said La Belle Isold, "but in fact we were wed on shipboard, and if adultery there be, it would happen only if I bedded with King Mark."

Her reasoning did exceed Sir Tristram's understanding, and he asked her to explain its process.

"Well," said Isold, "was it not God and God alone who did make all the ingredients in the love potion administered to us by the loyal Brangwain? And was it not He who gave to Brangwain the knowledge of how to mix them?"

"But mine own dear love," said Tristram, "is not this a sophistical philosophy? Can it be Christian to wed chemically and not by a priest?"

But Isold had grown impatient of argument, being no withered clerk who computed the number of angels who might dance upon the point of a pin, and she did leave off abstract theory now and step out of her ermine-trimmed robe, and the sight of her white body did stun Tristram thoroughly in his brain so that he had only one thought, that was to eliminate the separation between them.

Therefore he did lift his uncle from the bed, but he was

not so bereft of decency as to leave him on the floor, but rather carried him to a closet and laid him within.

And then Sir Tristram and La Belle Isold did join themselves in the connection which for true lovers can never be too close.

Now at dawn Tristram arose and left the chamber silently, climbing down the vines into the garden, and King Mark was still within the closet, for the lovers had forgot him utterly. But the loyal Brangwain, who had stayed the night in an antechamber for to guard them against intrusion, remembered the king, and after wistfully feeling with her hand the place in the bed where Tristram had lain, she did awaken her mistress Isold, and then she went to the closet and easily lifted the king's body, for she was of robust Irish stock, and she carried him to the bed.

Then she went away, and he soon woke up, at the which awakening Isold rose and left the bed.

Now King Mark did babble and slaver over the passionate episode he seemingly remembered, owing to the potion that had confused his wits, and he would have handled his bride further had she been within his reach, but you can be sure she was not, and complained of weariness and headache. And therefore he gloated over the evidence of her shattered virginity on the satin sheets.

Meanwhile, unhappily, Sir Tristram had been seen descending the vines by a vile dwarf named Frocin, who detested persons of normal size and forever lurked about Tintagel to spy upon their failures and if possible use such information for their ruin, for though he was powerless to punish God for making him with a tiny body and a large head, he could revenge himself on the handsome and gallant knights the like of which he could never be, and the beautiful and gentle ladies whose love he could never earn. And he did this secretly, whereas in public he performed as a buffoon, making those laugh whom he hated.

And this Frocin was in the garden now, where he came before the castle awakened to pull the blossoms off the roses and put lizards and toads upon the ground, for he was an enemy to all that lived in beauty, and seeing whence Sir Tristram descended, he was much pleased that Mark had been made a cuckold, for he wished his monarch no good, but he was all the same in a rage against Sir Tristram for his evident happiness.

Therefore Frocin went unto the royal bedchamber, for being considered no truly human person, he was admitted everyplace, like unto a spaniel or cat which doth scratch at a door, and when La Belle Isold had been dressed behind a screen by the loyal Brangwain and had gone out, Frocin went to the king, who was yet lolling in bed, and to amuse him he stood upon his head, waving his feet to produce a tinkle from the bells on the curly toes of his slippers.

"Tiny rogue," said Mark, and he amiably threw a satin pillow at him. "Minuscule monstrosity, what dost thou do for venereal pleasure? Never have I seen a miniature woman. Doth God make only little men, and are ye all therefore sodomites?" And he then did roar with coarse laugher.

Then Frocin rose upon his feet, saying, "Sire, herewith an epithalamium of my own invention:

> All brides are true—
> Sing cockoo!
>
> Isold's eyes are blue—
> Sing cuckoo!
> A stag is cornu—
> Sing cuckoo!"

"Bloody little bugger!" said the king in genial abuse. "There's bad rhyme in thy song and no reason. I shall have thee whipped, not wreathed, with laurel." But in truth he found Frocin an entertaining fellow and he called him to the bedside, but the dwarf's head rose not so far as the level of the sheets, and therefore he could not see what the king was pointing to thereupon.

"Wert thou taller, thou couldst see," said the king de-

testably, "the spoor of an Irish cat, late wild but now domesticated."

"Methinks," said the vile Frocin, "that after it was
wounded it leaped from the window and clambered down
the vines to the garden." He indicated the trail of blood-
stains that did lead from bed to the embrasure of the window, the which had been dropped by Sir Tristram from
his rose-torn hands on his entry the night before.

Now Mark did leap from bed and trace these, but he
could provide no explanation for them.

Therefore said Frocin, smirking evilly, "Sire, did you
see your nephew Sir Tristram in this chamber less than an
hour ago?" And of course King Mark had not. Then the
dwarf told him of watching Tristram's descent on the
vines.

"This I can not understand at all," said King Mark.
"Unless it be that my nephew did visit the loyal Brangwain, taking this route, but he is a very handsome knight
who might have any lady (except one) in the castle,
whereas Brangwain hath the face of a sheep." And he did
not tell Frocin that he suspected Tristram of being a
capon, for he knew the dwarf for a malicious gossip.

"Did you never close your eyes all night?" asked Frocin.

And divining his meaning, King Mark said, "Thine in-
nuendo, loathsome dwarf, will cause thy skin to be flayed
off and stretched to dry upon a wall. Sir Tristram is the
knight of most worship in all of Cornwall, as the queen is
the most virtuous lady." And he was about to call for his
guards to take Frocin to the torture chamber, where had
been installed an Iron Maiden the which Mark had got
from the Saxons, who had brought it from Germany,
when the dwarf said to him, "Sire, have you reflected
upon the inordinate long time it did take Sir Tristram to
bring La Belle Isold across the Irish Sea?"

And though this time had not been unduly long, men
are easily made suspicious in the degree to which they
know carnal passion. Therefore King Mark began to have
the beginnings of a doubt.

"Truly," said he, "I have some vague memory of a dream, in which I seemed to be locked within the closet, next a close-stool which had not been slopped out and stank dreadfully. Therefore I must have slept, if only briefly. Still, the tongue with which thou speakest this evil will be cut out, unless thou canst provide more evidence of my betrayal."

"Then pray spare my skin until tomorrow," said Frocin, "for tonight I shall collect what you require."

And King Mark granted this request, for it was true that the vile little man had previously furnished him much information that had been damaging to his barons and knights, and all of it had proved correct when the persons accused had been put into the rack and pulled apart, for God had not saved any of them at this time, as He would have done had they been innocent.

Now all that day the king did watch to see whether La Belle Isold and Sir Tristram behaved towards each other in a peculiar way that would suggest they had been illicit bedfellows, but he saw nothing untowards in the manner of either. And when he spake privately to the queen, asking her for her opinion of his nephew, Isold said, "I must accept him as your relation, and as the first knight of Cornwall, but never can I have fondness for him, for he did kill mine uncle the Morholt."

Reassured by this, Mark did plead the case of Tristram, saying, "My dear Isold, thy father himself hath forgiven Tristram, who triumphed in a fair fight, and the Morholt was the very brother of Anguish, a much closer tie than thine."

"My lord," saith Isold, "if you love me, do not mention to me the name of this knight unduly, whom I purpose to avoid."

Therefore King Mark was very happy with his wife, though he pretended to be distressed in complying with her wishes. And he was also pleased with the prospect of submitting Frocin to the torture and determining whether his Iron Maiden would perform effectively on a dwarf, for though he made use of Frocin's intelligences and found him entertaining, he would enjoy even more causing such a tiny man to suffer intense pain with the sanction Heaven doth give for the correction of liars.

Now when night came King Mark conducted La Belle Isold into their chamber, but before he joined her in bed he went to the closet for to bog into the stool there, and he seemed to remember it as the place he had seen in his dream the night before, and he was some vexed by the suspicion that he had sleepwalked there during the preceding night, as one sometimes does when nocturnally going to void urine, and there lingered unduly, dozing, while his nephew stole in and performed the uncle's office 'twixt the sheets with the aunt. O unnatural lese-majestical incestuous act!

But then wiping his breech he emerged from the closet and saw the beautiful Isold, her sable hair spread over the white satin pillow, and he could believe her the cause of no evil that could come to him.

And she smiled beautifully and gave him a goblet, saying, "My lord, the loyal Brangwain, who is an adept in white-witchery, hath concocted for us an aphrodisiacal potion, the which causes an increase in the passionate humors and, more, their long endurance."

And King Mark did grasp this goblet and gulp down the contents thereof, for he was not young, whereas his queen was but a girl, and in truth he did wonder, what with his memory of the preceding night, whether he could stand so soon again to the occasion, for all the ardency of his brain.

Now he had hardly swallowed the potion when he fell fast asleep, on seeing which La Belle Isold did go out upon the balcony and signal with a lighted lamp to Sir Tristram, who awaited in the garden below, and he began to mount the vines. But whilst he was climbing, Isold returned to the bedchamber and, to spare her lover the work of removing the king's body to the closet, she summoned the robust Brangwain to do this job.

Meanwhile the vile Frocin, who had concealed his tiny

body in the shadows of the balcony, did sprinkle flour onto the railing there and also upon the floor, and when Tristram arrived he did unwittingly make marks in it with his hands and boots.

Now Tristram and Isold did have their joy together until the coming of the dawn, and in the morning he departed, and Brangwain returned King Mark to the bed, where once again he awoke with the assumption that he had exerted himself all the night in the labors of Venus, which art their own reward, and he supposed he should soon have the further pleasure of torturing Frocin for his malicious prevarications.

Therefore so soon as Isold had gone away, he summoned to him the vile dwarf, saying, "Sirrah, prepare for thine agonies, for I did lie here all the night, not leaving bed at all, and therefore thou shalt die horribly for thy libels against the queen and my nephew."

But Frocin said, "Then what explanation for these footprints in the flour?" And he pointed to the traces of white on the carpet, and then led King Mark onto the balcony, to show him its floor and the railing. But a strong wind had come up during the night, the which had blown away the loose flour, and then some rain had fallen which dampened that which remained and made little particles of dough from it.

And looking at these King Mark said, "Caitiff, this is but the turd of birds. Beg God quickly to bring thee the balm of death, for I shall have thy tiny testes torn away with hot pincers."

"Hold you, for the love of Christ," cried Frocin. "If I take these pellets to the kitchens and have them baked into tiny biscuits, shall I have proved they are never avian mards but rather dough-balls, rolled by wind and rain from the flour I sprinkled here to show the spoor of adultery?"

Now King Mark was frustrated, certes, and perplexed as well. "Whoever did or did not creep here, I lay within that bed all the night."

"Sire," said Frocin, "may I suggest the possibility of your being captive of a spell?"

"Worked by whom?" asked the king. "For certainly La Belle Isold doth not have demoniac powers, and I was near no other person." But then he remembered the potion he had drunk, and also that Brangwain was an adept in white magic, but perhaps it was rather black, for the white came from God and could never be used to the detriment of a king. Therefore once again he had sufficient doubt to stay the torture of Frocin, and when the dwarf returned with the pellets of dough baked into little cakes, proving they were not the shit of birds, his suspicion burgeoned, and as to the traces of white on the carpet of the chamber, which came to and fro between bed and window, he was no longer certain they had their source in the Arabic powders used by Isold to dust her soft body.

So when Frocin begged his leave to prepare another trap, he agreed. But he said, "Yet if they are so cunning as somehow to have fooled me when I was here all the night, I have the paradoxical sense that I can never catch them at it unless I go away!"

"Or to pretend to, Sire," said Frocin, "while actually watching from a place of concealment."

Therefore did King Mark announce to all the court that day that he would leave before noon for to go boar-sticking in a remote forest and not to return to Tintagel until the following day. And with a great entourage he left, but he had not gone far beyond the horizon when he ordered them to halt and make camp, and he secretly returned to the castle, where in the subterranean dungeons he pleasantly passed the day in watching the punishment of malefactors, his presence there unsuspected by La Belle Isold and Sir Tristram, who as ever maintained only polite relations during the day if indeed their paths crossed at all.

But Frocin went to him who but for Tristram would have been the foremost knight of Cornwall, Sir Andret, and knowing he suffered great envy, said to him, "My lord, there is a game afoot the issue of which will mean the ruin of all who now have worship: not only Sir Tristram and our Queen Isold, but King Mark as well. For the first two will this night be proved foul adulterers, and when Mark discovers that his kicky-wicky doth bed with his nephew, he will order her burned at the stake. Sir Tristram will never suffer this, but will kill the king, whose other knights, restrained by you, will not defend him until he is well dead. Then you shall run Tristram through from behind, while he is distracted. You may then take the crown for yourself, and if you wish, La Belle Isold."

But this Andret, who was secretly a vile sodomite (which Frocin knew), did never lust for Isold, and also he was suspicious of the loathsome Frocin, of whom he worried that he might espy him with his varlets and report this impious perversity to King Mark. Therefore he asked, "And how would this profit thee, shameful dwarf?"

"You would perhaps reward me for making you king," said Frocin, "and you would rely on my subsequent intelligences to make your crown secure, so that treachery of the kind that we practiced against King Mark could never be performed by others against you."

Now Sir Andret pretended to agree with this plan, but privately he did intend to kill Frocin as well, for never could a dwarf be trusted.

And as for Frocin, he made the same suggestion to three other knights: Denoalen, Guenelon, and Gondoïne, with the difference that to each he gave the plan to kill the man who came before him, so that Andret would run Tristram through; then Denoalen would kill Andret; Guenelon, Denoalen; and finally Gondoïne would thrust his sword to the hilt between the shoulders of Guenelon. Thus would Frocin rid Cornwall of all its foremost knights but one, and then he would poison him, and so ruin the country absolutely for persons of normal size, and become himself the first dwarf-king in the British island, for of an evil race he was the evilest. (And the only good dwarf was the one who guarded King Arthur's treasure at Caerleon, who could turn into a dragon, and who was in the service of the Lady of the Lake.)

Now when night fell, though he believed that King Mark was gone away, Sir Tristram went towards Isold's balcony using his old route through the garden, for it would never do for anyone to see him in her hallway within the castle. And as he approached the wall the previously cloudy heavens opened to admit the light of a full moon, and though it was a windless night, a leaf fell from an oak in this light and looking aloft Tristram saw from behind a crouching figure on a high branch which did command a view of Isold's chamber.

And believing this to be a wretch who was up to no good, Sir Tristram shook the branch violently, and the king fell down to the ground and was knocked senseless, and not knowing who he was, for the moon went behind a cloud again, Tristram tied him fast with the king's own belt and threw him behind a bush, and then he mounted to the chamber of La Belle Isold, where he stayed till dawn.

Therefore the king was unconscious for another night, and when he awakened in the morning it was after Tristram had gone away through the garden, forgetting him in his transports of remembered bliss. And Mark did cry out for some hours before he was found and released by his gardeners, who thinking he was gone boar-sticking were malingerers.

Now, sore and dirty, he summoned to him the vile Frocin and would have sent him to torture had not the malicious dwarf blamed this latest miscarriage on Sir Andret, whom he did call a sodomite and traitor.

And King Mark swore a terrible oath, crying out in chagrin whether there was anyone he could trust? And a young page was there, who was one of Sir Andret's male harlots, and he stole away to Andret and reported this to that knight, who thereupon fled from that land. Therefore Guenelon became the second knight of Cornwall, and you can be sure he hated Tristram of being first, and conspiring with Frocin he did make many plans to discredit Sir Tristram, but they were all frustrated by God for a long time, for he doth not always permit the punishment of some sinners by others more evil, and He allowed Sir Tristram and La Belle Isold to enjoy their stolen love for many a year before demanding from them a grievous payment.

Now we must leave Sir Tristram for a while, for to consider the story of Sir Launcelot, who was an even greater knight but alas! certainly as great an adulterer, to an even worse end.

BOOK VII

*Of Sir Launcelot and Elaine the maid of Astolat;
and how the wicked Sir Meliagrant abducted the
queen.*

Now, as he had promised King Arthur, Sir Bors of Ganis
did travel to the remote monastery where his cousin
Launcelot was then immured of his own volition, for
Launcelot did ever despise the world and wish to be away
from it by any means that were not suicide, which was a
great sin. And therefore he would oft fight against giants
and other monsters, or if mere men an whole army, in the
hope that he would be killed honorably. But God, who
knoweth all, saw that these efforts were informed by the
yearning for death, and jealously He would not allow
Launcelot to exercise what was His own exclusive preroga-
tive. Therefore Launcelot possessed, unhappily for him,
what other men yearn for hopelessly: invincibility.

So when Bors came to his little cell, where Launcelot
prayed all the day and sometimes removed his hair shirt to
excoriate his sore back further with a scourge, he found
his cousin pale and weighing scarcely more than seven
stone, for he ate nothing but sufficient thin gruel to keep
him alive.

"Cousin," said Sir Bors, "I come to call thee forth into
the world, for to serve King Arthur." And he told him of
the Round Table and its company of worthy knights.

"Well," said Launcelot, "man is superior to animals

only in that he knoweth his wretchedness in the sight of God."

"But," asked Sir Bors, "doth God love a cloistered virtue? Thou art a young man, Launcelot. Shouldst thou not earn the right to condemn life by living it?" For Sir Bors was ever a wise knight, with a measured view of all things and a sense of the eternal equilibrium.

"Methinks that fighting evil is but finally to give it a reputation which unaided it could not aspire to," said Launcelot, who deliberated on such matters incessantly.

"Cousin," said Sir Bors, "carried beyond a certain point such a train of thought is necessarily heretical, for we know the right."

"True," groaned Launcelot. "I fear I am incorrigible." And he did take off his hair shirt and prepare to whip himself, and his cousin saw the festering sores on his back.

"Nay," said Bors, and he took away the scourge from Launcelot. "The greatest failing of all is not to use the gifts that God hath given us. Thou art the knight of most prowess who ever was in all the world."

"I do not know that I am," said Launcelot. "And I do not know that, being such, I could exercise my gift at arms for ought but vanity on mine own part, and envy on the part of others. Therefore, going into the world to fight against evil I should in a very real way but increase its sway."

"Cousin," said Sir Bors, "consider this: that vanity has rather brought thee, and keeps thee, here. Further, that man is born to sin, but some sins are worse than others. And finally, that there is at least some aesthetic if not moral distinction between squeezing life to make it groan and groaning oneself in private."

Now Launcelot did have great affection for Sir Bors his cousin, who was no slave to any passion and who could not see the essential differences amongst men, thinking them but accidental. And knowing that such men could be most marvelously persistent, with the strength of their innocence and ignorance, as to be so invincible morally as he was in the lesser struggle pursued with lance and sword, he realized he would be bested in this argument.

Therefore Sir Launcelot submitted to the suasion of his cousin Bors and bathed for the first time in a year, and he put on his armor, which hung loosely and did clatter upon his emaciated frame, and he said good-by to the good monks who kept this monastery, the which were called the Little Brothers of Poverty and Pain, and he did travel towards Camelot with Bors.

However they had not got far when Launcelot felt the effects of his self-imposed travail and he grew too weak to retain his seat upon the horse Sir Bors had brought for him, and therefore they stopped at a place hight Astolat and applied for lodging at the house of a knight called Sir Bernard, who granted them this freely for he was a man of worship.

And Launcelot was even more ill when he awakened next morning, but he concealed this from Sir Bors, saying he was too weary for to continue on to Camelot at this moment, and he insisted that Bors go on without him.

"Very well," said Sir Bors, "but I shall not leave without thy promise to follow when thou art strong enough."

And Launcelot did assent to this, with the provision that only death should inhibit him, for privately he believed that he was dying, and he was gratified in that belief.

Therefore Sir Bors left and when he was gone Launcelot did ask the daughter of Sir Bernard, who was named Elaine and who had come to nurse him, to fetch a priest to administer to him the last rites. But Elaine would not do this. Rather she went to the chapel and prayed to God to allow Launcelot to live, and God granted her plea, but what she could not know was that, as is His wont, He did place upon her an obligation to repay this gain by a certain loss. And Elaine had fallen in love with Launcelot and hoped to marry him.

So Launcelot began to recover under the care of the fair Elaine, who was (not that Isold had been married) the most beautiful maiden in the world, with hair of glowing brown and amber-colored eyes, and skin so soft that velvet did scratch it. But though she had fallen in love with him at first sight and continued to love him more, Launcelot was but affectionate to Elaine, and he thought of her with loving-kindness but not with passion, like unto the feeling for a sister. Nor did he understand that she loved him, for he was like King Arthur in that the ways of women were always strange to him, whereas he knew the quality of any man from watching him walk or ride.

Therefore the fair Elaine was ever more sad, and sometimes she felt so desperate as to consider committing the great sin of wishing she had never helped Launcelot to recover, if he were to be but a brother to her, of which she already had two.

And these two brothers, who were named Tirre and Lavaine, did admire Launcelot greatly, for they were but squires at this time, and whilst he was recovering they sought him out and talked endlessly of weaponry and war and all manner of such masculine things. Therefore Elaine had less and less of him as he grew stronger. Now the day came when he could go out of doors and instruct Tirre and Lavaine in the use of lance and sword and correct their style as they charged upon the manikin or quintain, which is to say, the post with a crosspiece that doth swing to smite the unskilled tilter as he charges upon it with an improper technique, and you can be sure that Sir Quintain did many times knock these varlets from the saddle with his circulating arms, and the men did laugh merrily, but the fair Elaine brooded only on her unrequited love.

Then Tirre did hear that King Arthur would hold another tournament a fortnight hence, open to all comers, and those who won their matches would take the place of certain knights of the Round Table who had died when upon quests (for a year had gone by since the previous tourney), and Tirre and Lavaine were eager to enter this competition. Therefore they begged Launcelot to take them to Camelot with him, for he did purpose at last to go there according to the pledge to Bors, being now entirely hale, thanks first to God but secondly to the fair Elaine.

"Very well," said Launcelot to the sons of Sir Bernard, "ye may go with me to Camelot, for to enter this tournament, and I have me an idea the which will provide some sport. With thee, Tirre, I shall exchange shields. Therefore thou shalt compete as Launcelot, and I with the blank shield of a squire."

Now, Elaine being excluded utterly from these matters, the which consumed all the spirit of the men, she did sit alone in misery as the fortnight dwindled, for Launcelot no longer needed her for nursing nor in any other wise, and she was benevolently neglected by him as if she were a hound—nay, he did caress the bitch which sat at his feet when he ate and he threw her bones, but he did not so much as this for the fair Elaine, who was sufficiently beautiful to break the heart of any other knight in the land, excepting Tristram.

Now the morning came when Launcelot and her brothers were to leave for Camelot, and as Elaine could not bear to bid Launcelot farewell she did remain in her chamber weeping. But to her surprise she heard a knock at the door, and when she opened it, there stood Launcelot himself, the last person she expected to see, and in her confusion she confessed her love for him.

But as it happened Launcelot did not attend carefully to her words, for he was altogether distracted by a wish to repay her for her nursing of him to health, the which he did not value as such, yearning for death; yet he could not suppose she would know that, and therefore what she had done had great moral worth.

Therefore he said to her, as if to a child, "If it would please thee, I shall wear thy token in my helm when riding in the lists."

Now herself distracted equally, the fair Elaine heard this as requital of the love she had professed, and she tore away from her best robe of red cloth-of-gold a sleeve and gave this to Launcelot, who affixed it to his helmet. Now to Elaine this was symbolic of her heart, but to Launcelot it was but the emblem of his affectionate friendship with a young girl who had brought him warm broths.

And while she swooned in happy thought of him, Launcelot rode to Camelot taking Tirre and Lavaine, and Tirre carried the shield bearing Launcelot's device of lions rampant, and Launcelot carried the one that was blank.

Now the tournament was begun with a great free-for-all that soon eliminated the less proficient knights, but both Tirre and Lavaine were still in their saddles when it was done, for Launcelot had stayed near to them in the press and unhorsed whoever came near, for he had no equal as a knight.

And King Arthur was watching, with Gawaine and Bors and Kay, and he said to Bors, "Thou hast told us of thy cousin, and I see that he is worthy enough, but scarcely as yet deserving of the highest praise, which should rather go to him who wears the red sleeve in his helm, who furthermore, on the evidence of his blank shield, is but a squire. More than once he has disposed of a threat to thy Launcelot."

Now Sir Bors recognized the style of his cousin's attack, which was unmistakable, in that of the knight referred to by King Arthur, and knowing of Launcelot's peculiar ways, among which was a dislike of public renown, he correctly divined the true state of affairs. However, not wishing to betray Launcelot, he said to King Arthur, "I confess I am amazed, Sire. Never have I seen such a knight as he who wears the red sleeve."

"No doubt," said Sir Gawaine, whose loss of envy applied only with Tristram, "he is good, perhaps very good, but as yet he hath never faced an opponent of great worth."

Mischievously Sir Bors then said, "Dost imply, my dear Gawaine, that he is not thy match?"

But Gawaine had learned to restrain the show of envy, and he replied simply, "He seemeth a worthy knight."

But Sir Kay did seethe and say, "Well, he hath not yet

faced one of us of the Round Table, and methinks the boy doth need a lesson in humility." And he thereupon donned his helmet, took up his lance, and rode to challenge the Knight of the Red Sleeve.

King Arthur groaned and said to the other knights, "Why oh why must Kay seek to prove himself upon the field? Prithee, Gawaine, go and follow him lest we be utterly shamed."

Now Gawaine was hoping for such a command, for he felt he would burst of chagrin if he could not try himself against this arrogant squire, and quickly he mounted and passed Kay at the gallop, shouting "Have at you!" to the knight with the red sleeve in his helm, then closing his visor and charging with lowered lance.

And soon Gawaine came crashing to the earth, being flung from his horse by a wondrous means, as if he had grown wings, for never did he feel the impact of the other's lance point. And when he recovered his senses he did rise and draw his sword, and the other courteously dismounted and took his own blade from the scabbard.

Now Gawaine was a swordsman of most marvelous merit, as had been seen in his fight with Sir Tristram, and he carried his attack to his opponent, hacking away great pieces of the blank shield until finally the other knight held little but its straps, and King Arthur watching was much cheered, and even Sir Bors began to worry that Launcelot had not yet recovered from his residence amongst the Little Brothers of Poverty and Pain.

(Meanwhile, denied the Knight of the Red Sleeve, Sir Kay did attack the man he believed to be Launcelot the cousin of Sir Bors, and he was soon thrown, for it was rather young Tirre, who had been trained by Launcelot.)

But the reasons for Launcelot's apparent setback were two: firstly, that Gawaine was so great a swordsman (as great, so went the jest of the pages, on the field as between a maiden's thighs) that even for Launcelot to defeat him was not an easy matter; and secondly, that Launcelot believed he here saw an opportunity to die without sinning.

O foolish man, for God doth detect every nuance of the sick will! And to His servant Launcelot He now made it known that the only unforgiveable sin is committed by the man who doth not use his gifts and therefore acts the coward to his own self, mocking the God who made him. So Launcelot with one great stroke severed Sir Gawaine's sword just beneath the hilt and knocked him to the ground. Then he raised Sir Gawaine's visor and putting his blade there he asked him to yield.

And Gawaine did so, saying with great graciousness, for as with Tristram his envy had been honestly expunged, "My lord, you are the greatest knight I have ever contested with, and perhaps the greatest in the world. Would that you were of our company of the Round Table."

" 'Tis for that purpose I have come here," said Launcelot, helping Gawaine to his feet and embracing him. "But, my dear Gawaine, I am sore all over from thy puissant blows. Never shall we fight together again except side by side against a common enemy and not each other, for never again could I expect that, just as I was about to surrender to thee, thy foot would slip on the grass and give me the advantage."

"Nay, dear Launcelot," said Gawaine, who now realized who his late foe was, "thou art my better, as is Sir Tristram, and I thank God ye are both my friends, so that I am that happy man who can love his superiors." Then he took him to King Arthur.

"Well, Launcelot," said Arthur, "thou didst have thy jest, which also had its serious significance, for given what we heard of thee from thy cousin Bors, methinks some opponents would have been overly wary of thee, and some overly eager to try themselves against the greatest of all. 'Twere better the way it happened, and the impersonal standards of quality have been maintained. We are sworn at the Round Table to fight for the Right, which is eternal, and not for the self, which is on temporary loan from Heaven." And he then knighted him.

"Sire," said Sir Launcelot, "I pray to God I shall never bring shame to the Round Table."

"It is curious to me," King Arthur said, "that thou, alone amongst my knights, and the greatest of them, doth have this worry. Modesty is a good, but methinks this goeth beyond that."

And Launcelot asked to speak with the king apart, and Arhtur granted this plea. "Sire," then said Sir Launcelot, "I have an awful secret, the which I may impart only to you. And that is that I am invincible."

"But for some place upon thy body, surely?" asked King Arthur. "Like unto Achilles with his heel or the German Siegfried who was made immune to wounds by dragon's blood except for where the linden leaf stuck to his back."

"Nay," said Launcelot, "I am not invulnerable to wounds, nor am I immortal. I can and will die, but I can not be defeated by living knight."

"I see," said Arthur. "Therefore thou canst take no pleasure in fighting. Gawaine, with his human envy, is the happier for it, being constrained ever to strive. But I ask thee to consider this, that God hath given thee the privilege not to be vulgar. O lonely man! Well do I understand this situation, being a king. Arthur and Launcelot shall be friends, joined in a unity like unto that of the head with the arms. I am thy king, and thou art my champion."

Then King Arthur took Sir Launcelot to meet Guinevere, little knowing that the common cause so lately identified was so quickly to be divided into parts.

But Queen Guinevere, who had fallen in love with Launcelot when she had heard Sir Bors's account of him, did not at first recognize the subject of her fantasy in the living knight, and but coolly accepted his obeisance.

And as for Launcelot, who had never been a passionate man, he saw only queenly condescension and not the woman, and that she was the fairest in the world did not occur to him, except in the abstract, which is to say, without carnality.

Then they left her presence for to go have their meat at the Round Table, with all their company. And the contest of Sir Kay with young Tirre, who owing to the shield he then believed was Launcelot, hath not been forgotten here: the former was soon defeated by the latter, and his brother Lavaine also won his own match, and both became knights of the Round Table.

Now the knights had all but reached the end of their meal, and the lackeys were only just serving the treacle tart, when a huge knight rode into the hall on an enormous horse, and both man and animal were all green in every particular.

Not only was the knight wearing green armor, but also his face was green within the opened visor. And the hide of his horse was green, as was the mane. And the only weapon carried by the Green Knight was a great green battle-ax. Indeed he was a wondrous sight and caused much amazement, and all the company of the Round Table fell silent except for King Arthur, who performed as he was required by the laws of hospitality.

"Sir knight," said he, "thou art welcome to sit down and eat, but I would fain have thine horse taken to the stables."

"Nay, King Arthur," cried the knight in a great voice appropriate to his size. "I come here not to feed but rather to find the knight who hath the courage to trade blows with me."

"The tourney hath ended," said King Arthur. "Prithee wait for the next, unless thy purpose be evil."

"My purpose," said the Green Knight, "is precisely that which you must determine by means of your own response, for I seek a knight with the heart for a peculiar adventure, the which he shall never understand unless he survives it."

"Well," said King Arthur, "that distinguishes it in no wise, for 'tis true of all adventures that deserve the name."

"Yet I believe mine is unique," said the Green Knight, "for what I propose is that one of your knights exchange blows with me. Now, he must strike me first, so power-fully as he will."

"Thou art an huge man," said the king, "and well armored, but methinks that Launcelot might well cut through thy steel and wound thee mortally."

"Indeed?" cried the Green Knight with much joviality, and he dismounted from his green charger and removed his helmet, and his hair was green as grass. "But to remove all possible obstruction I shall even bare my neck, and lie down prone. Now may I suggest that the weapon be mine own ax, for no sword has yet been made that can penetrate my skin." And he lay down on the floor.

Now all the knights were in a state of wonderment, but Sir Kay, who had lately brought in a great cheese of Stilton for to serve after the pudding, saw here an opportunity to prove himself as knight, and he went to the great battle-ax which the green giant had dropped, and he strove to lift it, but he could not.

And King Arthur urged Sir Launcelot to undertake this adventure. But Launcelot was concerned for the pride of his friend Gawaine, who he could see greatly yearned to have at the Green Knight but restrained by courtesy. Therefore Launcelot spake as follows.

"With respect, Sire, unless this be a command, methinks I am no match for this verdant giant," he said, innocent of vanity and therefore never thinking this might make him seem a coward. "Pray let me defer to Sir Gawaine."

King Arthur granted this request. Yet he did not, and would never, understand the modesty of Sir Launcelot, though he did love him for it. And all throughout their lives Arthur and Guinevere and Launcelot did love one another, though each pair in a different way, and men may be dear friends sans sodomy, as a lover and his cuckold be as brothers.

Therefore with great joy Gawaine did leap from his siege, take up the great ax, and with one blow strike off the head of the Green Knight, which went a-rolling the vast length of the great hall of Camelot, struck the far wall, and came rolling back unto the very feet of King Arthur. And the wondrous thing was that this head did roar with laughter throughout its journey to and fro! Then the green body rose and taking up the green head, placed it upon the green neck, and mounted the green horse.

"Well struck, Sir Gawaine," cried the Green Knight. "And now that I have felt the strength of your arm, I shall test your moral mettle. One year from today, you must meet me at a place of my choosing, there to accept one blow from me, or else be damned as an arrant poltroon!" And guffawing he did prick his horse and gallop out of the castle.

Now Sir Gawaine said, "Obviously there is some magic in this adventure, but whether wicked or benign magic is to be proved: for green is neither white nor black."

" 'Tis the color of vegetable fecundity," said King Arthur, "and this knight may well be of the druidical persuasion, his purpose being to challenge Christian principles."

"I shall meet him one year hence," said Gawaine, "and only God knows whether I shall keep my head after that meeting." And with a jolly laugh very like that of the Green Knight, he sat him down once more at the table and fell to his pudding with hearty appetite, for Sir Gawaine had yet a great zest for life.

And Sir Kay now came with the wheel of cheese, and said enviously, "But for the grease on my fingers, I should have lifted the ax and done as well as thou, Gawaine."

"Methinks," said Gawaine, "that God arranges each adventure for a particular knight, that chance doth never come into play. Now, I am the special defender of women. No woman is yet evident, but no doubt one will appear a year hence."

"And meanwhile," said Kay, "thou shalt prepare by jousting with as many females as thou canst find."

But Sir Kay could never provoke the greatest knights, who rather felt sympathy for him, and Sir Gawaine said now, "Thine adventure will come one day, and thou shalt perform thy role with courage and grace. Thou art a better knight than thou dost understand, my dear Kay."

But Kay's needs would have been better met by a malice which answered his own, and bitterly he went away, pushing the trolley which held the cheese.

"Now, blast him," said King Pellinore, "where doth he go? I wanted a bit of that Stilton for to nullify the taste of that damned sweet, which else will pollute my tongue all day. The Froggies eat their pudding last, but damn me if I can see that bloody custom."

And King Arthur chided him for his blasphemous oaths at the Round Table, for Pellinore though a devout knight was forgetfully foul-mouthed.

"I am concerned for Kay," Arthur then said. "His standards are such that he will not allow the lackeys to do some of the jobs that should be theirs. Any varlet could wheel about that cheese and scoop out and serve the portions, but Kay doth insist that only he can do it properly, with an eye to the veining and the ripeness and whatnot, the which seemeth to me inconsequential rubbish, for cheese is so much clabbered milk at bottom, whatever its coloration when it begins to go rotten. Indeed, I have always found it filthy stuff and seldom touch it." In such matters as this, Arthur confided only in Pellinore, the only fellow king at hand. "But look you, Kay insists on serving his brother knights, on the one hand, and on the other, he doth resent being in the situation of a servant."

But King Pellinore did merely roll his eyes and scratch at his louse-bites, for he had no patience with Sir Kay, not thinking him even a good seneschal so to take away the cheese before he could feed on it.

Now Guinevere though queen was a woman and therefore did not sit to meat with the assembled men of the Round Table, but she took her meals apart, with the ladies of the court, and providing for them with Sir Kay's especial pleasure, for though women understood nothing of the preparation of food, their tastes were more delicate and sensitive than those of men, and instead of the roasts of beef, joints of mutton, and gammon from wild boars that inevitably appeared upon the Round Table, for the ladies Kay had his cooks prepare turbot poached in court-bouillon, fowls scented with juniper berries, and gâteaux St.-Honoré.

But on this day they were eating a mayonnaise of chicken, which had been preceded by poached eggs in jelly and was to be followed by wild strawberries and clotted cream, for the weather was so warm that beneath their robes they wore only two silk petticoats and the fires had been allowed to dwindle to coals, for it was August in Britain and the sun sometimes showed itself through the rain clouds.

It was to the ladies' dining hall that Sir Kay now went though not with the Stilton, for that was a man's robust cheese. Instead he had a chafing-dish upon his trolley, in the which he would sauté mushrooms for a savory.

But scarcely had he bowed to the queen, then put his butter in the copper basin and waited for it to froth over the charcoals, when a knight burst into the hall in full armor, except that he did not wear his helmet but rather grasped it in his left hand, so that his head could be seen, and it was to a degree handsome, but there was an ugliness in his smile, which was very like a sneer.

And Guinevere said to him, "Knowest thou not that it is a thing most lewd and villainous to come to where ladies are eating and look at them. O barbarous wretch!" For he was an alien knight and not of the Round Table, and all the ladies did gasp at his unnatural act.

But far from being ashamed, the strange knight did snigger contemptuously.

"Caitiff, defend thyself," bravely cried Sir Kay, who confronted the knight with only a little paring knife, nor did he wear mail while frying mushrooms.

But this knight then feloniously knocked Kay senseless with a blow of his steel gauntlet, for he was a man in whom wickedness knew no limit.

Now Guinevere would not send to King Arthur for aid

against this contumacious rogue, for she did despise him too much for his lack of courtesy to herself and her ladies and for his cowardly assault on Kay. Therefore when next he drew his sword and presented its sharp point to her white bosom, she but stared at him in the queenly contempt that would have withered a man less vile.

But this had no effect on him, for he was quite foreign to all decency.

"Know you that I am Sir Meliagrant," said he, "and I am renowned for my beastliness to womankind. All my life I have mistreated females, for the reason that they are smaller and weaker than men and cannot defend themselves. Never will I fight a man unless the odds are vastly in my favor, as now with Sir Kay. Such injustice is my delight. I am in all things a thoroughgoing scoundrel, and by intention, never by accident. My sole pleasure is in being felonious."

And having concluded his detestable boast he proceeded to commit the criminal act of not only touching the queen, but grasping her around the waist and throwing her over his shoulder and striding from the hall. At this, a great many of the ladies fainted dead away, for never had they seen anything so evil in all their lives.

Now when Sir Kay came to his senses and he saw that the queen had been stolen and he reflected on his public shaming, he swore to get his own back on the evil Sir Meliagrant, and believing that this was, as Sir Gawaine had foreseen, that adventure which God had arranged for him peculiarly, he went and armored himself and he rode out of Camelot without telling a soul as to his mission.

And the ladies of the court remained in confusion for ever so long, so that neither King Arthur nor any of his knights but Kay knew that Guinevere had been carried off, and perhaps they would have continued to sit unwittingly at their meat until this day, had not King Pellinore, who was still out of sorts owing to his failure to get any cheese, gone to the kitchens in search of Sir Kay, and there he was told by the cooks, who were all blackened and greasy from the fires, where the seneschal had last been seen going, which was to the ladies' dining hall.

Therefore Pellinore went there and hearing the ladies making a clamor of grief he was so bold as to go within, and there he was told what had happened. Then he went to King Arthur, and when the king heard of this outrage his wrath knew no limit, for Sir Meliagrant had violated at once every law of God and man, and Arthur called for Excalibur to be brought and for his horse to be saddled.

But Sir Launcelot begged him to hold, saying, "Sire, certainly a knight who so boasts of his evil in your court hath a method in his seeming madness. I fear he might lure you, distracted by anger as you are, into some ambuscade. I pray you to let me undertake this mission, for though I find this crime heinous in the extreme, I have not the personal concern which would divert me from what should be a pursuit with the single-minded intent to recover the queen."

"Launcelot," said King Arthur, who returned to self-command, "thou art mine exterior conscience. Anger is a sin, certes, and a king can not afford to be its captive. This crime should be considered as being foremost one against the crown, and I must think of myself as exclusively monarch and not husband."

But Sir Gawaine did beg most ardently to be given this quest. "Uncle," he said, "'tis I who am the special champion of women!" And now all the other knights rose as one and each protested that he himself was uniquely appropriate for to be sent after Queen Guinevere.

But King Arthur overruled them all, first reminding Gawaine that he had an appointment to meet the Green Knight a year hence, and only God knew how long a time would be required for the queen's recovery, for no one could say to what land Sir Meliagrant had taken her. And the others he commended for their zeal, though it was to be expected from the company of the Round Table.

Finally he said, "Launcelot, I realize that coming when thou didst, thou wert sent by God to be of special service to Guinevere and therefore I designate thee to be from this moment on her protector, with the title Queen's Own Knight."

Therefore Sir Launcelot armored himself and rode in search of her who would be the only love of his life, although he did not know this yet, nor did King Arthur, nor did Guinevere herself. And the only person who loved Sir Launcelot in passion at this time was Elaine the maid of Astolat, who sat in her tower all the day and waited for his return from the tournament, holding the empty bowl in which she had fed him broths.

Now the abominable Sir Meliagrant took Guinevere to a kingdom that was not very distant from Britain but was cunningly concealed, tucked into a valley amongst mountains, entrance to which could be gained only by one pass not easily found, and before this pass was a rushing river over which was but one bridge, the narrowest in the world, for it was made of one long sword, the weapon of a giant, the which was mounted horizontally, keen edge upwards. Nobody had ever entered the country for that reason, and only Sir Meliagrant had ever left, for he had the only horse which could walk across this blade. (For like all wicked people he could do things which defied the means of honest men, for evil is always more easily managed than virtue.)

Now coming to this bridge, holding Guinevere on the horse before him, he crossed to the middle of it and then stopped, and whilst the sword and its burden swayed in the harsh wind that came down from the mountains, Sir Meliagrant said, "Think you that if you were dropped into this rushing stream your royalty and your beauty would save you from being drowned?"

But in the same disdain she had ever shown for Meliagrant, even while she was slung across his shoulder, Guinevere said, "What I think is only that I despise thee."

Now her contempt had begun to affect Sir Meliagrant, who did yearn to be hated and feared and could not abide being held in contempt.

"Well," said he urging his horse onwards, "I shall not drop you, my lady. I shall preserve you carefully for the hideous torture I shall inflict upon you when we reach my castle. I shall starve you, and I shall beat you, and I shall put a collar upon you and cause you to draw a cart. And these are but prefatory to the ingenious cruelties to come afterwards, the which it is my pleasure to plan as we ride."

But Guinevere said nought, nor did she have any dread in her heart, for to a great queen adversity is but an inconvenience.

Now when they reached the castle Sir Meliagrant secretly cast Guinevere into a foul dungeon, and then he went to see his father, who as it happened was the king of the country, and his name was Bademagu, and he did not know that his son was wicked, for the truth was that he was a bit dotty. Therefore when he saw Meliagrant he greeted him affectionately, and he believed that his son's recent enterprises had been of a beneficent nature.

"What a fine lad thou art, my son," said he. "Most chaps of thine age would be out wenching, gaming, and wassailing, whereas thou spendest thy days comforting the poor. But I worry that thou dost not get sufficient pleasure. Thou art a prince and one day thou shalt be a king and beyond the gathering of rosebuds. Soon enough one's youth is gone, the fingers are too rheumatic to squeeze a pair of bubbies, and one finds it difficult to remember being in the pretty imprisonment of a pair of white thighs."

"Father," said this false Meliagrant, "but for my duty to assume the throne one day—a day I pray be far into the future—I should take holy orders, being quite immune to the attractions of the world."

"Thy piety is praiseworthy," said old King Bademagu, wiping his eyes that were watery with age, "but 'tis not easy to be the father of a saint. I worry that thou wilt erect a pillar in the desert and go sit atop it for twenty years. Never have I known thee to practice the most simple amusements, not even hawking or pigsticking."

And Sir Meliagrant did simulate a feeling of horror. "I blench at the thought of such cruelties, Father. For everything that hath life is precious to God, and as you know I live only on milk, cheese, and sterile eggs, so that nothing must die to keep me quick." And with such detestable lies he continued to gull his father, whereas he spent all his waking hours in wreaking cruelties on whatever was living, and whilst he slept he dreamed of worse ravages.

"I must now return to my prayers in the chapel," said Sir Meliagrant, but when he left his father he went rather to his private store of torture-instruments and taking up a file, did sharpen the steel tips of his cat-o'-nine-tales, the better to lacerate Guinevere's white back, and then he oiled the threads of the thumbscrews he would tighten to crack the delicate bones of her fingers, and whilst he was doing this he became so aroused in anticipation (for his greatest ambition had been realized: to have the most beautiful woman in the world as his helpless captive), that he fainted dead away in bliss. And there we may leave him awhile.

Now, down in the foul dungeon, Guinevere sat serenely, though it was cold and damp and slime oozed from the walls and there were rats who lived there who were large as cats, but when they saw her beauty they became gentle and went away.

Sir Kay meanwhile was endeavoring to trace the route taken by Sir Meliagrant when he carried Guinevere off, and when King Arthur at last discovered his absence, he made great moan and he said to Gawaine, "Nephew, I fear that Kay has again bitten off more than he can chew. His zeal is commendable, but I am afraid that he will be killed if allowed to continue this quest unaided. Now Launcelot hath gone in search of the queen, but I ask thee to follow Sir Kay and preserve him against misadventure."

"Willingly," said Gawaine, and he did mount and leave Camelot, but he rode for many leagues without finding

any trace of Kay, though he asked every churl he encountered whether he had seen the seneschal, and though some
had seen a knight ride by, which in some cases had been
Kay, in some Launcelot, and in others Meliagrant with
Guinevere, and most of them had seen all three men (and
one queen), being churls they would not admit this,
should furnishing such information prove to their detriment and they be whipped for their pains, for the peasantry did not yet appreciate the difference between Arthur's
reign and that which preceded it.

Therefore Sir Gawaine continued to ride fruitlessly until
he reached Sir Bernard's castle at Astolat, where he was
welcomed with great cheer by that old knight and invited
to stay the night, for it was eventide already. And while
they were supping together Gawaine discovered that it was
at this place that Launcelot had stayed before he came to
Camelot.

"Indeed," said Sir Bernard, "'twas mine own daughter
who tended him in his illness, and at a great cost, I fear,
for she herself fell ill thereafter, and is at the point of
death."

Now Gawaine as the defender of women rose from his
meat and asked to be taken to her, for though he was no
physician the sickness of maidens was oft, he knew, rather
of the heart than of the body, and he was well equipped to
minister to such maladies. So he was conducted to the
chamber of the fair Elaine, where she lay and was whiter
than the sheets of samite on the bed, and she could hardly
open her eyes for feebleness.

And Sir Bernard made much grief. "She has been bled
repeatedly," said he, "and brimstone has been burned to
purify the air, and smoking feathers applied to her nostrils,
and nigromancers have made their incantations over her to
summon up the therapeutic sprites, and then the friars did
come to exorcise these demons and when she continued to
sicken counseled that she was so possessed of imps that
she must be burned alive to be rid of them. Upon which I
drove away the entire lot with a cudgel, damned jackals."

But Gawaine did not attend to the words of the bluff old knight, for he believed that Elaine, though ill, was the most beautiful maiden he had ever seen on earth, and he fell in love with her utterly.

"My lord," said Gawaine, "shall you permit me to minister to your daughter? For I believe I can cure her of this sickness."

"Sir Gawaine," said old Bernard, with a squint of his eye, "your reputation is not unknown to me. I beg you to do what you can to save my daughter's life, if you make this offer solemnly, but I promise that with this sword I shall make you a capon if your means be not honest."

"My oath on it, Sir Bernard," Gawaine said. "My day of impious lechery is done, and I am sworn to defend and protect all women, except that the queen hath her first champion in Sir Launcelot of the Lake."

At this name the fair Elaine opened her eyes and groaned most piteously.

"Lady," said Gawaine softly, "God will save you, else all beauty would be gone from the earth and ugliness regnant."

And Elaine did breathe the name "Launcelot" and took Sir Gawaine's fingers into her own white hand, then she closed her eyes again and slept.

"Pretty fool," said Sir Bernard. "My heart doth ache to see her so. Cure her, Gawaine, and you shall have whatsoever I can give you."

"Her hand in marriage," said Sir Gawaine, "is all that I want in the world."

"It is yours," said Sir Bernard, "for I can see that you are now a knight of the greatest worship. And now I shall leave you, for you have my total trust."

And Sir Gawaine spake the truth, though who knows whether if Elaine had been well he might yet have been able to overcome the carnal appetites with which he had been born, for God gives each of us a natural attraction towards a particular sin, to try our piety, and Gawaine's was ever the gaining of a woman's intimacy by means other than force.

Now he did stand by Elaine's bed all the day and all the night, and never dared even to sit down for fear it might disturb her, and by morning he was all but paralyzed in his limbs, especially the wrist of the hand held by Elaine. But at dawn the light came through the window and illuminated her face, and she awakened with a smile that was even more radiant than the sun.

But seeing Gawaine at her bedside she gasped and did drop his hand, relieving his ache of muscle but bringing soreness to his soul, for though he had correctly divined that a maiden whose illness could not be cured by bleeding did suffer from a malady pertaining to Love, he was wrong in his belief that for Elaine his own love would be the cure.

"Sir knight," said she then, "you are not Launcelot, and you were wicked to pretend to be he."

"Nay, lady," Sir Gawaine said, "Sir Launcelot is my friend and dear to me as mine own brothers, but never have I posed as that great knight." And he told her who he was.

"Forgive me, noble Gawaine," said Elaine. "I had me a dream, then, in which Sir Launcelot came and held mine hand all the night and said he loved me only." But she did then weep most piteously, saying, "But, 'twas an illusion, and I have awoke only to go back to dying."

And now Gawaine identified her illness, and he was hard put to overcome his disappointment, for he loved this maid with all his heart. But he was a great knight, and though he was yet capable of feeling envy in lesser matters, in those of the greatest substance Sir Gawaine was near to being the finest of all at the Round Table.

Therefore he said to Elaine, difficult as it was, for he loved her more than ever, "Dear lady, you must grieve no longer. Launcelot hath gone upon a quest, but he will return before you are much older. And I can tell you that he doth have no ladylove, having but lately left a remote monkery. When he comes back I shall bring him to see you, and how can he fail to fall in love with you? For you are the most beautiful maiden in the world."

Now Elaine found some cheer in Gawaine's words, but not much, for she said, "But he was here at Astolat for many weeks, and clearly he was not smitten or he should have come back ere now."

So poor Gawaine found himself in the situation of having to plead the cause of his friend, for the purpose of curing this maiden whom he himself loved but to whom Launcelot was apparently insensible. And little did he know that this would serve only to prolong and intensify Elaine's torment, for he who interferes in hopeless matters of love is more cruel than kind, if unwittingly.

Now it may be asked, Well, did not hearing of Launcelot's coldness encourage Gawaine's own hopes that Elaine might eventually transfer her love to him who was warm? But the answer to this is No, for Gawaine was not so vain as to suppose he could replace in her affections the greatest knight in the world. And Sir Launcelot did always inspire modesty in the best members of the company of the Round Table, for what all good men admire most is he who is best at what they do, putting him beyond envy.

Therefore Gawaine, because of love, became at this time as sad as Tristram had been from birth onwards except for brief interludes, and as melancholy as was Launcelot himself as a result of pondering on his invincibility. And this was unprecedented for Sir Gawaine, who amongst the foremost knights had ever been the most merry.

Now what Gawaine did was to assure the fair Elaine that Sir Launcelot though masterful with men was shy with women, and all the more so when he did care most for them. And poor Elaine's need was such that she heard this with great joy and soon she came to think that what she had formerly believed as Launcelot's indifference to her was rather the evidence of a love so ardent that he could not display it openly without shame, which was to say, without being seemingly effeminate.

"To be sure," said she, "he did ask me for a favor to wear at the tournament."

And remembering the red sleeve affixed to Launcelot's helm, Gawaine now understood whence it had come. "Well, there you are," said he. "If you are not his lady, then nobody is. 'Twas your sleeve that cleared the field."

Now Elaine soon felt well enough to rise from her bed and to take nourishment, and she continued throughout the succeeding days to improve in health, and Gawaine lingered at Astolat for her sake, believing that his general obligation to aid women took precedence over the particular command to look after Sir Kay.

Meanwhile Sir Kay as usual came to grief. Having arrived at the sword-bridge he saw he could never cross it, and therefore he dismounted, removed his armor, and put down his weapons, and leaping into the rushing stream he with great difficulty swam to the other side, but when he reached the far bank he was half-drowned and chilled to the bone by the icy waters, and in such a condition, and unarmed altogether, he was easily captured by the wicked knights posted by Sir Meliagrant to protect him against any pursuers sent by King Arthur.

And Kay was flung into another cell of the same dungeon where Guinevere was being held, and when Sir Meliagrant was awakened and told these news, he went to Sir Kay and taunted him vilely, but Kay though in his smallclothes and sopping wet did nobly disregrad this abuse.

Then Sir Meliagrant went to the cell of Guinevere and spake as follows. "Well, my lady, your champion hath been captured and humiliated and at this moment doth cringe and whimper in his durance. What say you now?"

"That thou art a liar," said Guinevere. "A knight of the Round Table doth cringe before God only."

And Meliagrant did writhe in hatred and gnash his teeth, and then he abused the royal Guinevere with loathsome epithets, such as Wench and Trull, and he threatened to go and heat his pincers, for to apply them red-hot to her proud paps. And lest it be thought that Meliagrant was but a vain braggart, be assured that bad as his bark was, his bite was worse, and if he had not yet put Guinevere to the torture, it was only that he could not decide which amongst his many instruments would produce the greatest pain for the longest time without rendering her insensible.

For his specialty was in maltreating ladies and now he had as helpless captive the most beautiful and gracious lady who was ever born, and therefore her agony must exceed all that he had ever brought to any female.

BOOK VIII

How Sir Launcelot rescued Guinevere; and of
their criminal friendship.

Now we will go awhile with Sir Launcelot, who reaching
the bridge that was a sword said to himself, Well, if God
will let me go across, I shall do it, and if no, then not, but
I shall not submit my faithful horse to this test.

Therefore he dismounted and taking off his hauberk and
the mail that armored his horse, with these he covered the
keen edge of the blade, which he then walked across like
unto a monkey using all his four limbs, two of which were
gauntleted in steel and the other two wore iron boots, and
so he went over the stream.

Now on the other side, having no steed, he began to
walk, and before he had gained a league, he came upon a
cart which waited at the side of the road. Until he came
quite close to it he could see only the horse between the
shafts and no person, and he believed it abandoned. But
when he drew near, he at last saw that its driver was a
dwarf, who had stopped and got down for to void his piss
on the verge.

"Ho, dwarf," cried Sir Launcelot. But to be so disturbed
at his pissing put the tiny man into a foul humor, he who
like all dwarfs was naturally peevish, and in reply he said
some surly word and returned to his painstaking urination,
the which he directed with his left hand while with his

right he did scratch his poll through his pointed cap, and his little figure was dressed all in motley. When he had done, and closed his breech with a varicolored codpiece, he leaped like a frog onto the cart, took up the reins, and would have driven away without further notice of Launcelot had not that knight detained his horse.

"I do not punish dwarfs unless they are rude," said Launcelot, "for there is no honor in it."

"Know you that I am attached to the court of King Bademagu," said the dwarf, "being his Fool, and I am under no obligation to strangers."

"Dost not observe the laws of hospitality?" asked Launcelot. "O barbarous little man!"

"What want you of me, then?" asked the dwarf.

"A ride in thy cart, for, as thou canst see I have me no horse," said Sir Launcelot.

Now the dwarf did smile to himself, for it was a great shame for a knight to ride in a cart, the which was used for hauling dung, the corpses of churls who died from the plague and other maladies of the common folk (whereas knights did perish only in battles and ladies from love), and other such rubbish, and he granted Launcelot's request willingly, for the purpose of degrading him.

Therefore he drove at a slow pace along the road and into the town below the castle, so that the populace could see the knight in the cart and jeer at him, supposing he was a felon en route to the block, for these carts were often used as such tumbrels as well, and the rascal many did take pleasure in taunting those transported in such wise. And quite a crowd collected and followed this cart, expecting to watch Launcelot be decapitated and to see his severed head mounted upon a pike.

But finally they arrived at the castle and the dwarf leapt down and went within and found Sir Meliagrant, for though he was indeed a Fool his first fealty was to the evil prince, and he did much wickedness in his service, of which King Bademagu knew nothing, being distracted by the dwarf's drolleries and cavortings. And now the dwarf told Meliagrant that he had brought one of King Arthur's knights in his cart.

"Well," said Sir Meliagrant, "what kind of knight would ride in this way? Dwarf, I am beginning to think these men of the Round Table are of no worship whatever. And that is a pity, for I must have virtue to shame and degrade, else what service can I render to evil?"

Then Sir Meliagrant went without, where Sir Launcelot was yet waiting in the cart, and he greeted him in this wise: "Welcome, Sir Knight of the Cart." And the people gathered there all bowed to Meliagrant and took off their caps, for he was their prince.

"Thank you, my lord," said Launcelot. "I come here in search of my queen."

"Well," said Sir Meliagrant, pretending to great cheer, "you have come to the right place, for your queen is indeed our guest here. Now come down from that dreadful cart, my dear man, and why if you lost your horse did you not send to me for another?" And this false knight did proceed to help Launcelot to the ground and to embrace him, and Sir Launcelot saw no reason to suspect him of evil. But while he was in Meliagrant's embrace, two men came with fetters and made them fast about him, and then he was led helplessly to a tower that stood by itself in a field and he was cast within, and it was a dark miserable place, with but one window, high above at the very top.

Now Meliagrant lost no time in telling Guinevere that he had captured another of the knights sent by King Arthur to deliver her.

"Thou hast taken these knights unfairly," said Guinevere.

"Indeed I have," boasted Sir Meliagrant in his wicked pride. "That is just my pleasure, for it is injustice that prospers in the world. If God disapproves of what I do, why doth He not allow you to be delivered from my infamous captivity? And do not speak of my subsequent punishment in Hell, for I believe only in what I can see at the moment."

"But," said Guinevere, "thou dost believe that the past has gone and that the future will come? And neither of them is at this moment. Therefore thou dost believe in two fundamental things that can not be seen."

Now Sir Meliagrant was confounded, not because of what the queen had said (which he did not think about), but that she had said it, for never had he previously met a metaphysical lady. But then he gathered himself and said, "Words, words, but the reality is that *I* have mastery over *you*. That is the truth and all of it."

"Nay," said Guinevere, "it is rather but a fact and, like all such, merely transitory."

And Meliagrant went away to ponder on a puzzling matter, which was, that if he killed or mutilated Guinevere, she would not be in a suitable condition to become his mistress, for indeed he had quite fallen in love with her.

And this was very chagrining to him, for he did not know how to go about winning her love in return. Which was to say, if he were kind and let her go, he would not have access to her. But if he kept her in captivity, she would hate him. Now thinking on this paradox he decided finally that there was nothing for it but that he become a man of virtue, so that she would stay with him willingly.

Now this was difficult for him because he had never his life long done anything decent, and he did not know where to begin, for he had done so much wickedness that he could properly atone for it only by emasculating himself and going to take residence in a monastery, but then there would be no point in thinking about Guinevere.

And while it was satisfying to bring pain, which was a thing of great variation and complexity, for each victim responded to it individually, there was a great sameness to the doing of kind deeds.

But finally he gave off his pondering and went down to the village below the castle in search of something virtuous to do, and he found a beggar who had no legs and who was seated at the corner of a wall and held his bowl out to passers-by. Now ordinarily Sir Meliagrant would have kicked this man in the stumps and then taken his bowl and thrown it away, for to amuse himself. But now he gave this beggar a bag of gold sovereigns, and the man opened the bag and took out one coin and tried to eat it but he could not chew the gold.

And this stupidity infuriated Sir Meliagrant, who drew his sword and was about to cut off the man's hands when he remembered Guinevere's beauty. Therefore he said, "This gold can not itself be eaten, but with it thou canst buy what thou needst."

The beggar thought on the matter awhile and then he dragged himself into the nearest shop, and again Meliagrant was sorely tempted to despatch him for his foolishness, but taking a strong hold on himself forbore. And soon the beggar reappeared, and he had bought himself a crossbow, into which he inserted a bolt, and then rising onto his stumps of legs, which ended not far below his belly, he took aim at Sir Meliagrant, saying, "Now I'll just take the rest of your treasure."

Meliagrant was not wearing his armor, and he did not want to be pierced, so while he was not carrying any more gold, he gave to the beggar his sword and clothes and horse. And after he had taken these, the beggar shot him anyway.

But the bolt did not kill Sir Meliagrant, going as it did through the fleshy part of his left arm, and with his right hand he plucked up a cobblestone from the road and with it he bashed out the beggar's brains before the rogue could swing his own sword at him, and then Meliagrant took up the sword and going into the shop, he cut off the merchant's head.

Therefore nothing was accomplished by his first effort to become virtuous. Yet he was fascinated by Guinevere's disdain for him, which he did not understand was his very reason for loving her, and he did not realize that she would never love him even if he became a man of virtue, that in fact he could be no more than totally inconsequential to her, however lovable or hateful he might be.

Meanwhile Sir Launcelot sat passively in his imprisoning tower, for he was again in a condition in which his will was benumbed. And if the truth be known, it was not horrible for him to be in this isolated captivity, into which he had been cast by trickery, for Launcelot despised deviousness and when it was used against him his tendency was to think, So much the worse for the cowardly trickster, who hath thereby won no honor and much shame!

Therefore the only person who was writhing in captivity was Sir Kay, who had been humiliated in the ladies' dining hall and even more so when he had reached this vile little realm. And he burned with the need to avenge the wrongs done against him.

Now it happened that Sir Meliagrant, still endeavoring to win the favor of Guinevere, decided to put Sir Kay at liberty. And he came to his cell and offered to do this, saying, "In return you shall commend me to your lady the queen."

Kay had never heard the like of this effrontery his life long, but he saw here a means of deliverance from his imprisonment, and therefore he agreed to do what Meliagrant asked.

"On your word of honor as knight of the Round Table," said Sir Meliagrant, and Sir Kay did so pledge. But so soon as Kay was let out of the cell he snatched Meliagrant's sword and smote him with it.

"O villainy!" cried Meliagrant, falling. But Kay wasted no sympathy on this evil knight, and he went to Guinevere's cell and took her from it.

Now of all knights Guinevere did least expect to see the seneschal as her deliverer, and she made him much praise, saying, "My dear Kay, thou art a knight of great prowess."

But Sir Kay was an honest man, and he confessed that it was rather guile which had freed him so that he could liberate her, and he said, "I have not yet proved myself in a passage at arms."

"Well," said Guinevere, "I was much pleased to be set free, but methinks that the means by which thou hast accomplished this were not proper, violating as they did thy word of honor. Therefore I must remain here." And she went within the cell again.

And Sir Kay was exasperated, saying, "Lady, lady, this is the most wickedest felon who hath ever drawn breath! Can anything be evil which defeats evil?"

"Thou art not evil," said Guinevere, who was even more beautiful in this damp dark cell than when at Camelot, for she was here the only source of light, and her golden hair and white skin did illuminate the gloom as if the sun did shine therein. "But 'tis a matter of style: there is much grace to the keeping of one's word, as breaking it doth seem inelegant."

And Sir Kay was abashed, for he abhorred the disorderly above all things. Therefore he said, "Forgive me, my lady. 'Twas well meant. Perhaps I should never leave the dining halls, for to be a good seneschal is as fine a thing as any, God wot. Yet I do know a yearning to achieve glory."

"And thou art no less a man for that," said Guinevere. "Thou hast most bravely come to the rescue of thy queen." And she honored him with her white hand, for him to kneel and kiss, and when he had done that he rose and he said, "I shall go to Sir Meliagrant, and unless he is dead, I shall try to cure him, and when he is well, I shall challenge him to fair combat."

So Kay left her in the dungeon and went to find Meliagrant, and he was a knight of greater worth for what his queen had told him.

But though morally mean, Sir Meliagrant was one of the fiercest knights on earth, and though he might with every foul device avoid a fair fight, if he took the field he was more formidable than anybody then alive but Launcelot and Tristram, and with Sir Gawaine he would have fought to a draw. (For God allows the force of Evil to be all but as powerful as that of Good, so that Heaven will be worth fighting for.) And there was little hope that Sir Kay would long survive the encounter which he now sought.

But Kay did not know that (and if he had he would have done the same), and he went to look for Meliagrant, but he could not find ought of him now but a few drops of blood on the stones of the floor. For evil made Meliagrant nearly invulnerable, and he had never been wounded at all until he endeavored to be kind to the beggar and then to Sir Kay, and he was not yet so virtuous that he could be hurt much. Thus he had got up soon after Kay had gone away, and the wound in his side quickly knitted and only itched like the bite of a bug.

Now Meliagrant was sorely tempted to make no further attempts to be decent for the purpose of winning Guinevere's esteem, for he believed he had proved that the entire world would resist his efforts to reform himself. And whereas he had been fearsome when vile, he was but a booby when he did other than ill.

However, such was his yearning for the fair Guinevere that he decided to make the supreme effort, and therefore he went to the tower where Sir Launcelot was imprisoned and he spake to him as follows.

"Sir knight, are you a man of honor?"

"Sir," said Launcelot, "that is not a question that a man may answer as to himself. Nor methinks would it be asked except by a mean fellow."

"Sir," said Meliagrant, "I find you lot from Arthur's court to be most exasperating. You are damnable smug about your own virtue, but you rebuff the poor devil who aspires to it."

"Surely," said Sir Launcelot, "you are not speaking of yourself?"

"I am indeed," said Meliagrant. "I would fight you fairly, but I fear the kind of treachery recently worked on me by Sir Kay."

"Well, I know nothing of that," Launcelot said. "But certes, it is the pot to the kettle, if true, for were you not as false as a knight could be when you embraced me only so that I could be put into fetters?"

"But to be wicked is my métier!" indignantly cried Sir Meliagrant. "Whereas Sir Kay did break his vow."

And Launcelot saw that he had reason in his speech. "Very well, then," said he. "Honor is most itself when granted to the dishonorable. I shall fight you. But I shall not seal this pact with an embrace."

"Have no fear," said Meliagrant. "I shall have a horse and armor and weapons brought without this tower and left here, after which my man shall withdraw. Then I shall meet you on the field, and we shall fight until one of us is overcome."

Then he went to Guinevere and told her of what he was doing.

"Now," said he, "when I win this fight you can no longer despise me, and therefore there remaineth no reason why we should not become lovers."

And Guinevere wondered at this statement. "Can it be?" she asked, and then, "Was this thine intent from the outset?"

"My purpose was to humble you," said Sir Meliagrant, "but I found I could not manage that."

And the queen asked, "Therefore thou hast fallen in love with me?"

"I fear that I have," said Meliagrant, "and thus far it is rather I who have been humiliated, and this love hath brought me nothing but two wounds." And he told her of his encounters with the crippled beggar and Sir Kay.

"Of the latter I have been apprised," said Guinevere, "and Kay would make amends and fight thee."

"This honor," said Meliagrant, "can be a taxing thing. Is it not remarkable enough that I fight fairly even once?"

"Then who is thine opponent?" asked Guinevere.

"A knight who is named Launcelot," said Meliagrant.

"My poor Sir Meliagrant," said Guinevere, "then thou shalt fight but once."

Now Meliagrant without knowing it at this point did indeed become virtuous, for he was doomed, and that is finally the sole means by which evil knights ever became converted to the good, for otherwise there was too much precedent for them to overcome. For example, in his heart Sir Meliagrant would always despise a crippled beggar and a man he had captured by deceit, whilst at the same time being indignant if the former perversely armed himself, and if the latter himself employed trickery.

Therefore in his ignorance he did thank Queen Guinevere for granting him this boon, that is, he believed that to receive her affections he had but to fight one of Arthur's knights, for he assumed that he had no equal on the field.

Now Sir Kay had been searching for Sir Meliagrant all this while, and by accident he came to the tower where Launcelot was kept confined, and he saw a horse there and a suit of armor, a lance, and a sword, and all of these he took. (The reason why Launcelot had not taken these things was that he was yet confined, for the malignant dwarf had delivered them but had intentionally omitted to unbolt the door of the tower, so that Launcelot could not emerge. Now if he did not come to the field to fight Sir Meliagrant he would be proclaimed a great coward, and the shame thereof would embrace the entire of the Round Table never to be expunged. And this was the treachery of the dwarf alone, which Meliagrant knew nothing of.)

Therefore when Kay, now armored and mounted, reached the field he found Sir Meliagrant waiting, and he lowered his visor and fewtering his lance he charged upon him, and Meliagrant did the same, and they met with a great shock, which came all from one lance, namely that of Meliagrant, which pierced Kay's shield and split it into two parts and hurled him from the saddle, while Kay missed his own target altogether.

Now Kay lay upon the ground, and Sir Meliagrant dismounted and came to him, saying, "Shall you submit?"

But Kay was senseless. Therefore Meliagrant opened the ventail and saw he was not Sir Launcelot.

And he called to him the dwarf and asked him about this, and the dwarf confessed what he had done and expected to be rewarded.

"Alas for thee," said Sir Meliagrant. "Thou hast made *me* seem the coward."

"My lord," cried the dwarf, "Sir Launcelot is invincible."

"Then," said Meliagrant, "we shall both die, thou and I." And raising his sword he cut off the dwarf's ugly little head with one stroke.

Then he went to the tower and released Sir Launcelot asking his forgiveness, which Launcelot gave willingly.

"Now I am told," said Meliagrant, "that you can not be defeated in a passage at arms."

"I fear that is true," said Sir Launcelot.

And Meliagrant thought about this awhile. Then he said, "Well, it is an honorable thing to die at the hands of the greatest knight."

"Methinks you have changed, then," said Launcelot. "I am only sorry that you did not live according to the principles of honor hitherto."

"I tell you I should think nothing of it now, but for the fair Guinevere," said Sir Meliagrant. "I have come to love her with all my heart, and I would gain esteem in her eyes."

"But she is Arthur's queen," said Launcelot, "and it is sinful to think of her as you do. Therefore even yet you care not for virtue." For Launcelot did not yet know the force of love, and he believed it but fecklessness in a man to feel it, and for a woman the occupation of virgins, properly abandoned when they put on the cap of marriage and took up the distaff.

"Look you," said Meliagrant, "I do not lust for her, else I should have taken her by force long ago, after submitting her to tortures most agonizing, for my loins are warmed only by bringing extreme pain to females. Indeed,

I can not perform the virile office in the absence of a woman's terror, horror, and pain. I have ever been of that nature, and therefore it was given me by God."

At this blasphemy Sir Launcelot gasped and crossed himself.

"But this disdain," Sir Meliagrant went on, "is unprecedented, and it is irresistible." But if he looked for understanding from Launcelot, he was disappointed, for that knight said only, "Alas, you are yet in the service of the Devil."

And then the two of them went to the field, where Sir Kay lay still unconscious and Sir Launcelot stripped him of the armor and put it on himself, and then mounted the horse. But before they fought, Meliagrant had the fair Guinevere brought out from the dungeon.

"Lady," said he, "I am about to die for love of you. Now, that gives you no obligation but some privilege: you are hereby freed from my restraint. If I did not do this now, whilst I am alive, I shall have given you nothing but discomfort and inconvenience."

"Well, this is nothing but what I had before thou didst remove it," said Guinevere, "and therefore it remaineth nothing." But then she did give him her white hand for to kiss. "But, poor Meliagrant," said she, "from a base fellow at the outset, thou hast attained to a certain nobility, and what is a queen for, except to inspire in knights an urge to moral improvement?"

Now Sir Meliagrant did hear this with great joy, and though he knew in his heart that he would die, he was no suicide, and therefore he fought fiercely against Sir Launcelot, and with such prowess that he might even have overwhelmed Sir Gawaine and held his own with the great Tristram, yet the outcome was inevitable, and as always Sir Launcelot fought not hotly but in the cold certainty that he was best in all the world, and therefore he knew no sense of triumph when with a final great stroke of his sword he cut Sir Meliagrant from hollow of neck to fork of legs and the body fell in two parts that were equal except that the head was joined to the right half.

Now, when this was done, Launcelot went to Sir Kay, who had not yet waked up, and he removed the armor and returned it to Kay's body, and he put the bloody sword in his hand as well. And then he had water brought and thrown into Kay's face, the which caused the seneschal to open his eyes at last.

"Ah, Launcelot," said Kay, "it hath been proved to me that I am no warrior."

"My dear Kay," said Launcelot, "look there where Meliagrant lieth in twain. Thou art a knight of the greatest prowess that I have seen." And Kay did sit up and stare in wonder, and he believed that he had unwittingly won this victory.

But Queen Guinevere summoned Launcelot to her, and she said in a privy voice, "Surely thou dost mean well, but is there any cruelty in this? In an erroneous sense of his prowess poor Kay would one day soon be overmatched again, and perhaps thou wouldst not be there to preserve him. This kindness might therefore cause his death."

Now Launcelot wondered that a woman had corrected him, though she was his queen, for never had he supposed that a female might speak with authority on male things, and he did bow, saying, "Lady, according to your command I shall inform Sir Kay."

But Guinevere frowned in annoyance. "Sir Launcelot," said she, "though thine outward behavior is beyond cavil, I find a hidden insolence in it. I would have thee apprise Sir Kay of the true state of affairs, by reason not of mindless obedience but rather because thou seest the sense in my judgment. Prithee, without fear of displeasing me by whichever opinion, give me thine honest mind on this matter."

"Lady," said Launcelot, "King Arthur hath named me your champion. In all things I am at your pleasure, and I have no private authority. If you tell me that ice is hot, then I shall warm myself before a fire made of it; if that dust be rather water, I shall wash in dirt. If—"

"Hold," said Guinevere. "I like this not. Methinks the late Sir Meliagrant had far more worth than a champion without a conscience. Thou dost mock me, Launcelot."

And Launcelot did start back in horror, for he was never an ironical man, and he was innocent of insolent intent. Of all the knights he was the most obedient and respectful. But perhaps he was the least intelligent, for in this case he failed utterly to derive any meaning from Guinevere's anger, except that she was willful owing to vanity, which was to be expected in a woman, even a queen, and this was not the great flaw it would have been in a knight.

Therefore he apologized and when Guinevere dismissed him (without however being appeased), he went to Sir Kay and told him how Meliagrant had actually died.

"Thank you, my friend," said Kay. "I'll tell thee that I am greatly relieved by these news. Had I continued to believe that while out of my senses I did overwhelm the ferocious Meliagrant, I might have challenged another knight as superior to me as he, and this gone to my death foolishly. My dear friend, thou hast saved my live by this hard truth, as thou might well have killed me by thy gentle prevarication."

Now Launcelot was struck by the similarity of Kay's sentiments to those voiced by Guinevere, and he was still baffled by them, for his purpose in trying to delude him had been but to help him to self-esteem, and it was difficult for Launcelot to understand the scruples of others because owing to his own invincibility he saw things otherwise than most.

And Launcelot and Kay did then escort Guinevere back to Britain, finding another route than the sword-bridge (and dotty King Bademagu never knew they had ever been in his land, and he mourned for his son Sir Meliagrant when he found him dead and believed him the victim of a dragon). And at this time neither the queen nor her champion yet was in love with the other, and both found Sir Kay's presence to be agreeable on the journey to Camelot, for they would have been bored if alone together.

Now when they arrived at court, King Arthur and the company of the Round Table greeted them with much cheer, and when Arthur was alone with Guinevere he said to her, "Having sent Launcelot to your aid, I did not fear for your well-being."

But Guinevere raised her fine white brow and said, "Methinks Sir Kay did earn some honor."

"I am happy for him," said Arthur. "I feared he might be despatched before Launceolt arrived. Now tell me of Launcelot's fight with Meliagrant, for he is much too modest to do so."

"Sir Meliagrant," said Guinevere, "died very well, in distinction to the way he lived."

"Yes," said Arthur, "I can understand that. It is a kind of glory to be killed by the noble Launcelot."

But this subject was tiresome to Guinevere and she took her lap dog and fondled him and fed him sweetmeats, and so endured much more talk of Launcelot by Arthur, who though her husband was the king and could not be interrupted except contumaciously.

And finally King Arthur said, "How blessed we are to have him, for Sir Tristram hath been rendered *hors de combat* by an adulterous love and doth stay in Cornwall in its sinful interests, and now even Gawaine (who went to aid Kay but never got beyond Astolat) hath returned ill, to which one might prefer his lechery of old, as being less debilitating."

"Is this not inevitable?" asked Guinevere. "You have cleansed the whole of Britain of evil. What's left to fight? The wicked must come as invaders, like Meliagrant, from elsewhere."

"A worser evil can come from within," said Arthur. "Tristram, that most noble of knights, hath been quite corrupted by the Irish witch Isold, and foolish Gawaine doth dote upon some chit of Astolat, who loveth not him but Launcelot!"

"What is this story?" asked Guinevere, who had now heard the first thing that had interested her in ever so long, and King Arthur related it.

"But you can be sure that the great Launcelot hath no attraction in return," said Arthur with a derisive chuckle. "Indeed, he knoweth not of hers for him, and he would not give a bean for it if he did."

Now Guinevere secretly waxed wroth at this smugness of men, but she exempted Sir Gawaine from her anger, for even as a lecher he did cherish women (which accounted for his successes with them, for never did he use force nor prevarication, but said simply, Come, sweet chuck, let us have some sport), and when Arthur finally went away Guinevere sent for the gallant Gawaine and asked him about this matter of the maid of Astolat.

"Lady," said Sir Gawaine, "I have lost mine heart to one who can only love another, and as in all matters of true love, methinks, nobody is to be blamed. For of all roads to sorrow, that of love is quickest."

"I am saddened to see the saddening of a joyful knight, who hath pleased so many maids and been equally pleased by them," said Guinevere. "When Sir Gawaine doth grieve because of a woman, the world is out of joint."

"Lady," said Gawaine, "my grief is rather due to a man, and would that he were base and ignoble, and that I were superior to him in any wise!"

"What is this adoration ye every one have for Launcelot?" Guinevere asked peevishly. "Is he a god and not a man?"

"At what all men try to do well, he doth best," said Gawaine. "Therefore he hath no envy. He hath no vanity, he hath no greed, he hath no anger nor gluttony, nor doth he have lust. For all of these do come from a lack of knightliness."

"He is then complete unto himself?" asked Guinevere, and her distaste for this paragon ever increased.

"But for sloth," said Sir Gawaine. "A tendency towards acedia is his only weakness."

"Well," said Guinevere, "and that were appropriate in one who so easily overwhelms."

But Gawaine did not hear her wryness, and when she dismissed him he returned to his chambers, where he found Sir Launcelot waiting.

"Most noble Gawaine," said Sir Launcelot, "the king hath told me of thy melancholy. Would that I might cheer thee some. Shall we go hawking? In the meadows without Camelot I lately saw many coneys, of which thy tercel would make short work. Come along, dear friend, let's to the mews."

"Launcelot, friend of my bosom," said Sir Gawaine, "I am too full of woe for sport."

"I am myself no stranger to the black humors," said Launcelot, "the which, when they are worst, I can not relieve except by scourging myself."

"As we are different in gifts," said Gawaine, "mine own being no match for yours, so are we otherwise in constitutions. Self-inflicted pain, I fear, would be irrelevant to my current condition."

"The king," said Sir Launcelot, "did tell me only that thou dost grieve, and not the wherefore of it, and he hath urged me to cheer thee if I can."

"My uncle is the wisest of kings," said Gawaine. "There should never be a division 'twixt Launcelot and Gawaine, else the Round Table could not preserve its integrity." And he winced. "But vanity, methinks, is not conquered once for all, but must every day be fought and brought down!" Here he had difficulty in continuing.

"What canst thou not tell to me?" asked Sir Launcelot. "I who would put his right arm into the fire for thee."

"In some matters," said Gawaine, "an enemy were friendlier than a friend to talk to." He smote his one hand with the other. "I love the fair Elaine."

Now Launcelot smiled in relief and he clapped his friend on the shoulder. "Well, Gawaine," said he, "I feared thou hadst some serious malady of the soul, such as we all, being born in sin, do know from time to time. Did God shed His blood fur us in vain? Are we beyond redemption? Each man must face these terrible questions. But thou art in anguish only over some little maid? My friend, worthy Gawaine, go to."

"And thou dost not even remember her," said Gawaine wonderingly. "Elaine of Astolat, who lately nursed thee?"

"Well now, certainly I do," said Sir Launcelot. "A fine girl, and virtuous, and I wore her token at the tourney. Gawaine, how pleased I am to hear this! Her father Sir Bernard is a loyal and God-fearing knight, and her brothers are splendid lads, and have joined the Table. Now bless me if I can see cause for melancholy in this anywhere."

But Gawaine groaned and looked away, and then Launcelot frowned as a thought came to him, and he said, "Ah," and did stare away. "Forgive me, my friend," he said finally, " 'tis a delicate matter, but is it the state of thine health that worries thee?"

"Health of the body?" asked Gawaine. "Methinks I am hale enough." But he was puzzled by the question, and he begged his friend for an elucidation of it.

"The fair Elaine is a virgin, gently reared," said Launcelot.

And then Gawaine's brow descended. "Nay, Launcelot, I have no boils on my privities! God did never so punish my concupiscence. He hath rather chosen this means: I love Elaine, but she doth love only thee."

Launcelot shook his head. "If true, this is most distressing," said he, "for I can not think of this maid except as my sister."

"Therefore," said Gawaine, "all three of us are miserable."

Launcelot pondered unhappily on this state of affairs. Then he asked, "Shall I go to Astolat and plead for thee?"

"Alas," said Sir Gawaine, "I fear that that would serve

only the cause of confusion, for I was lately there, pleading for *thee*."

"For me?" asked Launcelot in amazement. "I tell thee, my friend, I can not love this maiden, nor any woman, now or in any time, never." And this he said with notable intensity.

Now it was unthinkable that Launcelot was a vile sodomite, and therefore Sir Gawaine was puzzled. "Then I have done no kindness to the fair Elaine," said he. "But how could I have done otherwise, when she was dying for love of thee, than to give her the hope that thou wouldst return and requite?"

"God hath not made it easy to hearten some people," said Sir Launcelot. "For what they want they can not have. Sir Kay, for example, with whom I lately played the same part as thine here, but was properly corrected by our gracious queen, who is a remarkable woman, Gawaine, with a virile sense of justice. I was not prepared to find that, I confess, in someone female and passing comely."

Now Gawaine did wonder at this tepid tribute, and he said, "Certes, Guinevere is the most beautiful woman in the world."

"So be it, then," said Launcelot, "and God bless her always. But now, what are we to do with poor Elaine, if I can not love her, and she can not love thee, and thou canst love no other?" He frowned in compassion and said, "I do not speak in intentional absurdity."

"Yet, of course, 'tis absurd," said Gawaine sorrowfully, "the which is proved merely by hearing it said. And thou and I have better things to do, no doubt, when once we have determined we can do nothing here."

"Nobly spoken," said Launcelot. "But I think I have me an idea for the temporal salvation of the fair Elaine (for only God can grant the eternal). Near the monastery of the Little Brothers of Poverty and Pain, where lately I was in retreat, is, though segregated from them, a sisterhood of the same order. Now to this convent I shall urge old Bernard to send his daughter, where within this devout sorority, in the perpetual adoration of the Christ, whose brides they are, Elaine will find the true and the only happiness."

Now Sir Gawaine was himself all too worldly to be much cheered by this, though he knew that it was right, and he said, "But forgive me for asking this: Were it not even more kind if thou went to Astolat and with thine own lips talked of this matter with the fair Elaine?"

"She is a maid, Gawaine," said Launcelot sternly, "and under the management of her father. Only with a caitiff would it be lawful to abrogate paternal authority, to a virtuous end, but Sir Bernard is a most noble and pious old knight."

"Yet," said Gawaine, the defender of women, "the grief is hers primarily. Sir Bernard doth not understand her malady, nor methinks never will, for such old noblemen though honorable are coarse towards female sensibilities."

"Then, on thy plea, I shall go there," said Sir Launcelot. "But only with the permission of the queen, at whose disposal I am ever."

Therefore he did take himself to Guinevere, saying, "Lady, I would go to Astolat on mercy's mission."

"Ah," said Guinevere, "thou goest to thy little maid?"

"A maid, madam," said Sir Launcelot, "but not mine, by your leave."

"Thou shalt make her thine?" asked the queen.

"Nay," said Sir Launcelot, "I shall send her to a nunnery."

"Art thou a whoremonger?" asked the queen. "Fie, for shame!"

"O villainous commerce!" cried Launcelot in horror, supposing she had misheard him. "I did refer to a place where the good sisters immure themselves away from the vile world, a convent, madam, a female monastery."

"At London, I am told," said Guinevere, "this is oft the name by which a bordel went. But I know thee for a literal knight, Launcelot. Now tell me why thou dost disdain this maid. She is plain? But if she were, should Gawaine be so taken with her? She is foolish? But is that not the nature of all maidens, and why men do crave them, calling them in endearment 'pretty fool'?"

"Lady," said Launcelot, "I fear you do mock me often if not always, and whilst I can not properly protest, I must confess that I have noticed this."

"Were thy sword as dull as thy wits," said Guinevere, "thou wert not invincible. I grant thee, however, that I am unjust, for I am but a consort, which is to be as close to power as one might come without having any of it, and therefore to be farther away than the basest of slaves."

"Madam," Sir Launcelot said earnestly, "over me your power is not limited."

"Except by the king," said Guinevere, "who hath given me that much."

Now Launcelot was so puzzled that he said, in disrespectful exasperation, "Well, lady, what would you have?"

"The power to declare thee not my champion," said Guinevere.

"Lady," said Launcelot, "that is a matter between you and your husband, our sovereign, whom God hath put upon the throne, and to whom I am but a vassal."

"Sir Launcelot," said Guinevere, "dost find me beautiful?"

"Than whom no one is more so," said that knight.

"I wonder," said Guinevere, "whether thou art alone in that opinion?"

Now, believing this to be but womanly vanity, the claims of which not even a queen was immune to, Sir Launcelot said, "Surely not, madam, for 'tis asserted throughout the realm."

"Thou hast so heard," said Guinevere.

"Most lately from the noble Gawaine," said Launeclot.

"A lascivious knight," Guinevere said in mock disapproval.

"If so once, then no longer," Launcelot assured her. "Gawaine is the very man who would send me to Astolat, for he doth grieve for this maid."

"Who doth love thee alone, poor soul!" said Guinevere.

"But can not understand that thou wert made for finer things."

"Again I hear your mockery, madam," Sir Launcelot said. "Lady, I assure you that I have ever striven to be pious. My motive is good, however feeble (being but human) my means. But as I am your champion, your virtue must be my standard. Would you not have me go to Astolat? Then I shall not go."

"Sir Launcelot, I would never have thee oppose the direction of thy conscience," said the queen. "For in so doing I might cause thee to turn into a woman, thou who art (with Arthur) the model of virility, to the condition of which all knights aspire. Go thou to kill or cure this lovesick maiden."

But having got her leave, Launcelot was yet dissatisfied, though perhaps more with himself than with his queen. "Madam," said he, "know you that if I could return the love of this maid, I should. But I can not abrogate my vow. What is a man finally but his word? Hiw prowess at arms comes from God, but his oath is his own, and the seed of all his honor."

"Thou hast taken a vow of chastity?" asked Guinevere. "And hast thou sworn as well never to fall ill with the plague?"

"Lady, a sickness of soul can never be likened unto that of the body," Sir Launcelot said, "for the latter is but a wretched temporal thing, the which is necessarily corrupted by each passing moment and soon feeds the worms. But the soul can be polluted only by exercising wrongfully the liberty of choice given us by God."

Then Sir Launcelot went away, and Guinevere knew a great need to ruin him, being the most formidable and the worst enemy he ever had, except himself, and he had begun to understand that, for she had evoked from him a statement of his principles, which when put into words seemed fatuous in the extreme. Yet little did he know that what she found damnable in him was his strength and not his weakness.

Therefore at this time Sir Launcelot believed that Guinevere thought him a driveling fool. And for her part, she assumed that to him she was but a queen to be the champion of, and she bitterly remembered her dream, in which she had loved him before he became incarnate.

Now, as these things happen, in Camelot it was commonly known, as it was not in Cornwall, that Tristram and Isold were in love because they drank the potion brewed by Brangwain, the handmaiden and witch, and Guinevere was so exercised by her spite against Launcelot that she did entertain briefly the wish to send to her sister-queen for to get some of this liquid and feed it to him. But then she trembled with the thought of such wickedness, for, unlike Mark, Arthur was a great king, indeed the greatest ever or ever to be, and she did love him nobly, whereas what she felt for Launcelot was in another region of the heart. Indeed, it was rather hatred, was it not? as she did ask herself, and in grievous confusion she fell ill and she took to her bed, and no one, not King Arthur nor even her confessor, knew the reason.

And Sir Launcelot went to Astolat and he told Sir Bernard wherefore he had come.

But old Bernard said, "Well, my daughter is no longer ill, as you can plainly see." And he pointed to where she was walking in the garden and singing sweetly.

Sir Launcelot was overjoyed to know this, and he was pleased to put the matter aside and to tell Sir Bernard of the prowess shown by his sons at the tournament, who had won their seats at the Round Table. Now while they talked, a rain began to fall without, first gently and then in torrents, and at length Launcelot saw that the fair Elaine was yet standing in it, in the garden, and singing yet, though through the noise of the rain she could not be heard at all. And she was quite soaked, with her hair in string.

Therefore he called this to the attention of old Bernard, saying, "Methinks she will soon be ill again." And then they both went out to her.

"My lord," said she to Bernard, "I fear this drought will quite wither my blossoms." And the rain was streaming down her face. Then she plucked a wet pink rose and gave it to Launcelot, saying, "Sir, there you have my flower." And in withdrawing her hand from the stem she cut her finger on a thorn, and she said, bleeding, "Ah, I am well pricked."

Now Launcelot drew Bernard aside and said, "My lord, I fear she is perplexed."

"Alas," said Sir Bernard. "Come, let us get her out of the rain."

So they took her within, to her chamber, and they called her waiting-women for to remove her sopping clothes, and Sir Bernard and Launcelot went into an anteroom.

"I shall send for Sir Gawaine," said Bernard, "for he was her best medicine. Would that he were my son-in-law, but the daughter of a mere landed knight is of too low a station for the nephew of a king."

"Nay," said Sir Launcelot, "he would like nothing more than to wed the fair Elaine, but 'tis she who will not have him."

"The chit!" cried old Bernard. "I shall not brook this insolence." And he would have gone forthwith to chide her, ill as she was, had not Launcelot stayed him.

"My venerable friend," said Sir Launcelot, "your daughter suffers a malady of which you are not aware, and I fear it hath grown ever worse."

"'Tis true she doth seem distracted currently, but, believe me, 'twill pass," said Bernard. "Her mother was given to such transports, as are all women sporadically, owing to the changing phases of the moon, which doth move their blood as it moves the waters of the sea. One goes to women as one goes to fishes: they are slippery, silvery things, and do exude saline liquids."

"Methinks this is more than mensual disorder," said Launcelot. "Indeed, it was the noble Gawaine, always a great frequenter of females and now their special defender, who hath sent me here. We both of us agree that the unfortunate Elaine should be entered into a segregated community of the religious, such as the convent, just near by, of the Little Sisters of Poverty and Pain."

"I know these sisters," said old Bernard, "who do come here oft for to beg scraps from our kitchens. They live purely, but wretchedly, yet no doubt that is one and the same. And Elaine hath ever eaten like a sparrow. I had wanted to make a good match for her, Launcelot, for she is a comely thing and hath winning ways, or did have as a child. Blast the melancholy of her ways since becoming a woman!"

And Sir Launcelot privately deplored this unfortunate oath, though he knew that Bernard had good reason to be vexed. "But to be the bride of Our Lord," said he, "is to possess the greatest wealth, and such a woman knows a glory to which the most radiant queen cannot attain." And suddenly he did think of Guinevere, all golden, and he trembled as if in a chill.

"Well," said Sir Bernard, "and in her current condition, who else would have her?" He was a coarse old knight, but he was not unkind, and he added, "Poor wretch! Yes, this distress, having lasted more than a month, can scarcely be owing to a mere monthly. Then to the nunnery shall she go! I am grateful to you, noble Launcelot, among whose great missions this must be the least. Truly you are a knight of worship so to take pains for a provincial little maid."

And Sir Launcelot took his leave from Sir Bernard, and he did never see Elaine again. And when he returned to Camelot, he went to Sir Gawaine and told him what had happened, and he said, "I trust this hath ended in a fashion that will please God."

"I thank thee," said Sir Gawaine. "But forgive me, please, if I remain mournful awhile and, though I know it as sinful, to yearn only for the promised stroke of the Green Knight, the which will surely cut off mine head."

"Nay, Gawaine," said Launcelot, "there is some magic

in that, the green one being obviously monster, not man, and therefore thy best defense would be piety."

Then Sir Launcelot went to King Arthur, and when he had told him of the matter of Elaine and how he had treated it, Arthur said, "Thou hast performed well, my dear Launcelot, and now may I ask thee to go to thy lady Guinevere, who is ill as well, but will suffer no treatment by the physicians. Now, this is scarcely a mortal malady, but is rather methinks an access of the ennui that doth attack all women, even queens, and thanks be to God for making us men! Prithee go and amuse her, for she knoweth a great fondness for thee."

"Sire," said Launcelot, "have you no quest for me?"

"Pray do not be insulted," said King Arthur. "To bring a bit of cheer to the queen is not unworthy of thee, as her champion, and be assured that when a grander task must be done, thou shalt be relieved of the petty."

Therefore Sir Launcelot did dutifully go to Guinevere, in a kind of dread, for contrary to what King Arthur believed, he knew of her disdain for him, and he believed it of the kind that could not be altered except by a total alteration of himself, so that he would be a different man from what he was: the which was an impossibility. But when he found her, in her chamber, Guinevere was pale and drawn, and with great shadows beneath her eyes, and she slept fitfully with trembling and labored breath.

And looking at her, who was weak and ill and not at all radiant now, for the first time Sir Launcelot found her peculiarly beautiful. And while he stood there silently at her bedside, Guinevere did speak his name feebly, though still in seeming sleep.

And he answered, "Lady, I am at your service."

Now she stirred but she did not awaken, and she said again, "Launcelot."

"God save you, madam," he said.

Then in sleep she extended to him the lily of her hand, and he did bend and kiss it, and she withdrew her hand and put it into the bosom of her gown at the place where her heart was, and to Sir Launcelot it was as though she had put her bare hand on his own naked heart, and he started as if burned and he cried out.

Guinevere wakened thereupon and seeing him did wax wroth. "Wicked knight," said she, "what can be thy purpose, so to have stolen into the queen's bedchamber? O disorderly and contumacious man!"

"I was sent here by the royal Arthur," said Launcelot, but even so he knew a guilty confusion.

"Well, what a pretty piece of vileness this is," Guinevere said. "Hath the king become a pander?"

Now Launcelot believed her the captive of a madness to have spoke so, and he said softly, "Lady, lie back again and let sleep soothe this anguish. You are amongst friends."

But Guinevere would not be placated. "Thou harlot," she said, "thy wanton fingers were at my breast."

"'Twas your own hand, madam," said Launcelot, but in telling the truth he felt as though prevaricating, and he colored violently. "I am being wronged here, lady! Apply to the the king, I pray you. He sent me, for to cheer you in your melancholy."

"By fondling me criminally?" asked Guinevere. "Dost thou call Arthur a perverse felon?" And she did cry for her guards, who were ever without the door since the incursion of Sir Meliagrant, and when they came hastily within, she commanded them to arrest Launcelot and put him into confinement.

But for this they had no stomach though they were armed cap-à-pie and carried great halberds, and Sir Launcelot was naked of weapons, for such awe did Launcelot's presence inspire in mere kerns, and therefore with boorish cunning they pretended not to see him, and they fled as if in pursuit of an escaping rogue, and soon could be heard in the anteroom probing the tapestries and opening the cupboards.

Seeing this, Guinevere became no less distraught, and Launcelot's efforts to calm her were of no avail, because her haughtiness was such that she had rather be killed than touched intimately, and even the evil Sir Meliagrant had never done this while she was his helpless captive.

"Madam," said Sir Launcelot finally, "shall I then submit myself to the torture, to prove that I put mine hand on you at no time and in no wise, except to take the fingers you extended to me and to kiss them respectfully as the vassal's custom would have it?"

Then Guinevere herself did color, for her rage had made her even more pale.

"I did this?" she asked, and even as she spake she began to feel the infection of self-doubt, for no man would so offer to have himself broken on the wheel unless he believed his truth would thereby be established: for though this trial would kill him in any event, he would not go to Hell as a liar.

"Well," said she, "give me thine hand now." And he did so, and she examined it, saying, " 'Tis large, in truth, and horny. Such calluses would abrade." And she gave it back to him and stretching her bodice did look within at her tender skin whiter than the plumage of a dove and finer than samite.

Now Sir Launcelot did thrill with some terrible feeling, and he bit his lip till he felt the salt of his blood, and then Guinevere looked up from her white breasts to him and saw his mouth encarmined.

And she asked, "Sir, art wounded? Thou, who art invulnerable?"

"To a kind of death, madam," said Sir Launcelot. "Methinks you would kill me." And he wiped the blood from his mouth with his hand.

"If I commanded thee to love me, shouldst thou comply?" asked Queen Guinevere.

And Sir Launcelot swore the first oath of his life. "May God damn me, lady, if I do that not by your order, but by mine own need!" And he thrust his bloodied hand into her golden hair and cleansed it thereupon, saying, "Now we are both stained forever."

And Guinevere clasped him to her and demanded his fealty of body and soul, the which, transported, he could not withhold, and sinning against God and king, and in violation of all vows, they hastened together towards the littler death from which a mortal surviveth many times to continue his wretched progress towards the greater one, on which occasion he must justify himself to God Almighty.

And Launcelot and Guinevere were the most notable adulterers ever to be, for their joining was not in ignorance of the consequences nor as a result of a magical potion, but they came together from Envy and Vanity and the offspring of these: the hunger for mastery by man over women and visa versa.

And now we flee the spectacle of their calamitous first sinning, for to be the witness of such is in God's eyes to be no better than a participant, and go to the noble Gawaine, who though beginning as a lecher had grown ever more virtuous in the company of the Round Table.

BOOK IX

*Of Sir Gawaine's temptations at Liberty Castle;
and how he kept his appointment with the Green
Knight.*

Now Sir Gawaine did not soon cease to think about the
fair Elaine of Astolat, and he knew guilt for encouraging
her hopes that Launcelot would come to love her, for suf-
fering from it himself he believed that unrequited love was
a disease from which there was no cure. And though a
God-fearing knight, he was not sufficiently devout to believe in the efficacy of taking the veil if a woman, nor the
tonsure in a man, in which doubt he did sin grievously,
God save his soul.

Yet he knew that what Sir Launcelot had done was
right, as always, for that greatest of all knights could not
err, and in all the company of the Round Table,
Gawaine's faith in Launcelot was second only to that of
King Arthur, and it would be a terrible day when it failed.

But Sir Agravaine, the eldest of Gawaine's younger
brothers, was never fond of Launcelot from the first, having an envy in the name of his brother of which Gawaine
himself was innocent.

"Thou wert first knight," said Agravaine, "until he came
to Camelot."

"Hast thou forgotten the noble Tristram?" asked
Gawaine. "For he is another who hath bested me. And no
doubt there will come more. My dear Agravaine, a knight

of the Round Table doth his best, measuring his prowess against only his own capacity. God, and not men, establishes all hierarchies."

Now Agravaine, like all envious persons, was concerned for himself and not that person in whose interests he pretended to speak, and when his brother Gawaine was of a lower ranking, he himself was even less, and in fact he did from childhood on resent his elder brother's superiority within their family. And now he feared that Gawaine loved Launcelot more than he loved him of the selfsame blood. And secretly he bore no good will towards Guinevere, whom he desired lasciviously though she was his aunt by law. And as a result of all these negative feelings together, he did seethe within.

"Thou couldst overwhelm them all," said Agravaine, "wert thou not inhibited by courtesy."

"My dear brother," replied Sir Gawaine, "I fear that thou dost here reveal an ignorance of values, for courtesy is rather an honorable acceptance of order, and therefore a strength and never a failing, and it were rather weakness if I did think me nearly the knight that Launcelot is, in either prowess or piety."

But Agravaine did writhe in bitterness. "Launcelot is an hypocrite," he said. "I know that in my bones, and I shall one day prove it. God made no perfect man, Gawaine. We are all of us sinners, but some of us have not yet been caught out. Thy friend Tristram hath lately been revealed as but a vile adulterer."

"An adulterer he may be, alas!" said Sir Gawaine. "But I should never call him 'vile,' nor should he be seen as nothing more. And how much blame should be placed on one who unwittingly swalloweth a potion with magical properties? Is the poisoned one at fault, unless the liquid be self-administered?"

"Gawaine," said Agravaine, "thou art our older brother, and I honor thee as such, but oft I see a quality in thee that should rather be that of our youngest sib, baby Mordred, which in fact he himself hath never displayed (for he graspeth at weapons and not playthings, and hath wounded sometimes his nurses). Thou art naïve and gullible. Few men, and no women whatever, have ever commited adultery in defiance of their true hearts, irrespective of potions and spells."

"Well," said Gawaine in affection, "these negative thoughts, Brother, are but the fruits of idleness. Thou shouldst find thyself a quest to go upon and, fighting evil, not see it where it doth exist not. Poor Tristram hath been under a curse since the day he was born. As to the noble Launcelot, upon mine honor, when he offends God the Table will crack and fall apart."

And Sir Agravaine fell silent, but when he left his brother he went to the passage without the queen's chambers and he spake to the guards there posted.

"Fellows," said he, "know ye that such an incursion as that of the late Meliagrant is not to be regarded as uncommon. Evil rogues abound who would do harm to our gracious queen, for she is the embodiment of all virtue. Therefore keep ye a keen eye on all her callers, and furthermore, be they recognizable as even our own knights (and I assume ye shall repel all others), I would that ye report to me their names, for it is not out of the question that a felon will, through magic, assume the guise of a worthy man and so hope to penetrate unhindered to her tender presence, there to mishandle her vilely or perhaps even to murder her."

Now this false speech of Agravaine caused these guards, who were gullible boors, to become exercised with concern for their queen (and even more, if the truth were known, by a fear of what would happen to themselves if they allowed entrance to someone who would harm her), and they were quick to swear that no knight should enter without Sir Agravaine's knowing of it, and they also promised to tell those who would relieve them at the change of guard.

Now when Agravaine went away, one guard said to the other, "Here, thinkst thou we did wrong not to tell him?"

"Tell him what?" asked the other.

"Well, you great twit, that Launcelot's bloody well in there at the moment."

"In what?"

"In the queen's chamber, of course."

"And fucking well chamber'd he is!" said his companion. "For 'tis a rare queen these days can be told from a quean."

Now the other spoke close to his ear. "Dost believe he swyveth her?" (For these base fellows showed little reverence for their superiors, Devil take them.)

"Else I never heard a groaning," said the wretch.

"Well," said the other, "methinks thou hast never done, except at the breech of an ewe." And they continued this foul badinage (for the mean do love to jest vilely and in impious disrespect of the noble), and happy for them they were not overheard by a man of rank, else as punishment they might have lost their tongues at the roots.

And for many years only the lower orders knew of the adulterous love of Launcelot and Guinevere.

Now a twelvemonth having passed, it was time for Sir Gawaine to go and keep his fell appointment with the Green Knight. Therefore he bade good-by to his brothers, his friend Launcelot, and Arthur his king and uncle. And to all he said, "God alone knows when we shall meet again, whether on earth or in Heaven."

For he believed it likely that in return for beheading the Green Knight he would lose his own head, and his own could not be returned to his neck.

Then Sir Gawaine rode out of Camelot and he was about to cross the bridge over the river that flowed through the valley below the castle when he saw a barge floating downstream towards him, and what was strange about this barge was that it had no boatman to direct it and furthermore it was all draped with black velvet.

Now as it came ever closer to him on the gentle current Sir Gawaine could discern that beneath the black canopy lay a figure clothed in white stuffs, and soon he saw that it was a corse. And descending from his steed he went down onto the riverbank, and as the barge floated near by, he held his sword by the point and he hooked its handle onto the gunwale and he drew the craft against the shore.

Now that he could clearly see the dead face he recognized it as that of Elaine of Astolat, than whom he had never loved anyone more dearly, and he leapt aboard and he took the maiden's body into his embrace with much grief, and it was a long time before he lowered her again to the silken catafalque and collected his wits, the which had been lost in agony.

And only then did he see that she was dressed as a bride and wore a coronet of flowers on her sweet brow and she held in her crossed hands a bouquet of forget-me-nots. And to her soft bosom was pinned a letter. And this he took off and he broke its seal and he read through the new tears that welled to replace those which had dried, and for a while he was confused again in grief.

For what was written in that letter was as follows: "Not good enough to marry Launcelot, too wicked to marry God, I hereby give my virginity to Death."

Now Sir Gawaine did stay there with the body for a long time, but no one saw him, for this was a place on the river which was screened by a grove of trees from the castle above, and when he eventually came to his senses he realized he could not linger there, else he would never reach the Green Knight's demesne in time to keep his pledge. Yet if he summoned a chaplain from Camelot or went to the friary near by, to ask that this dear body be given a proper burial, no religious could do otherwise than to refuse it, for it was a suicide and in mortal sin, and therefore must be denied a consecrated grave. And as to Sir Launcelot, Gawaine saw great reason to conceal from him utterly and forever all knowledge of this sorry matter, for he was guiltless of it.

Therefore Sir Gawaine waited until night had fallen, and then in the darkness he entered the river and he pushed the barge ahead of him, so that, wading to the armpits, he reached the main stream. Then he allowed the current to take the vessel from him and softly bear it towards the sea. And he regained the riverbank and put on his armor, and he mounted his horse, and he went through the dark to his meeting with the Green Knight.

Now, as in all true quests, though he had no precise sense of where the Green Knight could be sought, he knew he would find him eventually by allowing his horse its head, and when at dawn he reached a castle, before which his steed stopped and pawed the ground and neighed, he applied for entrance to it.

But when the drawbridge was lowered and the portcullis raised, and he rode within, he was greeted not by the Green Knight but rather by a fine tall lord who welcomed him graciously and invited him to spend the night.

"I thank you, most noble sir," said Gawaine, "but I can not linger here. For I must needs meet an obligation within the next four days, and I do not know how much farther I must travel." And, because this handsome lord looked an honest man, he told him of his appointment with his verdant adversary.

"Sir knight," said the lord, "I tell you that I know this green man, whose Green Chapel is just near by, and it is there that you will find him, four days hence and in good time! Meanwhile you must accept my hospitality." And he led Sir Gawaine within the castle, which was the most sumptuously furnished place that Gawaine had ever seen, and the chamber where he was led was hung with silks and carpeted in fur soft as foam, and nightingales sang in golden cages, and hanging lamps burned Arabic oils with a delicious fragrance and in their glow, on a couch of wine-purple velvet, lay an exquisite woman whose robes were of pale-violet gauze and transparent, so that her voluptuous body was revealed in every particular.

Now Sir Gawaine was taken aback, for he believed that he had been conducted into a bordel and that this seemingly fine lord was rather a loathsome pander. But before he could draw his sword and smite him with the flat of it for this insult to a knight of the Round Table, the lord said, "Most noble Sir Gawaine, may I present my wife."

And therefore Gawaine was constrained by the laws of courtesy to greet this lady as he would any other, and he endeavored to ignore the indecency of her costume as she smiled at him and welcomed him to the castle, for her ivory body, scarcely screened, was far more beautiful than any he had ever seen in many years of intimate congress with maids.

"Now, Sir Gawaine," said the lord, "whilst you are under my roof, all that I possess is yours, and the only offense that you can commit against me is to refrain from using that which you desire. For this is Liberty Castle, and the freedom of my guest is absolute."

Now Sir Gawaine had never previously been given to philosophy, but since the beginning of the tragic episode with Elaine of Astolat he had grown ever more contemplative.

"My lord," said he, "do I understand that you are so addicted to the giving of freedom that you would impose it upon him who doth not seek it?"

"Ah," said the lord, "there is no such mortal upon the earth, for all are born free and become captives through denial."

Now Gawaine believed this an impious theory, but having a generous heart, he determined to ponder on it further. Therefore he now said only, "My sole desire currently is but for a basin of water and a towel, for my journey hath been dusty and I would wash."

"Then come with me, my dear sir," said the lord, and he conducted Gawaine to another chamber, which was even more sumptuously appointed than the one in which his wife lolled, and it gave onto a walled garden in which every sort of flower did bloom under a warm sun (though elsewhere the day had been damp and dreary), and in this garden was a pool in the center of which was the alabaster statue of a nude woman, and from each of her paps flowed a fountain of silvery water. And lovely soft music was heard there, though no musicians could be seen.

And saying, "Here you may bathe," the lord did clap his hands and a peacock spread its resplendent fan and strutted to him, carrying in its beak a little silver bell, the which he took and he rang it, and three naked small boys, all with golden hair and very white skin, came to Sir Gawaine, bearing towels as fluffy as clouds.

"Now," said the lord, "these tiny retainers will dry you, and kiss you as well, and when you have taken your pleasure with them, please ring the bell."

But Sir Gawaine did start back in dismay. "My lord," said he, "kindly remove these juvenile persons."

"Very well," said the lord, smiling. "I shall summon my wife to wash you."

"Nay, my lord, with all respect," said Sir Gawaine. But before he could say he would wash alone, the lord rang the bell again and a robust young man appeared, unclad except for an iron helmet and brass greaves, and carrying a bundle of birches, he smote his other hand with them whilst smirking in genial cruelty.

"This fellow," said the lord, "is late masseur to the court of Rome, and can soon obliterate the loins' memory of an arduous day in the saddle."

"Sir," said Gawaine, "I would wash me alone, and in a simple tin basin filled with cold water."

"I can deny you nothing," said the lord, and he summoned these things, and they were brought by a withered hag, and Sir Gawaine dismissed her and was left by himself.

Now when he had finished his bathe, he realized he had nought to wear but his smallclothes and steel armor, and therefore he reluctantly rang for his host, for to request the loan of a house coat. But in answer to his summons came instead a lovely young maid, her flaxen hair flowing over her white shoulders to part at her high round breasts so that the orchidaceous tips were revealed, for she was naked, and Sir Gawaine, who was an authority on such matters, judged she was in years sixteen, and in former times she would have been to him as a goblet of cool water to a parched throat, but now he hastily concealed his secrets with the coarse homespun cloth brought him by the hag to dry himself on, and he commanded her to fetch her master to him.

And when, as required by the laws of Liberty Castle, she complied instantly with his wishes, Sir Gawaine knew the first faint pangs of regret, for though he was no longer the unrestrained lecher of old, neither had he become as enervate as an eunuch.

Now the lord brought him a robe of fine silken stuff and trimmed with soft fur, and then he led him to a magnificent dining hall, where the table was laden with delicacies from all over the earth and the dishes were of pure gold, while the goblets were each cut from a solid diamond, and when they sat down they were served by a corps of unfledged maidens, delicate as primroses and with smooth bodies clad only in sheer lawn.

And hearing some slight stirring near his knees beneath the table, Sir Gawaine lifted the cloth and saw a beautiful child with a face of old ivory and dark eyes shaped like almonds.

"At the very edge of the world," said the lord his host, "on the brink of nothingness, live in great luxury a golden-skinned people called the Chinee. Now it is their practice to use infantile entertainers beneath the table top at banquets, to stir one appetite by provoking another. This can be especially amusing as prelude to an Oriental dish we shall presently be offered: live monkey. I shall strike off its crown, and we shall eat his smoking brains." And here the lord brandished a little silver ax. "I promise you that nothing is more aphrodisiac, and that soon you will be delirious with lust."

But Sir Gawaine declined to partake of the pleasure beneath the cloth, and he begged to have the dish withheld, but though he believed this lord monstrously unnatural he would not denounce him under his own roof, for after all no vileness had yet been imposed upon him, but rather merely offered.

And Gawaine also spurned the lark's eyes in jelly, the coddled serpent-eggs, the pickled testicles of tigers, the lot, and he asked instead for cold mutton and small beer, which he instantly was brought.

Now after this feast the lord led Sir Gawaine to a chamber where a lovely maid, dressed in many veils, played sweetly upon a flute while dancing gracefully, and one by one she dropped her veils until with the last one she was revealed to be a willowy young man, and when the dance was done, he bowed to the floor before Sir Gawaine but facing away.

But Gawaine said to his host, "My lord, I am no bugger."

Therefore the lord dismissed the young man, and then he said to Sir Gawaine, "Well, I would know what I might do for you."

And Gawaine said, "Nothing, my lord."

"So be it," said the lord. "And now I must leave you, for to go hunting, and I shall be away until nightfall. Pray remember that even in my absence you can be denied nothing at Liberty Castle." And he gave Gawaine the silver bell that had been fetched by the peacock. "Ring this for whatever you desire. But now I propose to you a bargain: that when I return we each exchange with the other that which we have got during the course of the day when we were apart."

Now Sir Gawaine could see no reason to do this, but he was aware by now that the ways of this castle were strange, so strange indeed as to suggest magic, but whether white or black he could not yet say: for though the beastly amusements offered him were evil, they may well have been temptations in the service of a higher good. And surely courtesy required that he respond amiably to this lord, until such time as he could determine his purpose.

Therefore he agreed to this bargain, for anyway he had no intention to do ought all day but prepare himself spiritually for the ordeal to come, when he must face the Green Knight.

"Good," said the lord. "Perhaps I shall bring you a brace of partridges."

"And if I have nothing to return?" asked Sir Gawaine.

"Then nothing shall be my reward," said the lord in a merry voice. "But do not forget that our agreement is to be considered literally, and that to conceal *anything* you have received would be to violate your pledge."

"My lord," said Gawaine reproachfully, "I am a knight of the Round Table."

"Indeed," the lord said, "and I should strike a bargain with no other!"

Then he left to go a-hunting, and scarcely was he gone when Sir Gawaine regretted not having asked where the chapel was situated within the castle, for he wished to pray there. But remembering the little silver bell, he rang it, and in answer to his summons the lord's wife appeared and she was no more abundantly dressed than she had been when he had seen her first.

"Lady," said he, "please direct me to your chapel, for I would fain pray."

But the lady came to press against him, and she put her arms about his neck, and she said, "Sweet Sir Gawaine, be kind to me, I beg of you."

And though Gawaine was far from being immune to the sensations caused by the pressure of her luxuriant body (and graciousness would not allow him to thrust her away), he had the strength of soul to remain modest, and he said, "Lady, this is not proper."

"I speak of kindness and not propriety," cried the lady, and she held him tightly and her warm breath was against the hollow of his neck.

"Lady," said Gawaine, "methinks I now understand the test to which I am being put at Liberty Castle, where all temptations of the flesh have been offered me, but in fact not even when I was a notable lecher did I frequent children, persons of mine own gender, nor other men's wives."

Now this beautiful lady did fall against him weeping. "You are the defender of women," said she, "and I am in distress."

"Then let me get mine armor and weapons," said Sir Gawaine, "and tell me who would abuse you."

" 'Tis no person," said the lady. "I am rather tormented by a sense that my kisses are obnoxious, for my lord hath avoided me lately." And she lifted her mouth to him, the which was moist and red.

"Your breath, lady," said Gawaine, "is fragrant as the zephyrs of spring, I cannot believe that your kisses are repulsive."

"Well," said the lady, "then there must be something offensive in the touch of my lips." And she pursed these for his inspection.

"Nay," said Sir Gawaine. "They are flawless as the rose."

"Yet," said she, "you can not be certain unless you press them to your own."

"Perhaps that is true," said Sir Gawaine. "But should I be the one to make this test?"

"But who other?" asked the lady. "I can not subject my husband to it, for it is precisely he who I fear finds me obnoxious. And any man who is not a knight of the Round Table could never be trusted."

"Trusted, lady?" asked Gawaine, endeavoring to loosen her clasp, which had now been lowered to his waist, to the end that their bellies were joined.

"A knight of lesser virtue, enflamed by my kiss, alone with me, my lord being in the remote forest, I attired lightly as I am, he in a robe of fine thin stuff that betrays the least stirring of his loins—" And so said the lady, and she heaved with the horror of it.

And Sir Gawaine said hastily, "Certes, I am trustworthy in this regard. Now, lady, your argument hath moved me. I shall accept one kiss from you, for the purpose of examining it."

And the lady forthwith crushed her hot mouth against

his lips and had he not clenched his jaws and so erected a barrier of teeth, she would have thrust her tongue into his throat so far as it would go, for it battered against his gums with great force.

And when he at last broke free, he said, "Your kiss is sweet, I assure you. But perhaps it is given too strenuously." (And truly, his lips were full sore.) And then he said, "As guest in Liberty Castle I have this wish, which must be honored, and it is that this test be taken as concluded." Therefore, as she was constrained to do by the law of the place, the lady went away.

Now when the lord returned from his hunt he came to Sir Gawaine, saying, "Well, here you are, sir knight, a brace of fine fat partridges, the which are my gain, and all of it, from a day in the forest. Now, what have you got here that, according to our agreement, you shall give to me?"

"As I predicted," said Sir Gawaine, "I have nothing to give you, having received nothing."

"I beg you to re-examine your memory," said the lord. "Surely you received something during my absence that you had not previously possessed?"

And Sir Gawaine was ashamed, first for his failure of recall, and then for what he must needs confess.

"I received a kiss, my lord," said he, coloring. But then he realized that he was not obliged to say who had kissed him (and the situation at Liberty Castle was such that there were many possible candidates).

"Very well, then," said the lord smiling. "Pray give it me."

Now Gawaine's shame was increased, for he understood that the terms of the agreement were absolute, but manfully he did purse his lips and press them to the cheek of the lord.

"Now," said the lord, "is this precisely how you received this kiss, and did the giver thereof make a similar grimace?"

Sir Gawaine hung his head and said, "Nay, my lord."

And then gathering his strength he lifted his mouth to the lord's and, doing his best to simulate the tender expression of the lady, he kissed him full upon the lips.

"Splendid!" said the lord. "You are a truthful knight of much worship."

Now the following day the lord came to Sir Gawaine once again, and he announced to him that he would make the same exchange with him as he had done the day before. But Gawaine did protest against this.

"Sir," said the lord, "I took you for a courteous knight. Are Arthur's men given to such rudeness?"

"With all respect, my lord," said Gawaine, "I am fasting for my appointment with the Green Knight, and therefore I can not eat game."

"Then I shall bring to you some other goods of the forest," said the lord, and then he looked narrowly at Sir Gawaine. "Sir," said he, "methinks you worry that you will have to give me another kiss."

Now though this was quite true, Sir Gawaine could hardly confess to it without being discourteous in the extreme, and therefore he bowed and said, "My lord, I make this pact with you once again."

But so soon as the lord left the castle this time, Gawaine, eschewing the use of the silver bell and hoping thereby to elude the lady, went alone in search of the chapel, but though he looked everywhere he could not find it. Therefore he returned to the chamber where he had spent the night and he knelt by his bed clasping his hands in the attitude of prayer, but before he could begin his orisons the lady appeared from nowhere and embraced him.

Then he rose with difficulty and freeing himself gently from her, he said, "Lady, it would be indecent for me to talk with you at this time. Pray let us wait until your husband returns from the hunt."

But the lady said, "Sir, remember your sworn duty to all women! Once again I require your aid, and the vows you have taken will never allow you to deny me." And she drew aside the transparent stuff that swathed her bosom, and she bared her breasts absolutely.

"Ah," she cried, "you start back, just as does my husband when I undress before him! Then it is as I fear: my bosom is hideous."

"No, that is not true, lady," said Sir Gawaine. "Between waist and shoulders you are very beautiful."

"Do you say my mammets are round?" asked the lady.

"Very round," said Sir Gawaine.

"And full?"

"Very full."

"Yet high."

"Oh, indeed high," said Sir Gawaine as he walked backwards, for she continued to approach him.

"But think you that the paps are discolored?" And now she held herself in two hands, so that the pink nipples did peek through the white fingers.

"Never discolored," said Gawaine, who was now against the arras and could retreat no farther.

"Not brown then?"

"Certes," said Sir Gawaine, "they are rather of the hue of the Afric orchid."

"Oh," said the lady, taking her hands away, "but they are cold! Methinks breasts should be warm, or if not, then warmed." And before Sir Gawaine knew what he did, she had taken his fingers and put them onto her bosoms. "Now tell me if they are cold."

"Lady," said Gawaine, "they are quite near burning." And for a dreadful moment he could not control his fingers, and finally it was she who drew back, saying haughtily, "Sir, I did not seek kneading. I wished only to know my temperature."

And Sir Gawaine was chagrined. "Forgive me, lady." He sighed with great feeling. "Now, by my privilege as guest, I wish to be alone." Therefore she vanished, and he fell to praying ardently.

Now when the lord returned from the forests he presented to Sir Gawaine the flayed hide of a bear, and he said, "There you have my day's spoil, and all of it. What shall you give me in return?"

And this time Sir Gawaine was ready for him, and he was relieved that it was not so distasteful a thing as a kiss. "I have for you a touch of the chest," said he. "Therefore if you will remove your hauberk and breastplate and raise your doublet, I shall give it you."

Now the lord did these things, and Sir Gawaine groped at his chest, which was covered with a thick mat of hair very like that of the bearskin.

Then the lord began to laugh, for he was ticklish, and when Sir Gawaine was done the lord said, "And is that all? Did I not know you as a truthful knight, I should wonder at this. Nor is it evident as to whose chest was so tickled in the original episode: your own, or that of another?"

"Mine obligation, methinks," said Sir Gawaine, "is but to give you what I had got, and so have I done. I am not required to explain it."

"Aha," said the lord, "methinks not even a sodomite doth toy with a hairy chest, and certes you are anyway not a sod. May I then assume it was rather a woman's full bosom which you fondled?"

"My lord," said Gawaine, "our agreement is to be kept to the letter, no more and no less."

And the lord did laugh merrily, saying, "Well put, my dear sir."

"And now," said Sir Gawaine, "may I ask you to show me to the chapel, for 'tis there I intend to stay at prayers until my appointment with the Green Knight, which is now but two mornings away."

But the lord said, "I'm afraid there is no chapel at Liberty Castle, good Sir Gawaine. We are pagans here, and furthermore we make no apology for so being."

Sir Gawaine crossed himself. "I should have understood that," said he. "Absolute liberty is the freedom to be depraved."

"But only if you choose to make it so," said the lord.

"One can also see it as the only situation in which principles may be put to the proof. No strength of character is needed to stay virtuous under restraint."

"But only God, sir, hath perfect strength," said Gawaine. And he was now vexed, and he said, "And how dare you, as a paynim, to test the virtue of a Christian?"

"Because I have no shame!" merrily replied the lord. "Which is a Christian invention."

Now Sir Gawaine began to suspect that this lord was the Devil, for never had he heard so much wickedness from any man. "Methinks," said he, "that you would weaken me for my encounter with the Green Knight."

"Well," said the lord, "if you are honest you will admit that it is a ridiculous thing. A charlatan dyes his skin and hair and dressed in green clothes bursts into Arthur's court to make a preposterous challenge. Would that be taken seriously anywhere but at Camelot? Now you are likely to die of this buffoonery, and *cui bono*?"

"For the Green Knight I care not a bean," said Sir Gawaine. "But to keep my oath I should go to Hell. And methinks I have done so in coming here."

But the lord did make much mirth. "It is so only if you choose to make it such, I say again," said he, "the which can be said of any other place on earth but especially of your Britain. But enough of this colloquy! And pray never believe that I do not admire you withal."

"Despite such flattery," said Sir Gawaine, "I shall leave you now."

"Ah," the lord said, "you well may leave me, but the one freedom not available at Liberty Castle is to leave it before the proper time hath come."

And Gawaine found that what he had said was true, for when he sought to go out of the gate he was arrested by a strange unseen force and could move only in the direction of the castle behind him. Therefore willy-nilly he stayed the final night, and the next morning the lord came to him again with the familiar proposal.

"Do I have a choice?" asked Gawaine.

And the lord answered, "Well, it is the last time." And promising to exchange with his guest what they each had come into possession of during the day, he went a-hunting in the forest.

Now Gawaine determined no longer to wait passively for the lady to seek him out, for he knew that she would do so, according to the pattern of the previous days: and all things in Heaven and on earth come in threes, and only the tripod is ever stable even though its legs be of unequal lengths. Therefore taking the virile initiative he did go in search of her, and you may be sure he was not long in finding her, for her sole purpose was to try his virtue (to which end all women, even the chaste, are dedicated) and thus all corridors at Liberty Castle soon led to the most private of her chambers, the walls of which were lined with quilted velvet of pink, the which color deepened and darkened as he penetrated the room, and the couch on which she lay was of magenta. But her body for once was fully covered, in a robe of the richest dark red and of many folds and trimmed with the sleek fur of the otter.

"Good day to you, sir knight," said she. "And for what have you come to me?"

"To offer my services," said Sir Gawaine, "the which you have previously required each day at just this time."

"Of that I have no memory," said the lady sternly. "And can your purpose be decent, so to seek me out when mine husband is away?" And crying, "Villainy!" she did clap her hands, and soon a brace of huge knights, armed cap-à-pie, burst into the chamber through a secret door and made at Sir Gawaine.

Now Gawaine understood that he had been tricked and mostly by himself, for he had come here voluntarily and unarmored and unweaponed. But being the truest of knights, what he feared was not the death that he might well be dealt here (for he expected to be killed on the morrow by the Green Knight, and we each of us owe God but one life), but rather that if he were not alive to meet his appointment with the verdant giant he would cause great shame to be brought upon the Round Table, for death were never a good excuse for breaking a pledge.

Therefore he seized a tall candlestick of heavy bronze, and he swung its weighted base with such force that the flange not only split the helm of the first knight to reach him, but also cracked his skull to the very brainpan, and his wits spewed out through his ears. Now taking the halberd that this man dropped, Sir Gawaine brought it up from the floor just as the other knight came at him, and he cut him from the crotch to the wishbone, and his guts hung out like ropes.

"Well," said the lady when this short fight was done, "do not suppose you have me at your mercy." And she found a dagger within her clothes and leaping at Sir Gawaine she sought to do him grievous injury.

But though he was the protector of women Gawaine saw no obligation to suffer being assailed by a female to whom he had offered no harm. Therefore he seized the dagger from her, and then, because she next tried to claw him with the sharp nails of her fingers, he restrained her hands behind her waist.

But hooking her toe behind his ankle the lady tripped him up, so that he fell onto the couch, and she was underneath him.

"Lady," he said, "I would not hurt you for all the world."

"Then release mine hands so that I might feel whether I have broken anything," said she. And he did so, but when her fingers were free she used them rather to bare her thighs, the which she then spread on either side of him. And whilst he was stunned with amazement at her strange behavior, she lifted his own robe to the waist, saying, "I fear I may have smote your belly with my knee, and I would soothe your bruises." And then she went to that part and farther with her white fingers.

"Lady," said Gawaine, "I assure you that I am not sore."

"Yet you have a swelling," said she, and she did forthwith apply a poultice to him.

And to his horror Sir Gawaine discovered that his strength of will was as nothing in this circumstance, and therefore he must need submit to this lady altogether. But this was a defeat which it was the more easy to accept with every passing instant, and before many had gone by he had quite forgot why he had resisted so long, in the service of a mere idea, for such is the eloquence with which the flesh first speaketh to him who ceases to withstand temptation, God save him.

But when the lady was done with him, and they lay resting, he knew great shame, and this grew even worse when he remembered he had agreed to exchange the spoils of the day with the lord of the castle.

Therefore when the lord returned from his hunting and presented to Sir Gawaine a splendid rack of antlers from a stag, and asked in exchange whatever Gawaine had got, his guest did prevaricate and say he had spent all day in prayer and therefore could give the lord only the peace he had thereby obtained.

"I am prevented by the laws of hospitality," said his host, "from impugning the veracity of a knight to whom I am giving shelter. Yet it seems remarkable to me that you have got no more tangible rewards during a day at Liberty Castle."

"Well," said Gawaine, "I cannot call it a reward when I am attacked by two of your armed men. Should you like me to assail you with a halberd and a mace?"

"Hardly," said the lord, but he smiled. "Yet you appear whole, whereas I passed their bodies being hauled away in a cart."

"My lord," said Sir Gawaine, "on the morrow I meet the Green Knight, and though I thank you for your hospitality, I shall be relieved to have it come to an end, for between us there is no common language."

And so he retired for the night. But while he slept he had bad dreams, for the ghost of the dead Elaine of Astolat came to him and chided him for his failure to confess to the lord what he had been given by the lady, thereby violating his pledge, and she reminded him that she had died for loyalty to an idea of herself.

Therefore when Sir Gawaine awoke, he went to find the lord for to tell him everything that had happened on the previous day. But nowhere could he find him throughout the castle, nor indeed did he see the lady or anyone else, nor the scented pleasure-chambers. In fact, the entire castle was but a ruin and covered in years of moss and vines, and it was apparent that no one had inhabited it since the days of the giants who lived in Britain before the first men came there after the fall of Troy.

Thus it was in sadness that Sir Gawaine rode to seek the Green Knight, for he realized that the last three days of his life had been spent in some magical test at which he had proved himself untrustworthy, mendacious, and adulterous.

Now he was not long in reaching a valley where a green chapel stood, and before it was tethered a green-colored stallion. And when he dismounted and went within he saw the same huge green knight who had come to Camelot one year before.

"Sir Gawaine," said the Green Knight, brandishing his great green battle-ax, "are you prepared to keep our bargain?"

"I have come here only for that reason," said Gawaine, removing his helm and baring his neck. "And I would fain have you get it over with quickly."

"Why for?" cried the green man. "Who rushes to his death?"

"Our bargain, sir," said Gawaine, "will be completed when you strike off my head. There is no provision in it for argument."

"I am no quotidian headsman," said the Green Knight, "and I do not crop necks for profit nor pleasure. Tell me why you are in haste to lose your self, the which is truly the only thing a man possesseth, if but temporarily."

"I am not pleased with mine," said Gawaine. "I have not done well. I have lately broken a vow and lied."

"Which is no more than to say, you have been a man," said the Green Knight and in a jovial voice. "And with only these failings, are better than most."

"And worse," said Gawaine, "I have adulterated with the wife of mine host." And with a groan he threw himself onto the stones of the floor of the chapel so that the Green Knight could chop off his head.

"Sir Gawaine," said the Green Knight, raising his ax high over his head, "you are the most humane of all the company of the Round Table, and therefore, unlike the others, you are never immodest. To be greater than you is to be tragic; to be less, farcical."

And with a great rush of air he brought the ax down onto Gawaine's bare neck and the blade struck the stones with a great clangor, and red sparks sputtered in the air.

But Gawaine was still sensible, and he flexed his shoulders and stretched his neck, and then he felt with his hands that his head was yet in place.

Therefore he sprang to his feet and drew his sword. "Well, sir," he said, "you have had your one blow. I am not to be held at fault if you missed me! Then have at you!"

But the Green Knight threw down his ax and laughed most merrily. "Feel your neck," said he, "and you will find that you have been wounded slightly."

And Gawaine did as directed, and there was a slight cut in the skin, the which bled onto his fingers.

"That is your punishment," said the Green Knight. "You are no adulterer, dear sir, for that was no one's wife but rather the Lady of the Lake. You did however break your pledge to the lord of Liberty Castle, and you did prevaricate. But had you told the full and literal truth and fulfilled to the letter the terms of your agreement, you would have been obliged to use the lord as you did the lady."

"Yes," said Sir Gawaine, and having escaped the death

for which he had been prepared, he felt an unique joy though his demeanor remained sober. "But I had done better to explain that at the time."

"Indeed," said the Green Knight. "And therefore, your slight wound. But in the large you performed well: a knight does better to break his word than, keeping it, to behave unnaturally. And a liar, sir, is preferable to a monster."

"Then can it be said, think you," asked Sir Gawaine, "that sometimes justice is better served by a lie than by the absolute and literal truth?"

"That may indeed be so," said the Green Knight, "when trafficking with humanity, but I should not think that God could be ever deluded."

Then Sir Gawaine knelt to pray, and when he rose he saw that the Green Knight had lost his greenness and had dwindled in size, and in fact was no longer a man, but a woman, and she was the Lady of the Lake.

"My dear Gawaine," said she, "do not hide thy face. Thou hast done nothing for which to be ashamed."

"Lady," said Sir Gawaine, " 'tis not all of it shame. I confess that I am vexed that once again you have chosen to gull me. Remember that on the first occasion I did seemingly kill a woman and now I apparently made love to another. Yet each of them was you, and both events were delusions."

"And from neither have you come away without some reward," said the Lady of the Lake, who in her true appearance was even more beautiful than in any of her guises. "And would you rather that each time the woman had been real?"

"No, my lady!" cried Gawaine. "But I might ask why my natural addiction to women must invariably be the cause of my difficulties. Methinks I was happier as the lecher of old. I have since been only miserable. And for that matter, what service did I render to Elaine of Astolat, whom I did love without carnality? Better I had made to her lewd advances, the rejection of which would not have altered her fate, but would have freed me!"

"Why," asked the Lady of the Lake, "didst thou assume thine overtures would have been rejected? Gawaine, thou wert never commanded to be a prude."

And so having made her favorite knight the more puzzled, the Lady of the Lake did void that place in the form of a golden gossamer, the which floated from the door of the chapel and rose high into the soft air without.

BOOK X

How the vile Mordred made common cause with his wicked aunt Morgan la Fey; and of his good brother Gareth.

Now King Arthur took every opportunity to bring Guinevere and Sir Launcelot together, for he admired Launcelot above all men in the world, whereas he believed that Guinevere despised that greatest of all knights, and it is natural for a husband to wish that his wife be at one with him in his enthusiasms.

But the queen showed more public disdain for Sir Launcelot than she had ever done, and not only because by this means she sought to avoid suspicion, but also for the reason that she could not understand the admiration which two men might feel for each other without being either of them sexually unnatural. For Sir Launcelot not withstanding that he had cuckolded his king held Arthur in great reverence, and whilst Guinevere insofar as she was a queen believed this was as it should be with a knight and his sovereign, as a woman she did wonder whether it was unmanly.

And so we leave them all in this situation, the which existed for many years.

But meanwhile Mordred the bastard was growing up in the Orkneys, those isles at the northernmost limits of the world, beyond which is the realm of the ice-monsters. And even as a wee child Mordred was wicked and when play-

ing with wooden swords he sharpened his blade and
hardened it over coals, so that it would not splinter when
he smote his playfellows, and he wounded so many of
them that the children of noblemen were kept from him,
and therefore he frequented the spawn of serfs, the which
if he hurt or even killed them had no recourse, for a
prince will be a prince the world over (except in Arthur's
Britain where there were none, for his only offspring was
Mordred).

Now Mordred's mother was Queen Margawse, and his
foster-father (who believed he was his real one) was King
Lot, and though neither of them was better than they
should have been, they recognized in Mordred a malignancy to which they could never attain, and it being generally true of all bad people that they dislike being in the
proximity of someone worse (for this maketh them feel
stupid, whereas in the company of good people they feel
cunning), Margawse and Lot decided when Mordred was
ten years of age to expose him in a waste land where a
wyvern was known to roam and to devour all things that
were quick.

Therefore they had their knights take Mordred to this
remote place, which was on the mainland, in the pretense
that a tournament would be held there. But even at this
tender age Mordred was quite clever enough to see this as
a ruse by means of which he would be disposed of.

Therefore when he was tied to a great rock by these
knights and then they rode away, and next the loathsome
wyvern came to devour him, he did not quaver in fear,
though this ferocious beast had the body of a serpent with
great leathern wings and a head like an horse's (if that
horse were ten times larger than naturally), and the nail
on the claw it thrust towards Mordred for to probe him,
as it always first did to its meat, was longer than his
childish body.

But Mordred, who knew that no beast was a match for
a man in shrewdness, said, "My lord Wyvern, think you it
is good husbanding of your resources to eat me, a mere

morsel of four stone, when more than fifteen hundred pounds of fresh fat knights are beyond yon hill?"

And the wyvern retracted its talons and in a trice flew over the hill and ate those knights along with their horses and armor, and then with a heavy belly it lay down and slept for three weeks, which gave Mordred more than enough time to loosen his bonds and to void that region.

Now he had traveled some distance afoot and he was hungry and weary, for this place was arid, but then coming over the brow of a hill he saw in a valley a beautiful palace of which the towers were made of spun sugar. And when he arrived before its portal he saw that the stones of which the walls were built were actually sweet cakes, and the trees which grew near by were weighted down with sugarplums.

Then the gate swung open, as if of itself, and Mordred went into the palace, which within was a place that any normal boy would have found jolly, with the pillars so many great peppermint sticks and merry music being played by elves on rebecs and flutes.

And a beautiful lady came to him, and she said, "Welcome, sweet boy." And then she sat down upon a silken couch, and she took him into her lap, and she did caress him dearly.

But in a moment she screamed and sprang up, and Mordred would have fallen to the floor had he not been so agile.

"Vile little bastard!" cried the lady. "Thou didst pinch my tit!" And she rubbed herself at her bosom.

"Well," said Mordred, "I am not so easily gulled, lady. There is but one reason why such a palace as this would be found in a desert, and that is to lure children within for to eat them."

And the lady raised her eyebrows. "Thou art an interesting child," said she. "If indeed thou art a child and not am imp in the temporary guise of one. If the latter, knowest thou who I am? I am in thy service, which is to say, evil."

"Lady," said he, "I am Mordred, and I am ten years old. Having lately been exposed by my parents, I owe no fealty to anyone. If this evil which you serve will give me an home, I shall be its willing vassal."

Now the lady did exclaim, "Mordred! I am thine aunt, Morgan la Fey. And though I am much pleased to see thee, do not expect an embrace, for I never touch another except to gain power over him and work his ruin."

"And for mine own part," said Mordred, "I always pinch or prick anyone who touches me in affection. But I am very happy to be with you, for I have always heard your name mentioned with loathing, and if people detest you so much, you must be altogether admirable."

"Thou hast the right instincts," said Morgan la Fey. "But these are not sufficient in themselves, for all children have a natural attraction towards evil, the race of mankind being a monstrosity upon the earth, but persons are often distracted when they grow older. I must undertake thy tutelage, so that as thou dost mature, thou remainest as rotten as thou wert born."

"Well," said Mordred, "methinks there is little danger of my acquiring any decency, though I might well hypocritically pretend to be a sweet child at times so as to gull certain persons into a belief that I am harmless."

"Splendid," said Morgan la Fey. " 'Tis a means which I myself use sometimes, and one of the most effective, for the reason that mortals, who live in fear, tend to dismiss from their attention him of whom they are not afraid, and therefore he can accomplish a great deal of wickedness without being detected. Whereas if he doth boast openly of his devilry, all will be on guard against him."

"My dear aunt," said Mordred, "you are the only human being with whom I have ever felt a common cause. Indeed, until this moment I have felt quite alone in the world, for though my parents can not be called good folk, methinks the evil they have done is largely a result of fecklessness and not a devotion to the bad. For example, exposing me to the ravages of the wyvern might be seen as wicked, for I am their child. But if they were malefactors of true mettle, they would have murdered me outright and not submitted me to an ordeal which might well go awry and fail in its purposes—as indeed it hath. And furthermore, it were the better service to evil to preserve me, for never since being born have I displayed the least decent trait."

"Yea," said Morgan la Fey, "thou seest these matters very clearly, Mordred, and though I have ever detested the thought of being a mother, I do wish I were thine, for thou art all I could ask of an offspring. My sister Margawse doth not deserve thee."

"Not to mention my father King Lot," said Mordred.

And Morgan la Fey did look sharply at her small nephew. "Dost speak ironically, Mordred?" she asked.

"Never to you, dear Aunt," said he. "But I see from your reaction that I have been naïve. Lot is not my father?"

"Now, Mordred," said his aunt, "doth it seem likely that thou wouldst be born in wedlock?"

"Then," happily asked Mordred, "my mother was a strumpet?"

"Nay," said Morgan la Fey. "She doth lack the imagination for that. Thy mother, Mordred, is merely an adulteress."

"These are nevertheless good news to me," said Mordred. "I trust my natural father is a more effectual rogue than Lot, whom I have ever despised."

"Thou art thoroughly indecent, I am pleased to say," said Morgan la Fey. "Yet thou art withal yet a child. The great purpose in doing evil is to defy the good, dear boy! Therefore thou shouldst be at a terrible disadvantage if thy father were a notable felon—indeed thou couldst have no choice in such a case but (unhappy thought!) to serve virtue. For the rule of human life, which can never be abrogated, is that the son will necessarily oppose the father, at least in principle if not in person, so that the issue of great lechers are prudes, the wise man is the scion of the foolish stalk, the hero generates a coward, and a criminal like thyself comes from the loins of King Arthur."

Now Mordred, who was yet a boy of ten, however vicious, here fell to weeping uncontrollably, and Morgan la Fey regretted that she could not touch him in tenderness, for despite her wickedness there was still some femininity in her. However she soon (and guiltily) repressed this obnoxious feeling and commanded her nephew to do the same to his grief, for in the service of evil such demonstrations of negative emotion are confessions of failure, and only positive gloating is permitted, as when one watches the excruciating torture of a helpless victim and screams in glee while he howls in agony.

Therefore Mordred dried his eyes and regained command of himself, and he begged the pardon of his aunt Morgan la Fey. "I shall not soon weep again," said he, "for nothing worse could possibly happen to me than to learn that I am the son of the finest king in the world."

"Well," said the wicked Morgan la Fey, "it is not however as unfortunate as it could be. Thou art not his legitimate son, but rather his bastard. Take comfort in the knowledge that thy very existence is a thing of shame to him, and that engendering thee is his sole stain. Were he as wicked as thou and I, he would put thee to death. But being good, he shall feel obliged to love thee."

"Now, my dear aunt," said Mordred, "is it not just that which will make it worst?"

"Nay," said Morgan la Fey, "for the pain that comes from love is the greatest on earth, and he who is loved hath the most effective instrument of torture that can be used on the lover, whom he can torment with impunity. The cunning device of the Christian religion is to maintain that love bringeth joy, while it is precisely the reverse which is true: that love doth bring only agony to the lover."

"Yea," said Mordred, "already I have divined that that is true of ardent passion, which is all pain if unsatisfied but boring if surfeited, but what of the paternal and other forms of familial love, and the loving-kindness of friendship. For though I am incapable of feeling any of those (except towards thee, my dear wicked aunt, but methinks our exchange of affection is due to a community of interest more than to blood), I am aware that banal humanity makes much of them."

"That these are feelings professed to by the rascal many," said Morgan la Fey, "should in itself be evidence of their falsity. A child 'loves' his father because he is afraid of him, and this fear is the other face of hatred. Whereas a father 'loves' a son while the boy is small, because he as yet has *no* fear of him, and this so-called love is therefore disguised contempt. Then the boy grows up, and he and his father arrive at a kind of equilibrium of power, and this truce is again called 'love.' Finally the elder becomes a dotard, which is to say that through age he has become as weak as a child, and in power (which is the only quality worth considering on earth or in Heaven) the father hath become a son, and he fears his new parent and is in turn despised by him. And once again this is called filial-paternal love."

And Mordred was enraptured by the brilliant intellect of his aunt. "I regret only," said he, "that because there is no such thing as love, I can not love thee."

"And be assured that thou dost please me quite as much," said Morgan la Fey, "and that at such a time I regret that I am not capable of sexual feeling, for on principle 'twould be a jolly thing to take thee into my bed and commit at once two crimes of which I greatly approve: incest and unnatural congress with an infant person. And 'twould only be improved upon were you rather my niece, thus affording the possibility of a third viciousness: female sodomy."

But then Morgan la Fey did smile merrily. "I jest with thee, dear Mordred. For the sexual appetites (though they might be used as means) are never ends in the celebration of evil."

"Indeed?" asked Mordred in wonderment. "In my innocence I supposed them amongst the very best."

"Well," said Morgan la Fey, "in a fight between two knights, when one kills the other has it been done by the sword or by the hand that wields it?"

"Both," said Mordred.

"And then again, in a fundamental sense, neither," said Morgan la Fey. "For oft the winner's hand is not so strong as that of the loser, nor is his sword as long, as in the celebrated combat between Sir Tristram and the Morholt. Nay, Mordred, 'tis the *will* that makes the difference. So with the sexual desires, for the encounters of lust are very like fights, and their outcome is determined by the wills of the participants and whether they conflict with the ethic of their respective peoples. By which I mean that for example the Morholt in good conscience misused sexually all manner of men, women, children, and animals (for this practice is permitted to a giant among the bawdy Irish), yet incest was an horror to him owing to its proscription by his people, and he avoided it. But amongst the Russkies all fathers swyve their daughters from the time of infancy, yet sodomy is abominable to them, whereas with the Greeks buggery is applauded by the men of greatest worship and it is performed publicly by philosophers and soldiers and priests, but carnal converse with animals is punished by death. And in Egypt men sluice only their female relatives and never a stranger, and any sexual association but incest is looked upon as a foul crime.

"The Vandals couple with mules, the Berbers with dromedaries, and the Copts with jackals. And the worst criminal offense in Rome during its Golden Age was for anyone, man, woman, or child, to deny his pudendum to anyone else who sought access to it. Therefore, 'tis not the nature of the deed but rather the attitude towards it of the doer, namely the will, which determines the interest served, whether it be good or evil."

"There is, then," asked Mordred, "no standard that is universally observed amongst mankind?"

"Only," said Morgan la Fey, "as pertains to power, the having of which is always desirable, however obtained and for whatever uses. And oft this is a matter of great subtlety, for there are those who enjoy being victims of extreme pain. Yet a keen eye will detect that oft the true power is in the possession of the victim and not his apparent master. Thus the Christian slaves destroyed the Roman Empire."

"Ah," said Mordred, "already thy tutelage hath done wonders for me, dear Aunt."

"But perhaps 'tis yet a finer game than thou dost appreciate," said Morgan la Fey, "for having said all of that, I confess to using lust (for I am beautiful) to ruin lesser men so that with their help I can destroy the king, who since his lone encounter with thy mother is immune to desire."

"But what can destroy King Arthur?" asked Mordred.

"His death, alone," said Morgan le Fey, "and brought about by some great shame such as by the machinations of a blood-relative."

Now at this moment Mordred made a sad reflection. "Well, dear Aunt," said he, "we too, you and I, shall die. Is evil then worth doing? What then doth it achieve that is greater than good: both are transitory."

And Morgan la Fey said in answer, "There are those of us to whom bringing pain to others is a remarkable satisfaction, dear Mordred. And do we not thereby serve Life? For only the dead are anesthetic, and whereas pleasant feelings are short-lived and never are vivid enough to escape a consciousness of the passing of Time, in the degree to which it is intense pain doth give at least the illusion of being eternal. And to a great man the greatest (and perhaps the only) pain be shame."

Then Morgan la Fey smiled upon little Mordred, and she said, "And now I shall demonstrate the sort of pain felt by persons without principles of virtue, such as thee, dear Mordred, and also I shall repay thee for pinching my dug earlier (though thou didst that in ignorance of mine identity, and whilst I have great admiration and affection for thee as a pestilent little fellow, it is my absolute obligation as an evildoer always to seek revenge)."

And with the sharp toe of her slipper she kicked Mordred full hard in the stones, from which savage blow he sank to the floor and writhed in agony for a time that seemed indeed eternal.

But finally he arose, saying, "I thank thee for this valuable lesson, dear Aunt. Now may I assure thee that I shall furnish myself with a dagger and that, with all respect, if you do assail me again, now that we are quits, I shall rip out your belly."

"As thou shouldst do," said Morgan la Fey with great approval. "At the tender age of ten years, Mordred, thou art the vilest little swine that could be imagined even in my venomous fancy, I am pleased to say. I can teach thee few more things, methinks, but perhaps I might assist thee to evoke some of the evil which, owing to extreme youth, as yet lies dormant in thy black heart."

And to celebrate their foul pact, Mordred and Morgan la Fey did go to the cellars of that castle, where a number of rats had been kept separate from one another and starved, and they brought them together in a cage and watched them devour one another with murderous fangs, much blood, and hideous noises.

And now we leave these vassals of Satan for to go with Mordred's half-brother (and full brother to Gawaine, Agravaine, and Gaheris), and he was a fine young man named Gareth, and he came to King Arthur's court for to become a knight of the Round Table.

But Gareth, who was King Arthur's nephew, did not wish to have this relationship known before he had proved himself, nor did he wish to be recognized by his three brothers who were knights, until he could join them as a full equal at the Round Table, for he was a young man of great independence and probity, having spent the years of his later childhood (by reason of his older brothers' absence and Mordred's infancy) by himself.

Now reaching Camelot at the time of Pentecost, when King Arthur was obliged to grant any boon asked of him by a person not a felon, Gareth went to the court and finding a moment when none of his brothers was there he asked the king to grant him three gifts.

"Well," said King Arthur, "these are two more than I am pledged to grant. Is thy need thrice as great as that of any other petitioner?"

And Sir Kay was present and he heard this and being already in a peevish mood owing to the many miscarriages in the preparations for the Pentecostal feast (for a great lot of cutlery had been ill polished by the feckless footmen and fifty firkins of clotted cream had got lost, &tc.), he said to Gareth, believing him an impudent knave, "Fellow, begone."

"Nay," said King Arthur smiling to Gareth, "I would hear thy requests."

Now Sir Kay, who did dislike things not done by the book, made a grimace, but of course he held his peace.

"I thank you, Sire," said Gareth, "and I beg your pardon for my discourtesy, which was not intentional, but I have been reared rudely and I am ignorant of the customs at Camelot."

"Thou art a comely youth," said King Arthur, "and from thy speech and carriage it can be seen that thou wert not basely born. And from thy white hands one could not say that thine upbringing was too rude. For I did myself have a rustic rearing, as my dear Kay doth remember, and mucked out the stables and slept oft with the hounds, and I think it was no loss to me." And here he looked fondly at his foster-brother and seneschal, and Sir Kay, who had not the same pleasure in remembering bucolic Wales, did scratch his nose.

"Sire," said Gareth, "with all respect, I should not like to tell you at this time of my provenance, nor to give you my name. As to the boons I would ask of you, the first is that I be permitted to stay here at Camelot for one year and to be put to service in whatever function you should choose, however mean or servile. Then, having proved my good intent, at the end of that twelvemonth I shall come to you and ask the remaining two boons."

Now Sir Kay was offended again, and he cried, "Sirrah, this is gross insolence to represent thyself as nameless. It is contumacious towards the king, and discourteous to the knights."

"Well," said King Arthur to Gareth, "what hast thou to say in self-justification of this peculiarity?" But the king was not angered but rather amused by the young man's strange ways, for he recognized that he was highborn (those of royal blood being ever able to identify their own kind), even though he did not suspect he was his own nephew.

"Sire," said Gareth, "I would prove myself with deeds, not words."

"Yet is it not thy word which thou wouldst have me to take now?" asked King Arthur. But he smiled and he said, "But I do like to encourage the zeal of youth. Most young men who come here apply for to become knights. Thou art unique."

"And base, methinks," said Sir Kay looking disagreeable.

"Very well, then," said King Arthur to Gareth. "I shall grant thy first request, if thou dost understand that at Camelot a man is asked to do nothing but to live up to his pledge. Thou canst leave at this moment with no loss of honor. But if thou dost main, be assured that I will take thee at thy word, and for one full year thou must work, without complaint, as a kitchen-lackey."

Now Sir Kay was offended that King Arthur had so little respect for the royal kitchens that he would send there a man for a taxing trial of character. But he must needs submit to the royal command, and therefore in ever worse humor he led Gareth to the kitchens and took him to the scullery, where there were countless dirty pots rising in stacks to the ceiling, and some of these vessels were so large that they could stew an entire sheep.

"Now," said Sir Kay, "these vessels must be cleaned and then polished to such a fine gloss that they might be used as looking-glasses. And when that hath been done they will be filled and put again onto the fires, and before thou hast got to the end of his lot, the first of it shall be back again, and so on *ad infinitum*."

And even as he spake, into the scullery came two cooks, in greasy singlets and running with sweat (for great fires burned all day in the kitchens, and those who worked there had skin the color of bricks), and these two men carried a great pot between them, the which had been used for breakfast porridge for an hundred and fifty knights. And this pot they hurled down with a great noise, and foully cursing as is the wont of cooks they went away, and though Sir Kay did not like this he could do little about their ways, for persons who work with food must needs be humored, else spitefully they may pollute the dishes.

And giving Gareth a pail of sand and a scrubbing-brush Sir Kay left him there and then he went to speak with the head cook about the menu for the feast of Pentecost, for which there were thirty-two courses, each separated from the next by the serving of an ice flavored with another fruit, and some of the fruits for these sorbets came from the ends of the earth, and there were no names for them, yet sometimes they were easier to find than certain local foods owing to the fecklessness of those who grew them conjoined with that of those who made deliveries, and Sir Kay continued to be in a bad mood throughout the day, and when in the middle of the afternoon he happened to be in that part of the kitchen where the lackeys peeled potatoes, and he espied Gareth there with a paring knife, he waxed wroth.

"Fellow," said he, "thou hast defied mine order, and never have I known such forwardness."

"Nay, my lord, with all respect," said Gareth. "I have followed your orders to the letter. But having polished all the pots I thought I should not sit idle, and therefore I came here to lend a hand."

"O mendacious varlet!" cried Sir Kay.

But Gareth asked him to look at the shining vessels which were mounted in great stacks against the walls, and Sir Kay went to them and he saw his mirror-image in their gloss.

But he was yet suspicious, and he had Gareth take every pot out from the stacks, and in every one the interior was bright as a looking-glass.

Yet by no means was Kay mollified. "Who saw thee at this work?" he asked. "Methinks thou hadst secret helpers, for this is a task which previously required six scullions, who took all day at it."

"My lord," said Gareth, "sometimes one man may do what many together can not, owing to his lack of distraction."

Now hearing this some other scullions who were peeling potatoes as slowly as possible, and who would steal away from their work as soon as they were not under the eye of Sir Kay or the cooks, began to hate Gareth with all their hearts, for already he had peeled twice as many potatoes as they had all together, and they determined to take revenge upon him. And their own hands were gnarled and of a dark hue (a deal of which was dirt), whereas those of Gareth, even after his labors, were fine and long-fingered and white as a lady's.

And Sir Kay noticing Gareth's hands found them an additional impudence, and he said, "Sirrah, how can thine hands have remained so white if thou didst labor so much? There is something about thee which is not honest, and I do not like it at all."

And Sir Kay went away then, but he determined to keep a watch on this varlet, whom he did suspect of trickery. And from that time forward he called him Beaumains, which is to say, Fair Hands.

Now when Kay had gone the other scullions gathered

around Gareth, and they said to him, "Is it thy purpose to mock us, shitpot?"

But Gareth replied sweetly, "Nay, my friends, I would work amicably amongst ye."

"Then," said they, "thou must reduce thine effort by four-fifths, for our rule is that we each of us peel sufficient potatoes to fill but one pail per day."

"But by working regularly one can fill at least two pails every hour," said Gareth.

And this speech was so offensive to them that they found some sticks and set upon him, for to beat him senseless. But Gareth was marvelous strong, and he seized each pair of them by the necks and he cracked their heads together until they begged for mercy.

And then Gareth released them all, and he said sweetly (for he was a gentle man and even when fighting he seldom felt ire), "I would not disturb your arrangements, for I am newly come here, nor do I expect to remain forever." And he did not say what he then thought, which was that they would all be here until they died, for he was a kind man. "Meanwhile, it is more interesting for me to work than to be idle, and though I have eaten many potatoes I have never before known how they were prepared for the cooking."

Now these scullions believed he was a great liar to say that, as if he were a nobleman and not as basely born as they, and they would have tried to beat him again did they not fear his strength.

"Therefore," said Gareth, "what I propose is this: that I peel all the potatoes, thus freeing all of ye to find more rewarding jobs, or indeed to go on holiday."

Now at first this proposal seemed attractive to them, for the negative reason that they should have to do no work, because none intended to look for another job in the kitchen or anywhere else. But soon the cleverer ones amongst them began to think of the consequences, for they had no idea what a holiday was except a time at which the noble folk ate a more elaborate meal than ordinarily, and therefore the kitchen-lackeys had to work harder than they usually did.

"Well," said they, "if we were found doing no work, we should be whipped, and if we sought other jobs, they would either be more taxing than potato-peeling, in which case we do not want to do them, or they would be easier, in which case the lackeys who now perform them would never surrender them to us. Therefore thou wouldst bring to us nothing but discomfort or pain."

And seeing the reason in this, Gareth knew shame. "I see I have intruded where I am out of place," said he, putting down his paring knife. "I hope I have not damaged ye much, and I thank ye for the lesson I have been taught."

But now Gareth wondered what job he might do at once well enough to satisfy his own need to allay boredom and yet not so well as to attract the resentment of those whose regular employment it was: for they would be sure to see what they did as dreary labor, while for him it would be amusement.

And he arrived near one of the great fireplaces where whole beeves were turning on spits, and a varlet held a long ladle, with which he gathered up the hot juices which fell from the meat into an huge copper pan, and these he poured back onto the roasting beeves, the which were all the while being turned slowly by another scullion, who held the handle of the spit.

And as Gareth came near and felt the heat of the fireplace upon his face, the varlet who held the basting-ladle dropped it and he fell fainting to the hearth.

And the other, he who turned the spits, cried to Gareth, "Wet him down, there's a good fellow." And taking one hand from his task he pointed at a pail near by. So Gareth fetched this pail and he emptied the water thereof onto the face of the varlet who had collapsed, but though he came to his wits he confessed to being sore ill, and he seized the empty pail and was sick into it.

"Well," said Gareth fetching up the great ladle, which was marvelous heavy whereas the boy who yielded it was a frail lad of no more than twelve years in age, "methinks the heat hath been too much for thee. Go to some cool place and rest, and I shall do this job."

And the boy went away and Gareth took up the work, but even though he was strong and fit the heat was hard to bear, and before long the other scullion who turned the spits did faint as well. And Gareth putting his ladle down took the pail and he filled it from a barrel of water and he soaked the scullion with it. And when he did this he saw that this man was a robust fellow of two- or three-and-twenty, and he wondered why he worked at such a job. But then, as the beeves were beginning to char, and the scullion was not quick to rise, Gareth turned the spits himself and he was forced to use all his strength to move them, and the handles though made of wood were so hot that they smoked, and the heat was even worse at that job than when doing the basting, for one must needs stand even closer to the fire.

But Gareth was happy to have found a task that required all of his physical strength and attention, for while he was turning the spits, the other scullion crept away and he did not return, and so Gareth did both jobs and you can be sure that he was fully occupied.

Now eventually came a burly great cook, who had both the basting-varlet and the spit-turner pinched by the napes, and he put them to their former work. Then he spake to Gareth as follows.

"Fellow, thou hast introduced a disorder here, and though under the laws of King Arthur we can no longer punish mischiefmakers so severely as we did once (and as they deserve), we are not obliged to suffer them helplessly." And so saying he did fetch Gareth a stout kick in the hindquarters, and the king's nephew went hurtling into a corner of the kitchen where an huge basin of white pudding had lately been put, and Gareth plunged into it head-first.

Now this was the demesne of the dessert-cook, and when he saw Gareth emerge from the pudding he equipped himself with a keen knife and he said that he would caponize him for polluting his blancmange, and though Gareth was a brave young man upon the field a kitchen was not the place he could defend himself well, nor would his social position allow him to do this, for in his current role he was much inferior to a cook. Therefore covered with pudding he fled and he finally took refuge in a pantry, the which was full of barrels containing tripes, and they were rotten and stank, and they crawled with worms.

Now this first day of Gareth's experiences at Camelot was typical of all that year he spent there working as a scullion, for though his intentions were the best and though he did well at every task he undertook he seldom failed to offend the people with whom he worked cheek by jowl, for the differences in principle (his being noble and theirs, base) were too great, and he came to understand that degrading oneself is a complex matter and does not necessarily serve the cause of modesty: indeed, it might well be more a thing of vanity to pose as a knave when one is by nature a knight.

Nor did he ever fail to annoy Sir Kay, and no matter how filthy the job he did, his hands when washed remained fine and white (and in distinction to all the others who worked in the kitchens he did bathe regularly and he had no fleas).

But finally a year had passed, the longest in Gareth's life, and the happy day came when he could leave the kitchens, and so he did with no regret, having learned little of value, except never to eat soup (into which the cooks when angered, which was oft, spat loathsomely) and to inspect all dishes served to him for foreign matter (for owing to the intense heat of the kitchen much wine was swallowed there, having been stolen from the cellars, and the staff were usually blind drunk).

Now Gareth had no clothes but those in which he worked as a scullion, and these were none too fresh, nor in his haste to leave the kitchen had he cleaned himself as carefully as he might have done, and he had no access to scents. Therefore when he came before King Arthur, who was again giving audience to those who sought boons, Gareth's fine figure was clothed meanly. And the guards were at the point of removing him forcibly when the king commanded them to hold, and he asked them why they would expel this varlet.

"It is a nasty dirty thing," said they, "and stinks, and is not noble but rather churlish." And these guards themselves were the sons of boors.

Now King Arthur chided them. "Ye know full well that all are admitted on my day for boons, irrespective of the orders to which they belong." Yet what he did not suspect (for a king in many ways is at the mercy of his retainers) was that most peasants were habitually barred at the gate and by servants who had been born into their class and were sometimes their very children.

Therefore these guards unhanded Gareth and he came to bow before King Arthur in his dirty rags, saying, "Sire, I now ask to be given a quest."

"Well," gently said the king, "though on such a day I give consideration even to the plea of a serf (for all my subjects high or low are my children), what is asked must be seemly and appropriate to the condition of the pleader. Thus a quest can properly be sought by a knight or by a squire who would earn his knighthood. For such as thou, my dear knave, I can do only what would be proper to thy station: I might, for example, make thee a kern in mine army, were it not stood down at the moment, owing to the absence of wars. Or wouldst thou work in the kitchens, where Sir Kay's staff are a kind of army, with him as general?"

"Nay, Sire," said Gareth with some feeling, "I have had sufficient experience of the kitchens." And then he reminded the king of his coming to Camelot the year before.

"Ah, 'tis thee!" said King Arthur. "Yea, I remember now. The lad whom Kay calls Beaumains." And here the king did smile. "I see that thine hands, despite the labors which have soiled thy clothes, are yet fair. Well, Beaumains, art thou ready yet to tell me thy true name?"

"By your leave, Sire," said Gareth, "I would first prove myself in some adventure the which would earn me a place at the Round Table."

"There be no aim more praiseworthy," said King Arthur. "Yet I have a good many knights any of whom would have prior claim to the next quest, and foremost among them is Sir Launcelot, who doth plead with me to find him a mission appropriate to his gifts. Now who but that great knight would find so taxing the companionship of the queen? Yet I can well understand his keenness for action, being myself condemned to stay here at court."

For King Arthur had taken a liking to young Gareth, in whom he could see obvious nobility, and since Sir Gawaine had returned from the adventure with the Green Knight (of which he had said little) his nephew had seemed more remote than when he had been the lecher of old. And though King Arthur had formally declared that Sir Launcelot was his best friend, he felt ever less close to him, owing to Launcelot's habitual distraction by melancholy.

And it is not always understood how lonely a king may be.

"Well, Beaumains," Kind Arthur said now, "thou must wait for the moment when thou shalt be summoned to possible glory. Patience in the young is as rare as zeal in the old, and the frequent situation in human affairs is that a man is asked for that of which he hath too little while being denied employment for that of which he hath a surfeit. Now, a knight is more than a warrior, else we are but barbarians."

"'Twas in that idea that I served as menial," said Gareth. "But methinks none too well, for though I was willing, nay, eager, my nature was alien to it."

"Indeed," said King Arthur, "demeaning oneself, except to God, is oft the mirror-image of vainglory."

"Yet," said Gareth, "did you not yourself, Majesty, do stablework as a boy?"

"Certes," happily said the king, "but I knew no other life at the time, Beaumains. Whereas it is obvious to me that thou hast been reared gently somewhere."

Now Gareth did not wish to reveal himself as yet and therefore he said nought, and furthermore at just that moment into the hall came a noble maiden who was in distress, for she wept copiously.

And Gareth did step to the side, to allow her to approach the king, which she did with a great plaint.

"Now," to her said King Arthur, "prithee collect thyself, for never canst thou be furnished succor unless we hear what ails thee."

"Sire," said this lady, "know you that my lands and my castle have been seized by a most notable felon and his three brothers, and he hath imprisoned my dear sister as well, and his name is the Red Knight of the Red Lawns, and he hath never been overwhelmed in a passage at arms, and he is the most perilous knight in all the world. Therefore," said this damsel, "it would seem necessary that no less a force be sent to deliver my sister than at least sirs Launcelot and Tristram and Gawaine, with sirs Bors and Gaheris in support."

"Lady," said King Arthur, "be assured that aid will be forthcoming. But, for one, it is not seemly that thou shouldst tell me how to furnish it. For another, any one of those great champions named by thee would be ashamed to have assistance in dealing with but four felons, the which he could manage nicely by himself, for any knight of the Round Table hath more strength than an hundred malefactors. But before I grant that for which thou pleadst, I would know thy name and whence thou comest."

"Nay," said the lady, "so much I will not tell you at this time, for I believe it is the boast of your court that any person requiring succor shall be granted it without condition."

Now King Arthur was nettled by this lady, whom he believed too proud, and he said, "Indeed, that is true, and I shall therefore aid thee to the letter." And to him he called Gareth, and he said, "My dear Beaumains, thy quest hath come sooner than expected."

Then King Arthur turned to the lady, and he said, "Here is thy champion. Nor will he tell his name to anyone."

And Gareth, in his ragged clothes and greasy, bowed to King Arthur and then to the lady, and he said to her, "Lead and I shall follow."

But the lady drew back from him in disgust, and in anger she said to King Arthur, "Well, this is a pretty boon! I beg you for five knights, and you grant me one filthy knave. If this is the kindness of Camelot then I shall go hurl myself upon the mercy of the Red Knight." And she went out of court in a fury.

Therefore Gareth did apply to King Arthur for what he should do.

"Armor and weapon thyself," said the king. "And follow that damsel and irrespective of her treatment of thee, relieve her of her molesters. For though she be proud to the point of discourtesy, she is a lady in need."

BOOK XI

*How Gareth fought four felonious knights each of
another color; and how he fell in love.*

So Gareth went to the armory for to equip himself, but as
it happened no decent armor was to be found there, nor
good weapons, for a tournament had lately been held and
the spare helmets and shields and swords had been taken
to replace those which had got broken, and all that were
left were rusty and battered. But of these wretched things
Gareth did fit himself out, and his helm was bereft of a visor and his shield was cracked, and his sword had a rusty
edge that was notched like a handsaw. And then to the
stables he took himself for to find a steed.

But no healthy horse was there, only tired old jades, and
the beast with which he was provided was lame and had a
sway-back, so that he sat so low in the saddle that he
could scarcely see over its head, and its rump rose up behind him.

And thus miserably furnished he went in pursuit of the
lady, and fortunate it was that owing to her despair she
had walked her palfrey slowly, else he should never have
caught up.

Now when Gareth reached the damsel her horse did shy
in fright, and when she regained her seat, the lady holding
her nose cried out in contempt of him.

"Lady," said Gareth politely, "I would be judged by deeds and not by appearances."

And the lady wept bitterly to see how this foul knave would persist in accompanying her. And then she said in great detestation of him, "Wretch! It is a great shame that thou shouldst be near me." And she rode ahead with all the speed she could manage and she vanished behind an hill, to reach which it took Gareth ever so long, owing to the condition of the jade on which he was mounted.

Now when Gareth did finally gain the summit of the hill and begin to descent the other side, he saw in the valley below a stream and on its bank was a silken pavilion in the color of blue, and a blue shield was hung outside it, and a horse with a blue hide was tethered there and its trappings were blue. And next to it stood the lady's white palfrey, but the damsel was not to be seen. Therefore supposing she was in the pavilion Gareth rode towards it, and when he got near he heard screams coming from within.

Then he dismounted and going inside he saw the lady upon a couch of blue silk, and she was bound by the arms and the legs so that she could not move, and her bodice was torn open so as to expose her white neck. And near by was an huge knight in the act of removing his armor, which was bright blue in color.

"Sir knight," said Gareth, withdrawing his rusty gauntlet and throwing it at the feet of the other, "there you have my challenge."

And the Blue Knight was astonished to see this mean-looking intruder, and was vexed to be interrupted at this moment, for he would ravish this damsel.

"O base fellow!" said he, and before Gareth knew what was happening the Blue Knight did lift him around the waist (for he was marvelous strong) and carried him without, to the bank of the stream, and then he threw him into the water.

"Now," said the Blue Knight, jeering from the bank, "I shall go and give that saucy strumpet a sound sluicing."

And with difficulty Gareth came out of that stream,

with the water pouring from his armor, and he said, "Sir, do you mean not to fight me as a man of honor?"

"Clown," said the Blue Knight, "'honor' be a vile mockery on the lips of such as thee, and thou hast begun to annoy me." Therefore he seized a great blue lance which was mounted outside the blue pavilion, and he mounted his blue horse, and before Gareth could reach his old steed, the Blue Knight rode down upon him.

But Gareth stepped aside from the point of the blue lance, and seizing the shaft he pulled it from the other's grasp, and with such force that the Blue Knight was thrown from the saddle as his charger galloped on, and so was his neck broken and he died.

Then Gareth went inside the pavilion and he would have quickly unfastened the lady from the couch, but she cried to him in fury, "Scullion! I shall have thine eyes put out if thou dost look upon my naked bosom!"

Therefore shielding his eyes with one hand Gareth took a long time to loosen her bonds, and the damsel denounced him for his slowness, and she held her breath so that she might not smell his kitchen-stink, and she was in no wise grateful to him for saving her from the mishandling of the Blue Knight.

And when she went without and saw that the Blue Knight lay dead she cried, "Fie, knave! Thou couldst not have done this except by treachery, for Launcelot himself would have been hard put to defeat this knight at fair combat."

And mounting her palfrey she rode away as fast as she could go.

Now Gareth possessed the Blue Knight's armor and weapons and horse by right of conquest, but he did not think it right for him to dress and arm himself with them, for the blue color of it all was peculiar to the man who lay dead. And moreover, Gareth had not yet overcome vanity, and he took some satisfaction in defeating a knight who was well equipped while he himself was furnished ill.

Therefore he climbed upon his wretched jade and set

out to follow the damsel, never understanding that because
of his vanity he was exposing her to a greater danger. For
she had gone over the next hill and into the next valley,
where beside the river a knight in brown armor waited,
and because Gareth's horse was so slow this felon had
time to seize the lady and tie her to a couch within his
brown pavilion, and raising her skirts and petticoats he did
bare her to the waist.

Now the Brown Knight was on the point of removing
his armor for to molest the damsel carnally when he heard
a noise without (which was the creaking of Gareth's rusty
armor as he rode down the hill), and this criminal asked
the lady whether she was followed by someone who would
protect her.

"Alas," said she weeping, "only by a stinking knave
from the kitchens. I am helpless against your vile ravages."

But arriving before the brown pavilion Gareth drew his
rusty sword and he smote the brown shield which hung
alongside the brown lance, and he cried, "Sir Brown
Knight, I challenge you!"

And at this clamor the Brown Knight came without the
pavilion and he saw Gareth, who was so wretchedly furnished, and with great insolence he said, "Scullion, come
and help me undress, and then I shall permit thee to watch
me swyve thy lady."

"Sir," said Gareth, "are you too cowardly to fight me?"

Now the Brown Knight was infuriated by what he believed the impudence of a greasy knave from the kitchens,
and therefore without putting on his helm he seized his
lance and mounted his horse, and he charged upon
Gareth.

And Gareth spurred his own beast, but the old horse
would not go faster than a slow walk, and his lance was
shorter than it should have been, for some of its butt had
broken off long since, and when he put it into the rest and
lowered it, the iron head did fall off altogether, for owing
to great age the wood had shrunk.

But notwithstanding these deficiencies, when they met it

was the Brown Knight and not Gareth who was unseated and thrown to the ground. Therefore, even more vexed than before, the Brown Knight rose from the earth and he drew his brown sword.

"Well," said he, "Fortune hath granted thee her last favor! Prepare to be sliced as if thou wert a joint of mutton."

"Sir knight," said Gareth, lowering his sword, "I can not fight you justly unless your head is protected. Shall you put on your helmet?"

"I shall not," said the Brown Knight with the greatest contempt, "for I have nothing to protect myself from." And he advanced on Gareth bareheaded.

Therefore Gareth proceeded to unlace his own helmet, for to remove it, but while he was so occupied the Brown Knight (defying all courtesy) would have smote him sorely had not the laces being old and dry soon burst, freeing the helm, and Gareth pulled it off with his dexter hand whilst raising the sword in the other and cutting off the head of the Brown Knight.

Now this severed head did leave the neck with such force that it flew within the door of the pavilion and rolled below the couch where the lady was tied fast. And she screamed when she saw it.

But when Gareth came within to free her she did not commend him for slaying her captor, far from it! Rather she commanded him to avert his eyes while he unbound her, and when she was at liberty she put her gown in order concealing her silken thighs, and then she said, "For the second time thou hast slain a knight by deceit. I would not be protected by ignoble means! Methinks the Round Table, if it is represented by thee, must be the basest companionship in the world."

And once again she mounted her white palfrey and she quickly rode away. But now realizing that if he continued on his old horse he might not reach her in time to preserve her honor on the next occasion, Gareth exchanged his steed with the fine brown charger that had belonged to the late Brown Knight, and he donned the brown armor and he took up the brown weapons, and just as the lady reached the bottom of the next valley and had been taken by the knight who guarded the ford there, who wore black armor, Gareth galloped over.

"Now, lady," said the Black Knight to her, "I can not understand how you got this far and eluded my brothers the knights blue and brown, unless you did so by some treacherous means. But be assured that I shall take you into my black pavilion, strip you naked, and then I shall dighte you soundly."

And the lady wept piteously.

But when Gareth wearing the brown armor came down the hill the Black Knight said happily, "Ah, there is one of my brothers now! Well, we shall share your sweet flesh."

And the damsel replied, "Sir knight, 'tis not your brother but rather a wretched kitchen-knave from Camelot, who hath murdered both Blue Knight and the Brown by treachery, and now, contrary to all laws of courtesy, hath stolen this armor and horse and these weapons." And she said, "Though I find you wicked in the extreme, I should prefer being mishandled by an evil knight to being saved by a base fellow."

And this lady, whose name was Lynette, can not be blamed altogether for having a low opinion of Gareth, because she had not seen him yet in a fight. And Gareth himself was not blameless, for owing to vanity he would not defend himself against her accusations, and Lynette was but one of the many human beings who distracted by a received idea must be patiently enlightened as to the truth.

Now Gareth was careful to come close to the Black Knight and with his visor opened to reveal that he was not the original wearer thereof.

And the Black Knight called him a caitiff and a wretch to murder his brothers by deceit, and he promised to kill him and to flay off his entire skin and nail it to a tree as an example of what happened to knaves who hoped to rise in the world against all human and divine laws and feloniously to represent themselves as their betters.

"Sir knight," said Gareth, "I commiserate with you on the loss of your brothers, for I have several of mine own and I love them dearly. Yet should one of them be killed in a just fight I should not call his foe a criminal! Know you that I have fought fairly and that I have won this armor by right of conquest. And now I challenge you to a fight, for I believe your intent is illegally to ravish this damsel."

But Lynette then cried, "Can it be that thou dost not understand that I do not desire thy protection, and that I find it greatly obnoxious? It is far more shameful to be saved by a scullion than to be ravished by a person of one's own class."

"Lady," said the Black Knight, "I very much like your sentiments, and know you that I should never misuse you were it not that I am obliged to do so to all maidens who seek to cross this river, for 'tis the law of our eldest brother, the Red Knight of the Red Laws, that no virgin shall long remain intact in his demesnes, for this would be a great insolence towards our virile family."

"Then here we are at odds," said Lynette, "for these lands properly belong to me and were wrongfully seized by your brother, and he holds my sister in captivity. And I confess that I would have him killed could I find a proper champion, the which this greasy scullion be not."

And Gareth, wishing to fight the Black Knight according to the rules of chivalry and fearing that the other would not agree to this (and the result would be again the ugly thing it had been with his brothers), asked this knight to dismount and to draw apart with him and speak privately, and when they did this Gareth said, "Know you I am Gareth, fourth son of King Lot of the Orkneys, nephew to Arthur of Britain, and brother to sirs Gawaine, Agravaine, and Gaheris."

"My lord," said the Black Knight, "then you are a prince?"

"Indeed," said Gareth, "and I am in disguise. But I have never been false, which is to say, I did truly work as a scullion for a twelvemonth. And having served amongst them I can tell you that I have no great love for lackeys, who are for the most part lazy and dishonest and with little feeling but self-pity. And though perhaps this character is due to their low position in the world, perhaps it is not, for methinks that there must always be some hierarchy amongst mortals and that a man might serve well whatever the situation into which he hath been born by chance. Yet my greatest condemnation must be reserved for those of higher stations who do evil."

Now the Black Knight heard little of the wisdom which Gareth though a very young man had gained since leaving the court of the remote Orkneys, for this knight was confused by the sudden change from scullion, too mean to fight, to prince, too far above him who was but the second son of a baron.

Therefore bowing low he said to Gareth, "Your Highness, shall you forgive me for not recognizing by your very seat on the horse (which quite properly you took by conquest from my brother) that you are the very model of all that is royal? I fear I am utterly disgraced!"

Now Gareth groaned in dismay, for he despaired that he could ever get this obsequious knight to fight him. But then he conceived a plan, and throwing back his head he laughed derisively and he said, "O gullible fool! I am but a mendacious knave!" and he tripped him up, so that the Black Knight fell down upon the ground. And Gareth said to him, "I shall mount now and take up the brown lance and unless you defend yourself I shall stick you where you sit."

And this ruse was successful, for the Black Knight rose in a fury and he mounted his steed, and they charged upon each other. Now the Black Knight's black lance did break upon Gareth's brown shield, but Gareth's brown lance hurled the Black Knight from his saddle.

And then Gareth dismounted, and they fought with

swords for only so long as it took Gareth to chop the Black Knight's blade off at the handle, and then he put the brown sword at his throat and he asked him to yield.

"That I do gladly," said the Black Knight, "for no one but a prince hath such prowess at arms, and I know you are right royal whatever your guise!" And he swore fealty to Gareth.

Now watching this the damsel Lynette was amazed, for it confounded all her prejudices, and she had not heard the Black Knight address Gareth by his proper title, so that she still assumed he was but a scullion. And yet she had clearly seen him defeat a formidable knight in the fairest of contests. And therefore several truths did here conflict, and in her confusion she swooned.

Now the Black Knight was as gentle and gracious as he had been brutal before, and he carried her within the pavilion and he bathed her temples with Cologne-water. And when she came to her senses she asked him whether she had seen him defeated by a kitchen-knave.

Now in commanding him to care for Lynette, Gareth had made the Black Knight promise not to reveal his true identity, and therefore this knight now said, "My lady, the man in the brown armor did overwhelm me in a fair test."

And Lynettte said in disgust, "For shame, sir knight! Begone! I now find thee more offensive than he."

And the Black Knight replied, "Lady, I accept your scorn as deserved, but you would do better not to disdain that man."

And he then went without, where Gareth said to him, "Go to Camelot and offer thy fealty to King Arthur, and be henceforth a knight of good repute, abstaining from all wickedness."

So the Black Knight did as he was commanded, and for the rest of his life he intended to serve virtue alone.

Now Lynette came out of the pavilion where Gareth did await her, and she was not quite so proud as before.

"Look here," said she, "perhaps I have judged thee too harshly. Thou hast some prowess at arms, though I do not know how thou couldst have got it in the kitchens. Never can I approve of thine exceeding thy station, but thou hast surely saved me from an evil fate. So much shall I grant thee. And now it is for thine own good that I say, return to Camelot while thou dost still live! For however thou wert able to vanquish the blue, brown, and black knights, the Red Knight of the Red Lawns is invincible. And though I can not say I am overfond of thee, I do not wish to see thee killed needlessly."

But Gareth saluted her from his seat on the brown horse, saying, "Lady, lead and I shall follow."

"Beaumains," said she, "why dost thou persist in this mad venture? Must I apologize for abusing thee? Then I do so freely. Thou art a brave man. Is that not enough? Then add to it this: dressed in that fine armor and mounted on a good horse thou wouldst seem to the manner born." And here she stamped her little foot in its satin slipper. "Now what lady could ever say more in condescension?"

"Lady," said Gareth, "you have been as generous to me as I could wish. And I am grateful to you for your kind concern, but nothing in the world could stop me from fighting the Red Knight of the Red Lawns, for that is my quest, and but one knight shall emerge from that encounter, only God knows which."

Now Lynette had never heard such a brave intent announced by any knight, let alone a scullion, and she would have fallen in love with Gareth then had he not been a knave.

"Well," said she, "come ride by my side, Beaumains. 'Tis the least I can do in view of thy destination. No longer will I seek to avoid thy company."

But in riding towards the castle which the Red Knight held criminally, Gareth nevertheless lagged an horse's length behind Lynette, for if the truth be known, he did cherish her illusion as to his inferiority.

So they crossed the last ford and rode over an hill and down into a forest, and from the trees in this forest hung the dead bodies of many knights, with their shields around their necks and upside down. And at this dreadful sight Lynette did gasp in horror and she brought her palfrey close to Gareth's horse, saying, "This be the fell work of the Red Knight. These were my loyal men, alas! I beg thee to flee, my dear Beaumains, for here thou seest forty valorous knights, and they were not enough all together to withstand him."

But Gareth said, "Lady, I will fight the Red Knight."

And despite her fear Lynette now was offended by him again. "Beaumains," said she, "there is a difference between true courage and reckless arrogance. Now, as a scullion thou perhaps couldst not know this, but that in itself is why the orders are distinguished one from the next. I confess that I did not believe thou couldst defeat thy betters at arms, and I was wrong, for thou didst vanquish the knights blue, brown, and black. Yet never allow thyself to believe that God will permit thee to flout the scheme of chivalry forever. Thou hast gone further than any other knave. Be content with that, Beaumains, and stay alive as the most valiant scullion who ever lived."

"Lady," said Gareth smiling, "with all respect, you do give too much worship to distractions." And for the first time he galloped on ahead of her, and he reached the place where the wood gave way to a broad plain, and there he saw a stately castle.

Now a great sycamore grew at the edge of the forest, and attached to its trunk by a silver chain was a large silver horn, and Gareth took this to his lips for to blow upon it, but Lynette rode to him and she spake as follows.

"If I can not keep thee from meeting the Red Knight," said she, "then at least do not yet sound the horn, which summons him to arms. At least wait till the sun begins to fall, when his strength will dwindle, for when it is high in the sky he hath the strength of seven men."

But Gareth said, "I shall never be more ready to fight than I am now." And he lifted the silver horn.

Yet Lynette was desperate to preserve him, for in great

perversity and defying her faith and her moral principles she could not forbear from admitting to herself (in great shame) that she loved him with all her heart, knave though he be.

And crying, "I am lost!" she leaned across her palfrey and sought to keep the horn from his lips by interposing her own pink mouth, and she was a maiden of the greatest beauty with long hair of the richest auburn color and flawless skin of perfect whiteness except for the rose of her lips and cheeks, and her eyes were as glowing gems.

But not yet had Gareth noticed her in the amorous way, and he did not now, when he thought only of fighting the Red Knight of the Red Lawns. And her palfrey stepped away at this moment, and Lynette was not able to kiss him.

So putting the silver horn to his lips Gareth sounded it towards the castle across the plain, and hardly had the last note died away when the great gates swung open and through them rode the Red Knight of the Red Lawns, and never did he gallop but rather he walked his blood-red charger towards Gareth. And all his armor was bright red and so were his weapons, and a red plume fluttered from his helm.

And he came to Gareth across the field, and he said, "Why, brown Brother, dost sound the horn? Didst think I might not yet be in possession of the castle? Didst not see the corses I have hung from every tree? No knight on earth can long stand against me!" But then he drew close enough to see that it was not his brother's face inside the brown helmet with the open visor, and he cried in rage, "O insolent impostor!"

"My lord Red Knight of the Red Lawns," said Gareth, "I overcame your three brothers honestly, and I would fight you now."

But the fair Lynette rode between them and she said to the Red Knight, "Sir, this person is not a knight but rather a valiant knave, the bravest in the world, and he is dear to me. Permit him to live, for killing him would bring you no worship. Further, if you grant me this favor, I shall put myself into your hands for whatever inordinate use you would make of me."

And the Red Knight roared in brutal rage. "Impudent bitch!" he cried. "I already possess thy castle and thy young sister is my helpless captive. What canst thou give me further but thy maidenhead, the which I shall anyway shatter at my convenience either before or after I take thy sister's? (Which I have not yet done only because my virility is so voracious that I must needs ravish two virgins at once.) And having once used a damsel, I find her subsequently loathsome, and therefore ye both shall be installed thereafter in a twopenny brothel!"

And so did this pestilent knight make his beastly boast.

And then Gareth said to Lynette, "Lady, will you void this field? For I would fight this knight."

So weeping hot tears Lynette withdrew, and she wept both in sorrow because this brave scullion, whom she loved, would soon be dead, and in a certain resentment that neither of these men, good nor bad, did count her as at all significant in their affairs, and she would rather have harloted herself to save the life of Beaumains than to have him preserved by any other means in which she did not figure, for such is a proud lady's hunger for mastery.

But the Red Knight cried, "Thou shalt kill me, puppy? Ordinarily I have the strength of seven, but now that I have learned of thy vanquishing of my brothers (which was surely done by deceit), in vengeance my powers are increased three times!"

And in fury he rode to an enormous oak which grew at the edge of the wood, and drawing his red sword he severed the trunk with one blow, and it could not have been encircled by four men joining hands, and this great oak, an hundred and fifty feet high, in falling felled a score of lesser trees.

Then the Red Knight went half a mile away across the plain, and he turned and began his charge, and whereas he was at the outset but a little speck of red on the horizon, he soon grew larger, and the speed of his red stallion was as the north wind and its hoofs made a sound like unto twenty drums struck at once.

Now Gareth waited till but an hundred yards remained between them, and then he began his own charge. And when he and the Red Knight met, it was with such force that the lance of each penetrated the other's shield up to the handle and plucked it away from each man's grasp and carried it away. And turning their horses each discarded his lance which was now impeded by a spitted shield, and both drew their swords.

Now with his first blow the Red Knight cut off the head of Gareth's brown horse altogether, and spraying blood from the stump of its neck the animal collapsed onto its forelegs and Gareth was projected onto the earth.

Now the Red Knight rode down upon him swinging his fell sword, but Gareth smote him in his right arm and he cut it cleanly off. But when it fell the Red Knight caught up the sword in his left gauntlet, and he turned his horse so as to bring the advantage to the sinister side. Then he swung at Gareth with full force, for his left arm was quite as strong as his right, and thanks be to God that Gareth was not struck by this blow, for had it hit him he would have been in two parts.

Then a blow of Gareth's did miss the Red Knight, but it cut the girth of his saddle and he fell from his steed, but though pouring blood from his severed arm he soon raised himself and with one swing of his mighty red sword he cut through Gareth's breastplate and the point went through the coat of mail beneath, and it scored Gareth's chest from high on the right shoulder diagonally down to his left hip. And fortunate it was that this wound but sliced open the skin and did not go deeper, yet copious blood ran out and down onto Gareth's greaves and it covered his boots.

And soon the field on which they fought was covered with blood from the both of them, and Gareth slipped and fell sometimes, but the Red Knight was in his own element, for his color was blood-red and he had so colored many lawns, and that his right arm had been lost did not distress him in any wise, and he smote Gareth more sorely than he himself was smitten, and he hacked away much armor and he wounded him often.

And whilst none of these wounds was mortal, Gareth was bleeding everywhere and he grew weaker, and though he did never lose heart (for he was doing his duty and there was no alternative) it seemed as though he might well be killed before the sun began to descend and the Red Knight lost strength (for as yet it was high in the dome of the sky).

Now you can be sure that Lynette did watch this fight with much dread, and never had she seen so brave a man as Gareth, and in the degree to which she had once despised him, she did love him now. And she was bitter against God for providing the finest man she had ever known and yet making him but a scullion (for Lynette had never met a man of her own station whom she could admire, the valiant having been all felons and the honest, effeminate), and she was punished for this impiety by not learning the truth until it was too late: therefore she can serve as a sorry example to all fair ladies who would judge a man only by his temporary situation!

Now this fight between Gareth and the Red Knight had gone on for many hours, and Gareth was continually forced back by the attack of his puissant foe, and so they went across that field and unto the very castle, and almost all of Gareth's armor had been hacked away, and he was so weak that he could not have remained on his feet were his back not placed against the stone wall.

And the Red Knight raised his red sword high over his red helmet with its blood-red plume at the crown, with a purpose to bring it down and to despatch Gareth altogether. And too weak to lift his own sword to deflect the blow, Gareth looked aloft at the red blade, but even in this moment of imminent death he was distracted by something he saw from the corner of his eye. And he turned his head and he saw in the window of a tower that did project from the wall of the castle the most beautiful face he had ever seen in his life, and it belonged to a maiden who was chained therein, and the window had iron bars.

Now Gareth fell in love with this maiden on the instant, and from that love, combined with hatred for the Red Knight whose captive she was, his strength returned to him and manyfold, and he raised his sword and chopped off the Red Knight's left arm, and then both of his legs, and then his head, and soon all that remained of this notorious felon was a pile of disjointed parts in red armor.

Then Gareth mounted to the tower and he freed the maiden from her chains, and then he hacked the iron bars from the window, and he threw open the casement and let the sun stream in. And the maiden made great joy.

"Sir knight," she said, "you have delivered me!" And her face was more radiant than the golden sun which came through the window, and her hair was more bright, and her eyes were blue as the sea. "Therefore I am yours by right of conquest!"

"Nay, lady," said Gareth. "I am of King Arthur's court, and we do not take such spoils. You are truly free, and you have no obligations."

"Then freely," said the maiden, "I would give myself to you, unless you find me obnoxious."

"Lady," said Gareth, "I would marry you, for I love you with all my heart."

And weeping with joy, for she loved him as well, the maiden fell into his arms.

Meanwhile Lynette, who had covered her eyes so as not to watch the Red Knight kill the young man she knew as Beaumains, had finally opened them to see the felon lying in many red pieces, whereas Beaumains was nowhere to be found.

Therefore Lynette went to the tower, and there she saw her sister in the arms of the scullion, and who can say which feeling was uppermost in her heart, jealousy or outrage that such a base fellow (though valiant) should touch a lady?

"Fie, Beaumains!" she cried. "Unhand my sister! Do not corrupt the memory of thy valor by acting shamefully now." And Gareth did as ordered, for the foolish haughtiness of Lynette had ever brought him contemptuous amusement.

But her sister, who was named Lynesse, clasped Gareth to her bosom, saying, "This knight hath delivered me, and we shall be married."

And Lynette gasped in horror and she said, "Lynesse, thou goose, dost not know he is but a knave who worketh in the kitchens?"

"I care only that I love him dearly!" cried Lynesse.

And therefore Lynette did appeal to Gareth. "Beaumains, this is but a foolish young girl who hath never left this castle in all her life. I beg of thee that thou be decent." And from her fingers she took her rings, which were of begemmed gold, and she gave them to Gareth. "Now, thou art the richest scullion in the world. Accept these as recompense for being the most valiant."

And now, for Lynesse was weeping piteously in the belief that her sister would drive her lover away, Gareth could no longer forbear from revealing who he was.

And when he had so done, Lynesse was overjoyed, but Lynette said reproachfully, "Why, my lord, doth a prince of the Orkneys and a nephew to the throne of Britain pose as a knave?"

"Perhaps," said Gareth, "to prove that he is no less."

"But so to delude a lady," asked Lynette, "think you this was chivalrous?"

"Lady," said Gareth, "(soon to be sister), methinks my duty was but to relieve you of this tyranny, and so have I done. King Arthur would never have given the quest to one who was unworthy of it."

"Well," said Lynette, "I am ashamed, and I confess I was at fault, but I do not think that all the wrong was mine." And she did go away for a while and weep privately, for now she could admit to herself that she had loved Gareth even as a scullion, and had she found him after he had slain the Red Knight (before he had found her sister) she might well have given herself to him knave though she believed him to be.

And it was not long before they all set out for Camelot, for Gareth's many wounds were slight and his love for Lynesse caused them to heal quickly.

Now it should be known that when Sir Kay learned that Gareth had gone off upon a quest, he realized that though he had been critical of him as a scullion he had rather liked him withal, and he did not want him to be killed in some rash venture. Therefore Sir Kay put on his own armor and he took up his weapons, and he went in search of the lad, for to aid him if he got into trouble.

Now Lynesse had found for Gareth a new suit of silver armor in the castle, and this he was wearing when he and the two sisters were traveling towards Camelot, and when Sir Kay came over an hill and saw him, the seneschal believed he was a felon who had captured these two ladies, and therefore he lowered his visor and he charged him.

Nor did Gareth recognize Sir Kay in the armor, and he answered the charge, and he soon unseated Kay, who was knocked senseless by his fall to the earth. And Gareth had defeated him so easily that he did not bother to dismount and wake him up and demand that he yield (for he believed him a knight of no consequence), and he desired to reach Camelot without delay and to be knighted and to marry Lynesse.

But meanwhile, learning that Kay had gone off again, King Arthur sent for Sir Launcelot, and he said to that great knight, "My dear friend, Kay has got away from us once again. Canst thou go and see that he is not hurt?"

"I can, Sire, and I will," said Launcelot, who was relieved to be away from Guinevere at this time, for she had grown ever more peevish of late and she did think him wanting in his attentions to her, notwithstanding that he did little else than to attend her (but this is the way of a

queen at best, and even more so when she hath nought
else to do). Nor for a long time had Launcelot gone upon
a quest. Therefore though this one was not for an exalted
purpose he was grateful to have it, and he accoutered himself and he rode to find Sir Kay.

Now it was not long after Gareth's encounter with Kay
that he espied another knight coming towards him and the
ladies, and this was Sir Launcelot. But Gareth did not
recognize his shield with its famous device of lions rampant. And further he was annoyed that he should be attacked again and so delayed. Therefore he said to the
ladies, "Have no concern! I shall make even shorter work
of this rogue than I did with the last." (For with his recent
successes Gareth, being but a young man, had grown foolishly arrogant.)

And fewtering his lance and pricking his steed he
charged upon Sir Launcelot, and watching his handsome
figure on the horse, both sisters thrilled with love for him,
Lynesse in joy, but that of Lynette was melancholic.

Now for his part neither did Launcelot know the identity of his opponent, but when he saw Gareth charge upon
him he lowered the most formidable weapon in the world
and he spurred his horse.

And when they met it was Gareth and not Sir
Launcelot who was thrown over the hindquarters of his
steed. And he rose unhurt and he drew his sword.

Now not until this moment had Lynette noticed Sir
Launcelot's shield, which she recognized, but she had been
distracted utterly by her unrequited love for Gareth.

"Gareth, Gareth!" she cried, and she rode her palfrey
onto the field and inhibited him from continuing the fight.
"You fight the great Launcelot!"

But Gareth's blood was hot from the humiliation he had
suffered in the presence of his lady love, and his wits were
so affected that he did not attend to the name of his foe.
And he cried, "For the love of God, Lynette, void the field
and let me slay this hound!"

And he went around the palfrey, and he rushed at Sir

Launcelot, who had meanwhile dismounted and drawn his great sword. But Launcelot heard Lynette cry out the young man's name, and he remembered that his friend Gawaine had a younger brother so hight, and therefore he lowered his sword, and he opened his visor, and he was about to ask graciously for quarter, so as to encourage this brave youth in his sense of valor. But Gareth was already setting upon him fiercely.

Therefore Sir Launcelot caught Gareth's raised wrist before the blade could descend, and he took the sword from him as if from a small varlet. And in shame and chagrin Gareth knelt and said, "My lord, I would you killed me quickly."

But Sir Launcelot raised him up. "Methinks thou art Gareth, the younger brother of my dear Gawaine, for I see in thee something of both his physical and moral qualities. Ye are a passionate family."

And it was as if Gareth had only now heard Lynette say the name of Launcelot, and he hung his head and he said, "Sir Launcelot, I have been a great fool, I fear. I love that lady with the fair hair and distracted by that love I became inordinate."

"Well," said Launcelot, "if this is the worst to which love has led thee, then count thyself the happiest of men." And then he remembered why he had come out of Camelot, and he asked Gareth whether he had seen Sir Kay.

Now when Gareth described the shield of the knight he had lately defeated, Sir Launcelot said, "Yea, that was the gallant seneschal. But from what thou tellest me I take it that he was not hurt badly. Therefore I shall not go to him, for he might be discomfited. And I know that thou art a man who will speak nought of thine encounter with him, for he is our friend."

For Launcelot was the most delicate of men with the feelings of his fellows.

Now the two knights and the two sisters rode to Camelot together, and when they arrived there the ladies related

Gareth's achievements to King Arthur and all the court, and Gawaine, Agravaine, and Gaheris were there, and they affectionately embraced their brother.

And King Arthur said, "When thou camest here, thou didst ask me for three boons. Thou hast received two of them. Which doth remain?"

"To be knighted by Sir Launcelot, Sire," said Gareth. "He hath ever been my model, which I say without prejudice to mine own noble brothers." (And while Gawaine and Gaheris did nobly approve of this, Agravaine was secretly much offended, for he did detest Launcelot ever more.) And then said Gareth, "Having lately had the experience I might say that only Launcelot can make one feel it a privilege to be unseated by him!"

And here King Arthur and the entire court (except for Guinevere, Sir Agravaine, and of course Sir Launcelot himself) did laugh most merrily. And Launcelot did knight Gareth as he wished, and the date was set for the wedding of Gareth to the fair Lynesse.

Now poor Lynette's heart was broken and having lost the one man she had ever loved she expected never to love another, and furthermore to be tormented forever by Gareth's proximity as her brother-in-law. But during the preparations for the wedding she became acquainted with Gaheris, who much resembled his younger brother except that Gaheris had a fine silken mustache and his voice was deeper and richer.

And having been a knight of the Round Table for some years he had performed many quests, and some had been quite as perilous as Gareth's only one. But his most attractive quality to Lynette was that *he* did admire *her* greatly.

And when the wedding was celebrated, it was a double ceremony in which Sir Gareth married Lynesse and the bride of Sir Gaheris was Lynette.

And these results, which were happy for all at Camelot, were very chagrining to the wicked Morgan la Fey, in whose service the Red Knight of the Red Lawns, and his brothers of the other colors, had toiled ardently. Nor was the evil Mordred pleased at the success of his half-brother Gareth, for he hated most those of the same blood (the which had turned to poison in his own veins). But the only harm that this vile pair could manage in this whole matter was to waylay the unfortunate Black Knight (whom Gareth had sent back to Camelot, it will be remembered, for to give his fealty to King Arthur), and to kill him by deceit, which they did in this wise: Morgan La Fey pretended to be a lady in distress, and the Black Knight stopped to give her succor, and she led him to one of her enchanted castles in a wood, where the pestilent Mordred stabbed him in the back.

"Now, my dear Mordred," said Morgan la Fey, "we have accomplished two pieces of evil hereby: firstly, we have despatched a knight who would henceforth have served virtue, and secondly we have made it seem to Sir Gareth that the Black Knight did not keep his word to do homage to Arthur. And with this Round Table lot, the latter is worse than the former, for they do believe that any life is soon over, but a man's honor be remembered forever, inspiring other men to come."

"Yea, my dear aunt," said Mordred, "but we must not pretend that this episode was in any large way a success for us. Was it not our purpose in instigating the Red Knight to seize Lynette's castle and to imprison the fair Lynesse, thus to lure out of Camelot the incomparable Launcelot? But methinks that if untried Gareth could overcome the four ferocious knights of the colors, Launcelot could have done so even more easily. Therefore what should we have gained even if it had gone as we did plan?"

"In the convent where I was reared," said Morgan la Fey, "I learned the black art of nigromancy, and using this means I have determined that there will be one knight in the world who can defeat Sir Launcelot. Now it seemeth to me well worth the effort to try to pit him

against every knight we find who hath hitherto been un-
beaten until we find the one who will whelm him."

"Well," said Mordred, who even at his tender age was
more clever than his aunt, " 'twould seem an inefficient
means, for no doubt Launcelot would kill thousands before that happened, and whilst we care nothing for these
lives, we must believe that with every victory his fame will
be ever greater. Should we not rather seek to ruin him in
another way?"

"Which way?" asked his aunt Morgan la Fey, and she
did resent being counseled by a child though she knew
him as already totally corrupt.

"In some fashion which doth not partake of physical violence," said Mordred. "For in fighting he hath no peer
(except for this one who will one day be found). But this
one who will come: can we assume that he will be an evil
man? He may be an even more virtuous knight!"

Morgan la Fey did frown. "Nay, Mordred, that is unlikely, for Sir Launcelot, damn him, is famous for being
without stain." (And in believing this she did unknowingly
demonstrate the naïveté of the very evil, which is founded
on vanity, for they think that they alone are capable of
wickedness.) And she said, "There is no means by which
Launcelot can be damaged morally, I fear. He hath no cu-
pidity, and he doth not yearn for power. And he is chaste
by natural inclination, and by vow as well. And that he is
merciless in this was shown by the history of the wretched
Elaine of Astolat, whom he could have saved with a few
embraces, and she was so desirable a maiden that thy
brother Gawaine hath been able to love no one else since
her death.

"Nay," said Morgan la Fey to her evil nephew, "let us
forget about Sir Launcelot the right arm and consider the
very head, my brother King Arthur: If it were struck off,
the body of the Round Table would soon wither."

And truly she had grown competitive with Mordred, for
she feared that his cunning might be more than an equal

BOOK XII

*How Sir Accolon, who was assotted with Morgan
la Fey, made an attempt on King Arthur's life.*

Now Morgan La Fey had long been married to old King
Uriens of the land of Gore, and he was as good as she was
evil, but he was not a shrewd king and he did never suspect her of wickedness.

And King Uriens gave little thought to ought but hunting, on which he was so keen that he did little else now
that there were no wars to fight, for like all other kings on
the British isle he was a vassal of King Arthur and under
his protection. And Morgan la Fey despised her husband
and therefore, though she knew no sexual pleasure, she
took to bed many other men for to make mock of him,
but if Uriens were aware of this (and she did nothing to
keep it secret) he did not so much as chide her, let alone
burn her at the stake, and he was indifferent to all that did
not pertain to the chase.

Now there came a time when he did invite his brother-
in-law and liege lord King Arthur to come to Gore to
hunt stags in his park, and King Arthur accepted this invitation with pleasure.

Now when Arthur told Guinevere he would be away
from Camelot her heart leapt secretly, for though she and
Launcelot had been lovers for several years they met always in a clandestine fashion. But as time went on she no

longer worried much, for never did King Arthur intrude
upon her privacy, and it was as if when Sir Launcelot
broke his vow of chastity King Arthur did assume its obligation. And in a strange way King Arthur and Sir
Launcelot were ever reciprocal.

And Guinevere first heard with pleasure of King Arthur's intent to go to Gore, but next she felt guilt for having such a feeling, and somehow it seemed less indecent
for her to make love with Launcelot when the king was
there to catch them than when he would be far away, for
never at any time did the queen forget that what she did
was a great sin and a crime against the state as well, and
there was in her heart a certain desire to be apprehended
and punished, and in this she was utterly different from
Queen Isold. (And unlike Sir Tristram, Launcelot was not
a passionate man.)

Therefore Guinevere did urge King Arthur to remain at
Camelot.

"Well," said he, "having accepted the invitation, I can
not now decline it except for a very grave reason, and do
you have such?"

Now Guinevere's protest had been the impulse of the
moment, and she had no argument to support it. Therefore she said quickly, "I have a premonition that harm
may come to you." Then she turned her face away and
she said, "Arthur, 'tis a delicate matter, and forgive me
please for treating of it, but your sister Morgan la Fey is
spoken of with small honor."

Now King Arthur was greatly vexed. "By whom?" he
asked angrily. "By the wretched mongers of court gossip?
So these mean tongues wag at Camelot as maliciously as
elsewhere? I had hoped that we might set an historical
precedent in this regard, as we have in so many others,
and be slander-free. But though the gaudy evils can be
overwhelmed, Guinevere, the squalid little ills persist!"

And not only did King Arthur have the usual sensitivity
to aspersions upon those who were of his same blood, but
any mention of *sister* served to remind him of Margawse

and his unwitting incest with her, and this was one reason why he so doted on Sir Launcelot, who rare amongst the leading knights was not his nephew. And sometimes he dreamed of Margawse, yet after all these years, and the terrible truth was that only with her had he ever felt desire, and therefore henceforth that feeling had ever been obnoxious to him.

"Forgive me, please," said Guinevere once more. "I share your distaste for this wretched thing." (As well she might!) And she said further, "But if gossip doth help to avert dangers, then 'tis justified to listen to it. I am sorry to say that Morgan's lack of love for you is known: your half-sister can not pardon you for being the son of the man who killed her father." (Now this explanation had only just occurred to Guinevere, for she had never heard it said.)

"That may well be," said King Arthur, "and if so, such a resentment is not altogether without cause, for my father's conduct (hence as elsewhere) was reprehensible. I tell you that privately, my dear Guinevere, and I do not advertise it, certes. For after all he was the king (and further, he can not be brought back from the dead to right his wrongs). But I have endeavored in every way to correct, insofar as that can be done, the injustices of old. I can not help being the son of Uther Pendragon, nor did I knowingly seek to become his successor. I was chosen by God, else how could I alone have been able to pull the sword from the stone?

"But I have neglected to show the great affection which I bear to my relatives who occupy the lesser thrones in Britain, and that is why I now must needs go to Gore. Perhaps when dear Morgan sees me there she will understand my benevolence towards her and her beloved husband my royal brother-in-law Uriens."

"But perhaps she will not," said Guinevere, who having invented her feeling of dread now felt it in truth, for she was a woman in whom the fancy was strong (and all persons of imagination oft create by accident that which becomes necessity). "And you would do well to carry with you a loyal guard, and who might be a better choice for that office than Sir Launcelot?"

"I do not share your fears," said King Arthur. "I can not think that Morgan la Fey wisheth ill to me her brother. And there is also hospitality's law, the which protects even an enemy when he is under one's own roof, not to mention Heaven's ordinance against harming the sovereign. But assuming for the sake of argument that harm doth come to me, might it not come to noble Launcelot as well? Then what would happen to Britain! And consider you this: if the Round Table hath enemies (for it is the Table that we serve, I and Launcelot and all the other knights, nor am even I essential to it), what better time to try to work its destruction than when both king and greatest knight are absent?"

"Yet there are Gawaine and his gallant brothers," said Guinevere, "and there are sirs Bors and Lionel, who are Launcelot's cousins, and Bedivere and Yvain, and Sir Lucan the Butler, and all together an hundred and forty-eight sans Launcelot and he who will come to fill the Siege Perilous. And have you not said that so long as one of its knights remains quick, the Table will stand? And what of Pellinore your friend, who was once himself a king?"

"And yet is!" said Arthur. "For royalty can not be taken away. But, Guinevere, I shall not go through the roster with you. Be assured there is some good reason why none of these, fine knights all, is not suitable to command at Camelot in mine absence. Gawaine, as you must be aware, hath been under a cloud for a long time. I can not regret the loss of his lechery, yet methinks he was a better knight when he womanized. I see some lack of character in Agravaine and an edge of bitterness therefrom. My two younger nephews are newly wed. As to Pellinore, he hath lately been again enthralled by what is perhaps a fantasy, the Questing Beast, and he hath once more gone in pursuit of it. . . .

"Nay, Guinevere, only Sir Launcelot will do, and I beg

you, knowing of your old aversion to him, to accept my judgment with as much cheer as you can summon."

"To 'command' in your absence, Arthur? Is this the proper term? Is Launcelot an alternative king?" And Guinevere's fine blue eyes did flash hotly.

"Well, is he not a prince and son of King Ban of Benwick? And I do not say 'to rule.' And then, who else doth remain who would exceed him in rank?"

"Indeed," said Guinevere, "none but the queen."

"To be sure," said King Arthur, "no man at all."

And then he called for the lackeys to prepare for his journey to Gore.

And when he left Camelot to go visit his sister and brother-in-law King Arthur's entourage comprised only his body-servants and a retinue of untried squires and yeomen and the like, and no knights at all, for he did not want his relatives to believe that he was invading their land for an hostile purpose.

Now when King Arthur arrived at the castle of Gore he was received with great cheer by his brother-in-law King Uriens, but Morgan la Fey was not in evidence.

"My lord and royal brother," said Uriens, "on the morrow I shall show you the loveliest damned stags in the bloody world! And if you have any better in your own parks I shall eat one raw, horns and all." And he smote his hands together in glee. "Damn me, is there anything in life worth doing but a damned bloody good hunt? Some say women, but stags do not have the damned pox! And some are gluttons, but all food soon turns to dung. And your damned drinking tints your nose and leads you only to your damned pisspot. Nay, only the hunt bringeth rewards that can not soon be revoked!"

And Arthur soon believed his brother-in-law the greatest bore he had ever met, as well as a vile blasphemer, for Uriens continued to speak in this wise without stint, before and at and after supper, and King Arthur did have no escape till he went to bed. And then he did smile in remembering Guinevere's fears for his safety while at Gore.

But little did he suspect that so soon as he had finished his prayers and fallen asleep, his evil sister Morgan la Fey would steal into his room (and she had been at the castle all the while, but she did not allow Arthur to see her, for her loathing of him was so great that she could not have concealed it). And she crept silently to where Excalibur was hanging on the wall, and she took it from its scabbard, and she replaced it with another sword which resembled it in every way but was made of poor steel, and though if its edge was held to the light it would glisten and seem keen, this was an illusion, for it was too dull to penetrate a ripe cheese.

And Morgan la Fey took away with her the real Excalibur, for which she had use in a wicked scheme the aim of which was to bring about Arthur's death. And why did she not simply slay him while he slept? Because she did not want her part in his murder to be known, for one, and for another she wished the crime to bring to grief two other men as well, namely King Uriens her husband and also a knight named Sir Accolon whom she had contrived to make fall in love with her. And she had pretended to be fascinated with Sir Accolon and she induced him to boast of his exploits, and she questioned him when he fell shy, and seeing himself reflected in her beautiful eyes (which he did not know were the windows of her corrupt soul) this originally modest knight became vain and he grew assotted with Morgan la Fey and because of her he confused his prowess with that of Sir Launcelot.

Therefore when the morning came and King Uriens took King Arthur on a stag hunt deep in the forest, Morgan la Fey came to Sir Accolon and she gave this foolish knight who was in love with her the sword Excalibur, the which she had purloined, and she spake to him as follows.

"Brave Accolon," said Morgan la Fey, and she came close to him so that he could smell the luxurious scents in which she was drenched, "I have been apprised of a treacherous plot against the life of my dear brother King Arthur as well as that of my dear husband Uriens, thy sovereign, who have gone a-hunting in the park. And Arthur hath left behind his sword Excalibur, only when armed with which he is invulnerable, as without it he is helpless. It is a magic blade, sweet Accolon, and I would that thou take it and with it slay these criminals before they reach the two kings."

And Sir Accolon took the sword from her and he swore that he would do as she asked.

"And furthermore," said Morgan la Fey, and sucking a magic pastille she breathed upon him a warm breath the delicious vapors of which no man unless supremely pious could resist (and Accolon was already madly in love with her), "thou shouldst know that these regicides have assumed guises in which they seem the mirror-images of King Arthur and King Uriens, for when they have killed them they would falsely take their places, O treachery, O perversity!"

And here Sir Accolon did gasp in rage and he brandished Excalibur in the air and he pledged that he would show these felons no mercy.

Then he asked how to distinguish the real kings from the false.

"There is but one means," said Morgan la Fey. "The false King Arthur doth carry on his hanger a false Excalibur, a replica which is exactly like unto the one thou dost hold, but is counterfeit. The real Arthur, who hath forgotten his sword, carries none." And then this wicked queen did take Sir Accolon's face into her two silken hands, and she kissed him hotly on the lips, saying, "Let this be a token of my gratitude, valiant Accolon. Thou shalt receive the full reward when thou dost return carrying the severed heads of these criminals." And she did obscenely writhe her lissome body against him, so that he might imagine it as naked and seethe with lust.

And poor Accolon might well have swooned in desire did he not have to leave forthwith. Yet he was an honest knight, and he said, "Lady, I ask no reward for defending my kings!"

"But prithee, bold Accolon," said Morgan la Fey, who was a cunning monster of deceit, "surely thou wouldst not deny me the pleasure of celebrating their deliverance with someone, and Arthur is mine own brother, and Uriens is remarkable old." And she put her hand on him immodestly, whereas in fact she intended to kill him with poison as soon as he returned with the heads of King Arthur and King Uriens.

Now thrilling with thoughts of Morgan la Fey and burning with fury against those who would plot against the royal lives, Sir Accolon mounted and holding Excalibur high he galloped in search of the felons.

Now Arthur and Uriens had got separated from each other, and from their retinue, for the latter had followed at great speed his baying hounds and his retainers were not mounted so swiftly as he. And as for King Arthur he had never been keen on bloodsports since the day long ago when his falcon had killed Guinevere's canary, nor with his manly British tastes did he care to eat venison except when cooked so long it was no different from mutton, and therefore he fell behind in the chase till the dogs were a league away and the riders were out of his sight. And then he dismounted and he sate him down upon a bed of moss beneath a great oak.

And he reflected on his reign. Now he believed that all his enemies had long been vanquished, and all notorious malefactors suppressed, and he thought therefore that the common folk were happy to be no longer ravaged, but he worried that his knights had sufficient employment. For the tournaments were mere games amongst friends, and virtue that doth not hone itself regularly against evil can not keep an edge. But was it not heresy to long for the devilish only to defeat it?

Then he did remember his late father-in-law King Leodegrance, who had owned the Round Table when it was but a great disk of oak and had no moral significance, and his hundred knights who had left Cameliard undefended to go on a quest for a thing which no one had ever seen and which nobody was certain as to its nature.

And though it was called the Holy Grail, and though King Arthur was of great piety, he had never heard of it since. Now he thought of this Sangreal with some interest, and what attracted him to it was that no one could describe it, nor had it ever been mentioned by the corrupt men who had held the principal bishoprics at the time when he assumed the throne, whereas pieces of the True Cross had been in sufficient supply to build from them a fleet of ships, and enough shreds from St. Veronica's sudarium, with which she wiped Our Lord's face, to make when sewn together sheets for all the beds in Britain; and old Canterbury had done a vast commerce in selling sprigs of straw from the manger wherein the Saviour was born.

But King Arthur's thoughts were interrupted here by the arrival of Sir Accolon, who seeing on the king's belt the false Excalibur cried, "Rise, detestable impostor, and prepare to go to Hell."

Now King Arthur was perplexed, and as Sir Accolon was a fine-looking knight he believed he must have spoken in error, and therefore he rose, saying, "Sir, for whom dost thou take me?"

"For a wicked traitor who would kill my kings," said Accolon.

"Well," said King Arthur, "I assure thee that I have no such intent, for what would be the purpose of it, when I am the king of all Britain, and I have no designs on the monarch of any other realm?"

"O mendacious, unnatural, and regicidal monster!" cried Sir Accolon. "Mount and fight me, else I shall cut thee down where thou dost stand in thy vileness."

Now King Arthur thought him a madman, and he sought to placate him further, but 'twas no use, for the wicked Morgan la Fey had perverted Accolon's reason so that he believed the real Arthur was the false one. And therefore the king was constrained to fight him or to be killed helplessly.

So he mounted his horse and having no lance he drew the counterfeit Excalibur from its scabbard. Neither did he wear armor nor carry his shield, and he was dressed for hunting in clothes of soft leather and he wore a huntsman's hat with a feather in it, and his only other weapon was a knife with a handle of horn. Whereas Sir Accolon wore full armor, and the sword he wielded was Excalibur.

And these two came together and they hacked at each other, and Arthur soon found that the sword he held was an inferior weapon, the blade of which had no effect against his adversary, for though he smote Sir Accolon with powerful blows that knight grew ever stronger, and had not King Arthur been so great a swordsman as he was, he might have been killed.

Then in fending off a puissant blow by Accolon, King Arthur's blade did shatter into many fragments, and he understood that it was not Excalibur that he held, and furthermore he recognized that it was his own proper sword with which Sir Accolon assailed him, for he knew it by its preternatural glitter and also by the peculiar sound it made when swung.

"Die, traitor!" then cried Accolon, raising the magic sword to the extent of his arm and charging upon King Arthur.

And expecting to die King Arthur sat his horse quietly and awaited the stroke that would kill him, for he had no weapon and a king can not in decency flee from a knight.

But just as Sir Accolon was about to reach King Arthur a hole did open in the earth and his horse stepped into it, breaking its leg, and being pitched to the ground, Sir Accolon lost his grasp on Excalibur. And King Arthur dismounted and picked up the sword before Accolon could reach it.

Now the king held Excalibur's point to the visor of Sir

Accolon and he raised it, and he said to the frightened face within, "Sir knight, this is my weapon, and I would know where thou hast got it and how?"

And Sir Accolon replied, "Morgan la Fey, the fair queen of Gore, gave it me, for to defend with it the lives of her brother Arthur of Britain and Uriens her husband and king of this land." And he told of the felons who impersonated those two kings. "Now," said he, "it is indeed Excalibur which you hold, and it doth belong to King Arthur, and you say you are he. Yet an impostor would say as much, and how can I know what is the truth?"

"Were I not the real Arthur," said the king, "would I not, having gained possession of the genuine Excalibur, now put thee to death?"

"I think that you would," said Sir Accolon.

"Well, I shall not kill thee," said King Arthur. "And thereby I establish mine identity." And he permitted Accolon to rise. "Now I ask thee to consider this reasoning which is somewhat more complex, but not so much. If my sister took Excalibur from me when I was sleeping and gave it thee without my knowledge, then does it seem as though she would have done this for my benefit or for my damage?"

"Sire," said Sir Accolon, "methinks some mistake hath been made, though in all good will. I can not explain it as yet, but I am sure the error hath been mine and mine only, for the fair and gracious Queen Morgan la Fey hath no fault."

"That is a commendable sentiment," said King Arthur, "for she is thy queen, and men commonly do well to have reverence for their superiors. Yet evil hath been known to have its servants in high places, for even amongst His dozen dearest Our Lord did find one traitor."

Now Accolon was yet assotted with Morgan la Fey, and his wits were clouded with his love for her, and therefore he did not understand the burden of King Arthur's speech,

and he feared that it was he whom Arthur believed treasonous.

"Sire," said he, "I hold treason in the greatest abomination, and I should willingly submit myself to the torture in
proof of this."

"Accolon," said King Arthur, "I believe thee absolutely.
Nor do we practice torture nowadays in Britain or in our
vassalages. 'Tis an outmoded means, to seek the truth
through pain, and justice is better served avoiding cruelty."

But this was still another thing which Sir Accolon, not
being of the Round Table, could not understand. "Great
Arthur," said he, "is not King Mark of Cornwall a vassal
of your own? It is well known that he shall soon put to the
torture none other than his queen Isold, on suspicion of
adultery with Sir Tristram of Lyonesse."

Now King Arthur was made full sore by these news,
and for a congeries of reasons, foremost amongst them
being his suspicion that Isold and Tristram were guilty of
this crime, for so went the gossip, and it was impossible to
forget a vile thing once one heard it, which was why he so
detested scandalmongering: was any good served by men's
knowledge of such a sin? (or never was it hidden from
God!) And then Arthur was reminded as well that Sir
Tristram was a knight of the Table, and finally that Mark,
who was self-elevated from duke to king, had never yet
sent him a pledge of fealty.

And yet perhaps it was Mark's use of trial by torture
which offended King Arthur most, for this displayed a difference of principle of more profound significance than
these other matters. And though he now rebuked Accolon,
and said, "Sir, we can not suffer thee, a knight, to speak of
kingly matters," he privately believed that the time had
come when he must march on Cornwall, for there was
nothing which King Arthur saw as more heinous than torture, and he believed that by its use the one who imposed
it became necessarily more evil than he to whom it was
applied. (And never was a prisoner taken by the knights

of the Round Table: all enemies were pardoned if they
sued for mercy, else they were slain honestly.)

Therefore King Arthur returned with Sir Accolon to the
castle of Gore. And when she knew that her brother was
yet alive Morgan la Fey had more hatred of him than
ever, but fortunately he soon returned to Camelot, for if
he had not, this wicked woman would have made more attempts on his life.

Now when King Arthur had gone Morgan la Fey called
Sir Accolon to her, saying she would know what had happened. And when he told her she made him great praise,
saying, "Thou art as wise as thou art brave and handsome,
sweet Accolon, for surely it would have been a great misfortune to have slain my dear brother King Arthur, and I
love you for preserving him."

And though Sir Accolon had told her that but for the
hole in the ground into which his horse had stepped he
should indeed have killed the king, he was so assotted with
her beauty that he believed her artful corruption of the
true state of affairs.

"Now," said she, "I would that thou ride after Arthur
and present him with this gift from me, the which I had
intended to give him while he stayed at Gore, but he went
away too soon."

And to Accolon she gave a rich mantle of silk on which
were sewn so many precious gems set so closely each on
each that the cloth beneath them could not be seen. "And
when thou dost return again to Gore, thy reward shall be
even more priceless than this, for I love thee dearly." And
once again Morgan la Fey kissed Accolon in a warm manner which was not seemly between a queen and her
knight, and Accolon forgot utterly to think about what
King Arthur had asked him, namely why Morgan la Fey
had had possession of Excalibur.

And furthermore this wicked queen now told him that
King Uriens was very old and that he could not live much
longer, and she intimated that when Uriens was dead she
must needs find a new husband and that someone very like

Sir Accolon would suit her perfectly. And then she said that because King Uriens would die soon anyway, it were no crime but merely an anticipation of the natural event, and really a kindness, if he were not suffered to linger in misery but rather swiftly despatched.

Now because of her persuasion, the which was honeyed to disguise its venom, the foolish Sir Accolon might well have been induced to murder King Uriens, did not that monarch return from his hunt at this very moment and in great joy, for his hounds had found a splendid stag and his archers had killed it. And seeing the king roar so joyfully, Sir Accolon decided he was not so ill at the moment that killing him would serve the good. (For Accolon though assotted was basically a decent knight.)

Therefore he took the mantle and he went towards Camelot, for to present it to King Arthur with the compliments of Morgan la Fey his loving sister.

Now Arthur had reached Camelot some hours earlier, and when he got there he had sent for Guinevere, for the matter of Tristram and Isold was weighing on his mind, and as yet he was not certain what he should do about it. And though he had at first believed that he must go to Cornwall with an army to compel Mark to swear fealty to him and hence perform according to Arthurian principles of merciful justice, he now considered that Mark's neglect of his obligations as vassal might have been due to his having been distracted by the criminal congress between his queen and his nephew.

And Arthur wished to speak of this matter with Guinevere, for he knew Sir Tristram to be a man of worship without a previous reputation for lechery, the chief mark of which appetite was the need for a succession of women, whereas Tristram was devoted to this one: and therefore the problem was love and not mere lust, which was to say, a feminine and not a virile matter. And thus King Arthur had the rare need for the counsel of Guinevere.

But the varlet he had sent to fetch her could find her nowhere, not at her chambers not in the garden.

"Well," said King Arthur when the boy returned with these news, "then she doth ride abroad attended by the faithful Launcelot as is her wont on these clement afternoons." And he sent the varlet without the walls to look for her.

Now this boy eventually came to the royal orchards the which had been cultivated under Sir Kay's direction, and it was the time of year when the trees were heavy with pippins and peaches and pears, and distracted by hunger this varlet picked him a lovely peach (which was illegal to do, and would have earned him a thrashing had he been seen by Kay or his staff), and he sate him down under a tree for to eat this fruit.

And whilst he was doing this he heard some soft gasps coming from not far away and rising with his peach he went to a near-by tree, where first he came upon a lady's clothing strewn on the earth and then that of a knight, and under the fruit-laden branches of this tree, which were so heavy that they came down as a screen on all sides, this page saw the heaving of the beast-with-two-backs, and this being a domesticated breed and not savage except to its own constituent parts, he observed its antics for a while, for he was but fourteen years old and he was curious to learn of the animal husbandry which lay in store for him as a man. But he could not see the twin faces of the creature, for they were obscured by the hair, the which was respectively gold and sable.

Then the varlet finished eating his peach, and thinking he might well be punished if detected at his observation, he dropped the stone and crept away. (And finding a secret place he polluted himself, the which he duly confessed on his next peccavi.)

Now it was not so much later that coming out from under the plum-tree, on their way to find their horses, which had been tethered at the edge of the orchard, Guinevere and Launcelot did pass where this fresh peachstone lay, and Sir Launcelot saw it, and he knew it as evidence that they had been observed.

And he said, "Lady, we are undone."

But though Guinevere did pale on seeing the wet red stone she never lost command of herself. "Well," said she, "I do not think the testimony of a peach-poacher would soon bring me to the stake. 'Tis illegal to pick fruit here without the order of Sir Kay, and even those who do the picking at his sanction are not allowed to eat ought but bruised fruits, and then they are forbidden to discard the stones here. *Ergo*, who ate this peach did so without the law, and as himself a miscreant, will never accuse his betters who are observed at other foibles."

And Sir Launcelot was once again amazed, and not only with Guinevere's quick wit but also at her self-righteousness, the which he supposed instinctive with royalty.

And he asked gently, "Is what we do then even less harmful than stealing the king's peaches?"

Now once her clothes were on her majestic body Guinevere was ever haughty with Sir Launcelot, nor was she altogether complaisant with them off, and because of this he felt at once less guilty of crime (for she was the queen and he but a knight) and more (for she was the consort of his king): which was to say he could neither defy her nor go without defying all that he believed in. And therefore indeed he was in love, and in the degree to which he was a lover he had become spiritually an eunuch.

"Yea," proudly said Guinevere, "a peach from this orchard is the king's property. He who takes it is a thief!"

"And hath Launcelot not stolen something?" asked the same.

"Nay!" cried Guinevere. "It is not a thing, and he did not take but rather was taken!"

And here her champion did stop and kneeling before her he said, "Majesty, accept the obeisance and abasement of your most miserable of lackeys."

And all of this had happened many times before, but now Guinevere was peculiarly irked, and she extended her slipper, saying, "Wretch, kiss my foot."

"Nay!" cried Sir Launcelot, now suddenly vexed himself (and with himself). "I shall not, for when doth the sword serve the scabbard?" Yet he did not rise.

"Dost refuse a royal command, Sir Froward?" asked the queen.

"Never," said Sir Launcelot. "And I continue to kneel to the queen but not to a spiteful woman."

"Well," said Guinevere, "they can not be separated, and therefore thou shalt die for this impossibility of discrimination. Thy blade, sir!" And she held her delicate white hand towards him.

Now Sir Launcelot drew his sword and he gave it her by the handles, and he said, "Madam, then be pleased to strike off mine head."

And the queen took his sword, the which was long and heavy, and she hardly could raise it, so massive it was. But a queen hath strengths which are more than physical, and Guinevere with the finest and whitest hands in the world (the which had lately done more gentle work) lifted the sword over Sir Launcelot's head, and only God knows whether she would have brought it down upon him in the next moment.

But at just that time the page came back through that part of the orchard and seeing her he said, "Lady, the king doth require you."

And Guinevere dropped the sword to the ground, saying, "Well, we are all subjects."

Now Sir Launcelot picking up his sword returned it to his scabbard, and then he shamed himself by addressing the little varlet in this wise: "Boy," said he, "the queen would show with my sword how she could knight a man were she the king. And so I knelt before her in the interests of this demonstration."

"My lord," said the page bowing.

But the queen with flashing eyes said, "Nay, varlet, Sir Launcelot doth jest! I was about to strike off his head for contumacy."

And the page did understand nought of this, for his wits

were confused so to be addressed by such high personages, he who otherwise received commands only, and he went to find their horses and to help them to mount. And when they rode back to the castle this varlet walked behind, and in his lowly situation he could never think that these were the two people whom he had seen swyving like goats any more than he could believe that angels did come together carnally.

Now Launcelot could not forbear from saying to Guinevere as they rode together, "So hath the king returned untimely. Therefore we were wise to go without the castle."

"To be found by this boy?" asked Guinevere. "Whereas when Arthur stays in residence, thou dost come to my chambers. I have told thee that the nearer, the safer."

"Perhaps I can not explain it," said Sir Launcelot, "but with the king away it seemeth peculiarly indecent to use his castle for this."

"Canst thou not," asked the queen, "think of anything in our love but the squalor of it?" And she began this question in anger, but she ended it in tears.

And Sir Launcelot turned to look whether the page was close enough to see, but he had now been left far behind.

Then he said to her, "Lady, God forgive us! For what we do hath never become less wrong."

And Guinevere then cried in awful blasphemy, "God damn thee to Hell, Launcelot. I would see thee nevermore!" And she rode swiftly away from him on her palfrey.

And while he could easily have overtaken her on his Arab charger, he did not, and he prayed to God to pardon her terrible oath, and he furthermore asked that all sins committed by them together be his burden and not hers, for he was a man and she but a weak woman like unto the first who had fallen to the temptation of the apple. And in the depths of his heart Launcelot knew great relief that their friendship was over, and that he could now return to the monastery of the Little Brothers of Poverty and Pain and for the rest of his life atone for the breaking of his vow of chastity.

For though he had loved her greatly, at no time was the joy comparable to the sorrow and the shame of it.

Now when Guinevere came to King Arthur he greeted her and he said, "I would have your thoughts upon the Cornish matter."

"My lord," said Guinevere, "you are soon returned from Gore."

"Yea," said the king, "I am sorely troubled by these news from Tintagel, where Mark would try La Belle Isold by torture for adultery. Now though this be not your proper concern, Guinevere, there are political consequences, and Ireland (an unruly king) will mount a host against Cornwall, I fear, and Mark is my vassal though unacknowledged by himself. And though I detest war I shall not suffer an invasion of my realm once again by the savage Irish. Therefore methinks I must go to Cornwall first and reduce Mark to his proper place, and to deliver Isold from the fire. Yet if she hath been guilty of this criminal trespass against the office of her husband (who if not royal except by self-anointing doth rule Cornwall), she must be tried, must she not? And if justly impugned, with proof, then banished. Or, think you, better sent to a nunnery?"

"My lord," said Guinevere, "I believe that I do lack authority to form such an opinion."

"Well, my dear Guinevere," said King Arthur, "I am of course not obliged to act upon your judgment, but I would hear your thoughts, for you are yourself a queen and a woman (and in those, though in no other way, God forfend! like unto Isold). And while the disposition of this matter be a kingly and male thing, the crime, if committed, is feminine."

"So be it," said Guinevere.

"Look you," said King Arthur, " 'twould be otherwise if Isold were but a noblewoman and Sir Tristram were rather a royal person (as he is by birth, to be sure, but he doth not rule in Cornwall), yet as it is these stations are reversed. A queen hath taken, as illegal lover, a knight!"

"But if as queen she took another king?" asked Guinevere.

"Yea," said Arthur, "and right you are, Guinevere, 'tis the felonious adultery that should concern us, and not the relative ranks of those who practice it. Dear friend, this is just what I wanted from you."

"Well," said Guinevere, "Sir Tristram is anyway a prince."

"Indeed, indeed," said King Arthur, "as are they all, my foremost knights, Gawaine and his brothers, and Sir Launcelot." And then he pondered for a moment, and he said, "Yet, withal, we do not know certainly whether this sinful liaison hath been instituted or is but the construction of malicious tongues. Methinks that Mark is a mean ruler, and that such a man hath meaner spirits around him. Sir Tristram hath ever been a knight of much worship, and only in such a company as the Round Table doth a man of prowess not inspire the envy of those nearby. Then Isold is a notable beauty, and a foreigner as well. Can plainer Cornishwomen forgive her for that?"

"My lord," said Guinevere, "no one can ever know certainly of privy things unless one be privy to them, and each man must decide alone how much evidence is necessary to establish a conviction."

"Well put, dear friend," said King Arthur. "You have aided me greatly, for what I needed here was to hear mine own thoughts as they were reflected from another, but only from another whom I could trust absolutely to have no corrupting bias. Launcelot and Gawaine, for example, are Tristram's friends and fellow-members of the Table, for one; and for another they neither of them would, or could, entertain the possibility that an otherwise honest queen were adulterous."

Now his audience with his wife having been concluded,

King Arthur went to his throne room, and there he found Sir Accolon waiting for him.

And when Sir Accolon had knelt and been recognized he rose and he gave to King Arthur the rich mantle he had brought from Gore.

"With this gift your sister the fair Morgan la Fey sends her love to you, most royal Arthur," said Accolon, "and she doth further command me to deliver these wishes with this coat: that you reign so long as you wear it, for it is sewn with the gems of immortality."

Now King Arthur was pleased that his sister would atone for her wicked and unnatural attempt on his life, and eager to think the best of her he even began to suppose that he had misunderstood the unhappy event at Gore. And yet the jeweled mantle was far too resplendent for his virile tastes, and therefore he did not put it on him, but seeing a lovely lady enter the court he called her to him and he asked her to put the coat of gems about her shoulders, and she came and did this.

Now this lady was marvelously beautiful in the mantle, but she soon did frown while wearing it. And to her she called Sir Accolon, and to him she said, "The weight of these rare jewels is too heavy for me to bear. It wants the broad shoulders of a brave and loyal knight, who is much loved by a queen."

And Sir Accolon in his vanity happily permitted her to put the mantle on him, and he smiled at King Arthur and he believed that one day soon he might be his brother-in-law.

But then the coat burst into hot flames and he was soon burned to ashes within it. For what had seemed lovely gems were really incendiary stones the which the wicked Morgan la Fey had sewn onto the mantle for the purpose of burning King Arthur alive.

Now King Arthur knew great anguish. And the beautiful lady came to him and she said, "This foolish knight hath received his just deserts, for he might else have been induced through his ambition and his lust to become a regicide."

"Who art thou," asked King Arthur, "to have saved my life?"

"Thy friend of old Arthur," said the Lady of the Lake (for it was she), "who furnished thee with Excalibur and who hath so many times provided instruction for thy knights, and who can protect thee from the grosser harms such as this, but who can give you no immunity to the subtler poisons undreamt of by Morgan la Fey."

And King Arthur lowered his head, on which there were already many gray hairs, but when he raised it again to thank her, she was gone.

And when Morgan la Fey heard of her latest failure to kill King Arthur she went into a fury, and she stole into the chambers of her husband King Uriens and sought to put him to death while he lay sleeping, but a loyal maidservant saw her and warned Sir Uwaine, the son of King Uriens by his first wife who had died, and Uwaine did obstruct his wicked stepmother from committing this crime. And subsequently Morgan la Fey was banished (for King Uriens was too kind to burn her, and anyway he wished only to go a-hunting), and she went into the wilds where she lived with her evil nephew Mordred and all the birds and all the animals did void that place, and even the trees withered and died thereabout.

BOOK XIII

*Of Sir Tristram and La Belle Isold; and how King
Mark discovered their love.*

Now King Arthur would mount his expedition against
Cornwall, but before he could do so the news came to him
that the trial of Queen Isold had already taken place.

For La Belle Isold and Sir Tristram had continued to
meet in the congress of adulterous love for so long a time
that it was not secret to anyone at Tintagel except King
Mark, and he was oft told of it by the vile dwarf Frocin,
who however could never provide evidence for his accusations. And every trap laid by this dwarf was evaded by Sir
Tristram, often unknowingly. And lying in wait to catch
him in criminal association with Isold, Mark was ever
frustrated. And once Frocin mounted a ladder placed
against the wall of the castle and climbed it to peer
through a window into the royal bedchamber and after
seeing the miscreants close-coupled within, he came down
to the waiting king. And then Mark himself climbing the
ladder, the which was stout enough to bear the weight of a
dwarf, it collapsed under him and he fell to the ground
breaking an arm and a leg.

And after this happened Mark in impulsive fury had
Frocin beheaded, the which he later regretted because he
would rather have tortured him to death slowly.

But then King Mark began to get anonymous notes

from other informants, and he was told therein just what the late Frocin had insisted upon: that he was a marvelous cuckold, on whom the horns had been put by his own nephew. Therefore he began to suspect that there was more in this than the malignancy of a monstrous dwarf.

But Mark could not understand how Isold could take Tristram into her bed when he himself slept beside her all the night, and during the day he kept her under observation at all times. But then finally one time when Isold brought to him the supposed aphrodiasiac he had drunk every night during the years since their wedding (for he had got older and he believed he needed it even more than at the outset: yet as we know all his swyving had been done only in fantasy), it occurred to him that this potion might be otherwise than it had been represented, which was to say, that it did not stiffen his yard but rather put him into a sleep so like that of the dead that he knew not what he did when under its influence.

Therefore to test the truth of this possibility he spurned the glass now, and fortunate it was that Isold observed his failure to drink thereof, and she spoke to him of this.

" 'Tis no forgetfulness, chuck," said King Mark, rolling up his nightshirt to reveal his yellowed privities and the white hairs on his protuberant belly. "Thine ardent labors shall stir me more than potions." And he commanded her to come and minister to him.

But begging his pardon for a short delay for to anoint herself with scented emollients, La Belle Isold went rather to an antechamber where she found the loyal Brangwain. And to her handmaiden she spake as follows.

"My dear Brangwain," said she, "it seems that the king will not drink of thy potion this night."

"Alas, my lady," said Brangwain, "then whatever shall be done?" And she was greatly dismayed, for this good woman was altogether devoted to the lady she had served since their girlhoods.

"Well," said Isold, "I have conceived of a plan that will suffice but only if we carry it out with great care, and it is this: that whilst I go in to Mark and distract him by taking off my robe before his eyes, thou shalt enter and secrete thyself behind a screen. Then when I have extinguished the tapers, we shall, thou and I, exchange places: which is to say, I shall go behind the screen and thou shalt come out from it and enter into the bed."

"With the king?" asked Brangwain in wonder.

"With himself," said La Belle Isold.

"And then submit myself to his embraces?" asked the loyal Brangwain.

"I fear thou must," said Queen Isold. "I see no alternative, good my Brangwain. Else I shall be the prey of that foul old man, and thou must agree that that were unthinkable."

"Indeed, my lady," said Brangwain, "such a beastly thing must never happen." Nevertheless she could not forbear from weeping gently.

"Well, Brangwain," said La Belle Isold, "was it not thee who fed me not the poison for which I begged, but rather the decoction of love?"

And Brangwain agreed that this had been the case, and she said, "Would that I had time now to brew me some potion the which would numb my conscience."

"Think thou," said Isold, "of the worthiness of the cause."

"I shall, my lady," said Brangwain. But then she said, "Is there not some difference between us in figure?" (For she was sufficiently robust that standing behind her Isold could not have been seen.) "Can the king be long insensible to the distinction, even in the dark?"

"Brangwain, my dear," said the fair Isold, "be assured that my performance in preparing for bed before his eyes will so heat this old man as to confuse his senses utterly and to render him incapable of entertaining any thought but to satisfy his inordinate lust."

And poor Brangwain did shudder at this indelicate speech of Isold's, for she was yet a maiden, and she had intended to remain so forever (feeling no desire for any man but Sir Tristram, who she could never have).

Now telling her to wait and to watch through a crack of the door until King Mark's attention was occupied, La Belle Isold went back into the bedchamber and standing where the tapers would light her to the best advantage she slowly and with provocative motions of her body began to lower her nightdress, the which was of white sendal (though not as smooth and white as her alabaster skin). But when her bosom had been bared to the rosy paps she stopped, and she had with her a flask of scented oil and from it she poured fine drops of this fragrant oil onto her breasts, the which she then caressed and manipulated slowly.

And this display did cause King Mark to moan in lascivious delight and to slap his old belly and his withered thighs. And whilst he was so occupied, the loyal Brangwain discreetly entered the chamber and she hid herself behind the screen.

Now knowing that her handmaiden was in place, Isold made shorter work of what remained of her disrobing, and gathering her dress below her ivory navel and at no time revealing her flanks she did pursing her orchid lips and leaning first this way, then that, blow out the candles. And then she slipped quickly behind the screen while Brangwain came slowly out from it and went towards the bed as if it were a gallows.

And no sooner had Brangwain entered the bed than the king did hurl himself upon her brutally, but being old and mean of body his assault was not so puissant as she had feared, and she was a most sturdy Irishwoman, and he but writhed upon her like a child at play. And when he sought to do more, Brangwain in defense of her maidenhead (and without thought) smote him between the eyes with her robust fist, and King Mark swooned.

Then she did fear what she had done, thinking she had killed him, and while that would be an occasion for much joy for Isold and Tristram, they would nevertheless be constrained to burn her for the crime of regicide, for which there was no justification on earth or in Heaven.

So did poor Brangwain lie sleepless with the supposed corse till dawn (for Isold had fled to Tristram), but when the first light came through the windows she saw that the king did but slumber, and happily, for he was smiling.

And shortly thereafter La Belle Isold returned, and she silently motioned for Brangwain to leave, which the loyal handmaiden did with great relief, but also with a marvelous new fear, for now that Mark lived he would soon awaken and remember that his bedpartner had knocked him senseless.

But as it happened, when the king awakened he was ecstatic, and he cried to Isold, who surely stood too far from the bed for him to reach, "My Irish tigress! Never have I known thee more ardent than thou wert last night! Nor may I say, never have I answered thy passion with even more. Indeed, I was quite out of my wits!" And in his horrid vanity he crowed and cackled, and he wished now that he had not killed Frocin, and he determined to get himself another dwarf to boast to, for a royal personage could speak on these intimate matters to none other.

Therefore was all well at the moment: with the king believing that his wife was his alone, and Isold and Tristram able to meet with impunity, and even the loyal Brangwain retained her virginity (the which was precious to her, being all she possessed of her own). And King Mark soon went away from Tintagel, for to hunt wild boars, and he invited Sir Tristram his nephew to accompany him (the boar being the very device which that great knight wore famously upon his shield).

But Sir Tristram wishing to stay near Isold declined, and he pretended that he was ill from the old wounds he had got years before from the Morholt, and therefore the king took along the second knight of Cornwall, he who hated Tristram, and he was named Guenelon.

Now this Guenelon knowing that so soon as King Mark had left Tintagel, Isold and Tristram would come together, did as if by accident separate himself from the king's party on the chase, and he rode back to the castle as fast as his horse would go. And when he arrived there he stole quietly to the royal bedchambers by a secret passage known to few, and therefore he eluded the watch of the loyal Brangwain, who served as Cerberus at the main door. And from behind a tapestry he saw the adulterous couple compounding their crime.

Then he left as silently as he had come, and he rode swiftly back to find King Mark, and he told him of what he had seen.

And King Mark thereupon returned to Tintagel in great haste, but Brangwain from her window saw the dust of his gallop and when he drew near she identified the rider. Therefore she pounded upon the door of the bedroom and she cried a warning, and Sir Tristram leapt from the bed and seizing his clothes he did leave by means of the balcony and he went down the vines and into the garden, where the gardeners saw him run bare and did marvel at it.

Now when King Mark burst into the chamber La Belle Isold was not there, and furthermore Brangwain had hastily made the bed, but so exercised was the king that he tore away the coverlet and the sheets, and he felt there with his hand, and indeed it was still warm. And he went to the balcony and looking down he saw the torn vines. Therefore he had the gardeners brought to him, and he questioned them closely. But these fellows, not being noblemen, held Sir Tristram in great fondness, for he always had been kind to them, and they would not betray him now, and they showed great courage in this because the king threatened to break them on the wheel.

"Well," said he in marvelous wrath, "then tell me why these vines are fresh-broken!"

"Well," said these gardeners, "the mason came there with a ladder, for to inspect the walls for cracks which needed mortaring, and his ladder did slip and tear away some leaves."

"Methinks ye do not need eyes which see false things," said King Mark, "and therefore I shall have them torn out."

And he would have had this done had not La Belle Isold come to him at that moment, and she begged him not to be cruel to these poor fellows.

"Very well," said King Mark, "but I must force the truth from someone, for I think that it will never be freely given me. Shalt thou then submit to the test of hot iron?"

And La Belle Isold said proudly, "I shall."

Therefore King Mark ordered that the preparations be made for this ordeal.

Now Isold went to Brangwain and she said, "Good my Brangwain, I would that thou compound for me some ointment the which I might put upon my hands to make them impervious to hot iron, so that I might withstand this test."

"Lady," said Brangwain, "I shall try to do this." And she proceeded to mix divers unguents from various ingredients such as the saliva of dragons (the which surviveth the flames that shoot from the mouths of those beasts) and the blood of the salamander who liveth in the heart of the fire, &tc., but when she rubbed these emollients into the palms of her hands and applied to them a red-hot poker she was burned sorely, for none of her compounds did turn away the heat.

And the loyal Brangwain was in great grief owing to these failures, for she believed her lady would be given the lie in the ordeal of hot iron and that she would then be burned at the stake for adultery.

Now Sir Tristram was in hiding, and he could not come out of it without being attacked by the many knights which King Mark had posted to guard the castle against him, and though he could have overcome them all, to fight would be but an admission of his own guilt and that of the queen, and therefore he determined to wait until the last moment before delivering Isold from the ordeal, should God meanwhile bring some other relief which would not compromise her. (For Sir Tristram was a devout knight, and though he knew that what he and Isold did was never right, he believed they were helpless to desist from doing it so long as they lived, and they must needs answer for it when they died. And so much did he love her that he would face Hell without bitterness).

And he lay concealed in the hovel of a churl whom he had befriended in the past, and he ate the gruel on which this boor and his family subsisted, the which was prepared by the good wife, who was of the age of Isold but in aspect seemed almost a crone, and he was kind to the many children there, who were at play in the mud.

Then on the day set for the ordeal Sir Tristram hired from this clown his host some of his ragged clothes and he put them on over his armor, and he hung a wooden cross on a thong about his neck. And he whitened his hair with chalk-dust, and when he walked limping and bent over he looked very like an hermit, and in this guise he went towards the place where the test of hot iron was to be held, the which was on a plain across the river.

And reaching the ford he waited there, where it was not long before a great procession came from the castle, with all the knights of Cornwall and all the ladies and the chaplains and the squires, and all the noble people. And then came King Mark, and lastly the bishop of Cornwall with his retainers who carried a bronze brazier in which the coals were already white-hot.

And all of these rode through the ford and onto the far bank before Isold appeared. And when finally she did come she was dressed in flawless white samite and her glistening black hair was caught behind with one gold clasp and it fell to her waist, and she slowly rode a pure-white palfrey. And attending her was the loyal Brangwain, who rode a donkey six paces behind.

Now they were all drawn up upon the meadow, and there they awaited her, but when Isold reached the ford she asked Brangwain to ride into the river to see how high the water reached, and when Brangwain did so she was wetted to the waist, and only the ass's head was out of the river.

"Well," said La Belle Isold, "I would not wet my clothes going to my ordeal."

Now Sir Tristram lingered there in his hermit's guise, and coming to La Belle Isold he said, "Lady, I shall carry you across the ford if you will."

And her heart leapt, for she knew him for what he was, and he took her from the palfrey and he carried her across the river, high in his arms so that no drop of water reached her, and then he put her onto the bank.

"Thank you, kind hermit," said Isold when she had regained her feet, and then stately she walked to where the smoking brazier stood, and near by was a table covered with a cloth of red velvet, the which was fringed in gold, and on this were all the holy relics of the land of Cornwall, and the bishop was there in his miter. And lackeys using bellows made the coals ever hotter until they were white, and into them they put a rod of iron.

Meanwhile the common folk had come out from the town, and they stood on the bank of the river, for they were not suffered to come closer. And they never quite understood the purpose of the ordeal, but they were entertained by it.

Now the iron was soon as white-hot as the coals in which it was embedded, and the bishop asked Isold to come before him, and then he said, "My lady, gracious queen of Cornwall, how do you swear?"

And La Belle Isold said, "I swear by God Almighty that the only man who hath held me in his arms, other than the king mine husband, is yon hermit, who lately carried me across the water!"

And so saying she plunged her two fair hands into the burning coals and took from them the iron, and she held it aloft for all the assemblage to look upon, and then slowly she brought it down and returned it to the brazier. And then she slowly opened her hands and she presented them to the bishop, and then to King Mark, and they were without blemish from the fire.

And kissing both of her hands King Mark cried out her vindication, but from the assemblage there rose no answering sound, for Isold and Tristram had no friends at Cornwall but the loyal Brangwain (who had swooned when Isold had lifted the iron), and all the rest of them knew that the queen was guilty but had employed some magic to seem otherwise.

And Sir Tristram let go of the handle of the dagger, the which he had been clutching beneath his clothes, for he had purposed to deliver Isold by means of it if the ordeal had gone against her. And so he went away without revealing his identity.

Now when they had all returned to the castle, where King Mark would hold a feast of celebration, Isold said privily to her loyal handmaiden, chiding her affectionately for her swooning, "My dear Brangwain, thou hadst less faith in thine ointment than I. Never did I doubt it would be efficacious."

Then Brangwain showed to her her own burns which she had got in her experiments. "Lady," said she, "your protection was the truth and never my compound!"

And hearing that, La Belle Isold did faint dead away.

Now Sir Tristram took off his rags and he returned to the castle as his own self, and his uncle King Mark embraced him joyfully.

And to him the king said, "My dear nephew, I ask thy pardon for entertaining this suspicion against thee, thou who art a paragon of virtue. Never shall I doubt thee again! Now I would that thou go to thy queen and aunt and escort her to the banquet ball on thine arm, in despite of all those who were wont to calumniate ye."

Therefore Sir Tristram sought La Belle Isold in her chamber, where she lay in her swoon upon the bed, and when he saw how beautiful she was he bent and he kissed her upon the lips. And thereupon she was awakened.

"Ah, my love," said she, " 'twas a near thing, methinks,

for only through the generosity of God did I escape burning."

"All good cometh only from God," said Tristram, "and indeed He hath favored us much till now though we are great sinners."

" 'Tis because we love each other truly," said Isold, "and if we sin, it is only in the formal sense, and never with the spirit, for our hearts are pure. And now I love all the people in the world, so happy am I! And I love Mark as the king, and I love our enemies as well. For this is what love doth to the soul, so saith Our Saviour Lord Jesus Christ."

Now Tristram was made uneasy by hearing this interpretation, and he did not think that God intended mortals to be happy except through love of Him, whereas it was Isold's opinion that a particular passion was prefatory to the general love of all creation. Yet he adored his sweet heretic, and but for having to escort her to the banquet he would have joined her to himself in this moment.

And unwisely he did whisper as much into the delicate whorl of her shell-like ear and she embraced him feverishly, urging him to become one with her regardless. And when he protested Isold said, "Well, did the king not say that he would have suspicions of us nevermore? And the meat will not be served immediately. And certes I may rest awhile after my cruel ordeal!"

Therefore she commanded the loyal Brangwain to go to the king and to tell him she would take some repose and then come presently. And so soon as Brangwain had gone Isold did take Sir Tristram into her bed.

Now when King Mark heard the message brought by Brangwain he said, "What an inconsiderate husband I am! I have been distracted by mine own joy. Indeed, 'tis no time for a public feast. 'Tis rather an occasion for familial intimacy, and therefore I shall join my wife in the bedchamber."

And in great dread Brangwain saw him send his seneschal to end the preparations for the banquet lately begun and to send away the lords and ladies who had already gathered in the hall. And she was not suffered to leave him, so that she could not warn the lovers who were locked together in the king's bed. And the king kept her by him so that she might hear his praise of Isold's stainless virtue and the impeccable honor of Sir Tristram. And King Mark believed that the talk against them had been due but to the envy that such noble persons inevitably inspire in the souls to which they are superior.

"For their honeyed natures are too sweet, Brangwain," said he, "for them to be properly imperious with the toads of standard humanity, the fealty of which is never freely given but must be taken by force."

And so he talked to the loyal Brangwain as they went towards the royal bedchamber, and she had no means by which to detain him. And then they reached that place, and he went in jovially, and there he saw La Belle Isold and Sir Tristram together in the bed, and he finally knew the truth.

And what King Mark did first was not to make a sound except deep in his throat as if he were strangling, and indeed he fell onto the floor. And he was the king and therefore Brangwain attended to him, smiting his back for him to induce him to expel what he was gagging on. But then rolling him over she found that he had swallowed his tongue in his rage, and therefore she put her finger in his throat and pulled it out.

Now while this was happening Sir Tristram and Isold did leave the bed and taking up their clothes they departed through a privy passage behind the tapestries, and so did they flee the castle of Tintagel and go into the wild forests of Cornwall.

And when King Mark was revived he formed an army and he pursued the adulterers for many days and nights without halting, for he was inordinate in his anger. And every time he was ready to go back, another trace of them was found, a torn piece of clothing on a thornbush or the like, and he was thereby encouraged to press on, but never could he find them. But after many weeks of this vain pursuit he had need to return to Tintagel, for the treacherous Guenelon, who had at first accompanied the king, soon had stolen back and had seized the throne of Cornwall.

And Mark could get back into his own castle only after besieging it for a long time, and when he did he had Guenelon drawn and quartered.

Now Tristram and Isold did at length find a cave in the heart of the wilds, and there they made their home. But no sooner had they moved into this than the dragon returned, whose cave it was, and Sir Tristram had a great fight with him and was sore wounded, but he killed it finally. But there was nought to eat save berries and roots, for the dragon had long since eaten or frightened away all the game. And the wounds that Tristram had got in the fight did not heal but got worse.

And their clothes were in tatters, and they could not wash often, for there was only enough water from the rainfall to drink and to bathe his wounds, and of ponds and brooks there were none thereabout. And had any Christians seen them at this time, they would have seemed savage creatures, this pair who had been so comely once.

And Sir Tristram lay with his shaggy head in the lap of Isold, whose legs were bare and cut with thorns, and her hair marvelously tangled and her eyes all red from the smoking fire in the cave, which had no proper draught.

"Well, my love," said he, "we are paying the wages of of sin."

But Isold, who was no longer La Belle, said, "My love, 'tis only a temporary inconvenience. At the least we are together and dissembling is no longer necessary. Truly we have some discomfort, but what of that, when nobody doth separate us one from the other?"

"But I am sore ill," said Tristram, "and soon there will be not even any more roots to eat, and I am too weak to go to look for food."

"Then shall I go," said Isold, "for I am hale though uncombed and sans scents and fine clothes, and for the first time in my life (which began as a protected princess, after which I became a queen against my will) I may have some use. And I shall feed and heal the man I love!"

Saying the which she made for him a bed of soft moss, and then she went out of the cave with his sword, with which she cut a branch from an ash tree, and she made a bow of this and the laces from her bodice, and then she fashioned some arrows and hardened their points in fire, and taking these weapons she went deeper into the forest, where there were partridges and coneys, and these she killed and brought back and nourished Tristram, who was almost dead, on their blood. And she ate their flesh herself, and she made garments and blankets from their feathers and skins.

Then from the bark of trees she brewed potions and applied them to Tristram's wounds, and gradually he grew better, and Isold was happier than she had ever been in all her life.

But at last Tristram was completely well, and so soon as he was he took back his sword from her, and he made a much stronger bow than hers, and he went farther afield to where the larger game roamed, and he killed a stag, and then they had hearty flesh to eat. And from the skins of this and other deer killed by Sir Tristram, Isold made stout clothes. And Tristram fashioned a spear and with it he killed a savage boar, and they made shoes from its hide.

And whilst Sir Tristram went hunting, Isold stayed at home in the cave and she was happy to have cured him. And Tristram was pleased to be well, but when his good health was no longer new, and he had supplied all of their needs, he began to think that it was deplorable for Isold to live forever in a cave in the wilds, for she was properly a queen.

But when he told her of this she said, "Mine own dear love, rather with thee in the woods than with anyone else in a palace! I care nought for courts as such."

"Yet," said Sir Tristram, "my love, thou art a royal person, whom God saw fit to make first a princess and then a queen. It can never be right that thou stay in this rustication, into which we fled on pain of death."

"I suffer not from deprivation," said Isold. "And obviously we can not return to Tintagel. Nor indeed may we go to Ireland now, knowing Anguish my father, who was much pleased by my Cornish match. Methinks he would now strike off thine head for carrying me away."

"The which I never intended to do, God wot!" said Sir Tristram.

"Prithee take no offense," said Isold embracing him sweetly. "Dear love, the fault was mine that Mark discovered us so. Thou hast acted prudently in all events."

"Yet methinks I might have done better," said Tristram. "'Tis not so virile to be such a victim of circumstances. But all the alternatives have ever been worse. I could not do without thee. Yet with thee I have done some evil. 'Tis pious to love one's fate, but I confess I am not always able to do that."

"And is it so dreadful here in our jolly cave?" asked Isold, for she could see his melancholy, and she feared its issue.

"But is it right that we live as savage creatures forever?" asked Sir Tristram in return. "Thou art a queen, as I am a knight."

And to this question Isold made no answer, for she was a woman and she did not share his sense of vocation.

Now when Mark had taken back his castle from the traitors and had killed them every one, he turned again to thoughts of Tristram and Isold, and the wondrous thing was that his heart began to soften towards them, for he came to understand that their love, though sinful, was malicious towards him only by accident and not by design, for his nephew could easily have killed him at any time and become king, and Isold might simply have introduced poison into the aphrodisiac he had drunk so often.

And of the many traitors which had surrounded him, they had not been two.

Now he sent for the loyal Brangwain (whom fortune had favored when it kept her by the king's side on that day when he had come upon the lovers abed, else she might have lost her head as a conspirator). And to that handmaiden he said, "Is there ought that I should know about La Belle Isold of which I am yet ignorant?"

"Yea," said Brangwain, "and it is that whilst en route to Cornwall from Ireland the princess and Sir Tristram did unwittingly drink of a potion that caused them to fall in love with each other, and for this there is no antidote."

"I see," said King Mark. "Then they are not evil in their hearts, and their purpose in adulterating together is not to make mock of my crown nor of me?"

"Nay," said the loyal Brangwain, "they bear you no ill will, Sire. They are helpless to do otherwise than they do."

"Well," said King Mark, "I am sorry to know this, for it doth make me feel worse. For they must be caught and put to death, and there is no appeal against the great crime of cuckolding the king. But I am relieved of all desire for revenge, and I can no longer hate them. Nor shall I actively seek them out for punishment."

And he was as good as his word, and he did not take up their pursuit again, and for a long time Tristram and Isold lived with impunity in the forest.

But then King Mark went pigsticking one day, and on the trail of a wild boar he had ridden deep into the woods, separating himself from his retainers. And finding himself before the mouth of a cave he dismounted and he went therein on foot, and he carried his naked sword should the boar be at bay there.

Now Tristram and Isold had lately eaten their rude lunch, and then they lay down side by side, for to rest, and both had fallen into a slumber.

And this is how King Mark found them, and he stood over their sleeping bodies with his sword in his hands, and looking at them in their clothes of deer hide and with their brown skins from the life outdoors, and seeing near by the coals of their fire and the bones of the rude meat they had

eaten, he was touched at the heart to know of the hard-
ships they had endured for their love. And he had no will
to put them to death as they lay asleep.

And if he took them in arrest and returned them to Tintagel for Isold's burning and the beheading of Sir Tristram, what cause would be served? 'Twould be but the
extinction of two comely lives who had been blameworthy
without conscious intent.

Now Mark was torn by these thoughts, for he knew that
his royal obligation was to punish these adulterers, and
being self-elevated from a dukedom to a throne he was
ever concerned with being kingly, and above all he wished
to avoid some failure which would shame him in the eyes
of King Arthur, whose esteem he most wanted.

But what he finally did was to bend over the pair and to
place his naked sword between their two bodies, and leaving it there he returned to Tintagel.

Now when Sir Tristram awoke from his nap and he
turned to Isold for to kiss her as was his wont when first
opening his eyes, he saw the sword between them, and
seizing it he sprang to his feet.

And Isold was awake as well, and she said, "This sword
is Mark's."

To which Sir Tristram replied, "I know it well."

"Dost thou then believe," asked Isold, "that 'twas himself who put it there?"

"I do," said Sir Tristram.

"Not stolen from him?" asked Isold. "And placed here
by some mocker?"

"Nay," said Tristram. "Mark was here, dear Isold, and
he saw us and he could have killed us in our sleep. Thus
he left his sword in significance of what he might have
done."

" 'Tis not at all like Mark," said Isold, "for he is a
vengeful man."

"Then he hath altered," Sir Tristram said deliberately
and with feeling. "This was a kind thing that he did, and
more than we deserved."

But Isold heard this speech with no pleasure. "Deserved?" she asked. "Who but God can say what are human deserts? We have done only what we have had to do! And we did never ask to be born."

"But we are not brute beasts," said Tristram, "notwithstanding the way we live now."

Then Isold looked at him for a long time, and she said sadly, "Thou wouldst return this sword to Tintagel."

"Never against thy will," said Tristram, and he looked dearly at her.

"I shall never exert it in defiance of what thou believest to be thy knightly principles," said Isold.

"But dost think that what I would do be the right?" asked Sir Tristram.

"Nay, Tristram," cried Isold, "I shall not say pro nor con of this! 'Twould exceed mine office to make such judgment. Do not ask it!"

"But we are not two but one," said Tristram.

"In some things but not all," said Isold. "Thy bosom doth not swell as mine, nor are thine hips as round, and I have a more slender neck and softer skin. And with thy greater strength thou hast made a stronger bow than mine and killed larger animals. Therefore we are something different in our obligations. If thou wouldst surrender to Mark, then do it of thine own volition unassisted."

"And shalt thou come with me?" asked Sir Tristram.

"Perforce," said Isold. "For what could keep me here in these wilds?"

Therefore, in the greatest sadness that ever any two lovers felt, they went out of the forest and they returned to Tintagel, where they came unto King Mark.

And Sir Tristram knelt before him and he offered Mark's sword in his two hands, and he said, "Sire and Uncle, I am sorry as I can be for my crime against you, and there is no excuse for it."

And overcome with feeling the king wept great tears, and he said, "There is the greatest excuse for it, Nephew, for I now know of the elixir of love the which ye both did drink unwittingly, and it was irresistible."

"Yet," said Tristram, "never did I try at all to resist it."

Now Isold did not assume the posture of submission, and she said to Mark, " 'Tis I who am solely at fault, for I am of the superior station. I was an Irish princess, and I have since been queen of Cornwall!"

"My dear Isold," said King Mark, "you are a proud woman, this I now understand belatedly. Your sin is God's affair and not mine. I shall make no reference to it further, and the decision must be yours whether to remain in Cornwall as its queen or to go away again with my nephew."

And now was Isold moved to tears, for Mark had become truly a fine king for the first time, in whom generosity was a strength and not a weakness.

And Isold turned to Sir Tristram and she bade him to rise, and then she asked him what he would have her do. And never had she looked more queenly, though she still wore the rude clothes of deerskin and her face was brown from the sun.

"Lady," said Sir Tristram bowing, "I shall love you all the days of my life." And here the tears welled from his eyes, and further he could not speak for some time. And then he said to the king, "Uncle, your kindness to me hath been too extravagant to repay in any fashion but by my departure from Cornwall forever. Mine heart is broken, but perhaps to the strength of my soul."

And they all three wept together awhile, and then Sir Tristram took his sad leave of Tintagel and he returned to Camelot, many years and much sadness after he had left, and he served the Round Table for a long time with more distinction than any other knight but Sir Launcelot, and his feats were many, for scores of monsters did he slay, both giants and beasts, and numberless fair ladies freed he from foul captivity.

But never did Sir Tristram fail to remember La Belle Isold in every moment that passed, and life without her was worse than death to him, and had he not remembered as well that he was atoning for the crime of adultery he would surely have committed the worse one of slaying himself.

And his friend Launcelot was almost as sad as Tristram, but for a reason that was the opposite: namely, that he could not permanently leave his own lady love, which was Guinevere.

And if God had made Sir Launcelot into Sir Tristram, and vice versa, then perhaps everyone would have been happier. But again, perhaps not. For what do mortals know, with their limited means? Except that earthly life, whether noble or base, is sad, and the oceans of the world are created from the salt tears of men.

and I doubt that his like will appear again at Camelot. Therefore there seemeth no need for Sir Launcelot to stand constant guard upon me, and this is stultifying to him, to be always with a lady like her lap dog. Is there not better employment for the greatest knight of all?"

"Than your defense?" asked King Arthur in amazement. "Nay, Guinevere."

"But what am I to be defended against?" said the queen. "Certainly he protects me not against boredom. I would that he be exchanged with Sir Gawaine, who at least hath some merriment in him."

"Then you have not seen him lately," said King Arthur. "Indeed, for some years, for Gawaine hath become and stayed dispirited." And the king sighed. "And not he alone. A certain spirit hath gone away from the entire company of the Round Table. Only to you should I confess, my dear Guinevere, that I almost regret not having to go to subdue Mark of Cornwall, for such a war, in a virtuous cause, might well have invigorated us all. But he sent me with Sir Tristram his pledge of fealty, and I can not deplore his change of heart in all ways. He hath now earned his claim to a crown, and he may keep his. And indeeed it is a fine thing too that Tristram doth no longer foully adulterate."

But King Arthur frowned and he shook his head, the which was now quite gray. "Yet Tristram is more melancholy than when first he came to Camelot," said he, "and he was then already the saddest man I had ever seen."

Now no sooner had Guinevere left King Arthur, having failed to stir him to do what she believed she wanted, namely, to send Sir Launcelot away from her, than Launcelot himself came to the king for the same purpose.

"Well," said King Arthur smiling, "one might suppose that thou and the queen were in a conspiracy in this matter." And then he grew sober. "My dear Launcelot, only to thee would I tell this, for I have no other confidant: I have a sister who doth wish me great ill. Now I can not say this to my nephews, for they are hers as well. And certes I can not tell it to Guinevere, for she is a woman. Therefore I tell it thee, my friend. This sister hath not long ago, using as her instrument a confused knight, tried to murder me. Having failed in this she might well, I fear, attempt to harm the queen."

"O unnatural sister!" said Sir Launcelot.

"Indeed," said King Arthur, "and I would that news of her not be bruited about, for I would not have a shame brought upon our court by the king's kin, as happened in Cornwall, though happily now 'tis there no more."

The king rose from his throne, and he said, "Come, Launcelot old comrade, and let us walk together in the gardens. I would see the latest roses, and I have not been without for a long time."

And Sir Launcelot did wonder at this speech, for it was late in the autumn, with the flowers all gone, but the king did not seem to know this until they had reached the outdoors. And then also King Arthur did falter and he almost stumbled against the stone curbing around a dead flower bed, the which was covered with leaves, but clearly visible.

"Thine arm, Launcelot," said he, taking him by the elbow. "My vision hath clouded some, no doubt but temporarily, as the result of some muck fed me by Sir Kay. The dear fellow and his rich sauces! Why oh why will he not feed me plainly! . . . Now tell me, my friend, what be thine opinion of Tristram? Should he be not happier to abstain from vile sin?"

And Sir Launcelot did shudder in his heart.

And high above them, from an oriel window in the chamber where she took her champion to bed, Guinevere looked down upon the pair, king and first knight, and she believed they looked for all the world, arm and arm as they were, like unto a pair of detestable sodomites.

So King Arthur and Sir Launcelot walked in the garden, and the king talked of the general dispirit at Camelot, but Launcelot did brood upon the matter of Morgan la Fey, for never had he known that such a wicked woman could exist.

Now King Arthur said, "Launcelot, dost know of something called the Holy Grail?"

And Sir Launcelot asked, "Is it the same thing that is called the Sangreal as well?"

"The same," said King Arthur, and his interest quickened. "Then thou dost know of it?"

But Launcelot confessed that he knew little but the name, having heard it mentioned by the knights who had been in the service of King Leodegrance the father of Guinevere.

"Yea," said King Arthur, "these knights were searching for it when Cameliard was under siege, and since we know they were not traitors, then their search must have been more important than the defense of their land, and what they sought was surely a thing of the highest spiritual value." The king stopped on the path between the flower beds, and he said, "But none of my chaplains, nor nobody from the friary near by doth know of this Sangreal, Launcelot, and how holy can it be when the religious themselves are ignorant of it?"

"Well," said Sir Launcelot, " 'tis I believe no disrespect of the clerics to say that as no one can know all of God, there must inevitably be matters concerning Him the which not even those with a vocation are aware of."

"Can it be," said King Arthur, "that this Grail is a thing of meaning to knights peculairly? For, Launcelot, it would be an admirable ideal: to quest for that of which the precise nature were unknown, yet holy in the large. And unlike the case with other relics, which are oft the pretext for charlatanism, no fraudulence can here come into play, for the reason that not enough is known of the Sangreal to misrepresent it."

"But," said Sir Launcelot, "could not then some false rogue give the name Grail to any object, for how could we know it was not it?"

"Nay," said King Arthur, "for from the knights of old Leodegrance I have learned that the Grail be known only when it is seen, at which time it is unmistakable, indescribable, and ineffable."

"Yet none of these hath ever seen it?" asked Launcelot. "And one might therefore say, how could they know?"

"Indeed," said King Arthur, "yet if thou thinkest on this state of affairs, my dear Launcelot, thy conclusion might be mine, *videlicet*, that it is just the imprecision which maketh it likely. By which I mean our human incapability of apprehending certain truths is the greatest evidence that they are true."

And Sir Launcelot believed that while King Arthur had begun markedly to fail physically though he was not yet so very old, his mind had grown ever more expansive.

And he said now, "Sire, I doubt nothing with the name of Holy."

"Thou art alien to shame, Launcelot," said King Arthur. " 'Tis why I speak with thee of such matters."

But Sir Launcelot averted his face as if in modesty. "You do me too much honor, Sire," said he. "For I am not without great sin."

"Well," said King Arthur, "being all men, we are all sinners, Launcelot." And saying this he did himself look away, for he could never forget what he had done with Margawse his sister, and in his heart he believed that he deserved to be plagued by Morgan la Fey.

And looking down upon them from her window Guinevere lost her bitterness and she thought that both of these men were without joy, the greatest king in the world and the greatest knight. And she wondered, Is this because they are men, or because they are mine?

And each of these three great persons was utterly occupied with obsessions of self at this moment, for Launcelot could hardly restrain himself from confessing to King Arthur his loathsome sin against him and begging that he be put to death for it; and as for King Arthur, who believed Launcelot a blameless knight, he felt an almost irresistible urge to tell him of how he had fathered Mordred. Whereas Guinevere considered whether she should not enclose herself in a nunnery, for she had known no peace for ever so long.

Then King Arthur and Sir Launcelot returned to the castle, each with his own burden of heart, and they went unto the Round Table, where no other person was to be seen at the moment, and the great table was empty in the vast hall, and all the hundred and fifty seats around it as well. And each of these had the name of the knight whose place it was emblazoned in gold on its back. Except the one on the right hand of King Arthur's chair, the which was blank.

"Can it be," asked King Arthur now, "that the Siege Perilous hath some reference to this Holy Grail? For it is another unexplained matter. No one has sat upon it since Pellinore did so and burned his breech. But thou art my first knight, Launcelot, and without stain. Go and sit within that chair. Obviously it was made for thee. Would that I had thought of it before now, my friend."

But Sir Launcelot, who feared no man in the world, was afraid of this siege, and he would fain have avoided it, yet he could not refuse his king's request. Therefore as if going to the gibbet he approached it, and the sound of his boots scraping on the stones of the floor echoed throughout the hall, where all else was silent.

But as he reached towards the siege, for to move it away from the Table so that he might sit down, a great flame burst from it and he fell back from the heat.

Now King Arthur was amazed, saying, "If thou canst not sit there, then who can?"

Nor could Sir Launcelot answer him, except to say, "Perhaps it must ever remain empty, as a reminder of our imperfections as men. Is there any complete circle except in Heaven?"

"I know only what Merlin said," King Arthur told him. "And between us," said he putting a finger alongside his nose, "Merlin may have been a charlatan. Many years have passed since we last saw him, I am reminded. All current magic is done by that woman."

And Sir Launcelot looked at him curiously, and he said, "The Lady of the Lake?"

"The same," said King Arthur. "But I have never known what to make of her. Merlin, whatever his sleight of hand, was never so inscrutable. Tell me, Launcelot, art thou truly at ease with any female?"

"Sire, I am not," said Sir Launcelot.

"Dost understand them at all?" asked King Arthur.

And Launcelot said, "Nay, I do not."

"Ah," said King Arthur, "what man doth? Yet we are charged to defend them. And since the wars have ended we do little else." He drew his own siege away from the table and he sat thereupon and he put his face into his hands. "Launcelot, methinks it is time that I declare for the Round Table a general quest, so that, whilst never neglecting the particular pleas to which we have hitherto devoted ourselves (we shall continue to deliver distressed ladies and to fight evil men and kill monsters), we shall pursue the Holy Grail."

And Sir Launcelot said, "Then may I give precedence to this quest, and leave upon it immediately?"

Now King Arthur looked up at him, and he said, "But what of the protection of the queen?"

And Launcelot groaned within, but then a thought came unto him, and though he was not guileful, so distressed was he that God answered his prayer to be provided with a good argument. "I am her particular champion, truly. But are not all the knights of the Table charged generally with her protection and defense? And should they not each of them have the privilege to attend her some time, for what greater honor could a knight have?"

"Dost speak of a regular change of guard?" asked King Arthur. "So that each of the company might take his turn as her attendant?" And then he smiled. "Wert thou not the friend of mine heart, Launcelot, and the finest knight of all I should never have assigned thee to her. Yet this honor hath to thee been of little worth—nay, nay, do not protest! I take no offense! No man can be blamed for having his natural inclinations, but he is judged rather by how he acts upon them. And thou art impeccable, Launcelot."

And King Arthur pondered on this matter and then he said, "Very well, my friend, thou art hereby released from this obligation. I shall replace thee first with my nephew Sir Agravaine, for I know that he doth hold his queen and aunt in the highest reverence."

And the queen did not know that Launcelot had gone away until Sir Agravaine came to her and he bowed and he said, "My lady."

"And what, sir knight, may I do for thee?" asked Guinevere.

"I have been commanded by the king to guard you," said Sir Agravaine, "for Sir Launcelot hath gone away from Camelot absolutely."

Now Guinevere turned biting her rosy lip, and she said, "Gone away?"

And Sir Agravaine spoke in malicious satisfaction. "Perhaps never to return," said he. "For who knows where the Holy Grail might be found, if indeed it doth exist at all? But being the soul of piety Launcelot will look forever." Now he said this simply because he was pleased by Launcelot's departure, and he knew nothing of the love between him and the queen, and his envy was as yet directed only to Launcelot's superior prowess to his own.

"Well, Sir Agravaine," said Guinevere, "I require no personal guard. Therefore I would that thou apply thyself to thine other duties." And she went into her inner chamber, where she wept bitter tears, for only with the superficial part of her heart had she wished to see the last of Launcelot, whereas profoundly she wanted him always, for the sickness of love is such that the symptoms oft disguise the disease.

And now Sir Agravaine was more bitter than ever to have his hope so dashed, for in fantasy he had seen himself defending Guinevere against another Meliagrant and her falling into his arms upon the deliverance, and unlike his brothers Gawaine, Gaheris, and Gareth he had no high conception of honor (though never was he truly evil like his half-brother Mordred).

But as he had been commanded to guard Guinevere by King Arthur, Sir Agravaine determined to keep his post regardless of her wishes, but to do it discreetly, even secretly, and therefore he concealed himself.

Now Sir Launcelot had not got far from Camelot when he heard behind him a galloping horse, and he turned and saw Sir Gawaine, who rode in great haste.

And stopping him Launcelot asked, "My dear Gawaine, art thou joining me in the quest for the Holy Grail? How happy I am to have thy company!"

"Nay, Launcelot," said Sir Gawaine, whose face displayed great unhappiness, "I go rather to do my familial duty, for my father hath been killed."

And Sir Launcelot made grief for a while, and then he said, "Hath he died of natural cause, Gawaine, or by some felon's foul hand?"

"Neither," said Sir Gawaine. "But I do wish it had been either, for since all men must die, the losing of a life be not in itself a great pity, and he was an old man, Launcelot. But what is peculiarly unhappy here is that he was killed in an honest fight, and by a comrade of ours at the Round Table."

"O terrible unnatural news!" cried Launcelot.

" 'Twas Pellinore who did it," said Sir Gawaine. "And what happened was this: as thou knowest full well King Pellinore pursuing the Questing Beast did long ago lose himself from his own country, and so did he eventually join the company of the Round Table. Now lately he left Camelot once again to follow the Beast, reports concerning which had come from the north, and going there he found his country from the which he had mislaid himself long ago. But meanwhile my father King Lot of the Orkneys had come upon Pellinore's land whilst searching for my youngest brother Mordred, who had been carried away by a wyvern, and finding that it had no king, my father Lot did annex it to his own realm. But arriving there soon after, Pellinore did challenge King Lot, and they fought in individual combat, and my father so was killed."

Now these news did cause Launcelot to feel an awful sadness. "Come, dear friend," said he, "let us find a chapel and pray for all concerned, for the soul of thy father and for King Pellinore as well, for surely he never knew of thy relationship to King Lot."

"Nay," said Sir Gawaine firmly, "I can spare no time for such. I go without delay to avenge my father's death."

"O friend of my heart," said Sir Launcelot, "vengeance belongeth to God alone! Do not do this impious thing, I beg of thee! Pellinore is our comrade. When we of the Table fight one another, then our purpose is lost." And he did clutch at Gawaine's bridle with his gauntlet. "Nay, dear Gawaine, I can not suffer thee to do this! I know that when Pellinore doth discover it was thy father whom he killed he will be contrite and he will beg thy forgiveness as a Christian and a brother knight."

But Sir Gawaine pulled himself away, and he lifted his lance offering to place it in the rest, and he said, "Launcelot, dearest friend, do not I pray seek to stop me, else we, thou and I, shall fight, and if thou art my superior at arms then so be it, but I shall not hold until one of us is dead."

And Launcelot would not fight Gawaine, whom he loved, and therefore he asked God to bring him peace, and they went each his own way.

And when Sir Gawaine reached King Pellinore's land he told him what he had come for, and Pellinore said, "Yea, noble Gawaine, I expected thee to come as Lot's first son. Now believe me that I never knew he was thy father when we fought. Yet what difference could that knowledge have made when he had taken my land and would not return it to me as its lawful sovereign?"

"Surely that is true," said Sir Gawaine. "I do not seek to justify what my father did. But mine unalterable duty is to avenge his death. I bear thee—(Forgive me for the intimate speech: you are now again a ruling monarch, but I still cherish the memory of you as our old comrade!) I bear you no malice, King Pellinore, as man and as knight. I confess that in mine early days of envy I had little affection for you, but I came soon to hold you in the same love with which we are all united at the Table. Therefore, that we now be enemies is not a personal matter."

"I share thy feelings, gallant Gawaine," said King Pellinore, "and I hope that mine own sons will be as zealous as thee to defend their family. Now, my friend, let us go to fight to someone's death!"

And they shook each other by the hand, and they went to the field, and there they fought all afternoon, for Pellinore though not in his earliest youth was a knight of great prowess, but he was finally killed by Sir Gawaine, who thus avenged the death of his father King Lot.

Now Sir Gawaine was himself sore wounded by the powerful blows of King Pellinore, and he must needs recover from them, and so he did in the course of some months, being nursed at the Convent of the Little Sisters of Poverty and Pain, and then he returned to Camelot.

And when King Arthur heard of the fight between Gawaine and King Pellinore he knew great sorrow. And then he became wrathful in the extreme.

"Nephew Gawaine!" cried he in a thunderous voice. "Thou of all knights! Then the Table Round doth mean nothing to thee! I had believed that this old savagery of blood-feud were gone forever from Britain. But beyond that, he who joineth the Table doth forsake all other obligations. When thou didst join its company, thou didst leave the base world where such wickednesses as revenge are practiced."

And King Arthur did shake with fury. "Was it not Our Lord who said we should forgive our enemies? Worse, Pellinore was not thine enemy but thy comrade and thy friend!"

"Uncle," said Gawaine, full of shame, "I submit myself to your correction."

"Yet art thou truly submissive to God?" asked King Arthur. "And Pellinore hath some sons who joined the Table, as thou knowest, and what of the first of those, Sir Lamorak? Shall he seek revenge from thee? And if thou dost slay him, then shalt thou fight the others in succession?"

"Yet, Uncle, King Lot was my father. And can a son be excused from his duty towards his parents?"

"Hast killing Pellinore, who was a good man, brought back King Lot?" asked King Arthur. "And further," said he drawing Excalibur from its scabbard and standing erect, "thy father was not so good a man, Gawaine. Now I have said it! Come defend thy family!" And he smote his nephew with the flat of his sword and he shamed him. "Have at thee! Thy father was a caitiff and a traitor. Scarcely had I assumed the throne when he brought an host to destroy me. And this Camelot where we are now was then Cameliard, of which thine aunt Guinevere was princess, and thy father besieged this castle for many weeks, and he would have taken it had I not come to drive him away. This is the man whose death thou wouldst avenge?"

And again King Arthur smote Gawaine with the flat of his blade. "Draw, Nephew! For I have determined to end this feud before it can go farther. Thy king and uncle will serve as champion of Pellinore's family. Now draw, else I shall cut thee down mercilessly where thou dost stand!"

"Sire," said Sir Gawaine, unfastening his sword belt and throwing it from him, and then he knelt before King Arthur and he exposed his neck. "I shall not stand against my king! Take mine head, for I know I have done wrong."

And Arthur stared down upon him for a long while, and then tears came from his eyes, and he laid Excalibur on the seat of his throne and he took Sir Gawaine by the arms and drew him to his feet, and he embraced him.

"Forgive me for insulting thy father's memory, dear Gawaine," said King Arthur. " 'Twas not personal, but rather in the interests of a principle. And I shall do the same with Sir Lamorak when he returns from his current quest."

And Sir Gawaine reflected that since the death of Elaine the maid of Astolat he who had been once the most personal of knights had become himself almost altogether only an abstraction.

Now at that point a weeping lady did apply at the castle and ask to be admitted to the presence of King Arthur, and she was so brought in.

And King Arthur, who was still shaken by his conversation with Gawaine, had little patience with her. "Lady," said he, "I can not hear thee for thy sobbing."

"Well," said she seeking to dry her eyes, "I am in the greatest distress, for mine husband and lord hath been overcome by an evil knight and he is being held prisoner in our castle."

"Then be of some cheer," said King Arthur, "for such matters are those in which we of the Table Round have a peculiar strength."

"Uncle, I shall leave at once," said Sir Gawaine, and he went to fetch the sword and the belt which he had discarded.

But the lady said, "I have not yet told you the whole of it, Sire, and I am afraid that Sir Gawaine nor any of your other knights can not answer the need. For 'tis you alone whom this wicked man hath challenged, and only for that reason did he allow me to travel here unmolested. 'Unless King Arthur come out of Camelot to meet me in single combat, he hath proved himself the basest of cowards in the world,' so saith this felonious knight."

But buckling on his belt Sir Gawaine said, "Uncle, I would that you disregard this challenge, the which could not have been made except by either a mad fellow (in which case be it not worth noticing) or some knight who hath a weird and devilish power by which he purposes to enthrall you criminally. I shall go in your stead, for in truth my existence is not essential to the Round Table, nor indeed to myself."

"Gawaine," said King Arthur, "do not anger me again. For one, thou art no less precious to God than I, and for another I love thee as nephew and as knight. But further, how may I of all persons turn away from a personal challenge? In the degree to which this felon doth the Devil's work, then I as God's anointed monarch must meet him with the sword which is invincible in the service of virtue."

And the king took up what he believed to be Excalibur, which he had laid down earlier onto the throne, but it was not his own sword now, for a vile dwarf had spirited himself secretly into the room whilst King Arthur had his impassioned colloquy with Sir Gawaine, and this dwarf had exchanged Excalibur for a counterfeit sword. For this dwarf was in the service of Morgan la Fey, and he had been sent to watch for a moment when the king let the magic weapon leave his hands.

"Then at least you will permit me to accompany you, Uncle?" asked Sir Gawaine now, "for I do not like what I have heard about this matter."

"Very well," said King Arthur. "But I want thy pledge, dear Gawaine, that thou shalt do nothing unless I am offered foul play." And Gawaine gave his pledge, and they set out with this lady to find the castle where her husband was held captive by the evil knight.

Now meanwhile the detestable dwarf who served Morgan la Fey had taken Excalibur to this wicked knight, whose name was Sir Gromer Somir Joure, and he was armed with it when King Arthur and Sir Gawaine and the lady came to the castle.

Now when the king demanded entrance to this place, Sir Gromer Somir Joure had the drawbridge lowered and he came riding slowly across it.

"Well," said he when he came unto the king, "shall we fight then?" And he was so insolent that Sir Gawaine could not endure him, and therefore Gawaine drew his sword and he would have set upon him to punish his contumaciousness had not King Arthur stayed his nephew's arm.

"Gawaine," said Arthur, "I shall not remind thee twice of thy pledge."

And Sir Gromer Somir Joure did sneer vilely at this speech, and then he made great insult to Gawaine, for to bait him into breaking his pledge, and he said, "Thou art

Gawaine, the notable eunuch of Camelot?" And he laughed vilely.

Yet Sir Gawaine would not break his word, and he suffered the evil knight to say this with impunity.

"Sir Gromer Somir Joure," said King Arthur, who had been told his name by the lady, "unless thou givest me some excuse for what thou hast done here I shall put thee to the sword."

"Which sword?" asked the evil knight.

And King Arthur drew from his scabbard that which he believed was Excalibur, but when he raised it the blade wilted and dropped like unto the lash of a whip.

And then Sir Gromer Somir Joure drew the genuine Excalibur, and he pointed it at King Arthur. But now Sir Gawaine drew his own sword and he sought to interpose himself between the king and the wicked knight.

"Gawaine," commanded King Arthur, "prithee move aside, for as yet I can not be sure this is foul play, for I have not been touched."

And Sir Gawaine must needs obey his king's command, and therefore he did as ordered, but he marveled at King Arthur's adherence to the letter even when his life was in imminent danger.

"Now," said King Arthur to Sir Gromer Somir Joure, "is it thine intent to compound thy felonies by smiting me with mine own sword?"

"King Arthur," said this felonious knight, "armed as I am, I might do anything I would, but as it happens I shall offer you no harm at this moment. For my purpose be not to slay you, but rather to humiliate you, the which, you will agree, is far more deleterious to a king of the greatest worship."

And King Arthur replied in his habitual dignity, "And how wouldst thou do this, sir?"

"By putting to you a question that is unanswerable," said Sir Gromer Somir Joure. "But so as to give it the appearance of justice, I shall give you one full year in which to seek an answer to this question."

"Unanswerable, sayest thou?" asked King Arthur. "Then however long I seek it, it doth not exist?"

"Well," said Sir Gromer Somir Joure, "in saying that I anticipate with malicious glee. There *is* an answer, but you shall never find it though it be before your eyes."

"And if I return in one year with the correct answer, what then?" asked King Arthur.

"In that unlikely event," said the wicked knight, "I pledge that I shall return Excalibur to you and you may deal with me as you will. But if your answer is wrong, you shall be at my mercy, and be assured that I have none."

Now again Sir Gawaine tried to ride between them, but King Arthur kept him away, saying, "Excalibur is invincible, Gawaine, and hath no conscience in its heart of steel. Thy suicide, nor mine, would serve no cause but folly."

Then the king turned to Sir Gromer Somir Joure and he said, "Very well, sir knight, give me this question."

And that knight smiled evilly, and he said, "It is as follows: *What do women most desire in this world?*"

And King Arthur marveled that the question was such a simple one, and he turned to put it to the lady who had led him and Sir Gawaine to this place, but she was gone. And he did not know that she had been Morgan la Fey in disguise, and that she had lured him here with a ruse. And Sir Gromer Somir Joure was but another knight who was the instrument of her wicked will, for she had used her beauty to deprive him of all honor.

Now King Arthur and Sir Gawaine rode back towards Camelot, and the king said, "Gawaine, there is something strange about this adventure, for I can not think that any evil person possessing Excalibur would surrender so easily. This question will be simply answered by the first woman I put it to. We may find some female before we reach the castle. If not, then Guinevere can answer it straightway, and I shall go immediately to find Sir Gromer Somir Joure and reclaim my sword."

"Uncle," said Sir Gawaine, "I once had considerable traffic with women, as is well known to all, and I tell you this: that I can not answer this question. Further, I gravely doubt that we shall find a woman who will answer it."

"Yea," said King Arthur, "that a woman doth not know her mind is an established truth."

"With all respect," said Sir Gawaine, " 'tis not so much that they do not know it, methinks, but rather that they would not tell it to a man. For why should they and so lose their greatest weapon?"

And King Arthur was not pleased with what Sir Gawaine had said, for he believed that he was jesting frivolously, and he said with impatience, "I purpose to spend no longer time upon this matter. Tis a grave thing to be deprived of Excalibur for such a foolish want."

And contrarily Sir Gawaine said, " 'Twas surely stolen whilst you were distracted by my recent failing, Uncle. Pray allow me to recover it by mine own means."

And King Arthur had not yet thought of how the sword had been taken and given to Sir Gromer Somir Joure, but now he realized that it must have been through the hateful devices of his sister Morgan la Fey, and he could not tell Gawaine of this, for she was his aunt. And he regretted that Sir Launcelot had gone from Camelot, for he was the ideal confidant, and the king mistakenly believed that Launcelot could answer the question about women.

"Thou canst render me great service," the king now said to his nephew. "Go and find Launcelot, and bring him back to me."

Therefore Sir Gawaine rode away on this mission and King Arthur returned to Camelot alone. And when he arrived there he went to Guinevere and he asked her the question put to him by Sir Gromer Somir Joure.

Now what Guinevere herself most desired was the return of Sir Launcelot, as it had been earlier his departure for which she most had wished. Therefore she said to King Arthur, "My lord, what a woman desireth most is not the same from one time to another."

Now to King Arthur this seemed to confirm his belief that no woman knew her own mind, for he was a man and did seek to find an universal principle for all things, which is to say, a fixity, an arresting of time; whereas it can be seen that Guinevere did speak from a female sense of fluidity (for women, like the sea, do know the tides, and their phases are no more capricious than those of the moon).

And next King Arthur sent for all the ladies of the court, and he asked them all the same question. And then he spake also with the women of the lower orders, even unto the wives and daughters of serfs. But never did he get an answer the which he believed satisfactory, for either all these women answered much as had Guinevere, or else they said that which King Arthur was shrewd enough to know was designed to please him as man and as sovereign, *exempli gratia:* "To obey their husbands, Sire! . . . To serve their king. . . . To care for men," &tc., &tc.

And though King Arthur believed that these were indeed the duties of women, given them by God, and that all British females performed them impeccably, yet he suspected that these truths were partial, for all women did descend from Eve who ate the proscribed fruit and so introduced the first shame into the world.

And then he did have nuns brought to him, to answer this question, and their answers were pious. And from Ireland and Germany and France he sent for strumpets (for he believed Britain to be clean of whores, whereas they were numberless in these lands), and to these drabs he asked the question, *What do women most desire in this world?* But their answers did not differ from those of honest women, and were not even to be distinguished much from those of the nuns and this amazed King Arthur, who thought them to be in the service of the Devil. (Nor were these harlots so vain as some of the ladies of Camelot, and they were dressed more modestly than most.)

Now all this questioning took a long time, and half the year was gone before King Arthur could find no more women to inquire of. And then having received no good answer he did purpose to find one from men.

Therefore he asked all of his knights who were at Camelot, and all the barons as well as the boors of Britain this same question, and he sent couriers with it to all the realms on earth, even unto the swarthy men in Afric and the yellow-skinned men who live on the edge of the world, and the men whose heads do grow beneath their shoulders and those with the hindquarters of goats and those who were so barbarous as to go about with their privities obscenely exposed as well as those in the towns who were so refined as to have become sodomites.

And though their answers were in many different languages, what all these men said that women most desired was *to be desirable to men.*

And though King Arthur believed that this was nearer the truth than what any of the women had told him, he thought it was not yet the correct answer. And he was in despair, for finally the year he had been given by Sir Gromer Somir Joure in which to find the answer had all but been exhausted without success, and it seemed as though he must soon go and be at the mercy of that evil knight who had none.

Now meanwhile Sir Gawaine had been seeking Sir Launcelot, who himself was looking for the Holy Grail and not knowing where to look had ridden aimlessly out of Camelot and very soon he found himself in a place no one of the Round Table had ever seen before, for this was easy to do in that time when the laws of geography were lenient. And Sir Gawaine could not find his friend, no matter where he looked, and he went all over Britain and he did discover no trace of Sir Launcelot.

And finally the entire year had passed during which King Arthur must needs find the answer to the question of Sir Gromer Somir Joure, and Gawaine returned to Camelot empty-handed. But then neither had he believed that Launcelot of all people could answer the question of what women wanted, for he had proved greatly ineffective in the matter of Elaine of Astolat, nor so far as Gawaine knew had Launcelot had ought to do with any woman his life long.

Now when Sir Gawaine reached King Arthur and told

him he could not find Launcelot anywhere, the king was sorry to hear these news.

But he said nobly, "Then I shall go to Sir Gromer Somir Joure with the answers I have collected, though methinks that none will satisfy him, not those of the women I have interrogated nor that of the men. But I have no other."

"Then, Uncle," said Sir Gawaine, "let me be your emissary in this matter. For this wicked knight will surely seek to do you great damage if you can not supply the correct answer. Whereas if it is I who confront him, what he does will be of no fundamental harm to the realm."

"Gawaine," said King Arthur, "I have given him my word. Now, my death could never be so damaging to what we believe in as the breaking of my pledge. All vows are made ultimately with God, even though His instrument be an evil man. I should be happy to die in honesty if the alternative were to live by means of deceit."

"Yet," said Sir Gawaine, "all this misfortune hath come about only because of the foul crime by which your sword was stolen. Hath a virtuous man no defense against criminality?"

"Twice hath my sword been stolen lately," said King Arthur. "To be sure, these thefts were wicked in the extreme. But were they not possible only because of mine inattention? And why was I inattentive? Because I arrogantly believed that all evil had been eradicated from Britain. If now I am killed by Sir Gromer Somir Joure, then it would be but a deservèd punishment for my pride, dear Gawaine."

And he prepared to go to his fell appointment, for the time was at hand.

But Sir Gawaine begged at least to ride in accompaniment with him, the which plea King Arthur granted, on condition that he not lift his sword to defend him.

Then they left Camelot together, and they had ridden to within a league of the castle held by Sir Gromer Somir Joure, and they reached a crossroads where was standing an ancient hag, and the closer they came to her, the more loathsome did she seem in figure, and her face was turned away. And when they arrived near her, and she turned and looked at them, she was so ugly that their horses shied from her.

For her nose was long and red as a carrot, and matter did run from her eyes, and her teeth were green as moss and her skin was purple, and her hair was like nothing so much as a thornbush. And foul as she looked, her stench was even worse.

And she did smile horribly and she said, "Hail, King Arthur and Sir Gawaine," and she raised in salute an hand like unto the claw of a cockatrice.

Now notwithstanding her loathly appearance, until proved otherwise she was a loyal subject of the realm, and therefore the king and Sir Gawaine returned her courteous greeting.

"I know where and why you go, King Arthur," then cried this hag. "And unless you can supply the correct answer to the question, you shall be a grave king indeed."

And Sir Gawaine clasped the hilt of his sword, for she was so vile-looking he believed her to be some felon in disguise, and he asked, "Dost jeer at thy king?"

But knowing no fear she cackled in shrill laughter, and she said, "Gawaine, remember how once you did kill a woman by mistake!" And Sir Gawaine was shamed, and he withdrew his hand from the sword.

"Well, lady," said King Arthur politely, "this is true enough. But if thou dost gloat over it, thou canst hardly be a virtuous dame."

"Do not mistake me, King Arthur," cried the hag. "It is I who can uniquely provide your deliverance, for I possess the true answer to the question of Sir Gromer Somir Joure."

"Then speak it," said Sir Gawaine, "for the love of God."

But King Arthur chided him. "I will accept no aid that is begged blasphemously," said he. And to the hag King Arthur said, "Lady, methinks thou hast some condition to providing this answer, else thou shouldst have given it me without ado."

"Indeed that is so," said the repulsive crone, and Arthur and Gawaine had all they could do to keep their horses quiet, for even those beasts did find her aspect obnoxious and they strained at their bits. "In exchange for receiving this answer, the which will save your life, you must pledge to marry me."

"Well," said King Arthur, "that I can not do, for the reason that I am married already."

"Which is no secret to anyone in the world," said Sir Gawaine, and again he clasped the hilt of his sword. "Uncle, methinks there be some treachery here."

And then the hag shrieked in the vilest laughter that they had ever heard, and the foul exhalations of her breath turned the green grass to brown on the meadow near by. "Gawaine," said she then, "remember your obligation to all women: that they be beautiful and desirable were no condition of it."

"That is true," said Sir Gawaine. "Lady, what would you of me?"

And the hideous crone did smile showing her teeth which were covered with slime, and there was a running sore in her ear, and her figure within the robe of filthy rags was as that of a blasted tree on a moor, and in her hair were the nests of many spiders.

And she asked Sir Gawaine this question: "Would you save your king?"

"With all mine heart," said Gawaine.

"Then I ask no less," said the hag. "I will give to King Arthur the answer to the question of Sir Gromer Somir Joure, if in return you shall marry me."

And holding his breath, so great was her stench, Sir Gawaine said, "Then I agree, lady."

"Nay, Nephew," said King Arthur. "I can not allow you to do this."

"Uncle," said Sir Gawaine, "you have forbidden me to help you otherwise in this matter, and I could not defy your command, but it is mine own affair if I choose to bargain with this lady." And to the hag he said, "I have accepted your proposal. And now tell us the answer to this question."

And therefore she did, and then she asked when Sir Gawaine would marry her, and she seemed to grow even more ugly by the minute.

"We shall go now to the felonious Sir Gromer Somir Joure," said Gawaine, "and if the answer you have provided be the correct one, and Excalibur is returned to King Arthur, then come to Camelot a fortnight hence and I shall marry you as promised."

"Then I have your word as knight of the Round Table!" cried the hag.

"Indeed," said Sir Gawaine, and then he said to King Arthur, "Uncle, come let us hie. Excalibur hath been gone too long from you."

Now as they rode King Arthur said, "Gawaine, I thank thee for this sacrifice. Long have I wished thou wouldst marry, but never in this fashion, thou who couldst have had the most beautiful maid in Britain."

But Sir Gawaine made an effort towards good cheer. " 'Tis little enough, Uncle, and perhaps God would have me atone for mine old ways, when comeliness was all I sought in a woman. No doubt this mine intended wife hath a strength of soul, a richness of spirit, for doth not God distribute human gifts so as to maintain a balance in the world?"

"Surely she is virtuous," said King Arthur, "and her wisdom must be remarkable, for she hath given us the answer to this question."

"Well," said Sir Gawaine, "let us determine whether it is indeed the correct one."

And soon they reached the castle which Sir Gromer Somir Joure seemed to hold illegally (though we know that it actually belonged to Morgan la Fey and she had installed him there).

Now the wicked knight awaited them in the middle of the drawbridge, and he held Excalibur across his saddle.

"Hail, royal Arthur and noble Gawaine!" said he. "The

time for answering the question is come at last. And if you have not the correct answer, King Arthur, then I shall strike off your head so that it will tumble into the moat and feed the serpents who live there." And to stir their appetites he now flung a piece of meat into the water below and it soon boiled with writhing reptiles which had red eyes and yellow fangs.

Now there was nothing in the world more loathly to King Arthur than serpents, for they had figured in the nightmare he had suffered after bedding with his sister Margawse. And his other sister Morgan la Fey had divined this through her art of nigromancy, and she had put these snakes into the moat for just that reason.

"Then put thy question, sir knight," said King Arthur, "and I shall try to answer it."

"What do women most desire in the world?" asked Sir Gromer Somir Joure.

But King Arthur would not first give the answer provided by the hag, because if he did not use it, then Gawaine would not be forced to marry the repulsive creature. Rather he began by repeating the divers answers he had got from women, "To obey their husbands . . . to care for men," &tc., and then he gave the answer he had got from male persons, "To be desirable to men," but at each of the answers the wicked knight shook his head and he raised Excalibur ever higher, until finally it was high as he could lift it.

And then Sir Gromer Somir Joure said, "King Arthur, you may give but one more answer, and if it is as wrong as these (and I expect it to be) your head will feed the serpents. Therefore I ask you to remove your crown and give it me."

And notwithstanding that he should have to marry the loathsome hag, Sir Gawaine prayed that her answer be the correct one.

"Nay, caitiff, do not be precipitate," said King Arthur. "I shall keep my crown so long as I am king of Britain, even if that be for but one moment more. Now, repeat thy question."

"What do women most desire in this world?" cried Sir Gromer Somir Joure, this knight who might have been a fine man had not his detestable lust caused him to surrender to Morgan la Fey his self-command.

And King Arthur gave the answer which the hag had given him in exchange for Sir Gawaine's promise to wed her: "What women most desire in this world is . . . *to rule over men."*

And with a terrible howl of chagrin Sir Gromer Somir Joure dropped Excalibur onto the drawbridge and he toppled from his saddle into the moat, where there was a terrible seething of the surface as the serpents tore all the flesh from his bones and the water turned bright red from his blood.

Then King Arthur took up his sword and he and Sir Gawaine voided this pestilent place.

"Well, dear Gawaine," said King Arthur when they had ridden for several leagues, "thou hast delivered Excalibur and preserved me, and I am most grateful to thee."

"Any knight would have done the same," said Gawaine.

Now when they reached Camelot the preparations for the wedding were begun, and they were lavish. And all the knights were curious to know who it was that Sir Gawaine was going to marry, but he did not tell them, nor did King Arthur.

And Guinevere, who had fallen ill for want of Sir Launcelot, of whom nothing had been heard in ever so long, determined to be well enough to attend Gawaine's wedding, for so fond of him was she. And she summoned him to her and she asked whom he was to wed.

"Madam," said he, "with all respect, I would not tell you now, so that you might be surprised at the appropriate time."

"Then very well, dear Gawaine," said the queen. "No doubt thy reason for this secrecy will appear in the sequel and thy bride shall amaze us with her beauty and her grace." And then her sweet smile did take on another character, and she said, "Alas for thee that thy dear friend

Launcelot is not at Camelot now! But perhaps he shall come home in time for the nuptials?"

"Nothing could please me more," said Sir Gawaine. "But I did search for him throughout the realm for an whole year. Were he not the invincible knight we know him for, I should fear he had been killed."

And Guinevere did shudder, saying, "Yet he is not immune to treachery."

"Let us rather think that he hath gone again to some monastery," said Sir Gawaine, "and there, secretly immured, doth spend his days in pious exercise."

But to Guinevere this was first a worse thought than if he had been killed, but next she knew an horrid guilt for having had the first thought.

Now the day of Sir Gawaine's wedding did come, like all anticipated misfortunes, soon enough. And all hope that the bride would not appear were dashed when the hag came a-riding into Camelot on a donkey that was the ugliest beast in the world, and it was lame and covered with sores. And the guards upon the gate sought to turn her away, for it was not seemly that such a pestilent-looking creature be admitted to the castle on such a festive day.

But King Arthur was waiting to escort her, and he gave her gracious welcome and he conducted her to the chapel.

And there Sir Gawaine in a handsome costume of fur and silk awaited her, and he bowed to this loathsome crone who wore a wedding gown of some mean stuff, which had not been white in many years, and it was tattered as well, and her shoes were covered with mire, and her veil was so torn that her hideous face, with its bursting boils, was hardly covered at all.

"Lady," said Sir Gawaine, "as you can see, I am prepared to keep my promise, for the answer you supplied was the right one, and I am grateful to you for saving King Arthur's life."

"Then, handsome Gawaine," said the hag, "mine husband to be, let us proceed in all haste, for I long to share thy bed!"

And then, her claw upon his arm, King Arthur conducted her to the altar, whilst Sir Gawaine was accompanied by his brother Sir Agravaine, who had known nothing of the hag until he saw her, and when he did he believed that Gawaine had lost his reason.

And all the knights and ladies there assembled did marvel at the sight of the hideous bride, and they could not believe what they saw, and therefore they would have murmured amongst themselves, but King Arthur silenced them with his stern countenance. And Guinevere believed that want of Launcelot had made her so ill that she had been affected in her brain.

Now the ceremony was conducted by the chief of the chaplains of Camelot, and you can be sure that he lost no time in completing it, for the stench of the bride was even more obnoxious than her appearance. And when he was done and he told Sir Gawaine, as he was obliged to do, that the husband should now kiss the wife, never had there been such an awesome silence, except for the gasps of the many ladies who fainted dead away (and a deal of these had first been made of women of, from girls, by Sir Gawaine in his robust days, and without exception they loved him yet).

Now Gawaine turned discreetly away for to take one deep breath, and then he turned back to kiss his abominable bride. And with her yellow talons she did lift her torn and filthy veil with all the dead flies in it . . .

But when her face was fully exposed her skin was white and flawless, and more delicate than sendal, and her eyes were the bluest of gems and her hair was the color of spun gold. And now a sweet perfume came from her, like unto that borne by a spring breeze which hath come through an orchard in blossom. And her rags were magically transformed as well, and now her loveliest of figures was clothed in white lace fine as a cobweb and it was trimmed with perfect pearls!

And when he kissed her Sir Gawaine pressed his mouth against the softest and the sweetest lips he had ever tasted, and they were the color of the most delicate rose, and no diamond was so perfect and white as her teeth.

And now the entire assemblage could gasp as one, in joy, and you can be sure that they did, for they all loved Sir Gawaine. Nor was anyone (except Gawaine himself) so happy as King Arthur!

"Well, lady," said Sir Gawaine when he had finished kissing her, "this is some change."

"Yea, and it is not an illusion," said his bride, whose name was Ragnell. "For this is my proper aspect, as the other was altogether false, and I was condemned to show ugliness to the world by a wicked queen who cast a spell upon me. Nor could this enchantment be altered in any way until one of King Arthur's knights would take me in marriage."

"Then," said Sir Gawaine, "how fortunate it was for both of us that this happened as it did!" And he displayed the greatest feelings of bliss.

"Thou hast nobly kept thy promise," said Ragnell, "but I fear that thou hast been rewarded but by half. For even though I am married, I must yet assume the beastly guise at times—indeed, I am sorry to say, for half the time, dear Gawaine! And now thou must choose whether this is to be by day or by night."

And so was Gawaine plunged into half-despair, and he asked, "Whether day or night?"

"Think carefully of the consequences," said Ragnell. "If I am loathsome by day, then I shall be an obnoxious sight to all at Camelot, shaming thee before thy friends, but at night I shall be beautiful for thee to hold me in thine arms. But reversing this, if I am comely throughout the day I shall bring thee much honor in court, yet in the nights I shall be so foul as to sicken thee when we are chambered together."

And they stood yet before the altar, and all the persons gathered in the chapel wondered at their delay in going to the wedding feast.

Now Sir Gawaine pondered on this matter, and then he said, "My dear sweet Ragnell, when thou art plain I shall not forget that thou wert beautiful not long before and that it will never be long before thou are beautiful once more."

And Ragnell was overjoyed to hear him say this, for another kind of man, less noble than Sir Gawaine, would instead have brooded always, even when beauty was present, on the ugliness to come (and life in general is always half of each).

And she said, "Dearest Gawaine, I love thee with all mine heart. Nevertheless I am obliged to ask thee to make a choice. Forgetting the ugliness, then when wouldst thou see the beauty, by day or by night?"

"Love of my life," said Gawaine, embracing her, "this can never be mine own decision, for thou art not an object which I possess like unto a suit of armor. Thou art one of God's creatures, and in all fundamental matters thou must answer only to Him. This choice therefore must be thine alone."

And Ragnell did cry joyfully, "Gawaine, mine own dear love! Hereby thou hast broken the curse altogether!"

And Sir Gawaine's heart did rise though as yet he did not understand this matter, and seeing his puzzlement Ragnell was in haste to explain.

"I shall never again be ugly at any time," said she, "but I shall be beautiful for thee always. For it was the condition of the wicked enchantment that had been put upon me that, first, I should be hideous at all times until a knight of King Arthur would wed me regardless, and that thou didst. But then I should be ugly half the day, the which half would be chosen by mine husband as my lord and master. But thou, dearest Gawaine, hath refused to use that power over me. And in allowing me mine own choice, thou hast liberated me in more ways than one. No free will can be held in the captivity of any enchantment, and no woman can be ugly who retaineth the mastery of herself."

And Sir Gawaine was overjoyed in his amazement, for he did not see that as a reformed lecher he could have done otherwise than he had!

And King Arthur had grown impatient to begin the wedding feast whilst Gawaine and his bride had been talking privately, and now he came and he took them each on a royal arm and so he walked with them to a dining hall, which was in another place than the Round Table (to which women were not admitted).

And the king gave them many costly gifts, and Sir Kay had had the bakers prepare a great cake which was twenty feet across and surmounted by the figures of a knight and a lady cunningly fashioned from spun sugar and as large as life. And great cheer was made that day by all the company at Camelot, and even Guinevere almost forgot her anguish.

And when they prepared for bed that night Sir Gawaine said to the fair Ragnell, who had in his eyes ever increased in beauty, "And who was the evil queen who put the terrible spell upon thee? For her name should be known to all, so that all may be on guard against her."

"Morgan la Fey," said his lovely bride, who did not know of his relationship to her.

"Ah," said Sir Gawaine, "then we must never make it public, for alas! she is the sister of King Arthur."

BOOK XV

*How Sir Tristram was married to Isold of the
White Hands; and of what happened then.*

Now Sir Launcelot had wandered far from Camelot, and
he had fought many knights, defeating them every one,
and if they were decent men who challenged him merely
to test their prowess he unhorsed them only and then he
shook their hands. But if they were wicked knights who
oppressed the weak and mishandled fair ladies, he killed
them without regret unless they gave him their pledge to
reform. And these latter he sent to King Arthur, for those
who had once served evil were all the more ardent in the
cause of virtue.

And Sir Launcelot asked everywhere he went for the
Holy Grail, but none had heard of it in no place, and at
the monasteries he was told by the good brothers that no
such thing existed, and instead they showed him the relics
they possessed, the shinbone of one saint or the petrified
toe of another.

And if he stayed the night in a monkish cell Launcelot
was wont to whip himself with a scourge till dawn, for
only then did he forget for a while his great sin with
Guinevere, which tormented him worse the longer he was
away from Camelot, for the reason that he desired her
more. And what was so terrible about the lust of Sir
Launcelot was that it was for one woman alone in all the

world, and no maid however beautiful could stir him, as we have seen in the case of the unhappy Elaine of Astolat.

Now one morning Sir Launcelot rode over an hill just as another knight came over the next hill, and on seeing him this other knight fewtered his lance, and therefore in self-defense Launcelot did the same, assuming that only a wicked man would attack him on sight, and each galloped down his own slope, and when they met in the valley below it was with a great shock. And though the other knight was thrown from his saddle by Sir Launcelot's attack, so was the latter unhorsed as well. And never had Sir Launcelot met a knight with this prowess, the which seemed quite as great as his own, and when they fought with their swords this other knight gave Launcelot blow for blow.

But Sir Launcelot was happy to have found an opponent so worthy at arms, and like his own this knight's shield was blank, so that he could not identify him. And they proceeded to fight all the day, and neither asked for a respite, and even the great Launcelot would have been exhausted but for the example of the other. (And this was the reason why one fine knight loved to fight another as good as himself, for it evoked his own best.)

And after many hours neither of them was hurt, so effective was each in countering the other's blows. But finally Sir Launcelot smote the other knight so violently upon the helmet as to rip it away from its lacings and turn it so that he could not see through the slits of the visor.

Now Sir Launcelot did call a halt and he lowered his sword, so that the other could adjust his helm.

And his opponent opened his visor then, saying, "You are a knight of much courtesy, sir, and can not therefore be the caitiff I took you for."

And it was none other than Sir Tristram!

"My dear friend," said Sir Launcelot removing his own helmet, and the two knights made much joy on seeing each other.

"Well," said Sir Tristram smiling, "how fortunate that

mine helmet came undone, for I could not have endured many more blows from the incomparable Launcelot."

"On the contrary," said Sir Launcelot, "I should soon have had to surrender to thee had not this happy accident occurred. I am amazed that I was able to endure so long against the great Tristram!"

And so they did exchange the typical expressions of modesty.

"Alas that we did fight at all in this fashion," said Tristram. "But I mistook thee for a very evil lord who hath ravaged the countryside hereabout."

And Sir Launcelot said, "Like me thou dost carry a shield with no device."

And Sir Tristram looked at the ground and he said sadly, "But for another reason." And then he looked into Launcelot's eyes, and he said, "Let us sit down here under this tree, my friend, and rest from our ordeal."

And they removed their heavy plate-armor and sat down in their chain mail, and their horses cropped the new grass in the meadow, and there were primroses near by, for it was spring again. And Sir Launcelot had been away from Camelot for half a year.

"Tell me, Tristram, hast news of the court?" he asked.

"Nay," said Sir Tristram. "I have not been there in ever so long. I like not the life in courts. In saying the which I mean no disrespect to that of Camelot, certes, but any court doth remind me only of that in which I knew mine only happiness. And that happiness was adulterous and wrong, Launcelot! And I should rather be happy that it hath come to an end, but I have a wicked heart, my friend, and it doth continue to bleed—to the degree that I wish thou hadst killed me awhile ago." And putting his face into his hands he wept copiously.

And Sir Launcelot made grief with his friend, for he did pity him and he had his own sorrow as well.

Then he said to Sir Tristram, "Well, happiness must wait for Heaven."

"But if I can not be with Isold on earth," said Sir Tristram, "I could scarcely meet her in Heaven."

"My friend," said Sir Launcelot, "thou shalt not desire there to be with her in the same fashion as here, and ye both will know nothing but the love of God."

"Then I am afraid I would rather go to Hell, Launcelot," Sir Tristram cried, "for there will never come a time when I do not love Isold!"

And Sir Launcelot shuddered at this impiety, but never did he chide Sir Tristram for it, for he understood that his friend could not feel otherwise, and Sir Tristram was a knight of the greatest worship and he would abstain from evil if he were able, and indeed he had acted with virtue in leaving Cornwall. What more could he have done? Yet he was miserable.

But Launcelot determined to think no more on this hopeless matter, for he was a Christian, and therefore he rose and he said to Sir Tristram, "Come, my friend, and join me in the quest for the Sangreal."

"And what is that?" asked Sir Tristram. "Is it some errand for the queen?"

Now Launcelot did stare at him briefly, but in the face of honest Tristram he could detect no malice. "Nay, my friend," Launcelot said then, "King Arthur hath relieved me as her constant guard. 'Tis an holy thing which I pursue."

And Tristram said, "In my state of soul I should repel it, methinks. Nay, regretfully and gratefully I must decline this honor, than which there can be no greater than to accompany the devout Launcelot on a religious quest. Thou art without stain, my noble friend, whereas I am eternally besmirched. I go now to a secular task, the which I have long neglected: the liberation of my native land, Lyonesse, from the tyrants who have ruled it since my father's death."

And Sir Launcelot did writhe in guilt when he heard Tristram's belief in his purity, and he embraced him. And he said, "My friend, I have a feeling that we have met for the last time on earth. Thou art the bravest man I have ever known, and the finest, as I am the greatest coward and the worst sinner." And then before Tristram could reply to this curious speech Launcelot taking up his armor piled it before him on his saddle and he rode swiftly away.

And thereupon began the period in which Sir Launcelot behaved like a madman according to the old scribes, and he lived as an animal in the forests, half-naked and hairy, and some hunting parties seeing him discharged arrows at him thinking him a beast of prey. And he ate roots and worms, and he slept in caves.

And in this condition we leave him for a while, for his ways were indescribably stranger.

Now Sir Tristram did as he said he would, and he crossed the sea to the kingdom of Lyonesse. But what he had not known was that long ago a faithful lord of his father's, hight Rohalt, had overthrown the tyrants and had since served as regent, awaiting Sir Tristram's return. And the faithful Rohalt made great joy when Sir Tristram came to Lyonesse, for he had never seen him since he was a boy.

But though Tristram was pleased to know that the wicked tyrants no longer ruled his country he was yet disappointed that he could not swing his sword in some good cause and thereby be distracted from his grief. For Lyonesse was now a land where all lived in peace and prosperity, and the people were all pretty and they sang and played on dulcimers and flutes all the day. And their bliss served only to remind Sir Tristram of his own sadness.

Therefore he went away from Lyonesse, having lost even his old gifts in music, and he left the country in the hands of the loyal Rohalt, who was also known as the Keeper of the Faith. And then Sir Tristram traveled all over the earth, and he did great feats of arms wherever he went, which are yet well remembered, and everywhere he went he was believed the greatest knight of all, but when he heard himself called that, he protested, and he said, "Then know ye not of Launcelot?"

Finally he came to the Lesser Britain, the which was also known as Brittany, which was separated from King Arthur's land by the sea, but where the people had the same Celtic blood (the richest and most brave) and spake the same tongue (the most melodious), and there he met a noble prince named Kaherdin, who was the rightful ruler of that country. But the power had been seized by a felonious usurper named Riol, and with inferior forces Kaherdin was fighting him currently.

Now Sir Tristram soon recognized that Kaherdin's cause was just, and therefore he made it his own, and he and the noble Kaherdin fought as comrades-in-arms.

Now whichever side was joined by Sir Tristram became victorious in not a very long time, and in the final battle Tristram unhorsed the caitiff Riol and then he struck off his head.

And Kaherdin did love Sir Tristram greatly for liberating his country, and he would know how he might reward him.

But Sir Tristram said, "My lord, I will take no payment. It hath been my privilege to fight in a just cause, and 'tis my métier so to do. Now I shall take meat with you, and then I shall go on my way."

Therefore Kaherdin ordered a great banquet to be prepared in his newly regained castle, and to this feast came all the lords and ladies of Brittany, and his own sister as well, who had been imprisoned by the miscreant Riol.

Now when Sir Tristram saw this sister of Kaherdin's he was taken aback, for she did look a twin of La Belle Isold as she had been when he had brought her to Cornwall from Ireland many years ago. And next another amazing thing occurred, for Kaherdin conducted the fair maiden to Sir Tristram and he spake as follows.

"My dear friend Tristram, may I present my sister, Isold of the White Hands."

Now Isold of the White Hands had never seen so handsome a knight as Sir Tristram, and it was he who had freed her from the imprisonment of the felon Riol, and she was fifteen years old. Therefore she fell in love with him on the moment.

And Sir Tristram loved her insofar as she was the image of the young La Belle Isold and had the same name, and seeing that love reflected on Tristram's face when he looked at Isold of the White Hands, her brother Kaherdin said to him, "Tristram my friend, if thou dost refuse a reward for liberating my land, then might I ask of thee still another favor? For methinks thou art a knight who must ever give and not take, most Christianly."

"Noble Kaherdin," said Sir Tristram, "I took something once, but in dishonor and unlawfully, and then I gave it back. And since then I have had no joy whatever, nor have I retrieved mine honor, for once gone it doth never return: and therefore I have carried a blank shield to signify the insignificance of my life."

"Well," said Kaherdin, "I know nought of thy past, my friend, but I can not think that ignobility did touch it at any point. But, whatever, the present is here and the future shall come. Now the boon I ask of thee, Sir Tristram (and thou canst not refuse it in courtesy!) is that, as we are brothers of the heart, we become brothers in the law. I would that thou marry my sister, Tristram!"

"Thy sister, noble Kaherdin?" asked Sir Tristram, and he was amazed.

"Isold of the White Hands," said Kaherdin, "the most beautiful maiden in Britain the Lesser, and she doth love thee greatly." For though Isold of the White Hands had said nought, her eyes spake for her adoration, and in offering her hand to Sir Tristram her brother served her own dearest wish.

Now Tristram could never love anyone in the world but La Belle Isold, who was married to King Mark, but this royal maiden of Brittany did resemble her so greatly and her name was the same, and never again could he hold the original Isold in his arms. Therefore he found himself agreeing to the proposal of his friend Kaherdin.

"Yea," said he, "I will marry thy sister, my friend."

And hearing this, though he did not look at her at this time, Isold of the White Hands did swoon in happiness, while Kaherdin made the greatest joy.

Now the wedding came and went, and it was a splendid occasion, and Kaherdin gave Tristram a castle on the edge of the sea, which was quite as grand as his own, and everybody in the land rejoiced, save Tristram who sat all day upon a stone which had been anciently carved by the Druids, and he stared across the water towards Cornwall.

And a year so passed, and then one day when Kaherdin came to their castle to visit Sir Tristram and Isold of the White Hands the weather was so fine that Isold had the cooks prepare food for to eat on a picnic (and this was *rillettes* and cold *pintadeau* and the cheese of Camembert and grapes and *gâteau breton*, and the wine of the Loire), and she and her brother went to a lovely glade in the forest where there was a crystal brook. And Sir Tristram did not accompany them, for he said he must attend to a certain duty, and what he did was to go and sit upon his stone on the precipice overlooking the sea, into which he did not throw himself only because he was a knight of great piety.

Now after they had eaten, Isold of the White Hands did see the water as so inviting on a warm day that she determined to splash her fair feet in it, and therefore she removed her satin shoes and she so did. And Kaherdin watched her affectionately, for he remembered when she had been a little girl and behaved merrily.

The Isold of the White Hands suddenly kicked the water with violence, and it splashed high on her leg, for she had drawn up her robe over her knees when sitting down on the bank of the brook. And she had been smiling pleasantly before, but now she laughed aloud, and the laughter did not have a jolly sound.

"Well, Sister," asked Kaherdin, "dost laugh in chagrin at the wetting of the fine stuff of thy skirt?"

"Nay, Kaherdin, I laugh at the boldness of the water,

which taketh more liberties with my limbs than doth the bold Tristram," said Isold of the White Hands, but she did not laugh further.

Now Kaherdin was disturbed by these news. Therefore he pressed her for confirmation of what they led him to suspect. And Isold reddened, but finally she told him that after one year of marriage she was yet intact.

At this Kaherdin did wax wroth, and he forthwith went to Sir Tristram, where he sat upon his stone, and he repeated to him what Isold of the White Hands had told him.

"Now," said he to Sir Tristram, "I have known thee as a knight of the greatest worship, and to thee alone I owe the return of my kingdom. But to avoid the bed of my sister is to make a grave insult to me and my family, who art of the Breton blood royal. Therefore I see no way in which this shame can be expunged except to fight thee, sorry as it would make me, for thou art my dearest friend and my relative in law."

"My dear brother Kaherdin," said Sir Tristram, "thou speakest with perfect justice, for I am afraid that as thy sister's husband I am an impostor. It was very wrong for me to have married her, for my heart belongeth to another, whom I can not have, and whom thy sister is very like in appearance and name. But no two of God's creatures are alike except superficially, and I can perform the virile office with but one woman only in the world. Therefore I see no alternative to a fight between us, by means of which thou canst recover the honor of which I have, though without malicious intent, deprived thee."

And Kaherdin did ponder on these words awhile. And then he said, "Tristram, my friend, now that I have heard the explanation for thy delinquency, I believe that a passage at arms must be only our last resort, for now lamentable it would be if brothers fought!" Then Kaherdin asked Tristram if he had lately seen the lady he so loved.

"Not for some years," said Sir Tristram, and though he knew the exact amount of the time unto the very minute since he had last seen La Belle Isold, he believed it would be offensive to Kaherdin to be so particular.

"Well," said Kaherdin, "the human heart is a subtle organ, my friend, the which oft groweth more ardent in memory of its past loves in the degree to which they are past. Now here is my proposal: that we travel together to see this lady, for methinks she be in some foreign country and not here in the Lesser Britain. Now it well may happen that if once thou dost see her again she may seem otherwise to thee than she appears in thy recollection."

And though Tristram knew that this could never be, he agreed with his brother-in-law Kaherdin, on whom he had brought shame, and he would do all he could to appease him.

Therefore Kaherdin went to his sister Isold of the White Hands, and he told her that he and Tristram must go upon a journey for to deal with the problem of which she had spoken, and that he had great faith that when they returned she would be made happy.

And Isold of the White Hands who was yet a maiden did therefore yet have a sense of love as being a gladsome thing if it were only consummated, and she was pleased to hear these news. And that Sir Tristram did not come to bid her good-by she believed was owing to his embarrassment, whereas actually he did forget to do this entirely, so eager was he (as well as full of dread) to see La Belle Isold once more.

Then Sir Tristram and Kaherdin sailed for Cornwall, and when they landed secretly there they did both attire themselves in ragged clothes and they stained their faces with walnut juice, and in the guise of beggars they made the journey to Tintagel on foot.

Now as it happened King Mark was at just that time removing his court from Tintagel to his other castle at Terrabil (at which it will be remembered that his predecessor Gorlois was once besieged by Uther Pendragon). And he was doing this so as to please his wife La Belle Isold. For not long before, a wandering minstrel had come to Tintagel, and King Mark having his old love of music had invited him to sing for his supper. But all singing was listened to by La Belle Isold with great sadness, for any music reminded her of Tristram, whom she loved every minute of her life, and the first thing they had done after drinking the magic potion on the Irish Sea was to sing together.

Now this minstrel had been to the Lesser Britain on his wanderings, and having seen the splendid wedding of Tristram to the beautiful princess Isold of the White Hands, he wrote a lovely song about it, and this was the first thing he sang at Tintagel.

And no sooner than she heard the first verses of it La Belle Isold put her face into her hands and she wept copiously, and even King Mark was affected. Therefore he stopped the minstrel and whereas in a former time he would have had severely whipped a singer whose song displeased him, he now rewarded this man with gold before sending him away.

"My dear Isold," said King Mark, "I would do whatever I could to make thee happy, but alas! I fear I can do nothing."

"You are a very fine king, Mark, and I hold you in all respect and affection," said La Belle Isold, "and that you have not required me to perform my wifely duties is the most marvelously kind thing that hath ever been done in the world."

And King Mark's eyes were wet as well. "Never hath there been such a love as thine and Tristram's since the world began," said he, "which though illegal in the extreme and the greatest offense against me, hath yet made me a better king, for so ironical is the truth, Isold."

And he smiled sadly at her, and said, "Tintagel hath so many unhappy memories for us both. I know that in thine heart of hearts thou didst hope that despite his vow Tristram would return to it once again. He will not, if he is married now. Let us then remove to Terrabil. 'Tis comfortable enough and with notable gardens, and from it one can not look hopelessly upon the sea."

Now with the news of Sir Tristram's wedding there was nothing on earth that meant ought to Isold, and hearing that he was married she now became in appearance an old woman, and her black hair turned chalk-white and her skin did wither and yellow. Yet King Mark saw her always as the young princess she had been when lately come from Ireland.

And when the court did remove from Tintagel for to go to Terrabil there was a great procession many leagues long, and this traveled along the very road used by Sir Tristram and Kaherdin in their disguise as beggars.

Now in the middle of this procession was an elderly royal personage on a palfrey, and a robust Irish waiting-woman accompanied her.

"Ah," said Kaherdin to Sir Tristram, "here cometh the queen, who is quite aged, but she who attendeth her is young and very beautiful." And it was the loyal Brangwain to whom he referred, and no other man had ever been taken with her, but beauty being in the eye of the beholder, the noble Kaherdin fell in love with Brangwain at this moment.

But then he gasped and he said, "Tristram, my friend and brother, of course this is thy very lady love! Well, I can believe in the depth and ardor of thy feeling, seeing her! By contrast, my sister, thy wife, is quite plain. Ah woe," said he. For love doth blind an otherwise keen vision, and his unhappiness was not only for his sister and Sir Tristram but for himself, for he loved Brangwain more every minute that he looked upon her robust face and rubicund complexion.

But poor Tristram made no response, for he had recognized La Belle Isold at a great distance, and he had looked at no one else nor heard no sound. And unlike Mark he did not see her as a young maiden but rather as she was, with white hair and yellowed skin, for his own love was not blind but clear-sighted and therefore tragic—*and he loved her more than he ever had before,* the which was more than anybody had loved anyone on the earth except Isold in her love for him.

And she rode slowly past him, where he stood in a ditch alongside the road, and her head was down and she looked only within. But when they came opposite to where Tristram and Kaherdin stood bowing, Brangwain did ride next the queen and tell her these beggars were there, for Isold did ever give money to those in want, and from her purse La Belle Isold took some gold coins and without looking to where they went she flung them into the ditch.

"Well, fellows," cried Brangwain, "ye may go and fetch that money, I'm sure."

And never had Kaherdin heard a more melodious voice. But Sir Tristram heard nothing nor did he see anybody in the great procession many leagues long but his beloved Isold. And he watched her until she could no longer be seen.

And then Sir Tristram and Kaherdin did sadly and silently return whence they had come, and when they were in Brittany once more, Kaherdin spoke to Tristram as follows.

"My friend," said he, "thy lady love is so beautiful that I can not find the heart to condemn thee for the insult to my blood. Thou canst not help thyself, that is clear. What man would not feel the same! But what I do not understand is why this maiden was forbidden to thee before thou wert married to another."

"Maiden?" asked Sir Tristram. "She is the queen of Cornwall! But alas! when she was a maiden she was first mine enemy, and then when next I came for her she was already affianced to King Mark mine uncle."

And only then did Kaherdin understand that Tristram's love was for La Belle Isold, and since to him the queen seemed an aged woman and ugly, he believed Sir Tristram to be a perverse knight and perhaps a felon, and therefore his honor was besmirched and he must needs challenge Sir Tristram. And this he did.

And Kaherdin went to his sister Isold of the White Hands, and he said to her, "Forgive me, little sister, for wedding thee to this knight, who is not a man of worship. I shall fight him, and though he is a knight of great prowess, may God give me the strength to overcome him in this virtuous cause."

But Isold of the White Hands did not join in this prayer, for as it happened she dearly loved Sir Tristram regardless, and she would have waited forever for him to return that love, not knowing that that was impossible. But as she could not hope that her brother Kaherdin would be killed, she was in grief all the night.

Now when Sir Tristram and Kaherdin fought together, at dawn on the following day, Sir Tristram refused to defend himself, and therefore Kaherdin's prayer was answered, as it might not have been had Tristram raised his weapons. (Nor would Kaherdin, being a prince of the greatest worship, have fought a man who did not defend himself, had he not been in a righteous fury to uphold the honor of his family.)

And therefore Sir Tristram fell with a mortal wound in his side, in the same place where he had been wounded so long ago in his fight with the Morholt.

Now when Kaherdin saw that he had hurt his brother-in-law so badly, he knew that his honor had been vindicated, and he grieved for his friend, and he had him carried into the castle and he called for his own physicians to come and to cure Sir Tristram. But they could do nothing.

And Isold of the White Hands sat with him night and day, and she washed Tristram's wound and she changed the bandages thereon, and she sought to feed him broths, but he could not eat and he ever grew worse. And Isold of the White Hands would have given her own life to save his, had she been able, for so much did she love him.

Now Tristram grew delirious and in his swoon he called for "Isold!" but if Isold of the White Hands came to him he turned aside and yet called for "Isold."

And when this had happened many times Isold of the White Hands told her brother that she feared Sir Tristram in dying had lost his reason as well. And Kaherdin went to his bed, and he felt great pity for his friend and he was sorry that he had had to bring him to this pass.

"Tristram, my dear brother," said he, "now that no dishonor stands between us, I would do anything to preserve thy life."

"My friend Kaherdin," said Sir Tristram, "would that I had never had to wound thee first in thine honor, the which wounding hath brought this about! For what troubles me is *thy* distress. The loss of the world is nothing to me, who did lose long since all of it that I cared about. I am ready to go to the kinder Hell. But before I do, I would see La Belle Isold once more."

And Kaherdin thought to himself that while he could not understand Tristram's love for the aged queen, there was something grand if he so persisted in it on his very deathbed.

"My dear Tristram," said he, "I shall go to Cornwall immediately and do all I can to persuade her to come back here with me."

And Sir Tristram's eyes were suddenly taken with new vitality, and he raised himself on his pillow. "Kaherdin, there is nought that would be immoral in this, for La Belle Isold is a notable physician, and she once before cured me of a wound as terrible as the one I have now."

"Well," said Kaherdin, who hearing this believed he now knew why Tristram was so devoted to Queen Isold, "then there is no reason why she would not come, for all physicians do have a divine obligation to treat the ailing. And she will cure thee, my friend! Therefore we can rejoice."

Now Sir Tristram had a more profound sense of things than did Kaherdin, and he said, " 'Tis wise to remain Greek, my dear friend, in regard to fate, and not to celebrate good fortune until it hath been established, for though our God is not the pagan idols whom they wor-

shiped, He doth methinks have much the same response to
hubris."

Then Sir Tristram said, "I would be taken to my stone
overlooking the sea, to await thy return, so that I might
watch for thy sail. And further I would have thee, when
thou dost come in sight of the cliffs of Brittany on thy return voyage, to display some signal as to whether La Belle
Isold be aboard. For the suspense I should feel when
seeing the ship on the horizon would thereby be relieved."

"Aye," agreed Kaherdin, "that can I do, for my ship
hath two different sets of mainsail, one in white and the
other in black. Now when approaching the coast of Lesser
Britain it shall show the white if Isold be aboard."

"And the black if not," said Sir Tristram, and he fell
back onto his pillow.

"But that is surely unlikely," said Kaherdin. "Thou must
be of good cheer." And soon he left to travel to Cornwall.

And Tristram was carried to his stone on the cliff which
looked onto the sea, and a pavilion was erected there to
protect him from the weather when it was foul. And there
he lay on his bed and he watched the horizon all day. And
Isold of the White Hands attended him, and she knew
only that he awaited the coming of a physician, but she
knew not who that physician was.

Now when Kaherdin reached the castle of Terrabil in
Cornwall and came to Queen Isold and told her that Sir
Tristram would surely die unless she came to treat him,
she agreed to leave for Brittany immediately. And King
Mark gave his hearty assent to this journey, for he grieved
greatly for his nephew.

And La Belle Isold and Kaherdin began the return voyage, and with them they took the loyal Brangwain, who as
we know was the source of the curative ointments and
portions used by La Belle Isold to heal wounds (and also,
alas! to drink and so to fall eternally in love).

Now Kaherdin was pleased to be near Brangwain,
whom he loved greatly, and in return that loyal handmaiden, who had never expected to attract a prince (or

indeed any other man) and who had adored Sir Tristram at a distance, was not long in falling in love with Kaherdin, who was a handsome man as well as the ruler of Lesser Britain. And were they not on a desperate mission they would have made greater joy together at this time.

Meanwhile Sir Tristram did weaken throughout the many days Kaherdin was gone, and finally his vision darkened so that he could not have discerned a sail had it appeared upon the horizon. And therefore he asked Isold of the White Hands to watch for him through a spyglass, and to tell him, so soon as a ship came into view, what be the color of its sail.

And his wife Isold promised to do this. But she asked him as to the significance of the respective colors.

"If white, I live, at least for a while," said Sir Tristram. "But if the sail be black, I am dead."

But Isold of the White Hands believed she still did not understand this scheme, and she questioned him further, and he was so weak that he fell into a delirium, in the which he came to take her for La Belle Isold at the time when they had been together in the wilds, and he spoke with great passion, and at length Isold of the White Hands came to know the truth in its entirety.

Now any truth concerning love is all but unbearable in the best of times, and to Isold of the White Hands, who had been gently reared and as yet had never been invaded by a man, the present moment was the worst in which she had ever lived. For she could have endured being an untouched bride had her husband been chaste for any other reason than that he could love only one other woman in the world.

And her great love for him turned into bitter hatred (for between these two feelings at no time is there the breadth of an hair). And when at last the ship appeared on the horizon and its sail was quite white, she put down her glass and she said to Sir Tristram, "The ship hath come, my lord."

And hearing this Sir Tristram found the strength to

raise his head and to take from her the spyglass and put it to his eye. But his vision was as of night and he could see nothing, and therefore he dropped the glass and fell back.

"Tell me for the love of God!" he cried. "Is it white, or is it black as death?"

And not knowing what she did in her hatred, for she was young and wounded in the heart, Isold of the White Hands spake but one harsh word to Tristram.

"Black," she said, and she went away, for she did not think he would die through one word (but in truth she did not think of him at all, but rather of herself, after hearing that he loved another: for in love there is oft little mercy, which must be sought in loving-kindness or nowhere. And Sir Tristram himself, in leaving La Bella Isold because of his principles of honor, had been ruthless towards everybody concerned and he had brought unhappiness to all).

Now Isold of the White Hands was wrong in her doubt that one word could kill a man, and the heart of that great knight Sir Tristram of Lyonesse did burst when he heard her single word, and his life, the which had been so sad throughout, ended there and then.

And when the ship came into the harbor and La Belle Isold and Kaherdin and Brangwain had climbed up the cliff, they found the corse of Sir Tristram, and his dear physician had arrived only to bury him.

And when Sir Tristram had been lowered into the grave La Belle Isold suddenly stopped weeping, for her grief was too much for tears to express, and then she died herself on the instant, and her body was laid with Tristram's and at last they were together eternally.

And when the earth was thrown onto the bodies, La Belle Isold was seen miraculously to be transformed again into a young maiden with hair of raven-black and cheeks of rose.

Now watching this, young Isold of the White Hands lost all of her hatred, and she might well have gone mad with grief at what she had done had she not been so pious, for God never intended that Sir Tristram should be made well upon earth, let alone happy, and in using Isold of the White Hands as His instrument He would not demand the loss of her reason as penance. Therefore she entered an holy order, and immured herself in a convent for the rest of her life, doing many good works, and she lived to a great age, but from the time of Tristram's death on, though she was but seventeen when that happened, her hair was white and her skin turned yellow and withered, so that she seemed much older.

Yet one happy thing did result from the sad love of Sir Tristram and La Belle Isold. For after the period of mourning had passed, the noble Kaherdin took the loyal Brangwain as his wife, and they lived together happily thereafter.

But as for King Mark of Cornwall, who had become a good king for a while, when he heard of the deaths of his queen and his nephew he first made the greatest grief, but then he came to reflect that being kind and decent had had no effect on the events of his life, and he waxed greatly bitter about this. And therefore he henceforth determined to be bad again, for he was alone in the world now and to be good by himself, with no intimates to share his virtue, did bore him, and he began to reign in a very cruel manner once more.

And you can be sure that King Arthur would have punished him had he known about this, but he did not. For King Arthur could think of nothing but the quest for the Holy Grail, which he had decided was to be the true work of the Round Table, and one by one he sent all of his knights upon it.

BOOK XVI

How Sir Launcelot was cured of his illness by
Elaine the daughter of the maimed king Pelles;
and how Galahad was conceived.

Now when we left Sir Launcelot he was living like a beast
in the wild, and though he had lost his weapons and armor
he was yet the most formidable man in the world, and
when he was attacked by lions and boars and great serpents he destroyed them with his bare hands or he crushed
them with great trees which he tore up by the roots, and
then he ate these creatures raw. And it may well have
been that, as some have written, he did lose his reason for
a while, yet never could he forget Guinevere, in which
feeling he was like Tristram with regard to Isold, but also
he hated Guinevere for evoking it from him, whereas Sir
Tristram did never hold hatred in his heart for anybody.

Now not even the great Launcelot had the kind of con-
stitution which would sustain him in this sort of life forever, and eventually he fell into a faint on the floor of the
forest and he lay there so long that the dead leaves of autumn did cover him up and then the first snows of winter,
and no doubt he would have been dead by Christmas had
not a party of poachers come there, looking for a bear in
hibernation, the which they might unearth while he lay
helplessly sleeping and take him captive and sell him to be
tortured for the public entertainment of children at
Yuletide, than which nothing would provide more merri-

ment, especially when the savage beast had been blinded and was then whipped while bound in chains.

And these poachers coming where Launcelot lay saw steam arising from the mound of snow-covered leaves, and believing it was an hibernating bear, they quietly uncovered it and threw a net upon it and dragged it along for some distance through the snow before they knew it for a man, so long had his hair grown and his fingernails, and his skin was black with filth.

But when they determined his proper breed they took him for a detestable felon who had been hiding there to elude punishment for his misdeeds, and therefore they carried him to the castle of the king of that country, who was named Pelles, and they hoped to be rewarded for his capture. And Sir Launcelot being very ill could not speak during this time.

Now the guards on the gate of the castle relieved the poachers of Sir Launcelot and they cast him into a dungeon. And when the poachers asked for their reward these guards said, "With pleasure," and they beat these men with sticks until they ran away.

And King Pelles, who was maimed and lay upon a bed always, was not told of this, and therefore Sir Launcelot might have died in the dungeons, where he lay forgotten by all, had not King Pelles had a fair daughter who did kind things at all times but especially in the season of Christmas, when she took warm clothing and sweetmeats to the poor wretches who were imprisoned.

And therefore after Mass on Christmas Day she descended to the dungeons beneath the castle, and there she found Sir Launcelot, who was covered with filth and hair and unconscious. But being a princess she could see that he was too fine a man underneath the filth to be a criminal, and therefore she had him brought out of that dungeon and carried to a chamber in the castle, where he was washed and shaved and put into costly clothing. And then though he was very pale and thin he was very handsome, and this princess fell in love with him, and her name was Elaine.

And so it came about that another Elaine was to save his life, for that is what this princess did, and she cared for him and she fed him from her hand for many days, and finally he was able to speak in a murmur though he still did not come awake.

And what he said was the name of Guinevere.

Now Elaine went to her ladies-in-waiting and she asked them had they ever in their lives heard the name Guinevere, and they all said surely it was the name of King Arthur's queen.

"Indeed it is," said the fair Elaine, "but is it the name of anyone else as well?"

But they none of them had heard of anybody else with that name in all the world, and they all believed it unique unto that noted queen (which it was, unlike Elaine, the name of this princess and also the dead maid of Astolat and the third half-sister of King Arthur, who was a good woman and did keep to her wifely duties and was never heard from in an ill way).

Therefore Princess Elaine returned to the sick knight, and to him she asked, "And what of Guinevere?"

And Sir Launcelot, who was not yet awake and in his right mind, said, "Alas! She is loved criminally by Launcelot."

And Elaine was therefore the first noble person to know of this illegal love (though it was well known to the base). But at this time she still did not know who this knight might be, for it was possible that he was a man so shocked by knowing of the love between Guinevere and Launcelot that he spake of it in his sleep-of-illness, for he looked to be a knight of the most austere virtue and when he spake the name of the queen he did not do so in tenderness.

And when he finally came to full consciousness in the succeeding days Sir Launcelot did not tell to Princess Elaine his true name, for he was full of shame when he learned of how he had been found and brought to the castle, and he called himself Sansloy. And when he talked with Elaine it was of piety. And therefore she did not believe that he was Sir Launcelot, and she did not wish to believe it, for she wanted his love for herself.

But it was again as it had been with the maid of Astolat (and as it would have been with any other woman named Elaine or indeed anyone else except Guinevere), for ·Launcelot had no interest in her as a woman, whilst her love for him grew ever stronger. And he returned her look of adoration with but distant kindliness, and she had the feeling that if she replaced herself at his bedside with any of her ladies-in-waiting Sir Launcelot would not have noticed the change.

And when at length he was fully cured he asked to see King Pelles, to thank him for his hospitality, and Elaine took him to the room where the king used a bed as his throne, for he had been maimed for many years and never could walk.

"Royal Pelles," said Sir Launcelot to his maimed king, "I thank you for the care I have been given at your castle. Obviously you are a king of great worship."

"Well," said King Pelles from his bed, "as decent folk we offer succor to any man of virtue in distress, but never have I seen such a fine-looking knight as thee! Methinks thou art of King Arthur's Round Table. And what is thy name?"

"Sansloy," said Sir Launcelot.

"And dost have a question for me, Sir Sansloy?" asked King Pelles, and shifting his position slightly on the bed he did wince painfully, for his old wound had never healed.

"I do, Majesty," said Launcelot. "I would know the names of the maids who attended me, so that I might reward them when my circumstances have improved. At the moment I have nought, having even lost mine armor and my weapons, and the clothes I wear were given me here."

Now King Pelles did look unhappy for a moment. "Alas!" said he, " 'tis not the question that would cure me, I fear. But thine is easy enough to answer: these maids which to thee in thy delirium have seemed many, are in truth but one, and she is my daughter the princess Elaine."

Now it can be imagined how disappointed was Elaine to hear that this knight had never distinguished her as being unique, when she loved him with all her heart. But this Elaine was of quite another character than the poor maid of Astolat (perhaps because she was a princess), and she determined to make her mark upon Sir Sansloy, though as yet she did not know how.

Now when Sir Launcelot left his presence King Pelles marveled on the name he had given him, the which signified "Without Law" in the French tongue, and thinking that this was hardly an appropriate name for a knight of the Round Table, he considered whether he might be an infamous impostor, come to his kingdom to do him great harm.

Therefore Pelles called to him a knight of his own who had competed in the tournaments held at Camelot, and he asked him whether amongst King Arthur's company there had ever been a knight named Sansloy, and this man said, Nay, not to his knowledge.

"Then go and look upon this knight who was lately ill but cured by my daughter the princess," said King Pelles, "and tell me if thou canst recognize him."

And so this knight did as he was commanded, and then he returned to the king, saying, "Sire, that is none other than the renowned Sir Launcelot, and well do I know him, for once at a tourney did I and five others ride upon him from all sides at the same time, and in the next moment we were all of us unhorsed, and he then dismounted and taking off his helm came to see whether we had been hurt. Not only is he the knight of the greatest prowess under the sun, but he is also the most kindest."

(And Sir Launcelot was ever celebrated in such terms by the knights he did defeat.)

"By Heaven!" swore King Pelles (who was not the most devout king). "The incomparable Sir Launcelot, here in my land under an assumed name! 'Tis a strange thing."

And then he determined to ask Launcelot about this to his face, for though he respected a man's privacy the king wondered that a knight of the Round Table would tell an untruth.

Therefore he had Launcelot brought to him, and he said to him, "Dost thou maintain that thy name is properly and solely Sansloy?"

"Nay, King Pelles," said Sir Launcelot, "I can not do that and so prevaricate."

"I am greatly relieved to hear it," said King Pelles, "for if the speech of a knight of the Round Table may be doubted in any wise, no matter how petty, then all virtue hath become the subject for vile mockery."

"Yet, Your Majesty," said Launcelot, "it would be an offense against God to think we are any of us perfect. I did not lie when saying I call myself Sansloy, but I do confess to misleading you."

" 'Twould seem then, not a greatly evil matter," said King Pelles.

"But," said Sir Launcelot groaning, "it was intended to conceal me, if only from myself, and to hide a shame is but to compound it."

"Shame?" asked King Pelles, and he did himself groan. "My dear Launcelot, what dost thou know of shame? King Arthur hath abolished it."

"For himself alone," said Launcelot.

But King Pelles believed this to be but the kind of modesty for which the knights of the Round Table were noted, and he called Launcelot to come sit near him on his bed.

"Sir Launcelot," said he, "in me thou seest a king whom shame hath maimed. I have me a wound which will not heal never, until a knight of great purity doth come one day and ask me a certain question. Despite thy modest opinion of thyself, thou art known to be the greatest knight on earth. Furthermore thou hast appeared here in a magical way. The great Launcelot, found exposed in a forest with neither sword nor armor, and brought here at the point of death—could this be possible unless a profound purpose was intended?"

But Sir Launcelot hung his head. "Believe me, King Pelles, nothing would please me more than to relieve you with the proper question, but as it happens I have none, and therefore I can not be the instrument of your earthly deliverance."

Now King Pelles was greatly disappointed, for if Sir Launcelot could not help him, then who could? And he believed that God did everything with a purpose, but why had Launcelot come here if not for this reason? For King Pelles, who could find no one to ask him the proper question, had many questions of his own.

Now learning that this knight whom she had saved would soon go away the fair Elaine did not suffer these news passively, but rather she went to the king her father, and she spake to him as follows.

"Father, know you that Sir Sansloy must be detained and punished, for he lately did make a vile and indecent attempt on my virtue!"

And King Pelles said in apparent wrath (though secretly he did smile into his beard), "Very well, I shall have his head struck off, for this is the most loathsome and felonious thing I have ever heard of!"

But Princess Elaine fell to her knees and seizing his hand and kissing it she cried, "Oh never, dear Father, for he is the very most bravest and handsomest knight in the world!"

"Well then, if this is so," said King Pelles, "then why would he force his attentions upon thee obnoxiously? For any maiden in the world would be overjoyed to have his love."

"I believe now," said the fair Elaine, "that I mistook his intentions."

"Is it not rather the case," asked King Pelles, "that thou hast fallen in love with him and wouldst keep him here for that reason?"

"You are the wisest of fathers," said the fair Elaine.

"But furthermore," said King Pelles, "he hath paid no especial attention to thee?"

And Elaine weeping confessed that this was true. "But until now he hath been ill, Father, and out of his right mind."

"Dear girl," said the king, and he patted her lovely head, "I am afraid that I too have been disappointed by him, but he is the great Sir Launcelot and surely he hath more important things to do than to treat our little ills in our obscure little kingdom."

And Elaine now arose, and with a great determination in her heart. "So he *is* Sir Launcelot!" she cried. And though she did not tell this to the king her father, she believed that there was nothing in the world more important than that she should have his love, for the fair Elaine though very young and beautiful and gentle did have a will that was marvelous strong.

And knowing that this knight was Sir Launcelot, and having heard from his own lips while he was out of his right mind (the condition in which the heart speaketh with perfect truth) that he loved Guinevere illegally, the princess Elaine did therefore believe that she would not be sinful (or if so, at any rate and at the worst, much less sinful than he) if she won his love by a device.

And so she summoned to her her handmaiden Brisen (who was to her as the loyal Brangwain had been to Isold), and she told Brisen what she must do, *scilicet,* to furnish her a means by which she could assume the guise of Guinevere.

"Lady," said Brisen, "this will I do gladly, for to make you happy I would lay down my life." And therefore Brisen, who was the greatest enchantress then to be found amongst the good folk of the world, did fashion a golden ring which was the exact replica of one worn by Guinevere.

And this ring she did give to a page, for to take to Sir Launcelot, who was about to leave the castle. And when the page had gone upon his errand, Brisen told the fair

Elaine to go to her bedchamber and to undress and to go to bed. And Elaine did this.

Now when Sir Launcelot was given this ring by the page he at first believed it a parting gift, the which King Pelles was adding to all the other generous things he had done for him, and once again he regretted that he could not ask the question which would cure the king's wound, and again he remembered why he could not: because he was not pure. And in shame and sorrow he put his hands to his face, and so was the ring, which he had put onto his finger, brought near his eye, at which time he recognized it (though, as we know, erroneously) as that of the woman whom he loved more than his honor. And in this instant he forgot all of his shame, and he ran to catch up the page, who had left, and when he reached him he asked, "Who is it that sends this ring to me?"

And this page had been instructed by Brisen to give the following answer if he was asked this question (and it was the truth): "She who loves you inordinately."

And Sir Launcelot demanded that he be taken to her from whom the page had come, for he assumed that Guinevere had come as guest to this castle, and the page believing that Brisen was the paramour of this knight, led Launcelot to her chamber.

But this room was an antechamber to that of the fair Elaine, and when the page went away and Sir Launcelot went within it, Brisen the enchantress put on him the most powerful of her spells, and when he went into the inner chamber and saw Elaine in her bed, he believed it was rather Guinevere.

And so great was his hunger for her that he made but one sob of passion and then he joined her. And Sir Launcelot and Elaine the daughter of the maimed king Pelles lay together all the night. And therefore had Elaine achieved her purpose!

But the dawn came finally, and with it the spell of Brisen lost its power, and when Sir Launcelot awakened and saw that he had held in his arms not Guinevere but

Elaine, he leapt from the bed with a great cry of anguish, and then his feeling turned to rage (which never did he feel towards his opponents on the field of battle), and he went cruelly to place his strong hands upon the delicate white neck of Elaine and he would fain have strangled her. For once he knew that he had been deceived, he knew again the shame he had forgotten, and he despised all women but Guinevere in the best of times, and his love for her was always near to hatred. And by throttling the fair Elaine he would punish all women for his failure to keep his virile vows.

But before his fingers could close around her white throat the enchantress Brisen hearing his cry of rage came into the chamber and she put a new spell upon him so that his fingers lost their grasp and he came away from Elaine's bed, and Sir Launcelot stood before Brisen like the obedient schoolboy which he had been as a child.

"Sir Launcelot," said Brisen, "know you that you have done a better thing this night than you have ever done with a woman, for the fair Elaine will conceive your child. And he will be a far greater knight than you can ever be, because his mother will rear him with all the love she beareth for you, and even more; for that part of him that is from you can never be separated from the part which is hers. And if she can keep only the son and not the father, 'tis better that she have the son, for though you are now the greatest knight in the world, he will be the greater."

And Sir Launcelot heard this quietly, and his wrath had been calmed, and indeed he was in a stupor.

"Now," said Brisen, "when you come out of the enchantment I have placed upon you, you will remember nothing of what happened here, except in dreams." And she led him outside and then she lifted the spell upon him, and it was as she had promised, for Sir Launcelot could remember nought of this remarkable event, and he rode out of that castle and went on his way.

And the fair Elaine was sorry to see him go, but his son was growing within her, and he was to be Sir Galahad.

Now soon after Sir Launcelot had left the castle of King Pelles there arrived there a knight named Sir Bromel, who had been smitten with a great love for Princess Elaine, and he came to sue for her hand.

But to him the fair Elaine said, "Sir knight, know you I can not love you nor any other man but one in the entire world."

And Sir Bromel asked for the name of this knight.

"Sir Launcelot of the Lake," said Elaine the daughter of the maimed king Pelles. "Therefore woo me no longer."

And in jealousy Sir Bromel lost his powers of judgment and he vowed to find Sir Launcelot and to kill him, and therefore he went in search of him, but luckily for him he rather encountered Sir Lionel, who was a cousin of Sir Launcelot. For Sir Lionel was seeking the Holy Grail and in that quest he had come near the land of King Pelles the maimed monarch.

Now Sir Lionel was a great knight indeed, and he made short work of Sir Bromel, who did not belong to the company of the Round Table, and in no time at all Sir Bromel lay senseless upon the earth. And Sir Lionel unlaced his helm and waked him up and accepted his cry of mercy.

"Thank you, Sir Launcelot," said Sir Bromel. "I can hate you no longer, when your mercy hath been shown me so graciously."

"Well," said Sir Lionel, "I am not Launcelot but rather his cousin. And I think that if he was your intended enemy you must now go and yield to him as a recreant. However, I do not know where he is. Therefore I would that you go to Camelot and present yourself to King Arthur, begging his pardon for your ill will against one of his knights and pledging to be virtuous henceforth."

"That shall I do," said Sir Bromel, and Sir Lionel permitted him to rise.

Meanwhile Sir Launcelot was himself returning to Camelot, for he had nowhere else to go, but he rode very slowly owing to his dread of seeing Guinevere once more (for in his mind he knew nothing of his intimate encounter with Elaine, and he was again as he had been). And therefore Sir Bromel did reach King Arthur's court before him.

But King Arthur was not at Camelot, for he had gone on a tour of his realm, and he was currently at Caerleon, where he still enjoyed exchanging chaff with the peevish but honest dwarf who guarded his treasure lode as of yore.

And meeting Sir Kay in the halls Sir Bromel asked him to whom he should go to perform the duty which Sir Lionel had given him. But Kay had grown more irritable over the years in pursuit of his household matters, and at the moment he was exasperated by the delay in a shipment of fish which was overdue, and a rat had drowned in a cauldron of court-bouillon in which the fish were to be poached, and therefore the lot had to be discarded. And for this reason Sir Kay rudely disregarded Sir Bromel, and Bromel would have taken offense had he not been awed by being at Camelot, which had already long been the source of legend throughout the world.

But then he met Sir Bedivere, a most gracious and fine knight, and he said to Bromel, "I think that in the absence of King Arthur you would do well to take your plea to the queen, for Sir Launcelot, whose mercy you would plead, is her special protector."

So Sir Bromel went to Guinevere. (And as we know, Sir Agravaine was guarding her now, though secretly, and from his place of hiding he heard all of this.)

"O gracious lady," said Sir Bromel kneeling before her, "in the name of Sir Launcelot I yield to you and I confess myself a recreant to have sought his life."

And Guinevere cried in grief and rage, "Caitiff! Hast thou done him damage?" And she looked for a dagger the which to plunge into his heart.

But Sir Bromel calmed her by saying, "Nay, lady, and happy it was for me that instead I fought Sir Lionel his cousin and was soon defeated."

Now when the queen had composed herself she asked Sir Bromel what his cause had been against Launcelot and if he had seen him, for Sir Launcelot had not been at Camelot since time out of mind. And she endeavored to seem indifferent about this, but she cared for nought else in the world.

"Never have I seen that incomparable knight with mine own eyes," said Sir Bromel. "But lately he was in the castle of King Pelles, where Elaine the daughter of that maimed king did fall in love with him."

And at these news Guinevere's feelings were such that she fainted dead away. And her waiting-women came to her and carried her to her bed, but when she awakened she did not stay there in the kind of illness she had suffered from before first becoming Launcelot's paramour and again when he had first gone away. Nay, now her fury gave her great strength, and she thought only of how she might harm Sir Launcelot in revenge.

And one of her schemes was when King Arthur returned to tell him that Sir Launcelot had taken her by force, in violation of the sternest laws of God and man. But then on further thought she abandoned this plan, for she did not want to test her credit with Arthur against his belief in Launcelot's honor, in the fear that being a woman, though a queen, she would have the weaker position. And in fact, it would have been a lie.

And next she determined to secrete a dagger in her bed, and when Sir Launcelot came unto her (if indeed he ever returned to Camelot), she would carve him into an eunuch—nay, she would kill him, and then herself. And so, as the scribes say, she "writhed and weltered as a mad woman."

And it was the worst moment for Sir Launcelot to make his return in, but so he did.

Now King Arthur was not at Camelot, but if he had been there Sir Launcelot would still have gone straight to Guinevere and not, as he was obliged to do, to the king to relate his adventures. But of Sir Launcelot's violations this would have been the least.

And if Sir Agravaine had been hidden in the chambers

of the queen at this time he would have known more than he did. But as it happened, after hearing the words that had passed between Guinevere and Sir Bromel, and seeing her great swoon at the news that Elaine, the daughter of Pelles the maimed king, was in love with Launcelot, Agravaine believed that he had evidence that Guinevere and Launcelot were lovers, and he lost no time in going to his brother Sir Gawaine to tell him of this.

Now Sir Gawaine at this time was living with his beautiful wife Ragnell in a castle not so far from Camelot, the which with its adjacent lands King Arthur had given him as wedding present. And though he was still a knight of the Round Table and would always be, he no longer went upon quests unless the king commanded him to especially. And what he did instead was to remain at home with the fair Ragnell, whom he loved greatly, and sometimes he hunted in his park, and he was keen on gardening, and if a fair was held nearby he might display his enormous marrows or his giant roses, and he might race his dogs there, wagering modest sums, and if he won he gave the proceeds to his serfs, who loved him greatly for all his kindnesses to them. And he was marvelous happy. And Gareth and Lynesse lived close by, and Gaheris and Lynette as well, and all of those families had many pretty children, and once in every fortnight the brothers and their wives and their children would come together and have great cheer.

But Agravaine would never get married, for he dreamed inordinately and outlandishly that he could find some means by which to take Guinevere as his own. And perhaps if he could confront her with evidence of her adulterous association with Sir Launcelot, Agravaine believed he might trade his own silence on this matter for her love—so went his mind, for he was not only a man with weak scruples but he was also a marvelous fool.

But he was not so foolish as to trust his own judgment completely, and therefore he went to his eldest brother, the greatest of the clan of King Lot, the noble Gawaine.

"My dear Agravaine," said Sir Gawaine when his brother had come to his castle, "thou art overdue in visiting us."

"Gawaine, I thank thee for thy gracious greeting, but I would speak of Launcelot," said Agravaine.

"I have not seen the incomparable Launcelot for a very long time," said Sir Gawaine. "And indeed I should like to, but I have been occupied here and have not visited at Camelot."

"Methinks thy true duty lies there, Gawaine," said Sir Agravaine.

"Well," replied Sir Gawaine, who was slightly vexed, "if the royal Arthur wants me he hath only to give me his command. Meanwhile my family is here, Agravaine."

And his brother laid a finger alongside his nose and he said, "But this is a matter of which the king would be last to know."

And Gawaine's vexation left him, for Agravaine had done this same thing often when they were small boys, for he had always some secret to impart, innocuous though it be, and the memory of it was amusing to Sir Gawaine.

"Well, dear brother," said he, "I'm sure that thy news are not so desperate that they can not wait till after we go to our meat. But before that happens which shouldst thou care to see first, the kitchen-garden or the mews? I say the kitchen-garden, for there are some splendid marrows just now at their peak of perfection (and well boiled they shall serve us at dinner). The flower-gardens are much too extensive to see in so short a time—as, certes, are the kennels. Yea, the mews are just the place, now that I think on the matter! I have a merlin I should like thee to have a look at it." For Sir Gawaine, once the notable lecher, had become quite domesticated.

And Sir Agravaine must needs suffer the seeing of Gawaine's entire estate and eat a number of meals and endeavor to speak courteously with his sister-in-law Ragnell, whom he found the great bore that a beautiful woman doth become when she is married happily. And he was obliged to notice his small nephews and nieces, who tended towards deafening ebullience, and Agravaine concluded that nothing was more obnoxious than to be a husband and a father. And it was ever so long before he could speak privily to Gawaine about the matter of Guinevere and Launcelot.

Nor did this happen until they had gone pigsticking together in Sir Gawaine's boar-wood, and in pursuing one hairy big beast Sir Agravaine's horse did step into an hole breaking its foreleg, and he fell to the earth, and then the boar did turn and charge upon him, with its furious red eyes and fóaming snout and great-yellow tusks, and it came so near that he could smell its foul stench before Sir Gawaine rode down upon it and impaled it through the ribs with his lance.

Then the huntsmen eviscerated it with their knives, and they flung its guts to the pack of dogs. And sirs Gawaine and Agravaine drew apart to celebrate this kill with a stirrup-cup.

And Gawaine said, "Agravaine, old fellow, we'll sup on boarchops this evening, smothered in blood-gravy and with turnips and sprouts fresh from the garden." And he patted his belly, which had grown thicker of late and bore his sword belt higher than of old.

And Agravaine despised him for having become so tamed.

"Gawaine," said he, "dost not sometimes long for the days of adventure?"

"Nay," said Sir Gawaine. "I am happy to have had them in my proper time, but of a life of adventure it can be said that there is no abiding satisfaction, for when one adventure is done, a knight liveth in expectation of another, and if the next come not soon enough he falleth in love, in the sort of love that is an adventure, for what he seeketh be the adventure and not the lovingness. And methinks this sequence is finally infantile, and beyond a certain age one can no longer be interested in games."

"And what of the adulterers, Gawaine?" asked Sir Agravaine.

"Of the uncommon kind like the unfortunate Tristram and Isold," said Gawaine, "one can but feel the greatest pity. I pray always for the soul of mine old comrade, and I think that God doth not hate this tragic pair, for 'tis said that from their grave, upon a cliff overlooking the sea in Lesser Britain, hath grown two rosebushes, a white and a red, and their branches are intertwined."

But Sir Agravaine, distracted by his bitter cause, was not moved by these news. Nor had he so great an affection for Sir Tristram, who so easily felled him at tournaments.

"Well," said he, "and what of the common kind, they who do not die for their passions but extinguish them by swyving together, and then, so soon as the humors have risen again, swyve and swyve once more, and unless they are taken in their detestable crime and put to death by burning, they continue so to mock their Faith and all right rule!" And he became so exercised that he did foam at the mouth as the boar had lately done.

Now seeing this Sir Gawaine did take it for the aftermath of Agravaine's fear at having nearly been killed by the beast.

"Well," said he, "of course such criminals must not be allowed to prevail in their disorder if it be so flagrant. But methinks their worse punishment must come from God, and not from man, for 'tis a greater sin than a crime."

"Gawaine," said Agravaine, "I shall leave off speaking theoretically. What if I can provide you with evidence that Guinevere doth adulterate with Sir Launcelot?"

And they were sitting beneath a tree and in its shadow, and yet Sir Gawaine's face blazed as if in the full sun.

And he said, "Agravaine, that is the most vilest accusation that could be made, and if thou canst not provide evidence to support it, then thou must go away from me, my dear brother though thou art. And if thou canst prove it, then God save us all. And since it must be one way or another, the outcome can not but be unfortunate."

Then Agravaine told him of what he had overheard pass between Sir Bromel and the queen.

"And is that all?" asked Gawaine. "That she swooned hard after hearing only that Launcelot was loved by Elaine the daughter of the maimed Pelles? This is no evidence of anything, Agravaine! For the queen hath ever been in delicate health, swooning easily."

"But only when Launcelot hath gone away from Camelot," said Sir Agravaine. "Never at the departure of King Arthur. And how would an innocent woman faint at the love of some other lady for a knight to whom she was herself indifferent?"

"Well, of course she is not indifferent to what happens to Launcelot," said Gawaine, "for he is by royal appointment the queen's champion. But further, Brother, thou dost not know of the fatal attraction the guiltless Launcelot hath for damsels named Elaine." And then he told Agravaine the unfortunate story of the maid of Astolat, the which he had never told another. "Doubtless, Guinevere did learn somehow of this," said he, "and therefore she swooned in pity for the maimed Pelles' daughter, for she knoweth (as who doth not?) of Launcelot's pious vow never to know any woman privily."

Now Sir Agravaine did jeer openly at Sir Gawaine's speech, saying, "Guinevere hath no pity in her heart for any human being."

And his brother Sir Gawaine struck him with the flat of his hand, and he said, "Brother, get thee hence, and never speak to me again so shamefully!" For his respect for the queen came even before his fraternal affections.

And surely this dispute with his brother Gawaine caused Agravaine to hate Launcelot and Guinevere all the more.

Meanwhile Sir Launcelot had come to the queen in her moment of greatest fury against him. But when she received him she did conceal the heat of her anger in a great coolness, and when he sought to embrace her she put up her hands, saying, "Knowest thou not it is death to touch the queen?"

And Sir Launcelot could not understand this, for as always he was distracted by the state of his own feelings. "Guinevere!" he cried. "I did all I could to escape my love for thee, but to no avail. I did live like a beast. I very nearly died. But when I was revived it was only to discover that I loved thee more than ever!"

"And why, sir knight, dost thou believe this were of interest to me?" asked the queen.

But Sir Launcelot was still immune to her display of coldness, and therefore he took this as a literal question to be answered straightforwardly. "Well, chuck," said he with utter insensitivity, "I can not avoid thee, do what I will."

And once again he sought to embrace Guinevere, but again she retreated from him. And now it seemed to him that she was being coy.

"Doth my return make thee girlish?" he said. "Shall I chase thee around the bed?" And though he loved her as he did he believed that she had lost some dignity.

Now until this speech the queen had been afraid to let him come too close and to embrace her, for she feared that he would thereby cause her to lose her anger against him. But hearing his last words she believed that the man was a monster of self-concern and that he took no account of her whatever.

And therefore she came to him, in seeming desire, and she disrobed, and together they went into her bed. But when he had been aroused to the point where he must needs have her or die, she sprang from the bed, and throwing a robe about her she cried, "Traitor! Felon! Go to thine Elaine!"

And Sir Launcelot was in the greatest throes of deprival. And when he could finally speak he said, "I have in my life long met but two Elaines, and neither has been 'mine.' "

And in a voice which was all but strangled by jealousy, Guinevere then told him of what Sir Bromel had reported to her.

"Well," said Sir Launcelot when she was done, "I can

not be held responsible for the delusions of a silly damsel! I had nought privately to do with her, Guinevere."

And the queen said, "Will you swear?"

"By my Faith," said Sir Launcelot, "though that be blasphemous! But I am anyway damned already."

And in the degree to which she had been furious, the queen so yearned to be appeased, and at length Launcelot persuaded her to return to bed, and when she did he presented her with the most effective argument in his own behalf for having been so long denied the provender of love (so far as he honestly remembered) he was now ravenous. And this was the only way in which this proud queen would submit to overwhelming.

And never were Guinevere and Launcelot so happy as in the succeeding months, for King Arthur stayed away from Camelot for ever so long, and from Caerleon he went to his castle at Winchester, in the which his father Uther Pendragon had died, and the great hall there was yet a memorial to his love of horses and dogs, for never had it been mucked out since in his last days he had used it as a stable and a kennel.

And now at last King Arthur revealed to his subjects at large that he was Uther Pendragon's son, as he had not done earlier, but he had begun to feel his mortality now. And everywhere he went men and women came to him calling themselves his brothers and sisters, for they claimed to be Uther's bastards. And to all of them King Arthur gave gold, and to those who could produce some evidence of their claim, such as a royal token given by Uther Pendragon to their mother, Arthur gave land.

And wherever he traveled there were long lines of petitioners who waited for an audience with him, and he turned no one away whether highborn or base. And when he came to his castle at London among the people there admitted to see him were an hideous hag with a young lad who had an exceeding pale face and glittering black eyes.

"And what boon do ye seek of your king?" he asked of them.

And the hag curtsied and the boy did bow, and the old woman said, "The varlet wished only to see his Sire."

"Well, I have ridden throughout the streets," said King Arthur, "and shall so ride again. Am I so different when sitting on a throne and not an horse that ye would wait many hours to see me here?"

"Majesty," said the hag, "the varlet would see you everywhere you go, for he doth idolize you."

"Thou art a good lad," said King Arthur, but he reproved him for his idolatry. "God alone is to be worshiped, my boy. When thou wouldst think of me, think beyond me to Him who is my king."

And the old woman and the lad made obeisance to him and then they went away, and they were Morgan la Fey in disguise and Mordred.

"Well," said Morgan la Fey when they were in a private place, "thou hast seen thy father at last. And what thinkest thou?"

"Of what?" asked Mordred. "Of him or how to kill him?"

"Both," said Morgan la Fey.

"It was no surprise to me that he is the finest-looking man in the world," said Mordred.

"Indeed," said Morgan la Fey. "And is that not disgusting?"

"Abominably so," Mordred did agree. "Now, as to how to do him in. . . . You are aware, my dear aunt, that your own efforts to that end have been disgraceful failures?"

"How typically malicious of thee to remind me," said Morgan la Fey, who had made herself beautiful again. "Canst thou do better, little shit?"

And Mordred smiled at the abuse, and he pursed his pale thin lips and narrowed his glittering serpent's eyes. "It may be a thing of time," said he. "Perhaps one day it will be old-fashioned to think of ourselves as unique in our monstrosity. Can there not exist monsters of the well-intentioned? Is not virtue finally a monstrous thing?"

"It is certainly to such as we," said Morgan la Fey, and she talked no further on this matter, for she was jealous of her command of evil, and she feared that Mordred as he got older would seek to gain mastery of her in this regard.

Whereas already he despised her methods, for Mordred did not believe in the efficacy of spells and enchantments and all such archaic rot. And he believed that kings could be better ruined by means that were quite reasonable.

BOOK XVII

Of Percival and his sheltered upbringing; and how
he became a knight.

Now when King Arthur toured his realm he was greeted
lovingly by his people everywhere, for they had been freed
of all oppression and their harvests had been great and no
plague had come since he assumed the throne. And the le-
pers came to him and fathers brought their idiot sons, and
the king touched these sick persons, and if they were not
cured then at least they felt less ill than before, and never
did he claim any curative powers that did not come from
God. And all the bishops were honest, and when King Arthur came near by the brothels did close, and some of
them never opened again, for the whores had become
nuns.

And everywhere he went his evil sister Morgan la Fey
tried to do him harm in some wise, enchanting weak men
so that they became traitors, and stones were dislodged
from battlements and fell down missing the king but narrowly, and noxious potions were introduced into his drink
and his meat was poisoned, but God always forwarned
him of these things, and therefore he spurned that which
was tainted. And if when judging contests in archery he
was the target of an arrow discharged so as to kill him, he
always turned at just that instant and it missed him. And
when his retainers arrested the felonious bowman King

Arthur accepted his plea that the shot had been made in accident, and he freed the man without punishment, as he forgave all others who, enchanted by his wicked sister, sought to kill him.

And this forgiveness broke the spell on these unfortunate men, and they swore henceforth to be exemplary Christians and some became honest knights and the rest, monks.

Meanwhile at Camelot, Guinevere and Launcelot did not resist their illegal love, and with Arthur being away they were never apart for a moment, and therefore it was no longer a secret to those who had eyes. But most of the knights of the Round Table were not in residence, being off on the quest for the Holy Grail, and furthermore no virtuous knight would gossip of the immorality of others, for he was concerned with his own sins and how best to atone for those of the past and to avoid committing them in future, though he well knew that to breathe was to sin.

But of all those who were present at Camelot, Sir Agravaine, though he spied incessantly on the adulterous pair, knew least about them: which is so often true of him who looks for infractions. And indeed though Launcelot spent every night in the bed of Guinevere, Sir Agravaine did never get positive evidence of this, though that was his sole aim in all the world at this time.

And the wondrous thing was that neither Guinevere nor Sir Launcelot knew they were being spied upon, for they had come to the point at which they did not care whether this happened, and therefore their very guilelessness provided a certain protection.

And as to Launcelot's notable scruples, they could only be called stunned now for a while. For though he knew he was damned, time for him had stopped. And so we leave him there for the nonce, like a fly who had ceased to struggle against the hardening sap in which he is immersed, and whether it turns to eternal amber we shall see in the sequel.

But now we go to the castle of the late King Pellinore

where his widow had but one son left at home, and his name was Percival, and he had been reared by his mother to know nothing of arms or of warfare, for his father had gone away when he was a small boy and had finally returned only to be soon slain by Sir Gawaine. And this queen's other sons had left her as well, for to search for their father who had gone to seek the Questing Beast, and one by one they found their way to Camelot and joined the Round Table, and these were sirs Tor and Aglavale and Lamorak and Dornar. Therefore she had no men at home at all, and she determined never to let young Percival leave her.

And so she kept him by her, and he never saw a sword or a lance, and he learned nothing of the knightly arts but rather was taught to sew and crochet along with his young sister and to talk only of womanish matters.

Now when his father King Pellinore did finally return and reign for that short time, Percival's mother did not tell him it was his father on the throne, but merely that it was the king. And when Gawaine killed Pellinore, Percival's mother kept this knowledge from him.

And never was there so naïve a boy as Percival, and he grew to the age of fourteen without ever having been farther from the family chambers of the castle than the private garden where no one else came.

Now one day he was in that garden, playing at dolls with his sister, when his sister left him briefly to go within the castle for to get a tiny muff with which to warm the hands of a doll that she believed to be cold. And Percival was happy to have this respite, because he was greatly bored and he idly watched a wren that did bathe itself in a birdbath and then hop to the top of the garden wall, where it stayed but a moment and then it flew over the wall and apparently landed on the earth without, for its flight could not be seen.

Now Percival was intrigued by this, and for the first time did it occur to him that there might be an earth outside the walls. That is to say he knew they were not sitting upon a cloud in the empty air, but he had never before considered what might be the nature of the world without. And therefore he now scaled the wall by means of the vines thereupon, and he looked over it, and he saw a broad meadow and a river running through it, and some knights were riding on the riverbank, with bright steel armor which shone in the sunlight. But Percival did not know they were knights, for never had he seen any.

Therefore he climbed down and he went to his mother the queen and he told her of these shining beings which he had seen and he asked her what they were.

Now his mother was determined that he should never take up arms, and therefore she spake to him as follows.

"My dear Percival," said she, "what a happy boy thou art! For thou hast seen a procession of angels."

"Well," said Percival, "they were quite the most beautiful sight that I have ever seen. How might I become an angel, Mother?"

"By living piously all thy life," said his mother. "And when thou hast died God will make thee into an angel for all eternity."

And Percival was pleased to hear this could be done so simply. But when he thought on it more he became impatient, and he did not want to wait so long to become an angel, because he was only a boy (and in fact he believed himself to be younger than he was, so protected had been his upbringing).

Therefore when he returned with his sister to the garden he found a large stone there and he gave it her and asked her to bash out his brains with it.

"O fool that thou art, Percy," said his sister, "for when the brains are bashed out a person doth live no longer."

"Dost not understand? I would become an angel quickly," said Percival.

"But can this be the proper way to that end?" asked his sister. "To make of me a murderess?" For his sister's wits were keener than his, because she was being raised as a maid should be, whereas he had been kept from all male things by his fearful mother.

"Thou canst not be a murderess," said Percival, "if it is I who have asked thee to kill me."

"Then thou wouldst be a suicide, fie on thee," said his sister. "And both of us would go to Hell." And thinking of the wickedness of this she burst into tears.

Now Percival was quite disappointed, and he scaled the wall again to see whether the angels were yet there, and so they were, for they were resting in the shade of a tree on the riverbank. And suddenly Percival determined to go closer to them so that he could learn more of their ways, and whilst his sister's back was turned he clambered to the top of the wall and then let himself down the other side.

And for the first time in his life he was outside the castle in which he had been born and kept, and for a while he was dizzy with the realization of this. Then from over the wall he could hear his sister crying for him, and fearing that his mother would send people to bring him back he ran as fast as he could to the river, where he hid in a bush. And the angels had tied their horses near by, and these beasts smelling Percival did nicker and stamp their feet. And a very large angel in a coat of shining metal did come to investigate, and he found Percival behind the bush.

"Well, varlet," said he, "why dost hide here? To do us ill?"

"Oh, never, Sir Angel," said Percival, and he rose and he bowed. "I have come to admire you."

"Thou art a fine-looking boy," said the knight, "and three-quarters grown, and thou wouldst seem strong enough. Why therefore dost thou wear the dress of a maiden? Art thou a detestable catamite?" And he spake with great sternness.

Now Percival understood nought of what the knight said, and his mother had always dressed him in the same fashion as his sister, and never having seen any other male persons he knew of no other mode.

And now the knight brought him amongst the others,

and Percival was awed by these large glittering beings, who clattered when they did move.

"And what do ye make of this, which I found behind a bush?" said the knight who had brought him there.

And all of these angels had heads made of metal, with windows in them which they looked out of. But then one of them took off his metal head, and underneath it he had an human face, the which was stern and strong, but looking down on Percival he soon smiled.

"Thou hast no need to be afraid of us, my boy," said he. "We are knights of Arthur's Round Table, and we mean no harm to anyone in this land."

"Knights?" asked Percival. "Are you not then angels?"

Now all these knights did laugh heartily, but not unkindly, and the one who had been speaking to him said, "I am Bors." And then he introduced each of the others. And he said, "Nay, we are not angels yet, though we hope to be when we have died, but God alone must decide that. Now what is thy name?"

"Percival," said the same.

"Well, Percival," said Sir Bors, "it would seem from the manner of thy speech that thou art of high rank. Yet from the content of it one might judge that thou wert ignorant of things that pertaineth to men."

"Sir, that is true," said Percival. "Until this moment I have never left yon castle in which I was born."

And all the knights sighed at these news, for they knew to whom the castle belonged.

"Thou art then the youngest son of King Pellinore, without a doubt," said Sir Bors.

"I did not know that," said Percival, "for I did not personally know the king, and I believe that he is gone again. But shall you all come to the castle now? For I am not allowed to be without it, and I would learn more of knighthood from you."

"Young Percival," said Sir Bors, "we all of us, and all men, are banned from the castle forever, by thy mother the queen."

"Alas!" said Percival. "Then I shall come along with you, for to be a knight is my only interest in the world."

"Thou canst not do that," said Sir Bors, and the other knights agreed. "For until a boy is full grown he must honor the wishes of his parents. He must do that even if he is being raised as a girl, which practice would seem to oppose the scheme of Nature. But when he hath reached the size of manhood he can then do as he will, and if he is made of the stuff of men he can be as good as any."

Now Percival was greatly disappointed, but he would have done anything these knights told him to do, so much did he admire them in their coats of steel and tall and strong as they were.

"And now we must leave thee," said Sir Bors, and he and the others mounted their great stallions above which rose their long lances on the right side, and on the left they bore huge shields which were painted in bright colors with their devices, and they wore plumes in their helmets and from their belts hung swords with golden hilts in scabbards of gold. And Percival had never seen so marvelous a sight in all his life.

But before they went away the strap broke on the shield of one of them, and it fell from his neck to the ground, and the knight would have dismounted to fetch it, but Percival ran there.

"Nay," said this knight, who was named Sir Lamiel, " 'tis too heavy for a boy to lift."

But Percival was already there, and he easily lifted up the heavy shield, which was made of iron and weighed many pounds, and he gave it to the knight. And all of them marveled that he should be able to lift it.

And Sir Bors said, "Percival, thou art a stout boy. When thou hast become a man, come to the court of King Arthur and join the Round Table, for methinks I see in thee a fine knight indeed."

And then they rode away, and Percival returned to the castle, where he found that his mother and his sister were in great consternation over his absence.

And when his mother saw him she embraced him weeping and then she waxed wroth, saying, "Wicked boy, to leave thy mother!"

"Mother," said Percival. "I shall not disobey you further, but I tell you this, that when I am a man I shall become a knight."

And his mother wept further, and she tore her hair. "So was thy father Pellinore killed," she cried, "and so have all thy brothers gone away and left me alone. And perhaps it hath been unnatural to rear thee with thy sister as two girls, but better that than to prepare thee for fighting, for that is what knights do." And then she composed herself, and she hoped she could keep Percival with her forever by misrepresenting his age.

And two years passed, and Percival was of the age of sixteen, and he had grown more than six feet high and he was of the strength of any two men, but his mother told him he was but twelve years old, and he had no way of knowing better, for he was kept from all other male persons and even his servants were all women, and they were ancient crones, and thereby his mother hoped to keep him always ignorant of sexual matters. And he was no longer even allowed to be alone with his sister, for she was fourteen and had become a woman.

Now in these circumstances poor Percival might have grown to middle age while still believing himself a boy, had not an evil knight, hearing that this castle was without men and therefore defenseless, come to ravage it. For while it was true that, as Percival's mother believed, knights did kill others, there is no defense against wicked men (with whom the world is ever rife) except good men who are as formidable. And the greatest delight of an evil man is to find some good person who is without weapons, and then he swoopeth down upon him as the falcon doth upon a coney and teareth at his flesh and devoureth him. Therefore knights who will defend virtue are always necessary on the earth, until we know the peace of Heaven.

And this felon came into the castle and he seized the

queen and Percival's sister and he put them into bonds. And Percival at this time was in the garden, a-sitting on the wall, watching for more knights to pass. But then he heard the cry of his womenfolk, and he went within, and he saw them in their bonds.

And the wicked knight was there, and seeing how Percival was dressed, he believed him a young woman as well, and he said to him, "Well, thou art an ugly wench with a growing mustache and great wide shoulders and no bosom at all, else I should mishandle thee as I shall do these two winsome women."

And Percival said to him, "I believe that what you would do is not right. Yet you are a knight and I think that knights serve the good."

And this wicked knight threw back his head and he laughed uproariously. "Thou great booby," said he, "there are virtuous knights and there are knights who serve evil. Obviously I am of the latter."

Now Percival had learned a new thing, and then he commanded the evil knight to untie the bonds of his mother and his sister. And the knight not only refused, but he drew his sword and he said he would slay Percival for having the ugliest body he had ever seen on a maid, and he made a great swipe at him.

But Percival evaded the sword's edge and he leapt at this evil knight and he lifted him up, armor and all, with his great strength, as he might have lifted one of his sister's dolls, and then he threw him through the window, and the miscreant fell to the hard ground without, for there was no moat, and his armor burst into many pieces, and in each piece was a member of his body, and therefore he died as a man of parts.

And then Percival freed his womenfolk, and he said to the queen, "Mother, methinks I am old enough now to become a knight."

"Nay, Percy," said his mother, "thou art yet a boy and must not leave me."

"But I am quite as large as the evil knight whom I

threw from the window," said Percival, "and I am as strong as a man."

"But manhood is not a thing of size," said his mother. "There are dwarfs who are tiny though being very old. And a child of the giants is already an exceeding large person at the age of five."

"But, Mother," said Percival, "even the wicked knight said that I was growing a mustache."

And his mother called him to her and she looked closely at his upper lip.

"Percy," said she, " 'tis no natural growth of hair on thy lip, but a malady of the skin which is caused by eating peaches that are underripe." And she took her sewing-scissors and she clipped off every hair.

And Percival was too modest to reveal to her that he had hair elsewhere on his person, his arms and his chest and his secrets, and he now believed that this was due to some similar cause from without, perhaps bathing in warm water, and therefore when next he washed he asked the crones who served him to bring him cold water straight from the well, and further to float in it a cake of the ice which had been saved, and buried in the earth, from the previous winter. But the season was late spring, and little of the ice was left, and therefore the water was not so cold as to freeze off the hair on Percival's body, and it continued to grow. And had he known of such a thing as a razor he would have shaved himself clean everywhere. And Percival was the most ignorant youth in the world, for he had no father nor brothers to teach him of male things.

Now two years went by and Percival had grown even larger, and unless his mother trimmed his face frequently he had a full silken mustache and a beard, and because her scissors could not work so closely as to make him smooth, she produced a razor and this was the first he had ever seen.

"Well, Mother," said he, "doth not this beard of mine mean that I am now a man? I had it not when I was a boy."

"Ah, Percy," said his mother, "thou hast no more hair on thy face than when thou wert a little child and I shaved thee during the night whilst thou didst sleep, so as not to frighten thee with this razor."

And Percival believed this, as he always believed everything his mother told him.

And then one day when he and his mother and his sister were seated in the garden, all working at their embroidery, they heard a great roar and looking up they saw the hideous head of a gigantic cockatrice the which was staring at them over the wall through bulging eyes as green as the deep waters of the tarn in which it made its home, and then it flicked its foul tongue at them, the which was long as an horse and covered with foul slime, and when drops of this slime fell onto the wall the stones were melted as if they were wax near a flame. And a great hole was being made in the wall, through which the dread serpent would enter, for to devour them all in a trice, for it was an insatiable monster.

Now the stare of a cockatrice, as is well known, doth paralyze its intended prey, and Percival's mother and his sister were as if frozen where they sat, but by some natural instinct Percival knew not to look at the foul serpent, and he was not frightened at all. And he went to where a stout sapling grew, and he tore it from its roots, and then going to that part of the garden in which an artful wildness had been arranged in contrast to the formal flower beds, he found a rugged stone and he raised it and he dashed it upon another rock so that it broke into jagged fragments, and one of these, with a sharp point, he fastened to the end of the sapling with laces taken from his dress.

And then he hurled this makeshift spear at the serpent, at whom he was careful not to stare directly, and nevertheless his aim was unerring. And his spear went dead into the left eye of the cockatrice and passing through it clove the evil head in twain, and from the great skull flowed a flood of foul yellow poison, the which splashing onto the earth dissolved an enormous hole in the ground, and the twisting body of the serpent plunged therein, the great scaly tail lashing the sides until they fell in upon it and covered the obscene thing entirely.

And except for the broken wall and some lingering smoke and a great filthy stench, the place was as before. And once the serpent's eye had been put out, Percival's mother and his sister were freed from the enchantment.

And the queen now said, "Thou art a good boy, Percy, to have driven off that naughty dog."

And his sister said, "We thank thee, dear Percy."

But Percival said, "Mother, methinks that was no dog, for dogs are much smaller."

"Well then," said his mother, "a toad, and 'twas a nasty thing which might give thee warts if thou endeavored to pluck the precious jewel from its head."

"A toad," said Percival, "is quite smaller yet." And then he smiled fondly. "Mother, I have a sense that you have been deluding me for some time, to keep me here amongst women exclusively. Nor can I blame you for so doing, for you are a woman, and you would wish to keep a man a boy, so that you would have your child by you forever. But I am grown now, for twice I have protected you and my sister from things which would do you harm. And now I think I must not wait for more evils to come here, but rather as a man to go and seek them out and fight them before they get this far. For I believe that this is a man's duty, and not womanly to stay at home."

And his mother knew the time had come when he would leave her, for all she had done to keep him. But she said, "Yes, Percival, and yet for all the brave men in the world who fight for the good, there is no less of evil anywhere."

"Well," said Percival, "if there were no evil, then what would become of bravery?"

"This hath a fine sound," said his mother. "And there is a certain truth in it, but not always is evil so easily to be identified, nor what is bravery, either. And where was the sense of the fight between thy father Pellinore and the noble Gawaine? For they were both good men and brave."

"Mother," said Percival, "with all respect, you are a woman, and you can never methinks understand the ways of men, their duties and their obligations."

"I think I know this," said his mother the queen. "That one day they will all slay one another, and all that women have done to preserve the world will be so rendered nugatory. But I know that I can not stay thee further, Percival." And weeping she kissed him and she wished him to go with God, and his sister did the same, and Percival went into the world.

And he walked on foot, for he had no horse, and he had no weapons nor armor, and indeed he was attired as a maiden. And after he had walked some leagues he met a tinker on the road, who drove a cart which was pulled by an ass, and in this cart he carried his tinware. And Percival greeted this fellow courteously, but the tinker abused him.

"Thou art either the hairest maid I have ever seen," said he, "or the most vilest effeminate sodomite, and in either case, a pestilence!" And he struck Percival with his whip.

Now Percival was not hurt nor was he angered, and he took the whip away from this fellow with one strong hand whilst with the other he lifted him from his seat on the cart, and he lowered him to the ground.

And this tinker turned pale and he shook with fear, for never had he felt such tremendous strength in any man. And then he begged Percival for mercy, and he said, "My lord, I meant no insult to you. 'Twas but a jest in the poor taste for which we traveling tradesmen are noted. And surely you will not punish me much, for I am old and furthermore I am feeling seedy at the moment, owing to a fish I ate lately, the which was putrid," &tc., &tc.

"I am dressed as a woman," said Percival, "because I have no other attire. Now look at my robe, which is of fine silken stuff, and this girdle is closed with a fastening

of pure gold. And then tell me where I might go to sell it
for money with which I might then buy weapons."

Now the tinker realized that Percival knew nothing of
commercial matters and he saw that the costly silk was
alone worth more than a fine horse, and there was enough
gold in the buckle to purchase an entire armory.

"These things, my lord," said he, "are worth not much.
But because I am your obedient servant I shall accept
them in exchange for my donkey. And if you are willing
to give me your bracelet as well, you might take my cart
as well, and all the tinware in it."

Now Percival seeing a use for all these things did strike
this bargain with the tinker, and therefore he undressed to
his smalls and he gave all his clothes and gold jewelry to
the fellow, and in return he took what the tinker owned.
And when the tinker left him (for to go into town and sell
these things), Percival made himself a suit of armor by
fastening many pans together, and for an helmet he put a
pot upon his head. And then he tore the cart apart, and he
used its floor for his shield, and from a stave in its side he
fashioned him a sword, lashing another stave across it for
an handle. And then from one of the shafts he made himself a lance, the end of which he sharpened on a rock.

And so equipped he mounted the ass, which was so low
that Percival's feet dragged the earth, and he rode in
search of knightly adventures.

Now when Percival reached the town some constables
had taken in charge the tinker, who they believed had
stolen the gold and silken stuffs from some noblewoman,
and they took him before a magistrate, who sentenced him
to be put upon display in the market square in the stocks
by day and to be thrown into a dungeon at night. And to
him the magistrate said, "Happy thou art that this is not in
the olden time before Arthur came, else thine hands would
have been cut off at the wrists!"

And the tinker was already in the stocks when Percival
arrived there, and when Percival found out what had happened he said to the constables, "Release this poor fellow

at once, for he speaketh the truth. 'Twas from me he got the things and honestly."

But thinking from Percival's costume that he was a madman they sought to subdue him with their staffs, and they would not listen to him until he took them together in the crook of his elbow by their throats and they could not breathe. And then they agreed to release the tinker from his punishment.

And thus Percival had righted his first wrong, though it was not in the knightly way he so desired, and then he left the town to continue his quest for adventures.

Now he had not gone many leagues along the road (and so as not to tire his little donkey he had got off and he walked alongside it), when he saw a bright red pavilion standing in a meadow and as he neared it he heard the sound of a damsel's weeping coming from within. And therefore he went to it and leaving his ass outside he entered the pavilion and there he saw a maiden who was tied with iron chains.

And having no tools about him Percival brake these chains with his hands and he released the damsel.

"Oh, thank thee, dear fool," said the maiden, who was very beautiful to Percival's eyes, and he was well qualified in this matter, for his mother and his sister were great beauties.

"But now," further said the damsel, "thou must run and fetch thy lord, for the wicked knight who holds me captive will soon return, and be assured that he would not be amused by thy motley, unique as it is in its tin construction, and he would visit dire punishment upon thee for loosing my bonds."

"Well," said Percival smiling happily, "then I have come to the right place, for I would fain meet a knight in honest combat!"

And the maiden did believe him a fellow of finite jest, for she knew her captor to be without a capacity for merriment. And she continued to beg him to flee, but then the thunder of hoofs could be heard, and Percival went without the pavilion.

And there he saw an huge knight who was dismounting from a charger.

And seeing Percival this knight said, "Ho, merry-andrew, come here." And Percival went to him courteously, and the knight said, "Now here is my proposal: that for every jest of thine which maketh me to laugh I shall give thee a piece of gold. But for every one which doth not amuse me I shall make thee eat a piece of my horse's shit."

But Percival bowed and he said, "Sir, I would fight you honestly."

And the night scowled darkly. "Well," said he, "that is not at all laughable. Prepare then to eat a great horse turd." And he went behind his charger and fetched up a steaming piece of dung from a newly fallen pile there, and he came to Percival to force him to eat it.

But Percival knocked him to the earth with the back of his hand, and then said to him, "Sir, again I say that I would fight you."

And the knight arose, and he answered, "Evil as I am, I do not slay poor madmen, the which are under an heavenly protection that not even the Devil, my master, dares to challenge."

"But I am not mad, sir," said Percival. "I am hung with this tinware because I have no proper armor, and my weapons are made of wood because I possess none of steel. But if I kill you (and I hope I can, for you are not a man of worship so to have kept a beautiful damsel in captivity) I shall take your armor and sword and horse."

Now this speech infuriated the knight, and crying, "Insolent puppy!" he leapt onto his charger and he rode upon Percival.

Now Percival mounted his little donkey and he lifted his lance which was made of the cart-shaft. And though this lance was made of wood only, without a steel head, when the evil knight finished his charge Percival's weapon had penetrated his breastplate and entered his heart, and all his blood poured down into his boots, and he fell dead to the ground.

And the maiden had watched this fight from the door of the pavilion, and when it was over she asked Percival to come within. And when he did she gave him the chains with which she had been fastened and she told him to put them about her once more.

"And with your great strength, sir, you shall pull them tighter than that weak knight, whom you have slain, was ever able to do," said she, and was breathing heavily and biting her lips. "And when you flog me, do it savagely with all your might, for more blood must flow with every bite of the lash!"

"Lady," said Percival, "I am your deliverer and not your tormentor. You are quite free now and may go whither you please."

"But what I please to do is to stay here," said the maiden, "and to be punished severely for my naughtiness."

"Well," said Percival, "I understand nought of this, and I see no sense in being chained when one might be free, nor in being flogged when one hath committed no crime."

"But I am a malefactress," said the maiden, "because I am a woman. And it was Eve who caused Adam to be expelled from Paradise, and all women since have borne her shame."

"But," said Percival, "without the woman, man would not have known the difference between good and evil, and therefore there would have been no virtue for knights to serve. And if in the cause of good I had not delivered you, I should not now have proper armor and weapons."

And he went without and he stripped the armor from his fallen enemy and he put it on himself, and he took his lance and sword and shield as well.

And the maiden came out of the pavilion and she said, "Sir, in delivering me you have gained possession of me, as of the armor and the weapons, and to leave me here were against the law of chivalry."

"Well then," said Percival, "I expect I must take you along with me." And he lifted her upon the ass. "But for this heavy armor and lance, which would be too heavy for this small beast, I should let you ride the horse." And mounting the charger which had belonged to the knight, he rode in the van.

And the maiden, whose vanity was as great as her beauty, felt no gratitude towards him for preserving her, whereas she had greatly admired the wicked knight who had abused her, for no one is more important to a tormentor than his victim. But to Percival she was but an encumbrance. And therefore, learning that he would go to King Arthur's court for to become a knight of the Round Table, this maiden determined spitefully to delay him as much as possible, and for every league they traveled she had another complaint, the answering of which required that Percival stop his horse and listen patiently, and then do what was wanted or explain why it could not be done.

Which was to say, he could fetch water to treat her thirst when a stream ran near by, but he could not make the road less dusty. And he could lead them off the road and through the meadows, but he could not defend her against the gnats which rose in clouds from the grass, and if they followed the bank of a river he could not guarantee she would not be offended by the sight of lizards and frogs.

And finally she refused to ride longer on the donkey, which was so short of leg that her robe trailed in the dust, and therefore Percival took her onto the horse and he held her before him, but she soon complained that his breastplate of steel was too hard and too cold against her back. And then he mounted her behind him, but it was not long before she said the back of his armor was no better and that clutching his sword belt she did hurt her delicate hands.

So Percival dismounted, saying, "Lady, take the horse for yourself." And then he walked alongside in the heavy armor and carrying the tall lance, but he was young and strong, and all he thought of was going to Camelot and applying to King Arthur for knighthood.

And the maiden had never known a man whom her beauty did not distract and soon made importunate, and had not Percival been so handsome and strong she might have believed him an eunuch.

Now they were still in the country when darkness began to fall in the evening, and the maiden stopped the horse and she said to Percival, "Sir, we have been traveling all the day, and now night cometh, and we have nothing to eat nor no shelter."

"Well," said Percival, "perhaps we shall soon reach Camelot."

And now the maiden quite lost her temper. "Methinks we are nowhere near Camelot! And if you believe that I shall ride farther you are mistaken. And why did you neglect to fold the pavilion and to bring it along, so that I should have had protection from the pestilent vapors of the night?"

"Lady," said Percival, "I did not think of that, for the truth is that being in the world is quite new to me, and I have never before been so long away from the castle in which I was born."

"Then," said the maiden, "I can see that you know nothing of chivalry, which is the law by which a knight is absolutely obedient to a lady which he doth serve."

"Well," said Percival, "I would learn about this law, for I long to be a knight."

And the maiden understood that he was but a naïve boy at heart, and therefore believing as she did that between a man and a woman one has the total mastery while the other is a slave, she said, "Thou must never address me without asking my leave. And when thou hast received permission to speak, thine head must never rise above the level of thy shoulders."

And Percival now asked to be allowed to address her and when this was granted he said, "Lady, I can not bend my neck so far whilst wearing this helmet."

"Then remove it," said she.

And so he did, and she then directed him to prepare for her a shelter for the night and with his sword he chopped down some trees and made a hut from them, and he gathered fruits and nuts for her supper, and from the fragrant leaves of a bush he prepared tea in his helmet. And after she ate, the maiden lay down upon a bed which he had made of soft branches and moss, and she went to sleep.

And Percival lay down upon the earth before the floor of this hut, like unto a faithful dog, and as he had no clothes but the armor he kept it on, and when rain began to fall during the night this armor filled with water and he was wet and cold, but he was not unhappy, for he believed he was doing what a knight should.

But then the maiden did cry from within the hut that she was cold and that he should bring something to warm her with. And therefore he rose and collected some thick branches, but when he brought these to her she abused him, saying, "Foolish wretch, they are sopping."

"Lady," said he, "I have nothing else with which to warm you."

"Then do it with thy large person," said she.

Therefore he lay down beside her, but this made her only the more furious. "Fool!" she cried. "Dost come here in wet armor?" And she commanded him to remove it from his body.

"But I wear only my smallclothes beneath," said Percival.

"Dost refuse a command from thy lady?" asked the maiden greatly indignant. And Percival therefore took off his armor and he lay down on the branches.

"Now," said the maiden, "put thine arms about me and hold me tight, so that I might be warmed. And take no liberties, on pain of being vile and grossly indecent."

Therefore Percival clasped the damsel to him, and as he had been quite cold himself he was warmed. But she still complained, saying, "I can not feel the heat of thy skin whilst I wear this robe." And so she removed her clothing and she commanded him to hold her again, and again she warned him only to clasp her in his arms and to do nothing impudent.

Now Percival found this an easy command to obey, for he knew not what else he might have done, and in his ignorance he was not aware what was the difference between a man's body and that of a woman, nor was he a sod who had interest in flesh of his own construction. But then he became aware that this maiden, who had seemed so slender when dressed, was considerably stouter when naked and lying down, and further that while she had commanded him to lie still she did herself begin to writhe. And she lay with her back to his front at first, but then she said that her spine had got warm and now she would do the same to the front of her body, and she turned to face him.

And now his own front was quite warm, in fact to the point of being queerly hot. And the maiden's face was against his chest, with his chin resting against her hair, the which was soft as silk and had the fragrance of flowers. And soon she complained again, and she moved so that she was beneath him, so that he could warm her better, and now she clasped him as tight as he held her, and whilst he obeyed her command not to move, she made incessant adjustments of her situation, and Percival felt as though he were in a pot being brought to the boil. And he was amazed by this, for it was at once both uncomfortable and pleasing, as when one scratched an itch till it bled.

And this matter was not finished before the dawn came, and Percival had not slept at all, yet in the morning he rose refreshed, and he donned his armor again and he made breakfast for them. And the maiden was not so peevish with him as she had been formerly, and therefore he believed that he was performing as a knight should. And when they resumed their journey she insisted on mounting the donkey and riding behind whilst he rode the horse.

Now it was not long before coming over an hill they

saw on the horizon the grandest castle in the world, which the morning sun did gild on all its towers and battlements, and Percival knew it must be that of King Arthur. And he made great joy.

And he said to the maiden on the ass, "Well, lady, soon I hope to be made a proper knight."

"Well, my lord," she said, "why then do not you ride ahead with all speed?"

"Do you give me leave to do that?" he asked.

"Ah," said the damsel, "you are no longer to be commanded by me."

But at that moment another knight appeared on the road before them, and he was Sir Agravaine, who believed that at last he had got proof that Sir Launcelot and the queen were paramours, and he was going again to see his brother Gawaine despite his earlier rebuff.

And Percival addressed him, saying, "Greeting, sir knight."

Now Agravaine was impatient to reach his elder brother, for he had seen Launcelot wearing a ring the which he had previously seen upon Guinevere's finger, and he believed this to be evidence of their illegal commerce, and he therefore spake disagreeably to Percival.

"Move aside, fellow," said he, "so that I, a knight of the Round Table, might pass."

And believing that this was the right thing to do, if a knight commanded him to do it, Percival did void the road.

But seeing the maiden on her donkey Sir Agravaine said to Percival, "And remove thy baggage as well."

Now Percival did not understand him, and he asked, "Pray, my dear sir, which is my baggage?"

And Sir Agravaine was vexed and he said, "Thou art an insolent fellow, and if I had time thou shouldst not go unpunished." And he rode rudely against the maiden's donkey with his great horse and he forced her off the road.

Now the damsel made no protest against this, and

indeed she looked at Sir Agravaine with much admiration. But Percival said, "Sir, if your behavior be typical of the knights of the Round Table, then I do not want to be one of them, for you have treated this maiden detestably."

And in great anger Sir Agravaine cried, "Well, thou hast brought upon thyself a sore punishment." And drawing his sword he swung it at Percival.

And not having the time to draw his own sword Percival evaded the blade of Sir Agravaine, and then before it could swing back the other way he seized Agravaine's arm and though it was encased in thick armor he brake it in his hands as if it were a twig.

Now Sir Agravaine did howl in pain and shame, and this greatly attracted the maiden.

"With your permission," said she to Percival, "I shall stay here and nurse this knight. Whereas methinks you are eager to reach Camelot."

Now Percival understood that his obligation to this damsel had been discharged and therefore he wished her the peace of God, and then he went along the road towards Camelot, for though he had been threatened with disillusionment as to Arthur's knights by reason of the poor performance of Sir Agravaine, he considered the possibility that this rude knight had not been of the company of the Round Table but rather served some other cause, and merely because he had been coming in the direction from Camelot did not mean that he had belonged there.

Now it will be remembered that Percival wore the armor of the knight whom he had vanquished on the day before, and he carried the shield of this knight, on which was displayed the curious device of an unicorn which was goring to death a lion, and whilst this meant nothing to Percival another knight who saw it now believed it was a challenge to him.

For King Arthur having long since returned from the tour of his realm, Launcelot and Guinevere had resumed their old practice of riding together into the royal orchards, and they had done so on this day, and they were

about to dismount for to pursue the end for which they
had come when Sir Launcelot heard the sound of creaking
armor not far away, and therefore he rode through the
trees and he saw Percival. And further, Launcelot saw that
the device on this knight's shield depicted the lion, which
was his own symbol, being run through by a unicorn.

Now the unicorn was the beast of Love, and its horn if
pounded into a powder was a cure for many venereal ail-
ments foremost among them being the malady which doth
cause the yard to wilt before it can perform its office. And
as it happened Sir Launcelot was no longer in his earliest
youth, and his powers were not so great as they had once
been, whereas the queen had grown more demanding with
age. And he was sensitive about this matter, and when in
the orchard he was ever worried that someone might spy
upon them, if not by design then by accident. And the
result of all these negative forces acting upon him was that
he was quick to take offense at the sight of this stranger.

And therefore Sir Launcelot cried to him to defend
himself, and then he did charge upon him with the most
puissant lance in all the world.

Now Percival, once again the recipient of inhospitality
in the shadow of Camelot, wondered whether this was typical of the treatment of aspirants to knighthood. But fewtering his own lance he answered Launcelot's charge with
his own. And this young lad, who had but lately left home
for the first time, and who had fought but once before and
that time with a makeshift lance fashioned from a cart-
shaft, now was about to meet the weapon of the greatest
knight of all.

But when they came together with a great shock it was
not young Percival who was thrown from his horse but
rather the mighty Sir Launcelot!

And Launcelot felt very old as he lay upon the ground,
and he did not spring up so quickly. And when he did rise
and draw his sword, and the Knight of the Unicorn dismounted and came to fight him by hand, Launcelot knew
his own blows to be not so powerful as of old, whereas his

opponent seemed even stronger than Gawaine had been when they fought long ago, and more. Did not Launcelot know his old friend Tristram were dead he might have believed it was he in disguise. And finally the moment came when he knew that this knight was even the superior of Tristram in strength, and there could no longer be any thought of defeating him quickly, for Launcelot must needs use all of his own force merely to keep from being overwhelmed.

And finally with a tremendous blow the other struck the sword from Sir Launcelot's grasp, and Launcelot's hand smarted sorely and his heart was stung no less in shame, and his sword flew over an huge oak tree.

And at this his opponent called a halt and went himself to fetch the sword, and he returned it to Sir Launcelot.

And greatly moved by this courtesy Sir Launcelot opened his visor and he said, "Clearly you are no caitiff, sir, for you might quite honestly have killed me."

And opening his own helm Percival said, "Nay, sir, I am no felon, but rather a squire who desires to become a knight more than anything in the world. My name is Percival, and I shall fight you further if you wish, but I should rather that you accepted my surrender, for I believe from your gentle speech that you are truly one of the knights of King Arthur."

And Sir Launcelot saw that though large in body he was scarcely more than a boy, and he wondered at him. But then he laughed and he said, "Percival, it were more just if I surrendered to *thee,* for methinks thou hast bested me clearly."

But Percival said, "Oh, nay, sir. Your sword slipped but temporarily from your grasp."

And Sir Launcelot was so amazed by Percival's prowess and he was so impressed by the lad's modesty that he took him straightway to King Arthur and he told the king what had happened.

And King Arthur looked at Percival and he stroked his

own beard, the which was now quite white, and finally he said, "Percival, dost know whom thou hast fought?"

And Percival said, "Nay, Sire, I know not."

"Well," said the king, "it was Sir Launcelot."

And Percival, who had fallen to his knees when admitted to King Arthur's presence and who had been told to rise, said nothing now.

"Dost not know who he is?" asked the king. "And why dost stand so, with thin head against thy breastbone?" And he was impatient with this boy, who acted like unto a cretin imbecile.

"Nay, Sire, I do not know, for I am ignorant of almost everything," said Percival, "including, apparently, even the proper fashion in which to stand before my king. But a maiden whom I lately served commanded me ever to keep mine head below my shoulders when addressing my superiors."

"Well," said the king, "a knight is obliged to protect a woman, and he is courteous and gentle with her at all times, but he need not to let her command him otherwise, else he might well encourage her in folly, to the which all women have a natural attraction owing to their vanity." And then King Arthur asked Percival how it was that he was so ignorant of the world.

"Sire, my mother did not allow me to leave our castle, and therefore I have had no association with anyone but her and my sister," said Percival.

"Then thou art to be commended for maintaining thy virility," said the king. And turning to Launcelot, King Arthur said, "He hath some ability with weapons, sayest thou?"

And Sir Launcelot answered, "With all respect, Majesty, what I say is that with a man of less generosity I might well have been slain."

But King Arthur could not but believe that his supreme knight did here, in the greatness of his heart, exaggerate most modestly.

"Percival," said he, "if thou wert able to stand a few

moments against Launcelot, then thou art obviously made of good stuff. Kneel then!" And the king drew Excalibur from its scabbard, and Sir Launcelot perceived that he had some difficulty with this, for his hands did tremble.

"Sire," said he, "may I . . ."

"Nay, my dear fellow," said King Arthur. "I've got it now. It has been a long time since I've done this, and my fingers are not so limber as they might be. Ah, there we have it. Now, young Purnival—"

"Percival, Sire," said Sir Launcelot, "by your leave."

"Percival, indeed!" jovially cried the king, and he lowered his sword towards the young man's shoulder.

"Majesty, your pardon," said Sir Launcelot. "Could you just turn the blade a bit so that the flat and not the edge will touch him? For Excalibur is marvelous keen."

"Certes," said King Arthur, and he did as asked, and he touched Percival on one shoulder and then on the other. "Rise, Sir Percinell, as a knight of the Round Table."

And Sir Percival's face did shine with joy. "And now, Sire," said he, "what be my first quest as a knight?"

And King Arthur had lifted Excalibur to look along its edge, and then he ran his thumb on it. "Well, look at that!" said he, as if to himself, " 'tis not so marvelous keen as once." And clapping his hands for a page he told the varlet to fetch him an armorer.

"Sire," said Sir Launcelot, "Sir Percival would know on which quest you would send him."

"Ah, yes, Purslaine," said King Arthur. "Well, I am afraid it hath been ever and a day since I have had at my disposal the quest of old. Whether this would mean that injustices are not nowadays so rife as once or merely that my subjects do not apply to me for rectification is perhaps moot."

"Sire," said Sir Launcelot, "with all respect. I think that it hath been a long time since you decided that Britain was free from felony."

"Indeed, Launcelot," said King Arthur, "but as I have grown older I have considered the alternative: that perhaps I do not hear as much as I did once. And perhaps the situation is rather that evil-doing hath got more subtle, perhaps even to the point at which it can not properly be encountered with the sword."

And considering young Percival, so eager as he was and so fresh of face, Sir Launcelot did feel, for the first time in a long while, the movement of his conscience. For he had fallen back into his old role as the queen's companion when he returned from the episode at the castle of Pelles the maimed king, and he had since gone no farther than the orchards. And when King Arthur had returned from the tour of his realm he made great joy on seeing Launcelot and he had indeed prevailed upon him to remain there, for now that most of the other knights had gone in quest of the Sangreal the king had no one to talk with.

And therefore did Sir Launcelot now suggest that Sir Percival be made the queen's protector, so that he might himself again seek the Holy Grail.

"Well," said King Arthur, "I should think that this young knight, who hath only lately escaped the imprisonment (though a benign one) of his mother and sister would desire anything but to be confined again with a woman. Nay, good Launcelot, I think I must give him the opportunity to exercise his new manhood!"

And to Percival he said, "The general quest of the knights of the Round Table at this time is for the Holy Grail. Now, ask me not what that be, for I can not tell thee except that it is something sacred, which pertaineth to Our Lord, and therefore there can be no greater employment for a Christian than to seek it, and if it is never found, then nevertheless there can have been nothing more virtuous than the looking for it. Canst thou understand what I say?"

And he asked this because Sir Percival, though a handsome young man and eager, did ever give the impression at this time of being slow in his wits.

"Methinks," said Percival, "that this is a thing which

though unknown at the outset may well be recognizable in the sequel."

And King Arthur smiled and he said, "Percival, perhaps thou art naïve in the important matters, as a young man should properly be, but thou hast a fundamental grasp of truth."

And an armorer came then unto King Arthur, and the king said to him, "Excalibur would seem to have dulled. I would that thou sharpen it."

And this armorer took King Arthur's sword and he held it so that the light was reflected from its edge. "Sire," said he, " 'tis not your everyday steel but rather some bloody magical metal. I can not think my grindstone will touch it, I'm damned if I do. Just what would do the job I can not say: perhaps a diamond, perhaps not, so bloody hard as it be."

"Methinks that cursing will never help," so chided him King Arthur, and begging his pardon the armorer withdrew, but in truth he was a fellow whom lack of worth had made lazy and blasphemous, and most of the staff at Camelot were much the same. And even the kitchens were no better than they should have been, for Sir Kay had pleaded not to be left behind when the other knights went upon the quest for the Sangreal, and though King Arthur worried for his well-being when afield he could not deny him permission to go upon this Quest of quests.

And now the king told Sir Percival to get from the armorer new furnishings to replace that which he wore, which had come from the wicked knight whom he had vanquished, and to provide him with a new shield on the which would be painted his own device.

"Sire," then asked Percival, "I ask your permission to use the device of my late father, the which was an eagle."

And the king said, "My friend Pellinore bore the eagle on his shield, and art thou his youngest son?"

"I am, Sire," said Sir Percival, "though I never knew him."

And the king spoke gravely. "Sir Percival, thou art now

a knight of the Round Table, and of a new generation. We who came before thee did as well as we knew how, but as we were beginners in chivalry, mistakes were made undoubtedly, and that all men are sinners is that rare truth which is without condition." And he stopped for a moment, and he looked down, and Sir Launcelot did stir uncomfortably as well, but Percival listened eagerly, for he yearned to hear all that pertained to the Round Table.

And King Arthur said then, "Dost know how thy father was killed?"

"In a fight with Sir Gawaine," said Sir Percival. "So saith my mother."

"Is it thine intent to seek revenge in the name of thy family?" asked King Arthur.

"Revenge, Sire?" And Sir Percival was puzzled. "Forgive me for mine ignorance, but I know not the meaning of that. If it is some phase of virtue, then I shall seek to perform it."

"Well, Percival," said the king, "would that the world were such as to make possible the survival of thy naïveté. But just as pure gold hath only a decorative purpose and for sterner uses must be alloyed with baser metals, so must the pure heart be made more sturdy by means of certain truths, which in themselves may be ignoble. To know evil sufficiently to fight against it, but not so well as to be infected by it, is the duty of the knight."

"Sire," said Percival bowing.

"But distinctions," said King Arthur, "are sometimes hard to draw, for our obligations do oft war each on each. 'Tis a good thing to defend relatives, but to join the Round Table is to forsake all others though they be even blood-kin. For to be a knight is to make a free choice, whereas one belongs *nolens volens* to a family." And the king said further, "Thy father King Pellinore was a fine man, and were he to have met his death at the hands of a caitiff, I should urge thee to seek out the miscreant and to put him to the sword. However, he was killed in a fair fight by another knight quite as fine."

Now Percival understood what the king meant, and he said, "My mother did confirm that the fight was fair, and I bear no ill will against the noble Sir Gawaine, who did what he believed he must do and was not dishonorable in any wise. Methinks it were in bad taste if I became his closest friend, yet when we meet I shall embrace him as my fellow knight."

And King Arthur was overjoyed to hear this, and not since Launcelot had first come to his court had he met a knight so virtuous as the ingenuous Percival. And he told him to go with God.

Now Percival was about to leave the court when the armorer, who had carried Excalibur to a window (not so much as to see whether he might think of a means of sharpening it as enviously to study the jewels with which its handle was encrusted), and deciding to return it to King Arthur without doing any further work, he called to Percival when he passed him.

"Ho, varlet," said he, taking Percival from his youth, and regardless of his size and his armor, to be merely a page, "take to the king his toothpick."

And Sir Percival did as he was commanded, and he returned Excalibur to King Arthur. Then he went back to the armorer, and he said, "I must have mine own suit of armor and a shield."

But this armorer was a base fellow and when they reached the armory he was rude and abusive, and at length Sir Percival found his presence to be disagreeable, and therefore he hung him by the collar on an hook high upon the wall where he thrashed impotently.

Meanwhile King Arthur looked again at the edge of the sword, now that Percival had carried it to him in his strong young hands, and he saw that its edge gleamed as of old. And then he plucked an hair from his beard, and he touched it lightly to the sword and it was cut in twain.

"Launcelot," said he, " 'tis a wondrous thing. Can it be. . . . ? Dost remember how, many years ago, when we filled the Table all but for one seat, the which was called the Siege Perilous, and Pellinore would sit upon it, but did burn his breech?" And King Arthur smiled at that memory, and then he was very sad at the loss of his old friend, and even sadder in the realization that many years had passed. And his memory not being what it had used to be, he asked Sir Launcelot which it was who had said the seat was to be kept empty for one who would come, Merlin or the Lady of the Lake?

And when he received no answer to this question King Arthur no longer looked into the middle distance, where he had been staring for some time, but to where Launcelot had been standing. But that great knight no longer stood there. Indeed he had asked for his leave some time before, and getting it he departed. But King Arthur did not remember that at all.

For what had happened was that Launcelot had himself suddenly remembered leaving Guinevere alone in the orchard, a long time before, when he had come upon Percival.

And when he went to the orchard to find her now, she was long gone. And therefore in great concern he went openly to her privy chamber instead of using the secret means behind the arras. (And had Sir Agravaine been spying at his post he could surely now have had evidence against these adulterers.)

And never had Guinevere been so insulted as she was now, to be left forgotten in a peach orchard for two hours.

And when Sir Launcelot came to Guinevere's chamber he said, "Lady, my neglect was inadvertent. A very great knight hath come to Camelot."

"Then send him to me," said the queen, "for I would have a new bedfellow."

And Sir Launcelot was greatly shocked to hear her speech. "Guinevere," said he severely, "there are times when I must be more than thy lap dog. Thou hast nothing to do but nurse thy vanity, which hath grown ever more valetudinarian throughout the years. My brother knights have all gone to seek the Holy Grail, but here I remain, the defender of a peach orchard. I have long since given up my claim to knighthood, and now methinks I can hardly even call myself a man."

And Guinevere was ever appeased to some degree when Launcelot was provoked into a display of any kind of feeling and especially if it was self-disgust.

"Thou art free to go away again," said she.

"Thank you," said Sir Launcelot, "for that which is as nothing when it cometh from a woman, even the queen if she be but consort and not the sovereign power."

And now he had delivered to her a telling blow, and Guinevere did grasp up an hand-mirror from her dressing-table and this she flung at him, and being a knight he would not flinch from the attack of a woman, and therefore this heavy gold-bound mirror did strike him in the front of his head and he fell on a carpet, bleeding from the first wound he had received in time out of memory, and in a boudoir, the which for some men is a more dangerous place than any field of steel.

And Guinevere, in the kind of contrition that was gratifying to her, did bathe his hurt in her toilet-water and she bound his head with a silken undergarment. And so we leave the great Launcelot, who was invulnerable except to his lady love, and we shall go abroad for a while.

BOOK XVIII

How Mordred came to Camelot and was knighted
by his father the king.

Now Sir Agravaine, felled by Percival, had been attended
by the maiden who had stayed with him, and she put his
broken arm into a sling the which she fashioned from her
petticoat. And she expected him to be grateful for this, but
he was not, for he believed that it was rather her privilege
to aid a knight of the Round Table, being obviously no
woman of high station if she rode an ass. Had she been
mounted on a palfrey and been accompanied by a proper
retinue, then Agravaine would have been obsequious.

Now as we know this maiden was either slave or
slaveowner with men—but she was not prepared for Agravaine's indifference, and therefore she was amazed when
he gave her a piece of gold for her services and mounted
his horse and rode away. And therefore she concluded (as
these vain women will) that he was a loathsome homosex-
ualist. And seeing him stop another knight who had just
come over the hill and engage him in conversation she believed he was importuning him to join him in an unnatural
act. Therefore she mounted her donkey and she went
away bitterly.

But actually it was the other knight who had stopped
Agravaine, and not for sodomitic purposes but rather to

ask him of the route to Camelot, and he was not a knight but rather a squire who carried a blank shield.

Now this squire was as young a man as Percival, but not so fit-looking nor so handsome, and his face was marvelous pale and his hair was black and his eyes were even blacker and so deep set as rarely to reflect the light of day, and at times they seemed more like holes without eyeballs. And yet withal there was about him something remotely familiar to Sir Agravaine, and he did not therefore feel for him the immediate dislike which he felt for most strangers. And in addition this squire was properly flattering to him.

"Then Camelot is just beyond yon hill?" said this squire. "I would fain go there and admire the gallant knights of the Round Table, of which company I should judge, my dear sir, that you are one, for never have I seen a finer seat on an horse."

"Well, indeed I am," said Sir Agravaine, "and when thou goest before King Arthur (for I suspect that thou wouldst become a knight), pray tell him that Sir Agravaine did meet thee and that he commendeth thee. For I am nephew to the great Arthur and not without influence upon him."

"Then I know great joy," said the squire. "For, dear Agravaine, I am thy brother Mordred."

"Can it be?" said Agravaine in amazement. "Wert thou not an infant only yesterday? Well, I did think that thou hadst a familiar look."

And they then dismounted and they embraced each other.

And Agravaine asked of their mother the queen Margawse, and he expressed satisfaction that their brother Sir Gawaine had avenged the death of their father King Lot.

Now Mordred, being detestably unnatural, cared nothing for his mother and even less for his foster-father and he considered that any revenge that was not his own (for which the whole world was the recipient) was without meaning for him. But recognizing that his brother was vain and a fool he believed that he might be able to use him for his own evil purposes, and therefore he gave voice to the conventional sentiments.

"Our three brothers," said Agravaine, "are every one of them now married, and all are fathers. But I have yet to find the woman for whom I would shed mine armor and lay away my sword, Mordred. The hearth is not my natural habitat. Give me the field, with its fluttering pennons and the drums of war!" For Agravaine was delighted to find a young relative to whom he could boast, and so he did this fatuously for some time. "I expect that," said he at last, "with Tristram dead and our Gawaine rusticated in this marriage, I am in effect the first knight of the realm."

Now Mordred, who though as young as Percival knew as much as the latter knew little, was quite aware that Agravaine spoke rot and to provoke him into even greater folly (and thereby to gain more power over him) he said, "I tell thee, Brother, I believed thou wert the great Launcelot himself until thou didst announce thy name."

And Agravaine scowled in hatred. "It is to me the greatest mystery," said he, "that Launcelot should enjoy his reputation, Mordred. But when thou hast got older thou shalt undoubtedly learn that the witless world doth oft applaud that which is not at all great. Launcelot's achievements, if examined without bias, are exceeding small. An ensample is his overwhelming of Meliagrant, who was an inferior knight to begin with, and furthermore he was lovesick at the time and distracted by thoughts of Guinevere."

"Ah, the queen our aunt," said Mordred. "Is she as beautiful as they say?"

And Agravaine had trouble with his breathing, for he did desire Guinevere so much, and so hopelessly, that he tended to suffocate at the thought of her. "She is comely, Mordred, quite fair to the sight. But I could tell thee—" And here he stopped, for as yet only Gawaine had heard his suspicions, as being the eldest brother, and though Agravaine was superficially foolish as Mordred believed him, he was not altogether a fool (for was he not correct in his suspicion of Launcelot and Guinevere?). Nor was he reckless, and finally Guinevere *was* the queen and despite what he said, he knew very well that Launcelot was the greatest knight in the world. (For Agravaine was one of those persons whose bitterness enables them to see the truth, as it doth keep them from knowing quite how to deal with it).

And therefore he would not speak further on the subject with Mordred at this time, until he knew him better.

But Mordred with his cunning sensed that Agravaine knew something damaging to Guinevere, else he would not have restrained himself, and he knew that he would be able to get Agravaine to speak of it sometime, for that he had begun to say it and then stopped was evidence of his weakness. If he had been strong in virtue he would not have said anything; and if strong in evil, he would have said it all.

Now Sir Agravaine wished to continue on to Gawaine's castle, and all the more so now that Mordred had joined him, for he believed that Gawaine would make great joy on seeing their youngest brother.

But Mordred had no interest in meeting Gawaine, for he knew him as a knight without reproach, and therefore there would be no way to use him in his schemes. And he asked Agravaine whether it would not be better to wait until he had been knighted.

"I expect thou hast good reason," said Agravaine. "Let us go unto our uncle." And he turned his horse back towards Camelot. And this was the first time that Mordred subtly asserted his dominance over his brother, but the second occasion came even before they reached King Arthur's court.

Now they came upon a peasant who was between the shafts of a cart, the which he was pulling along the road. And Mordred drew up and he said to his brother Agravaine, "Is it not an unfortunate boor who must serve as his own beast of burden?"

And Sir Agravaine shrugged. "I care nought for him, little Brother."

"Yet are we not Christians?" asked Mordred. "And is he not also a creation of God's?"

"Certes," piously agreed Sir Agravaine. "And therefore if he is too poor to afford a beast to pull his cart, then did not God make him so?"

"No doubt that art right," said Mordred. "But perhaps God made him poor so as to give us the opportunity to prove our charity."

"Ah," said Agravaine, "could this be so? And how might this be done, dear Mordred?"

"Well," said Mordred, "methinks thou must give him some gold, with which to buy him an ox. And I should give him some of mine, but I possess none, being but a squire."

"Thou art but a young man, Mordred, but thou hast a virtue that we of the older generation have forgot," said Agravaine, "(if indeed we ever had it), but our first task was to rid the realm of the larger evils. In thy purity of heart thou canst teach us much!" And so saying he took some gold from the purse which hung upon the saddle and he gave it to the peasant, who looked at it and then at him in bewilderment.

And then Agravaine and Mordred rode on, but when they had gained half a league Mordred stopped his horse and he said, "My dear Agravaine, methinks we did neglect to tell that boor to use the gold only for to buy him a beast, and not to squander it on strumpets or gaming or the entertainments of mountebanks. Now, as it was thy gold, let me contribute mine energy: rest here whilst I ride back and instruct him."

And Mordred therefore rode back along the road, and Agravaine believed him the finer for this.

Now when the peasant had finally understood that the gold was his to keep he dropped the shafts of his cart and indeed he set out for the nearest town where there were harlots and other entertainment, and this was in the other direction from Camelot, where all such things were banned. And because he was on foot Mordred soon caught him up.

And Mordred said to him, "Good boor, the money which hath been given thee is for thine hire as soldier, for I am Mordred and I shall one day overthrow the vile rule under which thou dost suffer. And thou shalt serve in my conquering forces."

"But, my lord," said this clown, "in truth I do not suffer as a subject of the great Arthur, whom I therefore love, and I have no reason for wishing him desposed."

"Well," said Mordred, "dost not want a beast of burden to pull thy cart?"

"Nay, my lord," said the rustic, "for then I should have to feed it."

Now Mordred was vexed, and he drew his sword and he put it at the belly of the peasant, and he said, "Then I shall explain this in a fashion which a simple head can easily understand: so long as King Arthur is allowed to keep the throne *thou art oppressed,* for I might cut out thy guts. But if he is overthrown thou shalt not only receive more treasure but thou shalt stay alive to enjoy it."

"My lord," said the boor, "I now understand this clearly and I am quite keen to serve you."

"Thou art a good churl," said Mordred, and he sheathed his weapon. "And thou shalt not go without profit if thou recruit thy fellows for this noble purpose, for I make to them the same offer and the same threat."

Then Mordred rejoined his brother Agravaine, and he said to him, "Brother, let us quicken our pace, for I would fain reach Camelot and be knighted by our royal uncle, and meet all the noble companions of the Round Table."

"Well," said Agravaine, "few of that company are in residence currently. They are away, Mordred, on the quest for the Sangreal, and God knows when we shall see them again."

"But thou hast remained?" asked Mordred. "And surely the king is protected by others as well?"

"I have remained there," said Sir Agravaine, "and doubtless one day I shall tell you why. And Launcelot is at Camelot as well. He doth protect his queen, Mordred. King Arthur needs no guarding, having no enemies for one, and for another with Excalibur he is himself alone an host of the greatest puissance. Dost not know that long ago, with a force of foot, mere kerns, he conquered great armies of horse?"

"Indeed," said Mordred, "I made all that pertains to King Arthur the constant study of my childhood. What better model for the British boy?"

Now Sir Agravaine commended his youngest brother for the reverence he showed towards the king, and he said, "But, dear Mordred, though Arthur be impervious against any threat from without, and invincible over all men, he can never be immune to another kind of danger: a very malignant type, for it cometh not with drawn sword and the scowl of war, but rather with the apparent smile of friendship, the bow of the vassal, the complaisance of the—" But Sir Agravaine would not yet say "wife." Rather here he broke off, and as at that moment they had gained the crest of an hill, when he next spake it was to say, "Look, Mordred, yonder."

For the lofty towers of Camelot had come into view, and the sun shone full upon them, and there was no grander vista in all the world.

And even Mordred was struck by the sight, but not with true awe, the which is an honorable emotion, but rather with an insuperable envy, and he thereupon determined that he should either become the master of this place or bring it down in ruins. And thus with the sight of Camelot his ambition took on another character than his previous aim, which had been merely to destroy his father the king for bringing him into existence. And Mordred was imbued with a purpose not only to kill King Arthur but thereafter to assume his crown! For was he not by blood the heir apparent?

And now he said to Agravaine, "I can not suppose that

in all the world there be a man so vicious as to desire King Arthur's downfall, but, dear Brother, this greatest of all monarchs is yet mortal and, alas! must one day die. And what of the succession?"

And Sir Agravaine said, " 'Tis a thing of which no one speaketh, Mordred. But thou art quite right that it should be of concern, for though Arthur is not so old in years, yet he hath too quickly grown aged. And I have not considered this before, but methinks that sin hath invisible emanations, the which do secretly poison those in its proximity though they themselves be blameless."

"Sin, brother?" asked Mordred. "Surely not at Camelot?"

But Agravaine grew guarded once more. "Little Brother Mordred," said he. "Being human we can none of us be without sin. It may well be that Arthur as king doth take upon his conscience all the failings of his subjects, in his role as God-appointed."

And then he spurred his horse and he galloped towards the great castle, and Mordred followed but only at the trot, for he did study each turret and machicolation and he looked for weaknesses therein and for the best places to let down ladders or to undermine the walls with galleries. And he was pleased to see, when he got closer, that the place did not look as impregnable as from afar, for there was evidence of neglect, and the walls had here and there notable cracks and stones were obviously loose on some battlements and on others the merlons had crumbled thus widening the crenels so that little protection was offered. And the moat had but an inch of water in it, and that was green with scum and foul with rubbish. (And all this was due to the absence of Sir Kay the seneschal.)

And Sir Agravaine who had got there ahead of him waited for Mordred at the drawbridge, which was ever down nowadays, and when they clattered across it, Mordred saw how many planks were rotten and that the chains were red with rust.

And he began to think that his coronation were soon indeed.

But then they went through the gate and into the great courtyard, and sensing rather than seeing at first that a golden light shone from above, Mordred did look aloft, and there on a high balcony, on a tower, was Queen Guinevere. Now, of her Mordred had not previously thought at all, for to him women meant nothing, because he had no sexual appetite and they were good for nothing else, having no power. And not even Morgan la Fey was an exception to this rule, for though she craved mastery what she had of it was but a negative form, and if she could ruin weak men, she did nevertheless not profit from it. And the result of her many attempts on Arthur's life had been only to prove him invulnerable against her and thus to confirm their relative positions.

And now Mordred, staring up at Guinevere (who did not deign to look down at him at all), realized that he must have her as his queen when he became king, else his rule would not be complete, for what he saw in her was the force she possessed, and he recognized for the first time that there was another kind of power beyond the crude and brutal kind sought by men.

And then a knight came onto the balcony at her side, and his head was in a silk bandage, and in comparison to her he looked quite mean and base, but unlike her he saw Mordred and Agravaine below, and he saluted them.

"Now which was that?" Mordred asked his brother, when they had dismounted and passed through the yard and entered the castle.

And Sir Agravaine, who was quite shaken by his own sight of Guinevere, so that he did go pale and trembling, said mumbling, "Launcelot."

Now Mordred, who had seen the effect of the queen on his brother, pressed Agravaine to speak again in a louder voice that might be heard above the noise of their creaking armor and clinking spurs.

And Agravaine cried, hatefully, "Launcelot!"

And now Mordred had seen enough to know that his brother lusted for Guinevere and had for Launcelot a jealous detestation. And he also knew that though Sir Launcelot might seem a base fellow when standing next to the most beautiful queen in the world, he had no equal as a knight, and ten Agravaines at once could not stand against him long.

Yet for all his cunning Mordred did not yet know, nor even suspect, that Guinevere and her knight were adulterers, and in this Agravaine was his superior. (And sometimes the shrewdest of malefactors fails to learn of an obvious and simple thing, possessing which he would be supreme.)

And then Sir Agravaine did with an effort shake off his negative feelings, and he said to Mordred, "Well, Brother, doubtless thou wouldst have a bathe and a change of attire before going to our uncle the king. Come then to my quarters, the which once housed all of our family at Camelot, before our brothers married and went off. They have been too spacious for me since, and I shall share them with thee happily!"

"Time enough for that in the sequel," said Mordred. "First I would meet our uncle the king without delay."

Therefore Agravaine, amazed at the zeal of his brother, conducted him before King Arthur, whom they found sitting alone at the Round Table, and Mordred's first view of his father was across the table at its widest, for they entered the great hall at its opposite end, and the king seemed the size of a pea. And then they walked to him, and this took a long time, and the sound of their progress did echo throughout the vast hall, frightening the pigeons who had long since got in through some broken windows and had taken up their roosts in the vaulting, from where they bedunged the Round Table below and dropped many feathers.

And also there was much dust on the Table, and sometimes in drifts like unto the sands in the burning lands of the heathens who have the heads of dogs.

Now as they got near to King Arthur, Mordred saw a king who looked very like a dotard, and whereas he had always hated the idea of him, and (because all hatred is complex) he feared him as well, now that he saw how decayed he had become in the flesh he despised him.

And as for King Arthur, he continued to stare into the distance in another direction than theirs until they had quite reached him.

And then Sir Agravaine said, "Uncle, have I leave to address you?"

And King Arthur was startled, as if they had leapt upon him out of a secret hole in the wall, and he sprang up drawing Excalibur as he did so. But then he recognized Sir Agravaine, and he lowered his sword, saying, "Nephew! Forgive me, my dear, I was quite distracted." And he embraced Agravaine and he kissed his cheek.

Now Sir Agravaine was most touched by this display of affection, the which was without precedent, and though he desired Guinevere he loved King Arthur and indeed he told himself that this was why he so hated the adulterers.

But what Mordred saw at this time was that when King Arthur stood erect he looked a marvelous powerful man, and he was much taller than Mordred and broader at the shoulder and his neck was like unto the trunk of a tree. And now with two fingers of one hand he lifted one of the great oaken chairs at the Table and he brought it near him and he told Agravaine to sit down.

"Uncle, do I defy your command if first I present your youngest nephew and my brother?" asked Agravaine.

For King Arthur in his distraction had not noticed the presence of Mordred, and Mordred (who like all truly evil persons had no vanity, for that finally is an all-too-human trait of the good but weak) took no offense in being overlooked by the king, as he had been ignored by the queen. And in fact he was pleased, for he believed this had been due to King Arthur's failing vision.

But now the king turned to him, and still without looking carefully at him, he seized him around the shoulders with his great hands, and he did embrace him, kissing both his cheeks, and King Arthur's beard was like unto a mass of wires and his grasp was very like a bear's and had Mordred not been equipped with the great weapon of diabolical cunning he would have been frightened by the great strength he felt in this man whose face seemed so old. And even so he was caused to thrust forward into the future his fantasy of deposing him, which when he entered Camelot had seemed so imminent.

And King Arthur was Mordred's father.

Then the king thrust him away, so as to look at him for the first time, saying, "Well, hath the late Lot's loins furnished me with yet another fine nephew and knight? And what is thy name, lad, and doth it (in the fashion of thy family) prominently employ the letter *g*?"

"Nay, *Sire*," said Mordred smiling slightly to think that he alone in all the world could employ that style of address in its literal sense when speaking with King Arthur, and that when he killed him he would uniquely be both parricide and regicide at once. "I am," said he, "the exception. My name is—"

And just at that moment King Arthur's vision, which was not what it once had been, did gain sharp focus on the features of the young man whom he held at arm's length and he saw the swart hair without gloss and the exceeding pale face and the little eyes which glittered so deep in their sockets when the angle was right.

And he dropped his arms, and he said, "Mordred! Thou art Mordred." And while King Arthur had not forgotten his existence, neither did he remember it as though it were an incarnate, breathing thing the which he would one day encounter.

And suddenly he became an old man again in body as well, and he bent, and drawing up his chair he sat upon it, and then he touched his eye and then his beard, and then he took away that hand with his other and he brought them both into his lap.

And at last he said, "Well, Mordred. Thou hast grown to manhood. And is it that long?"

"Long, Sire?" said Mordred. "Since what? I am yet young enough, methinks, and not quite old enough to give up the ghost." And his smile broadened and became quite ghastly.

And even Sir Agravaine, insensitive as he was and ignorant, saw that his brother had taken on a very strange character, and the king, who feared nothing in the world, did look as nobody had ever seen him.

And Sir Agravaine hastened to say, "Uncle, my little brother is quite new here at Camelot, which is a much grander place than our father's court in the remote and rude Orkneys. And to be presented to you is the greatest thing in his life." Then turning to Mordred he said, "Brother, we of our family address the king as 'uncle,' for though he is our sovereign lord he is yet our relative by blood."

But Mordred said, "Methinks, young and untried as I am, that I have not yet earned the right to belong to our noble family, that I am of it but willy-nilly."

And Agravaine did smile at this, which seemed to him ingenuousness, and he said, "Well, Mordred, is any family connection a thing of the human will? Are we not all put where we are in blood only by God? And thank God we are all the sons of Lot, decent men, for some good families have the odd rogue amongst them, yet he is still of their blood."

But King Arthur looked at Mordred, who resembled neither Margawse nor himself in any wise, and yet he was their son. And then he spake to Sir Agravaine, "Nay, Nephew, what he says hath reason." And he took out Excalibur, which he had put away, and he said, "Kneel, Mordred, and thou shalt be knighted."

And Mordred did so, his eyes seeking those of King Arthur, but the king looked instead at where he touched him, on both shoulders, with his sword.

Then King Arthur said, "Rise, Sir Mordred, as a knight of the Round Table."

And next a terrible thought came to the king, but he had an obligation to pursue it.

Therefore he said, "Sir Mordred, this seat to thy right hand, the which hath ever been known as the Siege Perilous, hath been empty since the beginning, and hath awaited the one who would come. I have the awesome feeling now that it may be thou who art destined to sit there."

But Sir Mordred was reluctant to try the chair to which the king pointed, for he despised any plan for his destiny that was not his own and privy to his own conscience, and he did believe himself in defiance of conventional augury, but his father was as yet the king and he must needs obey him.

And therefore he approached the Siege Perilous, but he had not got very near it when it blazed with a flame far more furious than any before, and it was the king's good fortune that he had previously drawn his own chair some distance away, else he might have been scorched so fierce was the heat.

And both King Arthur and Mordred were pleased that this had happened (though each in another way). Nor was Sir Agravaine made unhappy, for his envy applied to his brothers as well.

"Uncle," said he pleasantly, "perhaps this siege will never be occupied, but will continue to stay empty as God's reminder that perfection can never be achieved by men."

And King Arthur said, "Agravaine, methinks no sane man requires that reminder." Then he turned to Mordred and he said, "Mordred, thou dost want a quest. Hath Agravaine told thee of the Sangreal? Thou hast a keen look. Perhaps it shall be thee who finds it."

"And if I should," asked Sir Mordred, "then, Sire, what would you have me do with, or to, or concerning it?" And he endeavored to conceal the contempt he felt for this quest and to keep from his voice all suggestion of derision.

And King Arthur for his own part tried to conceal his awareness of Mordred's mockery, and the both of them failed at their efforts, for they were after all father and son.

"It is true," said King Arthur, "that as yet no one hath identified the Grail. But for many years I have been thinking on this matter, and as the time hath passed I have believed ever more ardently that the Holy Grail is the only thing in the world worth pursuing."

And Sir Agravaine said, "Uncle, I should think that the noble Launcelot being the greatest of all knights might well be first to discover the Grail."

"Launcelot hath gone forth," said King Arthur. "But he fell ill when near the court of Pelles the maimed king, and he was there nursed to health by the princess Elaine. Yet methinks he hath not since been altogether fit, for to Camelot he then returned and here he doth remain."

"And that was long ago," said Agravaine.

"Indeed," said King Arthur. "But perhaps this is a quest for the younger men, such as thee, Mordred, and that fine youth Pimpernel who hath but lately gone afield. It may be that we of the older generation have had our day." (Nor could King Arthur ever get the name of Sir Percival correct, he who was amongst the very greatest of the knights.)

Now Mordred was thinking of his vile ambition, to commit regicide and parricide and by marrying Guinevere to add incest to his loathsome crimes (for carnal congress with a stepmother was so regarded in that time, as in the day of the unfortunate Hippolytus son of Theseus the notable lecher). And Mordred believed the time had not yet come in which he could launch his attack, for as yet he led no forces, and the lone and unsupported malefactor could never overturn a throne so heavy as King Arthur's.

Therefore he said, "Sire, I shall go immediately upon the quest for the Sangreal."

And King Arthur commended him, but privately the king wondered why that he heard even this pious purpose with dread, when it was Mordred's. (And we know that he was quite right to have this feeling, for what Mordred purposed to do was to roam the countryside and corrupt the minds of the peasantry so as to disaffect these simple villeins against the king.)

Now King Arthur gave sirs Agravaine and Mordred their leave, and when they had gone out of his presence Agravaine said, "Alas! that thou didst never see our uncle when in his prime."

"Yet," said Mordred, "he seemeth not at all feeble today."

"Perhaps not in body," said Agravaine. "Nor perhaps not even yet in mind. But certes, his spirit's not what it was once."

"But he can not be very old," said Mordred, "for I am only—" But he halted here, and indeed he had startled himself by saying this much.

And occupied with his own obsession Sir Agravaine paid no mind to the interruption, and he said, "He hath but a few years more than Guinevere, yet she doth remain in appearance a young woman her life long!" And he said this as if in hateful indignation, but Mordred correctly identified it as rather the plaint of unrequited desire.

"Well, dear Brother," said Sir Mordred, "shall we to horse?" For he would fain have been accompanied by Agravaine, whose gold would be useful for foul purposes and yet who would be too foolish to understand what were done with it.

But Agravaine said, "Alas, I must needs remain here at Camelot for the moment, much as I should like to accompany thee." And he did not tell him why he must remain, but instead he gave him much pompous advice on how to conduct himself as a knight of the Round Table.

And after a while, when Agravaine stopped to think whether there be a detail of chivalrous practice which he had neglected to mention to his brother, Mordred brought this wearisome subject to an end by saying that which he had heard about the maimed King Pelles. (For he knew this by his aunt Morgan la Fey, who discovered all the shameful truths about all people in the world except the most important, namely the adulterous love of Launcelot and Guinevere.)

"Dost know of King Pelles, Brother? And how he received the wound which doth never heal?" So asked Mordred.

"Nay," said Agravaine, "I do not."

"When Pelles was but a young prince," said Mordred, "he had a great friend of his bosom, a very fine and loyal knight, and many times this friend had saved Pelles' life. And this knight met a beautiful maiden who was the daughter of an high lady of the court, and he would marry her, and Pelles having by that time become king, this knight his closest friend asked his permission. 'Certes, friend of mine heart!' saith King Pelles. And he commanded that a splendid wedding be held for his friend and this maiden, and so it happened. But when the knight went unto his bride that evening he found King Pelles lewdly bedded with his wife, and he had taken her maidenhead by the *jus primae noctis*, as though she were the daughter of a churl, and this knight grasped up a spear and he plunged it into the privities of King Pelles. Now this wound hath never healed since, nor hath the bawdy king (who formerly was lecherous as a sparrow) ever performed the virile act since that time."

And concluding this story Sir Mordred did smirk, the which was as near as he could come to merriment.

But Sir Agravaine owing to his obsession was not amused. And he cried, "O wicked knight to strike his king! Could Launcelot be so vile if discovered?"

"Launcelot?" said Mordred in amazement. "I speak not of Launcelot, and that was in another country besides. And was it not the king (and not the knight) who was here at fault?" And Mordred began to believe that his brother was not merely foolish but had gone quite dotty.

And then Sir Mordred took his leave of Sir Agravaine, and he went out of Camelot to work for King Arthur's ruin. But his scheme was not soon accomplished, for the churls whom he met were not quick even to understand his meaning, having no cause to hate the king who was the greatest they had ever known or were to know. And Mordred's great cunning, so effective amongst noble folk, was ineffectual with the loyal British peasant, who was a stubborn fellow in his virtue.

So now we leave this evil man and go with young Percival, who was to be the second most virtuous of all the knights of the Round Table, and the only reason he was not perfect was this: that he had during the night performed the act of darkness with the maiden whom he had rescued from her wicked captor on the road to Camelot. But he did not know what he had done, for never was there so naïve a knight as Sir Percival.

Now Percival roamed far and wide throughout Britain, and he went across the sea to Ireland, and then he crossed the British Channel and he went amongst the French, and thence to Germany notwithstanding that these people were benighted paynims, and everywhere he went he searched for the Holy Grail, and always he remained pure of heart and therefore totally ignorant of the ways of the world, and because people everywhere were offended by the presence of such a good man, and he seemed harmless, he was oft assaulted by those who did not learn, until it was too late to save their lives, that Sir Percival could be vanquished by no other knight at that time, including Sir Launcelot (as we have seen).

Now another of King Pellinore's sons, who was named Sir Lamorak and who was a fine knight, had also been upon the quest for the Sangreal, and at the time that Sir Gawaine had killed his father he was far from Camelot and therefore he did not hear of this occurrence immediately. But traveling upon a road in Wales one day he came upon some knights of the Round Table, and as they were on the same quest as he, joined their company.

And one of them, Sir Bedivere, made condolences with him on the death of his father, of which he believed that Sir Lamorak had been apprised, and as Bedivere had lately visited at Camelot he told Lamorak that his youngest brother Percival had been made knight.

"And that he is a very fine youth," said Sir Bedivere, "and hath a moral character comparable to his prowess at arms, can be seen by his response to the news that it was Gawaine who had overcome his father. ' 'Twas a fair fight,' said he. 'Therefore I bear towards Gawaine no hatred.' " And Sir Bedivere rejoicing said, "My dear Lamorak, it is not cheering to hope that Percival is representative of the new generation?"

But Sir Lamorak found these news to be evidence that his young brother, reared amongst women only, was effeminate, and he burned with revenge against Gawaine. But when he told as much to Sir Bedivere, that honest knight spake as follows.

"I am sorry to hear this, Lamorak my friend! Our Lord hath forbidden us in general to take revenge, or indeed to feel it. And in particular, King Arthur hath commanded that this feud between the families of kings Pellinore and Lot go no further! Two kings are dead, and one of them our fellow at the Round Table. He who raises another sword is condemned!"

And Sir Lamorak said, "Then I shall not violate my king's command and so go to Hell." Yet privately his hatred grew no cooler, and soon he left the company of the other knights, to go and deliberate on what damage he could do to Sir Gawaine's blood without shedding it. And he traveled north to the Orkneys, where in the castle of King Lot, Queen Margawse lived as a widow. And though she was no longer in her earliest youth Margawse did yet have a certain appetite, and Sir Lamorak was a comely knight in the prime of his years.

And it was not so long after Sir Lamorak came to the Orkneys that he became the lover of Margawse, who was the mother of Gawaine, Agravaine, Gaheris, Gareth, and

Mordred. And though he did this for revenge at the outset, for to bring shame upon that family, Margawse was yet as beautiful as when King Arthur conceived Mordred upon her. And this queen, who had never in her life been better than she should have been, now fell in love with Lamorak as well. And despite his weakness concerning revenge he was a fine and noble knight in all other respects, and therefore in loving him truly Margawse became a better woman than she had ever been.

And for all too short a time they were together in happiness, and what had begun as revenge had led to true love, but then her son Gaheris, come to the Orkneys to visit his mother, did arrive at her chambers unannounced. And seeing his mother in bed with her lover Sir Lamorak, the enemy of his family, and forgetting King Arthur's command in his fury and disgust, Sir Gaheris drew his sword straightway and he went to slay Sir Lamorak.

But Margawse hurled herself onto her lover's body for to protect him, and therefore Gaheris' keen sword killed his mother instead.

Now weeping in grief Sir Lamorak said, "O unnatural monster, what hast thou done?"

And Sir Gaheris, who was a good man whose decency had been overwhelmed by events which he in his human frailty could not control, cried, "Well, I meant to kill thee, and not her! But now that it is done, so be it, and the adulteress is punished. To go to bed with our worst enemy is the most foulest thing in the world!"

But then he fell to weeping uncontrollably, and he dropped his sword, and Sir Lamorak could have picked it up and slain him, but too much bloodshed had occurred, and none of it for a good reason.

Now Lamorak said to Gaheris, "For God's sake, is it not time we halt in our strife?"

And so they made a truce and then went to Camelot together. Now when they came before King Arthur and told him what had happened, the king was more enraged than anyone had ever seen him.

And he said, "It is all I can do not to wish a pox on both your houses! Now in what way is the community of the Round Table any better than the rest of the vile and vicious world? Do we not *envy* one another? Do we not know *pride* and *lust*? Is there any mortal sin that we have failed to commit?"

And Sir Agravaine, who was there, being in the grip of his obsession forgot himself now in great bitterness (and the death of his mother was as nought to him), and he said aloud that which he thought, "And is Launcelot not at least guilty of *sloth*?"

And King Arthur turned to him in a fury, saying, "And what of thee?"

Now Agravaine was ashamed, but rather of voicing his thoughts than of his feeling.

Then King Arthur said deliberately, "And one sin necessarily leads to the next, and so on, until we have the lot, for am I not myself guilty of *wrath*?" And he put his head into his hands awhile.

And moved by this sight Sir Gaheris took Sir Lamorak by the arms, and he said, "My dear friend, I ask thee to forgive me for my trespasses against thee and thy family."

And Lamorak clasped Gaheris by the shoulders. "My good friend," said he, "I beg thy forgiveness while accepting thy plea, and henceforward I shall never know ought but love for my brother knights."

And they did embrace each the other. And then Gaheris turned to his brother Sir Agravaine, for to ask him to swear eternal friendship to Sir Lamorak, but Agravaine had left that place silently after his rebuke by King Arthur.

And he went to spy again upon Guinevere and Sir Launcelot, but as usual he failed to find them in a compromising situation.

And indeed Sir Launcelot, who was only just leaving the queen's company, encountered Agravaine in a hallway. And he greeted him with much cheer, for Launcelot had no dislike for any other knight, unless some evil deed of theirs provoked it from him.

"My dear Agravaine," said Sir Launcelot now, "I wish thee a good day! I never knew thou hadst lingered at Camelot. We must, thou and I, go hunting together one of these afternoons, when the weather stays clement." And he shook his hand, and he said, "Now tell me of my noble friend Gawaine, who hath neglected his comrades since his happy marriage."

"He liveth," said Agravaine sullenly.

"Well," said Launcelot, and he clapped Agravaine upon the shoulder, "give him my love and chide him for an unfriendly rogue!" And he strode away in his velvet housecoat and slippers, for his armor had long hung in his chamber, rusting in disuse.

Meanwhile King Arthur sat as he was when the knights had left him. And now his half-sister Margawse, the mother of his son, was no longer amongst the quick. And he thought again, as he had thought so many times before, that a king should properly have no personal concerns whatever, for they inevitably introduce a corruption into his principles. And he hated Mordred, the son he had only lately seen for the first time, for being the issue of his lust. And he despised himself for having that feeling, and also for knowing only relief on hearing of the death of Margawse his lifelong sister and his brief paramour.

And even when most of his knights had been in residence at Camelot, King Arthur was ever peculiarly alone, for there is little that a king can share.

BOOK XIX

*How Sir Launcelot and the queen were discover-
ed in their illegal love; and how Sir Gawaine's
brothers went to arrest Guinevere; and how Gawaine swore vengeance against his
friend Launcelot.*

And now we go with Sir Percival, the most diligent of
the knights in searching for the Holy Grail. But we will
not travel with him everywhere, for he went across the entire world to its edge, beyond which is the eternal
darkness, and he had many adventures amongst men of all
stations and every color of skin and manner of speech.
And some of the men he met were fairly good, and some
were very evil, but most were a mixture of virtues and
vices whether they wore silk or rags, or lived in a palace
or an hut or a cave, and taking them all in all, all were
corrupt to a great degree, but none was without some
small virtue, and all were equal in that they lived in Time.

And Percival did not dislike any man, even though he
might have to fight him (and unless he yielded, to kill
him), and therefore he was thought everywhere to be a
great fool, and thus he was oft attacked without other
cause, for men did not understand that what they believed
folly could be a concomitant of great puissance.

And Percival learned nothing from each experience that
he did not already know, and therefore in his sense of
himself he was just as he had been when he had killed the
evil knight who had sought to capture and misuse his
mother and his sister when he was a boy. And he believed

himself to be greatly ignorant of all important matters, and therefore he was anything but a fool, for the only truth is that of God.

Now after many years he returned to Britain, not having found a trace of the Sangreal anywhere in the world, nor did he receive encouragement whatever in his quest, but never was he disheartened in the least, for every day dawned anew and each morning he had a great purpose to awaken to! Whereas most men everywhere sought only proximate things, and having got them were dissatisfied, and this was true of the drunkard with his cup, the lecher with his drab, and even the kings with their kingdoms.

Now having come back to Britain, Percival in his wanderings eventually came to a great castle, and he asked there for the farrier, for his horse was lame in one leg, and he was taken to the stables, where the farrier inspecting the hoof said it was sound enough but required a new shoe.

And Sir Percival said, "Well, I am relieved to hear that. For once in Saxony, amongst the pagan Germans, I was attacked by those savages with poisoned arrows, and I feared that my good beast had caught one of them."

"Nay, my lord, he's fit enough," said the farrier. "For your maiming, now, we know something about here. Oh, we're specialists in maiming, we are."

And Sir Percival said, "I trust thou dost not mean that ye maim people, for in that case I should have to consider ye mine enemies. For I am a knight of King Arthur's Round Table."

And at this the farrier did smile (and from the style of Sir Percival's speech he believed him simple-minded). "Nay, my lord," said he. "What I meant was that you are at the castle of the maimed king Pelles, and no more than that."

And believing it impolite of him, as a guest in this place, to inquire further, Sir Percival did not pursue this matter.

Now when the farrier had completed his work, Sir Percival would have left that castle and gone again upon his travels, but going back towards the main gate he passed a garden, and there was a youth there dressed in white velvet and with ribbons and bows, and for a moment Sir Percival did not know whether he was a boy or a maiden, for his skin was exceeding pale and his hair was long and golden.

Then this varlet called to him, and Percival going to him saw he was indeed a lad of perhaps sixteen years of age.

And the varlet addressed him, saying, "My lord, are you a knight?"

"Yea," said Percival, "indeed I am."

"Well," said the youth, "you are quite the finest man I have ever seen."

And remembering his own protected childhood, Sir Percival smiled and he said, "But canst thou have seen many?"

"Sir, I have not seen much," said the youth, "for my mother will not permit me to leave this garden."

"Well," said Sir Percival, "I was the very least of the knights of the Table when I was last at Camelot. They are the best men in the world, and I was remarkably fortunate to be allowed to join them, with my small endowments."

And this youth said with glee, "Then I know from your speech that you must be one of the greatest of all knights, for my mother hath told me that the more a knight's prowess, the greater be his modesty."

Now Sir Percival was embarrassed, and he said, "I expect, if thou art as I was at thine age, that thou wouldst be a knight, but that thy mother would keep thee in this garden for as long as she could?"

"Sir, that is quite true. My father, who was a knight of the Round Table, is dead. And my grandfather King Pelles hath lain maimed these many years. Therefore my mother the princess Elaine would keep me by her unharmed. But I think it is not so virile for me to stay in this garden forever, and I believe that it is I who should protect women, and not vice versa." And so said this pale young man, who did look quite sickly to the robust Sir Percival.

But Percival asked which knight had been his father, and when the youth said, "Sir Launcelot," Sir Percival made the greatest grief.

"O most noble of men Launcelot!" said he in his moan. "Can it be that you are dead, the greatest of all? And what wicked knight hath had the power to overwhelm you? And if you are gone, then doth the Table yet stand, and what of King Arthur?"

But the young man said, "No human adversary killed my father, for he was invincible. 'Twas God Himself who took him away, for to defend the fields of Heaven. He died in his sleep, many year ago, even before I was born."

And now Sir Percival (who was not a fool) did understand that this boy had surely been given this story by his mother, to explain Sir Launcelot's absence, for Percival had seen Launcelot since that time, when he knighted him at Camelot. And therefore he grieved no more. And he deliberated on whether or not to tell the youth that his father was surely yet alive.

And he asked him his name, and the young man said, "Galahad, sir. And, sir, did you know my father?"

"Thy father," said Sir Percival, "was the very man by reason of whom I was knighted! And methinks that having had such a father thou shalt be a very great knight thyself."

"Then shall you teach me the use of lance and sword?" asked Galahad.

But Percival said that he did not wish to defy the desires of Galahad's mother.

But Galahad said, "Sir, then in the name of my father?" And Sir Percival did not see that he could refuse him.

Therefore they went to the armory and they got weapons and armor for Galahad, and from the stables they got a fine charger, and then they went to a field, where Sir Percival showed Galahad how the weapons were carried and how they were brought into play in a fight.

Now Galahad was a slight youth and pale to the point of looking quite ill, and Percival feared that his slender arms were not strong enough to hold the long lance in the rest, nor to swing the heavy sword, nor to hold the large shield. Yet Galahad seemed to have no trouble with these when he tried them. And he had had but little instruction when he wished to joust with Sir Percival, and he begged so earnestly to do this that Percival finally agreed.

Therefore they both mounted and going each to opposite ends of the field, they charged at one another with padded lances. And surely Sir Percival did not use his full force, but hardly any of it, for he did not wish to hurt this frail youth his new friend.

But when they met 'twas Sir Percival who was lifted from his horse and thrown over its tail.

Then Galahad quickly dismounted and he came to help Percival rise from the ground. "My lord," said he, "forgive me for this, if you will! But methinks you did not charge me in earnest."

And laughing, Percival said, "Methinks thou hast much of Launcelot in thy blood!"

Then they mounted again and charged once more, and now Sir Percival used a quarter of his strength, and again he was thrown as easily as the first time. And again Galahad chided him politely for not jousting more earnestly.

So in successive trials Percival used more of his strength each time, and each time he was thrown. And each time he laughed more happily than the time before, for the greatest knights delighted when they found another who was superlative.

And finally Sir Percival charged Galahad as fiercely as he had ever ridden at any knight his life long, and he used all of his own great ability, which it will be remembered was sufficient to fight the mighty Launcelot to a draw, and once again he was easily unseated by this pale young man.

Now sitting on the ground in his armor, and he was

sore and tired, he said to Galahad, who had come to him again in concern, "Galahad, I jousted with thy great father once, than whom there was no greater knight under the sun. But thou art his superior!"

"Well, sir, I still suspect that you have not yet used much of your available strength," said Galahad, "and that, in kindness, you have favored me."

"I assure thee," said Sir Percival, "that I am much too tired to lift my sword. Nor, I suspect, dost thou need my instruction in that weapon, any more than thou hast required it in the lance." And Sir Percival was amazed at the strength of this slender youth. "When I have recovered my breath and soaked my bruises in a warm tub," said he, who had never since becoming a knight had ought but a cold bathe and usually in a mountain stream from which he had first to cut a hole in the ice, "I shall go to thy mother and urge her to permit thee come to Camelot with me, there to be knighted by King Arthur. For virtue, methinks, could have no greater companion than thee."

And Galahad was thrilled to hear this proposal, for despite his appearance he longed for a life of hardihood.

Therefore he took Sir Percival within the castle, and brought him to a chamber, where Percival did lie down upon a couch and sleep for many hours. And during this sleep he dreamed marvelously that a young maiden, all dressed in pure white, came unto him, and she carried a golden chalice, and she said to him, "Sir Percival, this is the Holy Grail, and because thou art almost perfect, thou canst see it, briefly, this once."

And Percival made great joy, but he was sad that this glimpse would be all he ever had.

But the maiden said to him, "Do not despair, for wert thou not as good a man as thou art, thou shouldst not see it at all."

And then before the vision faded the maiden spake once more. "Thou art good, Percival, because of thine ignorance, but thou art not perfect for the same reason: thou didst once commit fornication without knowing it. Thou

mayst be forgiven the act, but not the unawareness of it."
And having so said she vanished along with the Sangreal.

And then Sir Percival waked up wondering on this matter, but young Galahad had been eagerly awaiting the moment when Percival would go to his mother, and therefore he knocked him up so soon as he heard him stir.

And to Princess Elaine they both of them went, and she was still as beautiful as she had been when Launcelot had come to King Pelles' castle years before.

Now Sir Percival told her of Galahad's prowess, and she wept softly, saying, "I have always known that this day would come." And to her Galahad she said, "My son, I have prevaricated to thee for a mother's reason. Thy father is yet alive, by the latest news from Camelot, but in all my life he hath been with me only during his time of illness and one night following, before thou wert born. And now the time hath come when I shall lose thee as well."

And Galahad said, "Dear Mother, Camelot is not so far away that I can not oft return to see you."

And to be kind his mother pretended to be some cheered by that, but secretly she knew that despite his strength as a knight Galahad had no long life before him, for he had a mortal illness the which had taken all the color from his blood.

(Thus Galahad was to be one perfect knight, for God doth allow perfection only to him who is already dying, and even the most evil of men acquire more virtue with each of their final breaths, and no doubt God doth cure us all by killing us in the end.)

Then Galahad did take Sir Percival to his grandfather, Pelles the maimed king.

And he said, "Grandsire, this noble knight Sir Percival will take me to King Arthur, so that I might serve the Round Table. And I know now that my father is alive, and I shall join him!"

And King Pelles lay upon his bed sorely, both because of his incurable wound and because he had received the latest news from Camelot, and it was the unhappiest he had ever heard, but he would not tell it to his grandson Galahad.

Therefore he embraced him and he blessed him, and he said, "My dear Galahad, thou hast become a fine young man and without a father for thine upbringing, and alas! I could provide little guidance for thee maimed as I am in body and stained in soul. I am indeed a model of what thou shouldst at all costs abstain from: concupiscence, the which in me as a young man was unbridled. And thus I lost my closest friend and the use of my limbs as well."

Now Sir Percival, whose sole knowledge of lust came from the dream he had lately had, was ignorant of how it could maim a king and lose a friend, and though he would not have considered asking a question in other circumstances (for his mother had instructed him in courtesy), especially of a king, he now believed it were not rude to ask further of what Pelles had spoken so freely.

And therefore he said now, "I beg your pardon, Majesty. I do not understand why you suffer so."

And King Pelles did look amazed, and he thrust both arms at Sir Percival, and he said with great eagerness, "Yea, thou hast almost got it, but not quite! Now what was it that thou wouldst know? Pray ask me the question!"

Now Sir Percival being so ignorant of most things was always careful to follow instructions to the letter, and therefore he did as the king commanded, and he spake in the form of a direct question, in this wise.

"Why do you suffer so?"

And King Pelles cautiously stirred his maimed body, saying, "Almost I do not dare. . . . But I did not put the words into thy mouth. 'Twas a question as thou didst ask it first, was it not?"

And Sir Percival affirmed this. And then King Pelles slowly moved his legs from the bed, and when his feet touched the floor he pushed himself erect, and he stood unassisted, though swaying some with the novelty of the experience, for he had not risen from his bed in fifty years.

"Do I dare to walk?" said he, and he gestured that Percival and Galahad, who would help him, should stay away. And then he took one faltering step, and then another, and another, and so on until he positively strode about the chamber, and he was as fit as he had ever been, long before he did climb into one bed for half an hour and as result was condemned to another for half a century!

Now Sir Percival, who usually knew nothing, understood this extraordinary event very well: for some reason it had been his asking of the question, and in just the proper way, that had cured Pelles, who was no longer the maimed king, he who was the father of Elaine who was Galahad's mother.

But Sir Percival had not returned to Camelot for many years, and therefore he could not know that Sir Agravaine had at last got the evidence he sought of the adultery of Guinevere and Launcelot, and he would never have got it but for his brother Mordred.

And what had happened during the years that Sir Percival had been traveling across the earth and while Galahad was growing to manhood was as follows.

But first we must say that though it might seem that Sir Launcelot had seldom ever left the castle, that would not be true, and when he was younger he had gone on many a quest and freed many a damsel and defended the helpless and killed all manner of miscreants and monsters, and never did he fight unless the odds were greatly against him, and that is how he became the greatest knight in the world. (For it is only in the historical world that a reputation can be gained by talk alone, and in the realm of legend only deeds are counted.) And such an adventure the which happening but once would have made a man an hero, was routine to Sir Launcelot, and he did so many things that some were never known, there being present no witness who lived (and never did Sir Launcelot boast of himself), and many others were soon forgotten except by the persons whose lives he saved and whose kingdoms he restored and the women whose virtue he protected. (And sometimes it hath been said that he was under the guidance of the Lady of the Lake or that she had been his mother, and hence the style of his name Launcelot of the Lake, or *du Lac* by the French who claim him as well, but he was pure British from birth to death, and never was there any other knight of his like.)

And as we have seen, when he stayed at home with Guinevere he did greatly despise himself, but when he went abroad he could not endure his yearning, and as with all men and not knights only, as he grew older he dreaded the latter more than the former, and he accepted shame as being preferable to loneliness.

And by the time King Arthur had come back from his tour of the realm Sir Launcelot was so thoroughly debased through inactivity that he took small precaution against being detected in his criminal congress. And as for Guinevere, she had never.

For the queen was a woman of strong will, and lust was never her failing, but rather it was pride. And if she was ever apprehended and brought before King Arthur she knew what she would say to him, and it was, "I took Launcelot as my lover so that he could not be yours!"

But when that moment came she surely did never say that, for she was the greatest queen who ever served as consort and did not herself rule a country, nor indeed did she believe the truth was that simple.

Now Sir Mordred went about the countryside for a long time pretending to his fellow-knights that with them he searched for the Sangreal, but in reality he sought to corrupt the peasantry and to induce them to rise against King Arthur's rule. But in this he had no success. And if they took his gold they spent it at fairs on the various sorts of folly offered there, and they enriched the charlatans and mountebanks and gamesters and whores.

And his aunt the wicked Morgan la Fey had retired after many years of her failures against King Arthur (for she had got old and was no longer so beautful as to be able to pollute the minds of knights of weak character), and she did jeer at Mordred for his impotency to do any better than she had done.

And Morgan la Fey vilely cursed God for creating men, and she hated Him for being a male, and even the Devil was no better. And she established a nunnery for the worship of female black magic, and the house dogs were all bitches, and this convent was in a wild where the beasts were only hinds and vixens and savage sows. And Sir Mordred was the only man admitted there whose virile member and stones were not in danger of excision.

But Mordred told her, "My dear aunt, the gold is but a means to sway the baser fellows, which one must do in preparation for to deal with the higher orders, who can be corrupted only politically, which is to say, with the promise of gaining mastery over humanity in groups. For example, Mark of Cornwall and Anguish of Ireland, and the Picts and the Scots, and certes all the tribes of the savage Germans, none of these will come to support me against Arthur unless I have me an host of mine own, the which they will expect to engage him while they each take a part of Britain, and then subsequently, when I have defeated him, wipe me out and then fight amongst themselves for final supremacy. Until I assemble mine army they regard me as an isolated lunatic."

"The which thou surely art!" said Morgan la Fey cackling in shrill laughter, and her nose and chin had grown so that they almost touched each other, and she dressed in clothes of dead black and she wore a pointed hat.

Now what happened was that Mordred eventually despaired of raising a force amongst the loyal Britons, and (as the wicked do ever) he hated King Arthur his father more for being so beloved a sovereign that nobody could be found to rise against him, and finally this hatred grew so ardent that Mordred's very sputum became a corrosive poison, and if he spat onto the trunk of a mighty oak the bark dissolved and even the flesh and it toppled and fell to the ground.

So he came to believe that King Arthur could be destroyed in one way only, and that was by his son's own hand, and therefore Mordred went to Camelot for the purpose to murder him foully.

Now he went secretly and by night he descended into the moat, which through neglect was utterly dry, and he scaled the wall in a remote corner of the castle and he entered the window of a tower, and then he proceeded stealthily to creep through the corridors leading to the bed-chamber of King Arthur.

But at a certain turning he heard the soft steps of someone approaching, and the reflection of a light, and therefore he sank into an alcove, hiding himself under his cloak. Now when the person passed him Mordred saw in the light of the candle carried by him that he was Sir Launcelot.

Now if Mordred would kill King Arthur he must know where the greatest knight of all was going at this moment, lest by accident he meet his sword. Therefore he followed Launcelot, who as usual was going to the queen.

And it was only when Sir Launcelot had reached Guinevere's door and tapped softly upon it, and she did open it and for a brief moment her golden radiance was seen in the taper's glow, that Sir Mordred was at last possessed of that which, and only which, could bring down King Arthur and destroy the Round Table.

Thus he did not go to stab his king and father now, but rather he found the chamber of his brother Sir Agravaine, for he had an use for that foolish knight. And he woke him up carrying a candle, and Agravaine rubbed his eyes and stared in disbelief.

"Little brother Mordred!" he cried. "Not having seen thee for years I thought thou hadst gone to Heaven." But then he showed fear and he crossed himself. "Or art thou a ghost?"

"Now, Agravaine," said Mordred, "we have no time for

to exchange long greetings. The queen, Brother, is an adulteress!"

And Sir Agravaine groaned, and he said, "Yea, Mordred, I have suspected that since I was a young knight, but despite my long surveillance of several decades I have obtained not one whit of good evidence. And our brother Gawaine will listen to no accusation without some."

"Well, thy fruitless vigil is at an end, Agravaine," said Sir Mordred. "Now rise and clothe thyself, and take thy sword. For Launcelot doth bed beside Guinevere at this moment, and he is unarmed. We shall take him easily, thou and I, and he will soon lie under the headsman's ax."

"And what of *her*?" gasped Sir Agravaine in very much the same state as though he were mad with lust, and he flung himself out of bed and he would have thrown a robe over his nightdress had not Mordred stayed him.

"The bitch will be burned, certes!" said Mordred. (Who was prevaricating, for he would marry her after King Arthur was slain.) "But put on thy full armor. Launcelot unarmed is yet Launcelot."

Now Agravaine was not the worst man in the world, and he liked not to face an unarmed knight when he himself was armored cap-à-pie, for he had not even in the grip of his lifelong obsession forsaken all his noble scruples. And, now that the moment had come, he knew a reluctance to bring Guinevere to the stake, for what he held against her was not her adultery as such, but that it had not been committed with him.

And for a moment he had his old hope that with Launcelot gone she might turn to him to satisfy her lust. (For Agravaine was the simple-minded sort of knight who doth suppose that a wife turns adulteress to feed her carnal appetites, whereas the wise man knoweth that illicit swyvers, male and female, are ruled more by the needs of the mind than those of the privities, and under certain conditions can remain chaste more easily than the routine mortal.)

But as it was Mordred who now provided that which

Agravaine had sought for most of his life, so it was he who directed his older brother in how to deal with it.

And he said, "Adultery is a very vile crime ordinarily, Agravaine, but when it is perpetrated by a queen and the first knight it partaketh also of treason against the crown! These are the most heinous pair of miscreants in Christendom, Brother." And with such incendiary speech he heated Sir Agravaine's blood.

And Agravaine was so distracted by the high feelings with which he masked that which at bottom was envy, that he did not see that Mordred did not armor himself nor did he have any weapon but the short bodkin (with which he had intended to kill King Arthur).

So they went to the queen's door, and at the instigation of Mordred, Agravaine pounded upon it and he demanded that it be opened in the name of every law of God and man.

And within, where Guinevere and Launcelot lay abed, they awakened up and for a while they listened to the pounding.

And then Sir Launcelot said stoically, "We are discovered at long last." And then he rose from the bed, and he would have gone to the door to surrender himself for arrest, but the queen stayed him.

"Nay, Launcelot," said she, "we shall never submit to them. Flee through the privy passage behind the arras. Then I shall go to the door and decree death for these caitiffs who disturb the queen's repose."

"Flee?" asked Sir Launcelot in amazement. "Shall Launcelot flee? He who hath never fled from any man or monster?"

"Speakest thou of thyself as a third person?" asked Guinevere. "Hast thou lived as a man or rather as an abstract example for argument's-sake?"

"Whatever your opinion of me, madam," said Sir Launcelot, "there are certain things I will never do, and only insofar as I abide by those few scruples I am not totally corrupt. The loaf of mine honor hath long since been devoured by the teeth of my lust. Permit me to pluck at this crumb. I do not flee. I stand my ground."

" 'Tis an inappropriate term, for some years, this 'stand,' " said the queen. "Pray choose thy locutions with greater precision."

And Sir Launcelot did flush, and he said, "Did ever a woman in all the world so despise the man for whom she had nevertheless a lifelong addiction?"

"Doth not the drunkard despise the wine he so requires?" asked Guinevere.

"Nay, lady, not so much as he despises himself," said Sir Launcelot.

And Guinevere all at once lost her anger, and she wept softly, and she then said, "Well, shall I beg thee, Launcelot? Shall I say that I can not live without thee, that mine apparent disdain is merely the means by which I have endeavored to defend myself against becoming thy slave—and failed?"

"Nay," said Launcelot, "you shall never say that, for 'tis a jest, lady, and hath no comic application when the king's officer doth beat upon the door." And he went from her, but then he tarried and he came back. And he said, "I shall surrender and accept my punishment—but as one who took you by force, not as your lover freely accepted."

And now the pounding had become as thunder, and next the sound of a sword was heard as the very hinges were being attacked.

And the queen became as if angry once more. "Thou shalt lose thine head whilst I live stainless?" she asked. "Dost think that thou canst accept punishment better than I? And what of thy principles, Launcelot? Do they permit a lie?"

"Cast your memory back across the years, lady," said Launcelot. "Could one not, without utter disregard for the truth, interpret my first thouching you as a criminal assault on the queen?"

"Vanity," said Guinevere, "will ever be thy most flagrant sin." And she lifted her chin, and her throat was soft and white as it had ever been, and her eyes were as blue and her hair as golden, and her bosom as high in the nightdress of white sendal, and she was even more beautiful than when he had first become intimate with her. And for a long time they had not made love, for this soft life had made him an eunuch, and yet he could not leave it.

And the queen said now, "Sir Launcelot, I command thee to leave by the private way whilst I deal with these scum."

But Sir Launcelot said, "Lady, I defy thee in love!" And he went to the door and throwing the bolts he hurled it open.

Now seeing Sir Launcelot before him, if in sinful nightdress and at the scene of his crime, Sir Agravaine was for an instant stupefied. For to face Launcelot was to confront the greatest of living legends. And Launcelot was not an huge man with great shoulders and a chest like a tun nor exceptionally tall, and that was more the figure of Sir Agravaine, who exceeded him in all dimensions and wore full armor besides.

And Sir Agravaine was brave enough, and he had killed his share of formidable enemies, before his obsession had got so commanding as to keep him always at Camelot, and if we have not told about them here, it was because that his deeds did not distinguish him from his fellows at the Round Table, that company of the finest knights in the world.

But some few were greater than all the others, and they were sirs Tristram and Gawaine and Percival. But Sir Launcelot was the greatest of all, except his son Galahad, who was to come. And when any knight stood before him except in friendship, that knight was aware of dread peril, for all men of that time lived and died by legend (and without it the world hath become a mean place).

Therefore Sir Agravaine, to whom Sir Launcelot had always been friendly and kind, did tremble now within his steel, and for a moment he could not speak.

And Launcelot said to him, and not unkindly, "My dear Agravaine, what dost thou want at such a late hour?"

And Agravaine at last said, lifting his sword, "Methinks it is improper for thee to be in this place, Launcelot."

"Well," said Launcelot gently, "is it quite thine affair where I am?"

"Nay," said Agravaine, "unless thou art in some place where the honor of the Round Table be thereby affected adversely."

And now the queen came to the door, and she was full dressed in a daytime robe trimmed with ermine, and she wore her coronet (which was less golden than her hair).

And recognizing Agravaine through his open visor she said, "Nephew, thou dost not know what thou art doing. I give thee my word that nothing lewd hath here occurred. Now prithee void this place."

Now the reason that neither Launcelot nor Guinevere saw Mordred was that he lingered beyond the embrasure of the door, unseen, and therefore they believed that Sir Agravaine had come alone.

And at Guinevere's speech Sir Agravaine did lower his sword, the which he had presented to Launcelot's bosom, for if he found it difficult to stand without friendship before Launcelot, he could not do it at all before the queen, regardless of his certainty that she was an adulteress, for she was all that he found beautiful in the world, and on her command he would have groveled upon the floor. And now he was flattered merely by reason of her speaking to him to go away, for these were more personal words than she had ever addressed to him his life long.

And he colored in mixed pleasure and embarrassment, and he said obsequiously, "Lady, forgive me for making this alarum. It seems I was misled. I had woken untimely from a bad dream, and I fear my wits were confused."

Now Mordred in the corridor heard this with furious disgust, and he knew that if left to his own devices foolish Agravaine would soon go away, forsaking this unique opportunity to wreck havoc on King Arthur and the Round Table.

And therefore when Agravaine had finished his apology and Guinevere had turned away and Sir Launcelot had started to close the door, Mordred sprang into the embrasure and crouching at Agravaine's knee he thrust his dagger upwards and with all his force into the forearm of Sir Launcelot, wounding him to the bone.

Now Launcelot flung the door open and with his left hand he seized the sword which Sir Agravaine, distracted utterly by the queen, had not yet put away. And Sir Launcelot, believing that Agravaine had wounded him cowardly, knew great anger, and with his great strength he plunged the sword through the armor and into the breast of Sir Agravaine, and the blade went all the way unto its hilt and all of Agravaine's blood spewed forth from his mouth, the which was yet open in awe of Guinevere's majestic beauty. And he fell heavily onto the stones of the floor, and there he died.

Now Sir Launcelot had never seen Mordred, nor had the queen, and therefore they supposed that only Sir Agravaine, now dead, had known of their lying together.

And Guinevere said, "If the body be hidden in a privy place, none will know of this unfortunate event."

But Sir Launcelot said, "He was the king's own nephew, lady! 'Tis terrible that this happened, but what could I do when he cowardly smote me from behind? I did not believe that Agravaine, a noble knight, would be so base!"

But Guinevere would not dwell on why it had happened, but rather she thought only of how it could be concealed, and she flung aside the arras and she discovered the privy staircase leading to the cellars. "Carry his corse below," said she, "and deposit it in some remote place, perhaps the dungeons, the which are never used at Camelot."

"Lady," said Launcelot, "I have killed a knight."

"One of many such," said Guinevere. "And hast thou each time been benumbed with grief?"

"Agravaine," said Launcelot, "was my brother in the Round Table." And he stood looking at his body, and he made moan.

"That affiliation meant little to *him*, obviously," said the queen. "And did he not cut thee?"

"Yea, so he did," said Launcelot. "But he did nothing worse, and yet I thrust him through the heart! And why, lady? For he would not have come here at all had we not been cohabiting lewdly."

And the queen was in a great rage against him, and she cried, "All these years that we have been together, and thou yet see it as only lewdness!" And she raised her head and she looked at him with the greatest disdain, and she said, *"Thou squalid little man."*

And she went and she sat in the window and watched the dawn shorten the shadows in the courtyard. And Sir Launcelot knelt beside Sir Agravaine's corse, and he prayed for the souls of all of them, and the wound in his arm bled copiously.

And meanwhile Sir Mordred went to his father King Arthur, who was only just arising from his slumber, and he told him of the queen and Sir Launcelot.

And King Arthur raised his strong arm and he struck his son to the floor.

Then Mordred rose with a detestable smirk and he said, "Sire, I had anticipated your great trust in me (for I am of an honest blood). And now if you will put on your robe and crown and take your scepter, for in this matter surely you will rule *ex cathedra* and therefore you must needs have the proper furniture—"

"Toad that thou art!" cried King Arthur, seizing Excalibur and half drawing it from the scabbard. "Slimy thing! Have I the strength to restrain myself from slaying thee here and now?"

But Mordred was not in the least afraid. "Oh, I think you have! You are King Arthur and not Father Abraham. And you have already lost one nephew this night." And then he told the king of how Sir Launcelot had foully killed Sir Agravaine, as he had not told him previously, for Mordred did space his effects for their maximum advantage.

And the king made great grief, and he said as if to himself, "Such are the ends of such means." And he went to the hall of the Round Table, and there he sat down, and Mordred followed him leering.

And now he said to his father the king, "Do you command me to take them in arrest?"

And King Arthur lifted his white head. "Those dost sicken me to the death," said he, "thou pestilence, thou pox!"

"And so speaketh the greatest king of all time," said Mordred, who was much pleased to be so abused, "who ruleth with perfect justice! He blameth his bastard when his queen whores with his first knight. And what doth he care of adultery, when his only begotten son was born only by means of it?"

And King Arthur lost his anger in shame, and he put his head into his hands and he wept.

And Mordred cried, "She must be burnt, Majesty! Else you must abandon all pretense of your fitness to rule."

And Mordred did never believe that King Arthur would burn Guinevere at the stake, and therefore he believed that his father would abdicate the throne, thus forsaking it to him, who would receive with it the fealty of all the knights of the Round Table, leaving Arthur without defenders, and he would kill him and take the queen as his own.

But King Arthur amazed Mordred by assuming control of himself. "Yea," said the king, "I know that must happen before long. But I will not permit thee to gloat over it." And he raised his hand and he pointed at Mordred his son, and he said, "Thou art banished from Camelot."

"For telling the truth, dear Father?" asked Mordred. "Very well, then! You have Excalibur, and I am armed but with a tiny bodkin."

And King Arthur stood up and he unbuckled his sword

from his waist, and he threw it from him, and he said, with a loathing in the first words, "My son, shall we contest the point?" And his limbs no longer trembled.

But now Mordred was sore afraid, as he had not been when King Arthur was armed, and he fled from Camelot.

Then King Arthur sent couriers to Sir Gawaine and his other nephews Gareth and Gaheris, and he commanded them to come to him. And when they arrived he told them of Sir Agravaine's death.

And they all mourned for their brother, and sirs Gaheris and Gareth swore to avenge his death and to kill Sir Launcelot.

But Sir Gawaine said, "Brothers, let us first make certain in what fashion he was killed, for it is not like Launcelot to be a foul murderer. Agravaine was a good man and our dear brother, but yet I know that he did nurse a great bitterness in his heart, for what reason I did never understand, and perhaps this caused him to act rashly."

And Sir Gareth chided Gawaine, saying, "Thou hast for a long time stayed beside thy good wife, Brother, at a warm hearth. And so have Gaheris and I. But can we therefore ignore an heinous offense against our father's family? Have we exchanged our honor for our comfort?"

But Sir Gawaine said, "My dear Gareth, I have killed in the heat of wrath and I have killed in the cold certainty that revenge was necessary, and I was wrong to do either. By accident I killed a lady once when I could not control my anger against her knight, and it has not been long since I killed King Pellinore because he had justly fought for his own land against our father. A knight should protect the persons of his family, but when his line of blood hath become a mere abstract principle he should move cautiously. And I have learned by living some years that sometimes Honor is real, but sometimes it is an illusion, and when lives are lost for the latter, can any purpose be served but the Devil's?"

And Sir Gaheris was caused by this speech to reflect on

his late encounter with Sir Lamorak, and how in inordinate anger he had killed their mother Margawse accidentally. And his spirits were chastened now, and he agreed with Sir Gawaine. But Sir Gareth did not, even so, and though he would not dispute with his older brothers, his anger was unabated against Launcelot, the man he had once so worshiped as to wish to be knighted only by him.

Now King Arthur said, "Nephews, our beloved Agravaine can not be brought back to life, however he did leave it, and revenge is forbidden by our holy Faith."

And then the king's head fell to his bosom and he closed his eyes. Then after a long time he lifted his head again and he said, "Sirs Gawaine, Gaheris, and Gareth, I command ye to go to Queen Guinevere and take her in close arrest."

And then he told them of the criminal cohabitation of Guinevere and Sir Launcelot, and that she must be burned.

And Sir Gawaine asked the king how he knew of this, and the king said he had been told by Mordred.

Then Gawaine said, "I do not know our brother Mordred well, but methinks that like Agravaine he too doth have some inexplicable grudge. Could it be rather that the noble Launcelot had gone to the queen's chambers for some honest reason, but owing to the lateness of the hour and the privacy of the place his errand might seem lewd to one who looked for infractions against decency? Sir Launcelot is the queen's defender. Could she not have sent for him because she feared the incursion of some Meliagrant, now that Camelot has long been void of most knights?"

"Well," said King Arthur, "I know now that thou hast always been my best knight, Gawaine, and I undervalued thee of old, perhaps because thou wert my nephew and I would avoid nepotism. Thou properly lovest Guinevere as thy queen and thine aunt, and I know how thou hast rightly always loved Sir Launcelot."

And here King Arthur looked as though his heart would break.

"But thou dost know full well that though we have made gentle many of the harsh laws of the olden time," the king said, "and no longer are the hands of thieves struck off at the wrists and no man is beheaded for insolence to a superior, there are yet some crimes the perpetrators of which must receive the extreme punishment, else a mockery is made of right rule. And one of them is treason, and Guinevere hath committed it, and therefore she must be burned. It is beyond my power to pardon her from this sentence."

And King Arthur wept piteously.

But Sir Gawaine said weeping, "Uncle and Sire, I shall not obey this command! Let Gaheris and Gareth go if they will, but I shall not arrest the gracious queen my aunt, whom I have always honored above all women and whom I love."

And King Arthur would not punish him for this defiance, but he sent Gaheris and Gareth to take Guinevere.

Now when Sir Launcelot would not hide Agravaine's body and sat all the night beside it praying, Guinevere believed the end was nigh of their being together. And when she understood this she was no longer spiteful towards him. And in the morning tenderly she commanded him to leave her for his own safety.

But Sir Launcelot refused, for he said that he must make Agravaine's death known so that he might have a decent burial in hallowed ground, and that once the king learned of this he would send to arrest them both.

And Launcelot said that he would willingly accept death as his own deserved punishment, and he would not resist arrest. "But, lady," he vowed, "never will I allow you to be taken and burned."

And they disputed over this matter, with Guinevere refusing to leave the castle and go into hiding, and Sir Launcelot refusing to leave her. And never had they been closer in all their lives together than they were now, when each grieved over the doom that threatened the other, and at last they had conquered their vanity and their envy.

Thus they were still there when sirs Gaheris and Gareth came to take Queen Guinevere, for this must needs be done first, and as for Sir Launcelot, he was a knight of the Round Table, and they purposed merely to tell him that his honor required that he arrest himself. But Guinevere being a woman could not be put into her own custody, for she had none in the eyes of the law.

Now they knocked upon the door of the queen's chamber, and Sir Launcelot opened it with his left hand, for Sir Mordred had grievously wounded him in his right arm, which wound had not healed but had grown worse.

"Sir Launcelot," said Sir Gaheris, "greeting."

"My dear Gaheris," Sir Launcelot said. "Thy brother Agravaine is dead, I fear. I loved him as I love you, but alas! we came to blows, and in the sequel he fell. I shall regret this all of my life, and I shall do whatever atonement thou wouldst ask of me."

"Nothing," said Gaheris, "will bring him back amongst the quick, and I know thee for a knight of the greatest worship, and thou art my brother too, in the Table. What we have come for now is not revenge for Agravaine, but rather to arrest the queen in the name of the king, for she hath illegally cohabited with thee and therefore she must be taken and burned for committing treasonous adultery."

"Sir," said Launcelot, "I can not allow this to happen."

"Sir," said Sir Gaheris, "dost thou defy the king's command?"

"Sir, I do," Sir Launcelot said. "And in the name of the only greater power than his, and that is Love."

And Sir Gareth, who had not sworn to forgive Launcelot for killing Agravaine, and had not spoken yet but stayed silently seething with hatred against him, now cried, "Felon! Defend thyself! Else I shall cut thee down where thou standest!"

And though his brother Gaheris sought to restrain him until Launcelot had the time to reconsider his defiance of the king's command, Sir Gareth found Agravaine's sword where Launcelot had dropped it after killing him, and this he gave to Launcelot.

"Now, sir," said he, "lay on, and be prepared to meet the righteous fury of him whose family thou hast offended!"

And thereupon he attacked Sir Launcelot with all his strength, and Sir Gareth was as we have seen one of the most puissant of all knights, and though he had got married and had lived bucolically he jousted for sport with visiting knights and therefore he had kept fit. And Sir Launcelot had not fought in many years, and not even for amusement at tournaments, and his prowess might have suffered from inactivity and his person had gone soft, and he could not use his right hand at all owing to his wound.

And for a few moments Sir Gareth forced him back, but with one great blow of his sword Sir Launcelot cut down through Gareth's skull and parted his brains, and Gareth plunged dead to the floor, this fine man who had been knighted by Sir Launcelot and who had once adored him.

And seeing this Sir Gaheris could not stand by, and he attacked Sir Launcelot with a power which had vanquished giants and monsters, but it was not long before Sir Launcelot smote him backhanded cutting him through mail and flesh and bone, and his bosom opened and his heart and lungs fell out, and he gave up the ghost.

And Launcelot threw down his sword and he looked at the reeking corses of two more of his friends, and he said weeping, "O my God that it hath come to this."

And then he carried Guinevere away from Camelot and he enclosed them both in a castle called Joyous Garde, and he summoned there his cousins Sir Bors and Sir Lionel, and an host of other knights who were his especial friends, and he said to them, "If ye love King Arthur ye will stay with me here in this place and defend it against him when he cometh to take it."

And Sir Bors and the others did not understand this at first, and therefore Sir Launcelot explained it to them.

"Believe me," he said, "when I say that I love King Arthur and would do him no further harm, and I know I shall suffer in eternal Hell for the offenses I have committed against him. Yet I will not surrender the queen for to be burned! Therefore it is better when the king cometh to besiege this place, to hold it against him, for fewer of his knights will die than if we fight afield. Now I ask ye to repel his scaling ladders with long poles, so that none of his knights will be badly hurt (for they are all our old comrades), and if ye hurl spears, ye shall seek to avoid human targets, and ye must yourselves keep well shielded against his missiles. For remember we are all of us friends, and that this war hath not come about because we hate one another."

And Guinevere was there, and she thought to herself, Nay, it hath happened because of men and their laws and their principles! And she wondered whether those who were not knights did not have it better, living according to their appetites, for the common folk and the beasts fought only for food and sometimes their lusts, and being a woman she could not understand honor and justice, for they were invented by men.

And now that she and Sir Launcelot were truly together for the first time in their lives, they were soon estranged, for he was distracted utterly by the preparations for the defense of the castle of Joyous Garde, and he had no time for her at all. And this reminded her greatly of what had happened when she had married King Arthur.

But now we return to the grief of Sir Gawaine when he learned of the deaths of his brothers Gaheris and Gareth. And Sir Gawaine had been the happiest of the knights except for intervals of sadness, the which no man born into this vale of sin can escape utterly. And all in all he had lived a very good life, and when young he had fought and wenched as much as any man could ever, and he was loved by all at the Round Table, and he had married one of the most beautiful women in the world, who was almost unique in that she was satisfied to have him for her husband, and he now had six sons.

But Sir Launcelot had killed three of his brothers, and Gareth, whom he remembered as the varlet who had worked uncomplaining as a scullion in the kitchens and then endured the disdain of Lynette and overwhelmed a series of the most ferocious knights of all time to win his own knighthood, had been especially dear to him. And though Gareth was now himself a father and the lord of his own castle, Gawaine still saw him as the young squire with bright eyes, and to whom winning a place at the Round Table was the only thing worth doing under the sun.

And now his brains were splattered across the floor of Guinevere's bedchamber. And brave Gaheris was dead as well, than whom few knights were more noble, and stout Agravaine, rash intruding fool perhaps, but a good man withal, and all of them bore honorable scars from fighting evil in the cause of virtue.

Now when King Arthur heard of the deaths of two more of his nephews and of the escape of Launcelot and Guinevere he turned as if to stone.

But Sir Gawaine, who had been a kind and genial man, knew for the first time in years what it was to feel wrath, and in the degree to which he had loved Launcelot over all men, because he was the greatest knight, Sir Gawaine now hated him with all his heart, and he vowed to fight him until one of them died.

But King Arthur was in his stupor of grief, and when Gawaine urged him to gather an host and to march on the castle of Joyous Garde, the king looked at him as though he did not know him.

"All is lost," said King Arthur, "and all we have done is to establish the truth that men can serve but one cause alone, and that is futility."

"Well, Uncle," said Sir Gawaine, "perhaps you hoped for more than any king should, but yet you achieved more than any king ever has. And did we not know full well at the outset that there would be some limit, for are we not Christian knights and not pagans, and is not just that knowledge of the human condition the difference between those who believe in God and those who worship idols?" And Sir Gawaine had never been amongst the most devout of knights, for always he had loved life too much.

"Nay," said King Arthur, "we have done nothing, for I see now that mine hath been a shallow philosophy. To the profound vision there is no virtue and no vice, and what is justice to one, is injustice to another. And even God Himself is ruled by Time, for not even He can change the past."

"Well," said Sir Gawaine, " 'tis true enough that the interests of men are oft naturally opposed, and that only one knight may be the greatest and only one woman the most beautiful, and only one king can have the most power, for do not human beings think only in superlatives? And can envy and vanity and wrath and sloth and all the other modes of sin ever be abolished? And yet does not each of them have its peculiar value if exercised in a certain degree? Is it not envy which doth cause us to strive towards the attainments of our fellows? And is not vanity an incomplete step towards acquiring self-respect, which is a good?"

And King Arthur came out of his stupor then, and he said, "And now thou wouldst go to kill Launcelot, Nephew, and what can be the purpose in that? Our reign can never be restored again to what it was once, and thy brothers shall remain amongst the dead."

"Yea," said Sir Gawaine, "you call me back to a sense of duty, Uncle, and therefore you still rule as a great king should. I am wrong to feel wrath against Launcelot, and I know that. Yet I am an human being, and I know that but for him my brothers should live. Is it not human for us all to have two minds, the one that sees an aspect of eternity, the other that must deal with the life which is measured in Time? According to the former, I do forgive him for doing what he could not refrain from, but whilst I live I shall seek his ruin."

And King Arthur then said, "Launcelot hath ever been ruined, since the first, as have I. But thou, good Gawaine, hast a command of reality the which I think will be a better model to those who come after. Therefore I should not want thee to die untimely. And reasonable man that thou art, thou knowest that thou canst not defeat Sir Launcelot at arms."

"Well," said Sir Gawaine, "is that a good reason why I should not fight him? And if he kill me then he hath the blood of us all on his hands!"

And said King Arthur, "It is true that to Launcelot that would be the worst revenge, for he doth not value his life at all. But does that justify the commission of the mortal sin of suicide?"

"Nay, Uncle, pray do not misunderstand me," cried Sir Gawaine. "I do not go to die. Launcelot hath not taken the field in years. Surely his great prowess hath not gone unaffected by the sloth in which he hath lived. I have some merit with lance and sword, and I have kept fit. But beyond all of that I fight in a righteous fury, and what moral mettle be left to him *now*?"

"Yet," said King Arthur, "it is written that he can not be overcome—"

"Where?" said Sir Gawaine. "And by whom? Some lily-livered scribe who hath never held a sword? Some romancer who would confine us to a myth? I defy such augury! And now I have asked too many questions. I go to provide an answer."

And Sir Gawaine thereupon caparisoned himself for to go and besiege Joyous Garde singlehanded. But in love for him, and great concern for his life (and not to take Guinevere and Launcelot for a condemnation of death), King Arthur called in all of his knights who had not gone to help Launcelot, and he marched on the castle which Launcelot held against him.

BOOK XX

*How Sir Percival and Galahad came to Camelot
in King Arthur's absence and met Mordred; and
of the colloquy between the king and the queen;
and how those two great knights Sir Launcelot
and Sir Gawaine fought together until one of
them fell and gave up the ghost.*

Now all of this trouble had happened before Sir Percival
had come to the castle of Pelles the maimed king and had
healed him inadvertently by asking the right question, the
which had been much too simple for any other visitor to
think of in fifty years, but Percival was too naïve to do
the expected.

And King Pelles knew of the tragic matter amongst the
knights of the Round Table, for it was the worst thing that
had ever happened in all the world, and the fall of Rome
to the heathen was as nothing to it, for this was the only
time that a king had set out to rule on principles of absolute virtue, and to fight evil and to champion the good,
and though it was not the first time that a king fell out
with his followers, it was unique in happening not by
wicked design but rather by the helpless accidents of fine
men who meant well and who loved one another dearly.

And there were many who did blame the woman, for
without her King Arthur and Sir Launcelot would still
have been friends, and some of these persons who blamed
Guinevere were themselves women and their motive was
envy, for they would have liked themselves to have
brought down a rule of men. But most of her accusers
were men, and for many their motive was lust, and they

would have liked a beautiful woman for themselves, so that they might betray their best friend for her, but not having one they spitefully wished that the queen would be burned for adultery.

And everybody everywhere in the world knew of this sad matter, and all disputed over it and took one side or the other, except for the wicked, derisive persons (who abound in all eras) who believed it laughable that the greatest king of all time should realize the great dread of all husbands, which is to say, to wear the horns of the cuckold. (And in France the malicious wits did jest as follows: that when Guinevere was taken and burned, Launcelot's grief would be the worse, and to console him King Arthur would say, "Dry thy tears, my friend! I shall soon marry again.")

And Princess Elaine, the mother of Galahad, had known of Launcelot's sinful love since the time when she had cured him of his illness, but never had she told anyone about it but her hand-maiden Brisen, by means of whose magic potion she had taken him into her bed, and she did not meanly exult now that it had become a scandal. For she knew that Launcelot could love none other than Guinevere, as she Elaine could love no one but him, and she believed that no great love could be enjoyed unconditionally and forever. Therefore she believed herself fortunate to have spent one night with Launcelot, and she was the only woman aside from Guinevere to have had that much of him, and it was even so much more than the queen had got, for Elaine had borne his only child.

And now this son would leave home and become a knight of the Round Table when that table had broken into two parts! But Elaine his mother could not find it in her heart to tell Galahad what had happened, and neither could his grandfather King Pelles, who was no longer maimed but whole.

And therefore she kissed Galahad and wished him to go with God, and she bade Sir Percival farewell, that good knight who was armed with his ignorance, and they left the castle of King Pelles.

And the king accompanied them to the gate, and he was so pleased with his newfound ability to use his legs after fifty years that he did not walk slowly but rather scampered ahead like a young varlet, and he confessed to being quite giddy over having the opportunity to ride again and to do all the things a king should do but which he had not done for five decades. And he could not thank Sir Percival enough for having asked the proper question.

But he did not say that now he had been cured of his wound, he did not regret having swyved that little maiden before her husband had got to her (though he was sorry for having slain him subsequently), for she had the sweetest flesh he had ever enjoyed, and King Pelles was of the old school of monarchs, of before the coming of Arthur, and who knows if he were not the better for it, for he loved the life God had given him and he had paid for at least one of his sins while he lived.

Then Sir Percival and Galahad traveled to Camelot, but when they got there they found it a deserted place, for King Arthur and all his knights were at Joyous Garde, outside it with the besiegers or within amongst the besieged. But Sir Percival, who knew nothing, did not know this, but he believed that if King Arthur and his knights were away, then it was as it should be, and therefore he saw no reason for worry.

And he took young Galahad into the castle and he showed him all that was there to be seen, and the youth marveled, and finally they went into the great hall where the Round Table was kept. And Galahad felt faint (for he was dying, which no one but he and his mother knew), and he must needs to sit down and to rest, and therefore he drew a chair to him, and he sat down upon it.

And letters in fire appeared across its back, and they spelled the name

GALAHAD!

Now Sir Percival spake wonderingly. " 'Tis the Siege Perilous, Galahad, my friend! Thou art the one who would come, and for thee this seat hath been kept empty for all the years."

And Galahad smiled to hear this, but he was not well, and he said, "I wonder where King Arthur hath gone, and my father, and all the other knights of the noble company, for I would fain see them soon."

"I expect," said Sir Percival, "that they have all gone out to look for the Holy Grail, for that hath been the principal quest of the Round Table for a long time."

"Alas then!" said Galahad. "We have missed them in both places. But it is a wonder that we did not meet them upon the road as they went towards the castle of my grandfather and we came to Camelot."

"And why, pray," asked Percival, "should they go to Pelles (until lately the maimed king, now whole owing to the question which I asked naïvely)?"

"Because," said Galahad, who was feeling some better now owing to the strength he drew from the Siege Perilous, "that is where the Grail is kept, as everyone knoweth."

"Then my dream of seeing it was not a dream but reality?" asked Sir Percival.

"I expect it was, if you have seen it," said Galahad. "Was it carried by a maiden dressed in white samite?"

"And she had golden hair," said Percival agreeing.

"Well, surely that was the Sangreal," said young Galahad, "for there is only one golden-haired maiden there and she never carries any vessel but it, for the reason that she is the Grail Maiden."

"Well," said Sir Percival, "is it not amazing then that all the knights of the Round Table have looked for this for years, when it was only a few score of leagues away from Camelot? And I myself have gone in search of it to the ends of the earth, but then I am the most ignorant of knights and have been thought by many to be purely a fool."

And Galahad smiled. "But if you had known where it was immediately, would you had so many interesting adventures?"

And Percival thought about this, and he said, "I think I was happy in not finding it straightway. For all I ever wanted was to be a knight and to have adventures and not to stay effeminately in the garden with my mother and my sister."

But Percival marveled to himself that this most sacred of objects should be kept at the castle of King Pelles, who was maimed through concupiscence, but he said nothing of this to young Galahad for fear of offending him. And then, for he was naïve but not stupid, he came to understand that King Pelles was an appropriate host for the Grail Maiden, for owing to his wound he had not been able to mishandle her.

And having understood this Percival was no longer so naïve as he had been, and now he believed that it was very queer that Sir Launcelot had never come back to see his son Galahad, for Pelles' castle was not so far from Camelot and it was well known that Launcelot had not gone questing for many a year, and therefore what had he done instead?

Then when Galahad had rested they left the hall of the Round Table and they went to the throne room, and there, on a cushion of red velvet, on the golden throne of Britain, sat a man wearing a robe of ermine and a crown! But it was not Arthur but rather a man whose skin was so white that it looked almost blue in the crepuscular light of the chamber, for the curtains were drawn and only a few tapers did burn, and his hair and eyes were black as midnight at the dark of the moon.

And Sir Percival clasped the handle of his sword, and Galahad did so as well.

But seeing them the man on the throne did cry, "Hold, brave knights! Do not commit a treasonous display of arms against your sovereign!"

And Percival and Galahad were amazed to hear this. And Sir Percival said, "Is this not Arthur's throne?"

"It was so formerly," said the crowned man. "But my father is no longer amongst the quick. King Arthur is dead. Long live King Mordred! Vassals, to your knees!"

But they remained standing, and Sir Percival said, "I am the most ignorant of knights and I do not understand many things, but with all respect I find it difficult to believe that King Arthur hath died so quietly that we never heard of it."

"Well," said Mordred, "did ye not know that he went to besiege Sir Launcelot at the castle of Joyous Garde?"

And young Galahad did gasp at these news, and Sir Percival said, "Sir, I would that you say no more. I shall go to Joyous Garde, and if what you have told me be true, then you shall receive my obeisance."

"Nay, good sir," said Mordred, and he rose from the throne, "prithee linger here awhile. Thou canst not aid Arthur now, who is beyond human help. And as it happens, I have found the Holy Grail and brought it here to Camelot. Can this have been done by any but the rightful king and heir?"

And Mordred clasped his hands and there entered into the chamber a beautiful lady, and she wore no clothes at all, and she carried between her naked breasts a cup encrusted with countless gems of rare brilliance but none was so scintillating as her ruby-red paps.

And Galahad threw his arm across his eyes and he turned away in shame.

And Sir Percival cried, "Felon! Liar! Impostor!" And he drew his sword and he would have slain Mordred had not that false knight quickly disappeared behind an arras, and when Percival cut it to ribbons and then looked behind it, no one was there. And the lady vanished as well (and she was Morgan la Fey).

"Galahad," said Sir Percival then, "we must with all speed to Joyous Garde. Surely this wicked knight hath not told the truth as to King Arthur and thy father Launcelot, than whom there were never greater friends. But methinks that if both are absent from Camelot, and all the other knights as well, and even unto the queen, some great emprise hath that castle as its locus."

Therefore Sir Percival and Galahad set out for the castle of Joyous Garde.

And when they were gone Sir Mordred came out from hiding, along with his evil aunt Morgan la Fey, and she was no longer beautiful but rather an hag again.

And Morgan la Fey said to him, "Mordred, I shall help thee no more, for thy schemes are no better than mine have been. If I know Arthur he will make his peace with Launcelot and even with Guinevere, for to be a cuckold is no great shame for him, and to hold his kingdom together means more than anything else."

"Nay, Aunt," said Mordred. "His kingdom no longer exists. The crown is mine and I shall reign in Britain henceforth."

"Well," said Morgan la Fey, "this is but the play-acting of the child thou art yet, and I shall perform no further in it. When Arthur returns thou shalt be but the same little bastard thou hast ever been."

"Nay," cried Mordred, "I shall kill him and marry Guinevere."

"Guinevere!" cried Morgan la Fey, and she laughed in derision. "She be too much woman for thee!" And so saying she went out of Camelot, and she soon changed her witch's clothing for the habit of a nun, and she entered herself into the Convent of the Little Sisters of Poverty and Pain, for after a long career in the service of evil she had come to believe that corruption were sooner brought amongst humankind by the forces of virtue, and from this moment on she was notable for her piety.

But Sir Mordred was not in the least discouraged by her defection, for she was but a female, and whilst he hated all men, he despised women, and even Guinevere was to him only a royal piece of furniture like unto the crown and the scepter, to possess which was the king's right.

However, he did suspect that he might need more power than he yet had to keep the throne of Britain, for Sir Percival had shown no fear of him, nor did he like the look of the pale youth who accompanied him, who he could see was dying, for Mordred had a great fear of death like all vicious persons who had no claim to Heaven, and he knew that a dying man could not be threatened with worse than he already had.

Therefore he left Camelot to recruit him an host, and as he failed ever to stir the loyal British churls to revolt, he went to Germany amongst the detestable Saxons and the loathsome Angles, and by making them large proffers he collected an army amongst these villainous peoples who had always coveted Britain, the which was a gem in the mud of the world, and these he brought across the British Channel to Kent.

Then he went to Cornwall, to the court of King Mark. Now owing to his witness of the love of Tristram and La Belle Isold, Mark became a kindly king, but when it had a tragic end he became embittered, for his grasp of philosophy did not exceed the near-at-hand, and he became an enemy of virtue and therefore he did not love King Arthur.

So when Sir Mordred came unto him and promised that in exchange for his aid against King Arthur, Mark could divide with him the entire island of Britain, the Cornish king did agree. And he did not know of the Germans who were camped in Kent.

And next Mordred went to Ireland, where King Anguish still occupied the throne, and he made him the same proffer as he had made to King Mark.

But King Anguish said, "I am too old for to go to battle, and I already have the finest land in the world. I made an error in sending Isold to Cornwall. Ireland for the Irish! I shall not fight unless some bloody buggers try to invade my lovely kingdom." And he had Mordred stripped and taken to the sea and thrown therein.

And Mordred had no more success amongst the Picts

and the Scots. Therefore he went back to join his precious Angles and Saxons, and he formed an host of these beastly men, and they feloniously marched toward Camelot.

Now King Arthur had gone to the castle of Joyous Garde, the which he had besieged for many months, and between him and Sir Launcelot, who was therein, a stalemate existed. For Launcelot would not surrender the queen for to be burned, and King Arthur could not go away without her. And yet they loved each other, so that they would not fight to determine whose will should prevail, nor did any of the knights on either side fight those of the other, for they were all dear friends.

And when King Arthur learned that the supply of foodstuffs within the castle had been exhausted he sent in great stores of meat, and Sir Kay though loyal to Arthur went along with these stores, and he prepared many a delicate meal for Guinevere and her ladies-in-waiting (whom King Arthur had sent to attend her), for to please the queen's fine palate had ever been his greatest joy.

But Sir Gawaine that noble knight did not love Sir Launcelot any longer, and he would fain have fought with him, but Launcelot refused to meet him, and from the battlements of Joyous Garde he spake to him as follows.

"Gawaine, my dear friend," said he. "I believe that I could not have done other than to defend myself against the attacks of thy gallant brothers. Yet I know a terrible shame that I did slay them, for they were all three fine knights and my friends! I shall henceforth never have a moment's peace from anguish. But that they would have taken the queen for her burning I should not have resisted them, and even now I should surrender myself to thee for whatever punishment thou wouldst bring me, were it not that I must protect the queen, who is blameless in all our troubles."

"Sir Launcelot," said Sir Gawaine, standing below the wall, "I do not seek to punish thee, which is something only God may do. But I would fight thee honestly, to the death of whichever one. I can not live with honor when thou hast killed all of my family, for what would my sons think of a father who forsook his duty?"

But Launcelot said, "My dear Gawaine, I will not again raise my sword against anyone of thy blood. I have shed too much of it!" And weeping copiously he went within.

Now this colloquy had taken place many times in the weeks in which King Arthur had besieged Joyous Garde, and neither changed his opinion, nor did King Arthur in his dutiful conviction that Guinevere must be taken and burned at the stake. And only God knows how long they all might have remained *in statu quo* like unto figures woven into a tapestry were it not for Mordred.

For Sir Mordred marched on Camelot with his Germans from the east, and King Mark had come with an host of Cornishmen from the southwest, and these forces had converged on Salisbury Plain, near Stonehenge (for which Merlin had brought the great stones from Ireland many years before, and which was sometimes thought to be a druidical monument, but which was actually an immense and cunning calendar).

And reports were brought to King Arthur by the loyal Britons who lived in that region and who had escaped the murder and rapine wreaked by the Germans on the land.

And hearing these news King Arthur said to Sir Gawaine, "Nephew, the realm is in dire peril. We must needs leave the seige of Joyous Garde and go to repel the foe."

Now Gawaine, having heard who led the enemy host, hung his head in shame, and he said, "Doth it not seem futile that I am here to defend the honor of my family when my youngest brother is a vile traitor!" And he was so tormented by this that his uncle the king at last made an admission that he had never made before to anyone, so that he might relieve that good knight his nephew.

"Gawaine," said he, "thou shouldst know that Mordred is thy brother but by half. Like thou and Agravaine and Gaheris and Gareth, his mother was Queen Margawse, but he did never come from the loins of thy father King Lot.

Nay!" And his noble countenance become the seat of a shame much greater than that of Gawaine. "God forgive me," said King Arthur, "for Mordred is mine own son! And begat in incest he has lived in unnatural bastardy, and I can not but hate him, for he is the creature of mine own detestable lust. And now I must go and kill him, and then methinks I am ready to die myself."

And he wept greatly, and Sir Gawaine though in great grief himself sought to comfort him, but he could find no way in which to do it. And then Gawaine thought of his old friend Launcelot again, and how that he filled a need for the queen, who else had been alone all her life, for King Arthur had been unmanned through his unnatural connection with Gawaine's own mother. And Sir Gawaine, first the merry lecher and then the satisfied husband, understood that he had been a rare man in being made happy by all women he had ever met, and few knights and fewer kings could say the same.

But then thinking further, he believed that if Sir Launcelot had not engaged in an illegal congress with Guinevere and then carried her away when it was discovered, the detestable traitor Mordred could not have gone so far in his design to ruin King Arthur and destroy the Round Table.

Now King Arthur soon dried his eyes and he prepared to march on Mordred's host, for he was the king and kings can not allow the accidents of personality to obscure the essence of their rule.

And he said to Sir Gawaine, "In this extreme situation Guinevere's crime must be seen as a mere foible, and furthermore we require the service of the many good knights who joined Sir Launcelot at Joyous Garde. Therefore go to him and say that King Arthur doth withdraw the siege, and that he shall not fear punishment on the condition that he void Britain absolutely and stay in banishment forever."

"And what of the queen?" asked Sir Gawaine.

"She may go anywhere she listeth," said King Arthur, "except to return to Camelot. I will not lift mine hand against her now or in the future."

And Sir Gawaine went below the wall of Joyous Garde and he called to Sir Launcelot, who came onto the battlements, and he told him of King Arthur's decision. And Sir Launcelot was pleased to hear that the queen would not be burned, and therefore he had the gates opened and all the knights that had been with him came out and they joined the king's forces without prejudice.

Then Guinevere rode forth alone on the white palfrey, and on that morning when the sky was leaden it was as if the sun had appeared upon the earth. And she came to the pavilion of King Arthur, and she dismounted and she went in unto him and she fell upon her knees.

Now King Arthur protested, "Rise, Guinevere! You have nothing for to beg of me, for I would do you no harm, having taken my oath upon it."

"Arthur," said Guinevere, "I kneel before you because you are the king and I am your subject like any other, but what I beg of you is nothing for myself. Indeed, with me you have been more merciful than any other king would have been in all the world. But I beg you not to banish Sir Launcelot, and not for mine own sake, but rather for yours. To overcome your enemies you will need his sword, which is invincible. Nor is he guilty of wrongdoing, for what he did was by command of his queen, to whom you had sent him as her own knight. *And I had nobody else to rule over!* Therefore he bears no responsibility for this shame, and all of it is mine."

And though kneeling in entreaty Guinevere was humble in no wise, but rather she was as proud as she had ever been, for she was the sort of woman who could not be otherwise to save her soul.

And King Arthur came to her and taking her hands he lifted her to her feet. "My dear queen," he said, "you do embarrass me and not for the first time. Of late I have considered whether you would not have been a better sovereign than I, and whether were our situations reversed I should as consort have acted as well as you.

"But to proceed further with this fantasy would no doubt be blasphemous, God having decided which must rule and which must serve. And power came to me by surprise: until I drew the sword from the stone a second time that fatal day, I never knew I was so much as a prince, let alone a king."

And King Arthur looked very old and weary, and he sat down upon the portable throne which he used when afield.

"Indeed, though I was proficient with weapons when a boy I did not foresee a career as a knight. I expected to be a farmer, Guinevere! And I confess to thee alone that I have never felt so comfortable with men as with animals, and the best friends I ever had in all my life were the hounds of Sir Hector my foster-father, R.I.P., and the horses, and even the sheep and the swine. And it is a curious thing that my father Uther Pendragon, with whom I have shared little else, did also have a great love for his beasts."

And King Arthur smiled awhile, but then he came out of his reverie, and he said, "But when rule was thrust upon me by God, who had arranged that no one else could withdraw the sword from the stone, I must needs accept it. Yet, though one must never question the decision of Heaven, I have ever believed myself a strange choice for the throne of Britain. Power, Guinevere, hath never been to my taste."

"But perhaps," said Guinevere, "that is because you have always had all of it! Those who crave power are neither those who have none, like the churls, nor those who have all, like you, but rather those who have some claim to it but can not get enough."

"Yea," said King Arthur, "like Caesar, for whom Europe was not enough, and therefore he came here to our blessed island, which God permitted the Romans to take and hold briefly only so that the Christian religion might be brought to our stout Britons, so that when Rome fell to the barbarians we might be the only bastion in a world of utter savagery."

But then King Arthur said to the queen, "Enough of this, for this is a matter which is of concern to men and not to women, and now I must go to war."

And she did therefore believe him to be the most innocent of men though the greatest king of all, and perhaps there was some connection.

And she said to him, "Arthur, I am sorry to have committed an offense against you."

But the king said, "Nay, Guinevere, not against *me*, for what I am in myself is nothing, but rather against the crown, which is all. Therefore I can not permit Launcelot to fight at my side, much as I need his sword, indeed much as I love him dearly as my friend, for that love is merely personal."

"And what of me?" asked Guinevere. "Where shall I go now? And if I ask, Is there a place for me in all the world?, then I wonder whether there has ever been one!"

"What you do now is a matter between you and God," said King Arthur. "It were truly impertinent for me to think about this." But then he looked softly upon her, and he said, "I have thought too much in time past. I loved thee greatly, my dear Guinevere, in mine own fashion. And I love thee yet. Never have I pronounced an animadversion upon thee! We must part now, never to meet again in this life. As a man and lately thine husband, I say only, Go with God!" And then he became stern though not unkind, and he said, "As a king my counsel is to cultivate discretion."

And then he strode from his pavilion and he commanded his knights to assemble and to march on Salisbury Plain, there to meet the host assembled by the vile Mordred.

And Guinevere, alone in the pavilion, did think King Arthur not so innocent after all, and she forgave him as he had forgiven her.

Now last of all to come out of Joyous Garde was Sir

Launcelot, and he was alone as well, for now that he had preserved Guinevere from burning they had no more reason to cleave together.

But Sir Gawaine was waiting for him without the gate, and when Launcelot rode out, Gawaine said to him, "Sir, we have an appointment."

"Dear Gawaine," said Sir Launcelot, "must we fight? All of it is finished now, for whatever the outcome of King Arthur's war with Mordred, the Round Table is no longer a perfect circle, if it ever was, for at its finest moment there was one seat unfilled. But methinks there was a moral continuity amongst us, and that such a company of knights could come together in the common cause of virtue for even an instant was unique in the history of the world."

"Well," said Sir Gawaine, "the principle was noble and we all of us did uphold it each in his own fashion, and perhaps we did well as we could, being but men."

"Alas!" said Sir Launcelot, "certes, that is true of thee and the others, but I could not have done worse! And to say that I could not help myself is no excuse before God nor man. I did what I did, and I can not undo it. And now, having caused this great peril to come to King Arthur, I can not even defend him against it."

"Nay," said Sir Gawaine, "thou didst not cause it, Launcelot, but thou didst give an opportunity to a vile knight to use for his cause, and that caitiff is my only remaining brother. And though I can finally forgive thee for killing Agravaine, Gaheris, and Gareth in self-defense, I can not pardon thee for assisting Mordred, though unwittingly, in his detestable scheme. Unless I fight thee now, this greatest of all shames to my family will never be expunged."

"Gawaine," said Sir Launcelot, "methinks thine ethic is exceeding complex, and that somehow, whatever the situation, it finds me peculiarly at fault. . . . But perhaps it is only right that thou dost, for now that the queen hath been saved and I am prohibited from joining King Arthur, I have no use in the world but to give thee satisfaction. May God strengthen thine hand!" And saying this he drew apart from Gawaine on the field before Joyous Garde.

And both of them closed their helms and they put their lances in fewter and spurring their horses they charged on each other. Now the wound in his right hand which Mordred had given him stealthily had never properly healed, and therefore Sir Launcelot could not fight so well as of old, and when his lance met Sir Gawaine's shield it was ripped from his grasp.

But Gawaine's shaft did break when its point struck Launcelot's shield, and therefore wheeling their chargers they drew their swords and they came together with flashing blades. And so they fought fiercely for two hours, hacking at each other.

Now when the fight had begun Sir Launcelot did purpose to allow Sir Gawaine eventually to overwhelm him and to kill him, for in no other way could they both be satisfied, Gawaine in his sense of honor and Launcelot because he fain would die. And furthermore Sir Launcelot believed that he was no longer necessarily the better knight. And the reason that he would not let Gawaine vanquish him quickly was that his former friend, who had fought him once long ago, would not fail to notice if he did not use his full strength, and he would believe it a great insult. And Launcelot had offended Gawaine too much already.

But the longer they fought the less Sir Launcelot felt like losing voluntarily, for he already seemed to be losing in fact, and his hand felt as if it had already gone to Hell and was being burned in the fire which did not consume, and he could not change hands without Sir Gawaine's wondering why, for he had not wounded him in the right arm, and therefore he would believe he was being offensively given an advantage!

And Sir Launcelot, who had never been given to thought (as opposed to religious contemplation) believed that if Gawaine's morality were complex, it was because chivalry in general was more complicated than it seemed, for it is not easy always to know what is the noble thing, or what is brave and generous or even simply decent. Yet if a knight gave way to his impulses, as he had done once with Guinevere, he might bring down a kingdom by chance more certainly than a caitiff like Mordred could do it by design.

And though other persons might believe that his life had been grand (for he was the greatest knight of all), and all the more so now that he was known as the lover of the greatest queen in all the world and the most beautiful woman, Sir Launcelot thought that it had been largely squalid, with intervals in which it rose to banality. And for the first time he pondered on the differences amongst men, and how though a company of them might hold the same principles, each member might honestly interpret these in another way. (But he did not think about women at all, though he was here fighting one of his best friends only because of one.)

Now at this moment Sir Launcelot was finally wounded in his right arm by a savage blow of Sir Gawaine's, the which cut through his armor and penetrated his flesh, and he dropped his sword upon the ground.

And when he dismounted to fetch it, Gawaine descended from his own steed and he waited till Launcelot picked up his blade in his left hand, and then they proceeded to fight on foot. And Sir Gawaine seemed to grow ever stronger, while Sir Launcelot weakened owing to his wounds.

And we shall leave them there at this moment, for this fight would go on all the day and it was to be the longest in the history of the world, for Launcelot and Gawaine were living legends, and one of them must die in this encounter, and with two such men you can be sure that this was not a thing of a minute.

Now King Arthur and his knights had ridden towards Salisbury Plain, but Guinevere still sat in the silk pavilion he had left behind, for he did not expect to rest during the fight with Mordred's host, and if the truth be known, King Arthur did not expect ever to lie down again except in death, for he had a premonition that this fight would be his last.

But he did not know that Mordred was not on Salisbury Plain with his Germans, but rather had come to spy on Joyous Garde, and when he saw King Arthur march away, stole into the pavilion where the queen sat defenseless.

And drawing his sword Mordred put the point of it at the white neck of Guinevere, and he said, "Lady, you are mine."

And looking at him without great interest, Guinevere asked politely, "And who art thou?"

"I am Mordred," said the same.

"Well, Mordred," said the queen, "what wouldst do with me, mishandle or murder?"

"Neither, lady," said Sir Mordred, who was amazed by her calm.

"And is there a third possibility when a lady is captured by a felon?" asked Guinevere. "Or by any man?"

And Mordred perceived that she was rather more clever than he had supposed King Arthur's queen would be. "Yea," said he, and he smiled the smile from which even most men did turn away in distaste if not in horror (for his face seemed to be leering from an uncovered grave), but this had no effect on Queen Guinevere, to whom all men were as boys. Then Mordred said, "Lady, know you that I am the new king, your late husband Arthur having fallen dead on the road to Salisbury Plain. You are therefore a widow, and I intend to take you for my queen."

And Guinevere rose in all her stateliness, and she said, "Sir, thou art a liar, for I am sure that King Arthur is yet alive. Thou art a criminal to come to me in this way, and thou wouldst be an usurper and a traitor. Nevertheless I shall go with thee freely, for two reasons. Firstly, that by thy look thou art a ruthless caitiff who would kill me if I did not do thy will, and I do not wish to die before my time. And the other reason is that if thou dost wish to marry me, thou threatenest me with no worse than I have ever had. Therefore lead on, and I shall follow."

And for the first time in his life Sir Mordred was confused, for he had expected that taking Guinevere would be a very difficult task, and when they left the pavilion it was Guinevere who led and he who followed.

And Mordred helped her onto her palfrey, and then he asked her whether she had waiting-women to attend her on the journey they must take.

"They are all yet within Joyous Garde," said she, "and surely they now sit at the windows, watching those two knights yonder, who are trying to kill each other though they be dear friends, for truly most women are foolish as men." And looking down on him from her palfrey she asked Sir Mordred where he would take her.

Now Mordred with his elaborate schemes had nevertheless given this matter no thought whatever, and his horse was not near by but rather hidden in a thicket half a league away. Therefore he must needs lead Guinevere's palfrey there while going afoot himself, and so he began his association with her by serving as lackey.

And when he arrived at the thicket he saw that his beast was not there, but had got loose, and was strayed or stolen. And he was constrained to walk on foot all the way to London in his heavy armor, for though Guinevere taking pity on him offered to share her palfrey he could not endure the shame of riding into a city behind a woman, even the queen, and her richly decorated saddle did offer no place for another rider, and therefore he must needs have been perched on the horse's arse.

Now finally they reached that great town, and there they came unto the Tower of London, the which had been built by Julius Caesar, and in this place all the British kings from Brute to Uther Pendragon had kept their crown jewels, but King Arthur had used them to build hospitals and orphanages and asylums for the insane, and the jewels were not there any more, so that the guards had been removed. And nobody at London noticed their queen being led through the streets by a knight who was weary and limped, for the lords were busy in doing good works and the common folk were laboring happily and whistling like so many birds.

And Mordred did close Guinevere into the Tower of London, but she did not protest at any time. Indeed she spake not at all from the moment when she had told him she would follow, and as for Sir Mordred, neither did he speak to her, for the reason that he could think of nothing to say to this great queen which would not make him seem foolish, and he did dread her scorn.

And having locked her into the Tower he went without and coming upon a fat merchant who rode an horse, he knocked him off it and he got on the animal's back and rode towards Salisbury Plain.

Now before the castle of Joyous Garde, Sir Launcelot and Sir Gawaine had continued to fight all the day and into the evening, and Gawaine had surely gained the advantage as the sun fell through the western sky, and Sir Launcelot's right arm had lost so much blood that the field was covered with gore and in the wet grass both knights oft slipped.

And Sir Gawaine halted frequently for Sir Launcelot to bind his wounds, but his friend declined this courtesy. But finally when he had opened his visor to reply to Sir Gawaine's kind suggestion Gawaine saw that his face was dead white from the loss of blood. And therefore he insisted that Launcelot be bandaged, and he called out from the castle the waiting-women of Guinevere, who had been watching the fight from an oriel window.

And these ladies came forth and they tended to him, and one tore some stuff from her petticoat and she made a dressing for Sir Launcelot's arm.

Now some of these ladies had wagered on him, and others on Sir Gawaine, and all of them loved one or the other of these supreme knights, and many loved them both. And if Sir Gawaine had been the lecher of his youth he would have had a choice of bedfellows. But he was older now, and more sober, and he was happily married. But beyond that, having to fight his great friend he knew no joy, nor did he believe he would ever know it again, whoever survived this fight: for he who won would be the killer of his friend.

And if Sir Gawaine was victorious, he had no brothers left but the vile Mordred, and the Round Table was shattered forever. And perhaps the best thing he could do for his sons was to give them an example by dying nobly. Now this was the first time that Sir Gawaine had ever thought in this fashion, for he had loved his life in all its phases.

Whereas Sir Launcelot, who had always hated life and wanted to die, now that he was bleeding to death he began to think otherwise, for actually dying is not so romantic as is thinking about death when one is invincible, and Launcelot had never been in real danger before in his life. Therefore he began to see himself in a new light, and he came to think that his invincibility might be a myth, and that he had previously overwhelmed his enemies because they were half-conquered by the myth before they met him.

Now the lady who had bandaged Sir Launcelot with her petticoat had placed a sizable wager on him in this fight, and therefore she greatly desired that he should win. And she had seen Sir Mordred take the queen out of the pavilion and lead her away, and she now gave these news to Launcelot, thinking that he would thereby be inspired to win, so that he might go and rescue Guinevere. But with wicked greed she did not speak so loudly that Sir Gawaine could hear, for she knew that that noble knight would end the fight there and then knowing the queen was in peril.

And because of her greed one of those great knights died that day. (But in the years to come God visited a sore punishment on this lady, for a brutal Saxon mishandled her and gave her both an idiot bastard and a disease.)

And she was right in thinking that Sir Launcelot would

fight with new vigor, for he realized then that he *was* invincible when fighting so as to protect Guinevere. Therefore when he again joined battle with Sir Gawaine his left arm had all the strength that his right had formerly possessed, and with one great blow he brought his sword down upon Gawaine's helmet so mightily that though the steel was not cut through Sir Gawaine's head was broken within.

And this great knight fell into the swoon of death. And going to rescue Guinevere, Sir Launcelot wept piteously for his friend. And the waiting-women found some peasants to carry Sir Gawaine home to his castle and his wife the Lady Ragnell and his young sons, and there he lay dying for some days, but never did he become conscious again.

And Sir Gawaine, one of the very greatest knights who ever lived and the finest man of the company of the Round Table (for he had all the virtues and of the vices the most natural), was greatly mourned on earth by all the brave knights and all the beautiful ladies, whilst in Heaven the angels rejoiced to have him amongst them, with his great virile integrity.

BOOK XXI

*How Mordred stabbed King Arthur from behind;
and how the battle began.*

Now Sir Launcelot went to London and there he
found the merchant whose horse had been feloniously
taken from him by Mordred, and he was told by this merchant that the wicked knight had come out of the Tower.
And Sir Launcelot gave this man some gold for to pay for
his horse, and then he went to the Tower and he broke the
lock on the portal with one wrench of his mighty fist, and
he climbed to the top.

And there was Guinevere, who sat by the window and
looked across the river Thames, nor did she turn to see
who had entered her prison.

And Sir Launcelot said to the back of her golden head,
"Well, I have delivered you."

And though she recognized his voice she continued to
look out the window, and she said, "From what?"

"From your captivity," said Launcelot. "Lady, you are
freed."

And now Guinevere turned and said, "Thou hast done
thy duty, Lancelot. And now?"

"Lady," said Sir Launcelot, "I am commanded by King
Arthur to void the realm. I have been banished from Britain, but the rest of the world is open to me. Perhaps I
shall go to the land of mine old friend Tristram, across the

sea, which methinks is yet governed by his brother-in-law, the noble Kaherdin. Such a ruler can ever use another sword, for his enemies, if he be virtuous, are ever rife."

"And is he not married, Launcelot?" asked Guinevere.

"Yea," said he, "and to Isold's former handmaiden the loyal Brangwain."

"Not a beautiful woman, by all report," said Guinevere.

"Nay," said Sir Launcelot, "but Kaherdin loves her dearly."

"Methinks then," said Guinevere, "that she be grateful and not proud."

And Sir Launcelot said, "Lady . . ."

" 'Twas not my beauty which attracted thee," said Guinevere, "but rather my pride. Therefore can it be said that thou shalt never be banished by Prince Kaherdin?"

"Lady," said Launcelot, "perhaps it was neither thy beauty nor thy pride, but rather thy sense of power to which I addicted. I am not a leader, but am always led. I was Arthur's mastiff, and then I became thy spaniel. I shall offer my neck to Kaherdin for whichever collar he might fasten around it."

"And dost not propose to take me along as thy bitch?" asked Guinevere. But she smiled upon him, for she was done with him forever.

"Madam," said Sir Launcelot, "I do not think you would be comfortable in any place where you were not the queen. But if you require my services at any time, for defense or protection, you have but to send for me and I will come on the moment."

And he bowed to her, and then she put forth her hand so that he might kiss it, which he did.

"Now, Launcelot, prithee tell me this," said she. "Dost think we together brought down the Round Table?"

Now she did not ask this in mockery, but neither did she feel a great guilt about it, for Guinevere was proud (for she really was the most beautiful woman who ever lived).

And Sir Launcelot answered deliberately, "Nay, lady.

We were great sinners but we were not heretics! Had we not done what we did, God would no doubt have found another pretext, for is He not jealous of Heaven as the only perfect place?"

And saying that he went away from the Tower of London, and he left Queen Guinevere for the last time.

But he did not yet take ship for Lesser Britain. Instead, though the most loyal knight who ever lived, he did disobey his king again, as he had disobeyed him when he was commanded to surrender Guinevere for burning. And he did this for to save King Arthur's life, as he had saved that of the queen. For Launcelot believed that without his help King Arthur would be overwhelmed by Mordred, and perhaps that was his vanity.

Now we return to Sir Percival and Galahad, who had arrived at the castle of Joyous Garde too late, for Percival could not find the road there for a long time, and Galahad was too ill to travel fast, and he coughed much and he must needs to stop oft and to rest.

And so when they reached Joyous Garde they were told by the ladies of the fight between sirs Launcelot and Gawaine and of the death of that great knight Sir Gawaine, and of the abduction of the queen by a detestable felon.

And these ladies all were weeping, even unto those who had wagered on Sir Launcelot, for all of them grieved most piteously for Sir Gawaine. And young Galahad heard of this fight with unhappy wonderment, and then finally he heard why his father had been at Joyous Garde and of his criminal attachment to the queen.

But Sir Percival drew him aside, and he said to him. "Galahad my friend, do not listen to this gossip, for though these be decent ladies, who can say what is the truth? Methinks it be unlikely that thy father would change from being the greatest knight into an adulterous traitor. I tell thee I have met Sir Launcelot and there is no finer man alive. I can not think that he fought against that great knight his dear friend Sir Gawaine. Rather, these ladies being in a state of female giddiness owing to the time of the full moon, conjoined with the dampness of the days here at this castle (which seemeth more grim than joyous), they suffered from an optical fantasy, and the knights they saw fighting were rather two wicked men, and 'twas the winner which abducted the queen."

Now Galahad, who was too young to know the ways of the world, was some cheered by what he was told by Sir Percival.

And Galahad said, "Well, Sir Percival, we must go to the succor of one or the other, king or queen, for Arthur is challenged at Salisbury and Guinevere hath been carried away illegally."

"Now," said Sir Percival, "according to these ladies both crimes are the work of the vile Sir Mordred! And how can this be possible? Therefore, how can they be believed as to the fight?" And he clapped Galahad on the shoulder, and he said jovially, "Come, my friend, let's to the war! For if Sir Launcelot hath gone in pursuit of the queen, she has nothing to fear. And we, thou and I, are warriors. Come, we shall let some Saxon blood!"

And Percival mounted his steed and Galahad mounted his own, and they both of them spurred their animals towards Salisbury Plain. But they had traveled no great distance before Galahad was ill again, and he coughed blood, and seeing a convent near by Sir Percival took him there, and there Galahad was nursed in a cell by a saintly old nun who bathed his head with Cologne-water and fed him warm broths.

And neither Percival nor Galahad recognized her as Morgan la Fey, whom they had seen walking obscenely naked through the throne room at Camelot whilst Mordred had posed as king, for she had reformed absolutely. And with her tender care she restored Galahad at least temporarily, and then both knights prayed with her, and then they resumed their travel, and they carried with them a crucifix she had given them to take to King Arthur.

Meanwhile Sir Launcelot had reached the plain at Salisbury, where the two armies were drawn up opposing each other, King Arthur on the one side with his small band of valiant knights, and on the other all the Angles and Saxons in the world and with them King Mark and his host of Cornishmen.

But the battle had not yet begun, for the reason that King Mark and the Germans, when they first saw one another, were unhappily amazed, for each side had supposed that they would fight King Arthur alone and, when he was dead, get all of Britain for themselves. And Mordred being at that time many leagues away and occupied with the abduction of Guinevere, the ensuing quarrel had got so heated that these felons were ready to war on each other, for there is no love amongst criminals.

And these allies were at swordspoint and were about to slaughter one another when Sir Mordred returned having ridden in such great haste that the stolen horse dropped dead with the effort.

Now with the eloquence of a serpent Mordred did convince each party, by speaking to each aside, that he loved them the better, but that they needed the other's help to defeat the fierce Arthur and his puissant knights of the Round Table. But to each he promised that when King Arthur was dead he Mordred would lead them in an attack on the other, whom they would destroy. (But privately he believed that the battle would be so deadly as to kill everybody but himself, leaving no one in Britain but the churls, over whom he would rule with Guinevere at his side.)

Now when Sir Launcelot arrived there he came near the Saxon camp, and seeing one lone British knight (and not recognizing the device on his shield) an hundred German dastards did rush at him, with an intent to kill him foully, but though his right arm had been crippled by Sir Gawaine, so that he could not use it but rather carried it in a sling made from the petticoat of a lady-in-waiting, Sir Launcelot using his left arm only slew fifty of these felons from his horse, but then one of the remainder, who could not reach him with a weapon, did cowardly hamstring his steed with a battle-ax. And therefore Sir Launcelot fought the rest of his opponents on foot, and with his flashing sword he destroyed them all, and severed Germans heads did strew the field like unto melons at harvest-time.

And Sir Launcelot would continue on to join the knights of King Arthur, but because of the command that he be banished, he believed he might do better to disguise himself, and therefore he hid his proper shield, with the lions rampant, and he took up a Saxon shield the which was round and in its center was a heavy iron boss all red with rust (for this backward people knew not how to make shining steel, nor did they have stuffs for their clothes, but wore hairy hides closed with thongs).

Now though Sir Percival and Galahad were delayed by Galahad's illness, they had made good time in coming to join King Arthur, and when they reached the knights of the Round Table, Sir Percival brought young Galahad to the king straightway.

And though he was a naïve knight, and did not for a moment believe that Sir Launcelot had an illegal attachment with the queen, Sir Percival forbore to mention to King Arthur that Galahad was the son of Launcelot, for he wished not to distract him on the eve of battle.

Rather he said to him, "Sire, this young man is named Galahad, and he is the finest knight in the world, for at Camelot he sate upon the Siege Perilous with impunity. Nay, it burst into fiery letters which spelled his very name!"

And King Arthur was amazed. "Then he who will come hath come at last," said he, "and in the hour of my greatest need! Well, Galahad, kneel and become my last knight." And the pale young man did so, and he looked so ill that King Arthur could not have believed him a knight were it not for his having sate in the Siege Perilous. Then he touched him with Excalibur, and he said, "Rise, Sir Galahad."

And Sir Galahad gave to King Arthur the crucifix

which had been sent by him from the Little Sister of Poverty and Pain who had been formerly Morgan la Fey, and King Arthur looked at the figure of Our Lord and he saw above His head not the letters INRI but rather ACRB, which was to say, not Jesus of Nazareth King of the Jews but Arthur of Camelot King of Britain. And King Arthur thanked Sir Galahad for delivering this, but privately he put it aside, but he believed it blasphemous, for one, and for another he did not consider himself a martyr.

And after this ceremony Sir Galahad must needs go and rest, for he was ill and sore weary, and taking his horse he went within the circle of Stonehenge and he lay down upon the ground and he slept.

Now King Mark and the Cornish host foolishly attacked King Arthur and the knights of the Round Table without warning, for they seethed with indignation at their Saxon allies and would cleanse their bad blood in battle. And there were five thousand of them.

But after they had charged upon King Arthur's force their number was reduced by half, for at the far left extremity of Arthur's shining line was Sir Launcelot (and he had gone there because he could use only his left arm), and he singlehanded slew two hundred men of Cornwall. And at the right end was Sir Percival, who did kill an hundred ninety-nine of these enemy and he wounded one mortally, who died within half an hour.

And the other two thousand one hundred and one were killed in the center by Arthur's line by sirs Lionel and Bors and Bedivere and Lamorak and Lucan the Butler, and sirs Gahalantine, Galihodin, and Galihud; Sir Nerouneus and Sir Plenorius, Sir Urre, sirs Blamor and Beloberis, both of Ganis; Sir Villiers the Valiant, Sir Harry le Fise, Sir Bellangere le Beuse, and Sir Clarius of Cleremont; and sirs Lavaine and Tirre, who were the brothers of Elaine the unfortunate maid of Astolat; and all the others, and all of them were knights of the greatest worship, including Sir Kay, who at this time did finally gain the prowess he had always longed for, and he destroyed ten of the enemy as if they were Cornish pastries.

And then King Arthur looked sadly at the results of this carnage (for though he wished to defeat the enemy he deplored the bloodshed), and he sent a courier to King Mark asking that he meet him in the middle of the field under conditions of truce. And Mark agreed to this, and the two kings rode out alone to join each other.

"Mark, my greeting to you," said King Arthur.

And King Mark replied, "God give you good day, royal Arthur."

"Now look you, Mark," said King Arthur, "you are properly my vassal, yet never have I demanded tribute from you, and never have I punished you for your long-withheld expression of fealty. And I did not do this, because I have always been sensitive towards Cornwall owing to the unjust treatment of your predecessor Gorlois by my father Uther Pendragon, which resulted in my birth. But I can not tolerate your shameless treason."

"Well, Arthur," said King Mark, "I think you a bad king for Britain, for else why should one of your knights come to me for help in overthrowing you? Clearly the Round Table hath not been a success, if one of your hand-picked knights doth revolt against it." (And King Mark was an hypocrite, who had thought of this reason on the moment, for his true purpose here was to seek power.)

"Now, Mark," said King Arthur, "you know full well that I am the lawful king of Britain, whether good or bad, and that to take up arms against me be vile treason for whatever the cause." (And Arthur could not tell him that Mordred was his bastard.)

"But laws, Arthur," said Mark, "are made by those who win battles."

And King Arthur said, "Even so. Look about the field and see your fallen, and none of my knights hath a scratch. Now what I propose to you is that we, you and I alone, meet in individual combat. I want no more of your Cornishmen killed on this field, for they too are my subjects. And if you so desire my crown on your head, then you must have the stomach to take it, or else be known more for your poltroonery than for your contumaciousness!"

And King Mark waxed wroth at this taunt, for in truth his strength was not a thing of principle but rather his emotion at any given moment (and he had had a few fine impulses in his life, along with many bad). And he lowered his visor angrily, and he fewtered his lance, and then he charged on King Arthur.

And when Mark rode down upon him King Arthur swung Excalibur twice. The first time he cut in twain the shaft of King Mark's lance, and the second time he cut off his head.

And then King Arthur went before the host of Mark, who had been watching this fight, and he spake as follows.

"Cornish subjects! Ye have seen what happens to all traitors. Therefore return to your land of Cornwall and live there in peace, without fear of punishment, if ye promptly void this field. Stay, and ye shall all die. Leave, as my loyal subjects, and know my love."

And therefore this Cornish host did fall to its knees as a man and do homage to King Arthur, and they all swore their fealty to him. And then they rose and they went towards their home in Cornwall.

But when they went over an hill and into the valley and were out of sight of King Arthur, their late allies the Angles and the Saxons seeing their depleted force fell upon them from ambush, and this German host did outnumber the men of Cornwall ten to one. And though Cornishmen were valiant warriors and each was worth nine Germans, these odds were too great and they were killed every one.

But King Arthur nor none of his knights knew ought of this massacre, and many knights commended him for making peace with the Cornishmen without more fighting. And he was encouraged to believe that he might make a similar truce with the Germans, for whom he had no hate (though much contempt), and to convince them that they should return peaceably to their own land.

And therefore he sent a message to them, but this was intercepted by Mordred (who had sent the Germans to destroy the host of the late King Mark), and when the Saxons returned with smoking swords and the high passions aroused in such a beastly people by killing, he said to them, "I have received from King Arthur a message in which he maketh great insult to the Angles and the Saxons, of whom he says those who are not vile sodomites are despicable cuckolds, and all are cowards!"

Now the Germans did take no great offense at these words, because they knew themselves as just the men so characterized, and they were so shameless a folk as to believe this a mere description of themselves and not a judgment upon them, for they knew no moral scruples and were entirely pagan.

Now seeing this Sir Mordred understood that he must give them something to fight for which would appeal to their felonious greed and vicious lust. And therefore he said, "Amongst the knights of the Round Table are many handsome men, and some of them are but youths with fair skin, and after this battle ye may use them as your catamites." And the many sods amongst the Angles and the Saxons grunted in pleasure to hear this.

And next Mordred said, "And for those of ye who like females, the British women are the most beautiful in the world, and when we destroy these few knights of the Round Table, ye may ravish all the mothers, wives, and daughters and sisters in the land." And the Germans did cheer vilely at this promise.

But some were more interested in treasure than in flesh, and to them Sir Mordred said, "King Arthur keepeth, at the castle of Caerleon-upon-Usk, which is virtually unguarded, the lode of the Nibelungs, the which was stolen from Germany when your Sir Siegfried was foully murdered from behind by a cowardly British assassin!" For Mordred had made a study of the lore of this people, and he spake to them in their own tongue, the which was called Anglish and was so many grunts and squeaks.

Now with his serpent's tongue Mordred soon brought these pagans to a murderous frenzy in which they would have smote their own brothers. And they built huge fires and they erected altars to their obscene gods and they made barbarous blood-sacrifices. And they sounded horns and they screamed and howled whilst dancing in circles detestably naked, with their privities exposed indecently.

And this noise was heard in the British camp, and King Arthur and his knights believed that it signified the Germans' joy that there would be no war, whereas it was just the opposite.

And King Arthur said, "Come, let us visit these fellows and embrace them in friendship, for a Saxon despite appearances is human and if he be a heathen yet, it is doubtless only for the reason that the missionaries have not yet reached his wild land."

And Arthur and his knights did ride across the field, and they were not in the order of battle, and the king did carry below the point of his lance a banner with the picture of the Mother of God upon it.

And the Germans were so distracted by their heathenish rituals that they did not see the British until they arrived before their camp. And had his purpose not been peaceful King Arthur could have killed them all.

But seeing him Sir Mordred did call the Saxons to arms, and they soon formed a line the which stretched to the horizon on each side, and behind it were several more, for in number they were twenty thousand, and each man was armed with a lance and a sword and an ax, and the iron boss on his round shield protruded six inches and it served as a weapon as well.

But seeing this array King Arthur was not dismayed, for he believed that these foreigners did not understand his pacific intention. And he rode to where Mordred was, and he held his banner high with both hands so that Mordred could see he did not approach him in hostility.

And to his son he said, "My dear Mordred, this is a strange place to see thee."

Now notwithstanding that he had twenty thousand armed men with him, Sir Mordred did greatly fear his father, whom lately he had watched swipe off King Mark's head with one blow, and he well knew that Excalibur was yet invincible. And he could not ignore that decisive truth, for unless King Arthur were killed he would have achieved nothing. And though the king held the banner with both hands Mordred did not believe he could smite his father so powerfully that he would not be able to seize Excalibur before he died and to kill his bastard.

Therefore Sir Mordred offered him no attack, but rather he greeted him courteously, saying, "King Arthur, sire of Britain and myself, good day."

"Mordred," said King Arthur, "thou shouldst know that Mark hath gone home to Cornwall. I urge thee to urge thine Angles and Saxons to do as much and thus to avoid dying today on the blessed soil of Britain."

"Well," said Mordred, "Mark did not travel far, but rather met with great mishap beyond yon hill, and the flower of Cornwall alas! hath withered and died."

"Can this be so?" said King Arthur. "These are most mournful news! For Mark was not a caitiff at heart, but misguided, a victim of his own inordinate humors, but for which he might have been a worthy man." And then seeing Mordred's derisive smile he said, "Yet he brought this unhappy end upon himself! Now, I would avoid further bloodshed here. I have no quarrel with the Saxons, and long ago I drove them from this land and wreaked no revenge on them thereafter. I desire no part of Germany, and if they leave Britain now I shall love them."

"They are poor fellows," said Mordred, "and their land is arid and they have nought to eat at home, and as you can see they have no clothes but coarse hides."

"I see them armored cap-à-pie," said Arthur, "but if they be naked underneath, then we shall furnish them with good British woolens. And from my granaries they may take so much corn as they need; and from my herds, fat beeves and stout ewes. And they may eat their fill and take more food home to Saxony, for I accept thy word for their plight though their breastplates do bulge in massive convexity."

"But food alone doth not make the man," said Mordred, "nor doth clothing which is merely warm meet their need. They would be gentlemen and wear velvet robes and silken hose and gold ornaments."

"Well, I think overmuch of these be effeminate," said King Arthur, "but perhaps so adorned they would be less warlike. Therefore I shall open to them my treasury at Caerleon, for which indeed I have ever had little use, for all Britons are naturally rich, even unto my churls, who till the most fertile soil in the world, and they have no wants the which God doth not supply them, and when early in my reign I sought to abolish serfdom, no serf would leave his master in the entire realm, for he loved him too much."

And Sir Mordred was sickened to hear this, for he knew that it was too true!

And yet he said, "Methinks the lower classes be depraved! Do they not go to fairs and consort with gamesters and strumpets?"

"Yea, they do this sometimes," said King Arthur. "For men in their station require the odd holiday. And while in the zeal of youth I sought to outlaw all debauchery I soon came to understand that in moderation it doth serve a salubrious purpose amongst the lower orders, who can never be expected to live on the stern principles of knights."

"Such as adultery?" asked Mordred. "Yea, that is true! To sin one must be of an higher sensibility, above the herd but below the angels. And do you not hold the very image of Her who was married to the cuckold St. Joseph?"

Now King Arthur was sorely tried by Mordred's blasphemous and obscene taunts, but he was stayed by his own guilty conscience towards his bastard.

"Mordred," said he, "the Germans, and the late Cornishmen as well, are only pawns in thy game with me, I know full well. Thou hast been ill used all thy life, and I regret that with all mine heart! But I believed it needful for my reign not to acknowledge thee as my illegitimate issue. For I did think that the sovereign must be beyond reproach."

And then the tears fell from King Arthur's eyes. "But shalt thou permit me belatedly to give thee that which thou hast been denied all these years? Before my assembled knights I shall acknowledge thee as my son and embrace thee as the first Prince of Wales!"

"Now that your wife hath been proved an whore," asked Mordred, "and your first knight hath crowned you with antlers? I thank you not, Father."

And despite the vileness of this answer King Arthur was touched in the quick of his heart to be so addressed.

"Yea, mine own son," he cried, "I am thy father and I would do anything I could for thee. The very throne of Britain be thine! Mordred, my dear, put down thine arms and send away thy foreign confederates, and I shall abdicate in thy favor."

Now Mordred's own heart leapt, and not in love or in virtuous joy, but rather in the realization that he was now very near to getting the means to kill King Arthur, for he would not that power be given him, but rather he wished virilely to seize it.

Therefore he said, "Well, Father, this is a fine speech and very cunning. But can I trust you to keep your promise if I send my Germans home? For I have learned that power comes only to him who already hath a deal of it, and not to him who is unarmed and naked."

"Nay, my son," said King Arthur. "All power comes from God, and He distributes it through His love."

"Then, Father," said Sir Mordred, "in proof of your love for me shall you dismount and taking your sword from its scabbard lay it upon the ground?"

Now King Arthur, who was sincere in his promise to

abdicate and give his crown to Mordred, and who using all of his faith had come to love him, was nevertheless not yet so trustful of his bastard that he would readily put Excalibur down whilst Mordred stayed mounted and armed before an army of twenty thousand barbarians, whose savage steeds could scarce be restrained during this colloquy. And these horrid Saxons were themselves biting their lips, and the froth at their mouths was bloody, for heated by the slaughter of the Cornishmen they lusted to slay Arthur's fine knights and tear their smoking hearts out and eat them, for these Germans were ferocious as wild beasts.

"Well," said King Arthur, "I trust thee, my dear Mordred, but canst thou control yon bloodthirsty lot? For that reason I did never consort with foreigners much, and when thou hast assumed the throne I urge thee to spurn such alliances with un-Christian folk. Let the British knight, always outnumbered but never vanquished, be sufficient for thy needs."

"Father," said Mordred, "I am afraid that I require some earnest of your good intentions. Else I might think you merely a prating old man, clutching at the shreds of your rule beyond your proper time."

And it was finally this stinging insult, rather than his real or supposed love for Mordred, that caused King Arthur to dismount and to take Excalibur from its jeweled scabbard and to lay it upon the earth.

Now Mordred was so thrilled to see this as to tremble violently in vicious glee. And indeed he was all but shaken from his saddle, and therefore he could not ride down King Arthur with his horse, the which he had planned to do so soon as his father was disarmed. And the king was nearer the sword than he and could pluck it up in a trice and kill him.

Therefore Mordred dismounted and taking out his own sword he threw it at King Arthur's feet.

"Now, Sire," said he, "may I not chide you for your delay? For there, freely given, is mine own earnest! And now I shall send my Germans away." And directing King

Arthur's attention to them he cried to them in the Anglo-
Saxon tongue for to attack and do much killing and gain
much plunder. And King Arthur, who did not understand
this coarse language and knew only melodious British and
the tongue of God, which was Latin, was amazed to see
these Germans give to their horses the heads, and their
charge began.

But quickly he understood that his bastard had tricked
him feloniously, and he turned to seize up Excalibur from
the earth.

But Mordred had acted the sooner, and he already held
the magic sword, and when King Arthur turned to him he
ran his father through the bosom till caught by the hilt the
blade could go no farther.

And then King Arthur fell, with the sword in him, and
it was held so tightly by his muscles and bones that
Mordred could not withdraw it, and therefore Mordred
ran away like the coward he was. And King Arthur's banner, the which displayed an image of the Virgin, fell onto
the ground.

And so the battle began, and when the scribes say it was
started by the sting of a serpent, they were not in error,
for that snake was Mordred.

Now twenty thousand Angles and Saxons charged the
knights of the Round Table, who were in the number of
an hundred eight and forty (for Galahad was ill and sleeping, and Mordred was the foe), but when the charge was
over, ten thousand Germans lay bleeding dead on the gory
field of Salisbury, while but fifty of King Arthur's knights
had fallen, and all of them struck from behind.

And Sir Launcelot, with but his left hand, skewered ten
Saxons at a time on the end of his lance, and then he
hurled them all away dead and he pierced ten more. And
many times he did this. And Sir Percival, who broke his
lance after killing two hundred Germans with it, then
drew his sword and holding it at the level of the neck he
rode along the Saxon ranks lopping off heads as if he were
in a wheat field with a scythe. And soon there were so

many severed heads upon the field and so much blood that a thousand Germans did slip and fall into it and they could not get a footing in their heavy armor and they every one drowned with their snouts in this gore.

Now the horses' hoofs tore all the grass from the field and turned the earth to dust, and a great cloud of it obscured the sun, and the day became night, and the darkness was a place of crashing steel and terrible cries from men and animals, but the dust was settled by the torrents of blood which poured from the bodies when the flesh was hacked and limbs were severed. And when the sun reappeared the field was as a lake of red mud, and everywhere were enmired dead men in whole or in pieces.

And Sir Launcelot's cousins Bors and Lionel killed many hundreds of Angles and Saxons, and Sir Bedivere did fell whole ranks at a time, and Sir Kay did himself kill scores, for being Arthur's knight of least prowess was yet to be a great champion amongst foreigners, and he ran through Saxons as he had once spitted capons.

Yet the dastardly enemy did surround some knights two hundred to one, and while those in front distracted an hero, those behind did hamstring him with axes, and when he fell they filled every part of his body with blades till there was room for no more. And so eventually perished an hundred of the knights of the Round Table, the finest men on earth, who never fought except for the cause of good.

And after three hours there were left only fifty of King Arthur's men, and only one thousand Saxons, and all the horses on both sides had gone down, and all fought on foot.

Now amongst these bodies lay King Arthur, and he was not dead though mortally wounded by the hand of his bastard son Mordred, the most wicked man who ever breathed. And Mordred was hiding behind one of the great stones at Stonehenge, where he watched everybody else killing one another, for this gave him great pleasure, and he looked forward to the hour, which must come soon, when all other noblemen would be dead and he would be unique in his existence, and emperor of all of Britain and Germany as well.

Now lying in his swoon of death King Arthur was visited by the ghost of Sir Gawaine his late nephew.

And seeing him as a shade King Arthur said, "My dear Gawaine, I am unhappy to see thee thus! I had hoped that thou, left behind, might assume the throne when I died, and preserve it against the great felon Mordred."

"Nay," said Sir Gawaine's ghost, "I can do nothing palpably, Uncle, for my body lies rotting and provideth dinner for the worms. I have come to give you spiritual succor."

"Alas!" said King Arthur, "we shall all join thee soon in Purgatory, Gawaine, for methinks we have today gone the noble Pyrrhus one better! For he survived his terrible victory, whereas I am dying. But Mordred liveth!"

"Then you must not die yet, Uncle," said the ghost of Sir Gawaine. "You have one duty left."

"Yea," said King Arthur, "to kill mine own son. Well, I think I can not, Gawaine. Perhaps there was some justice in the triumph of perfect evil over imperfect virtue, which is to say, of tragedy over comedy. For have I not been a buffoon?"

"Uncle," said the shade of Sir Gawaine, "there is no man who hath not believed the same of himself in very bad times, and verily we are all fools for we live but temporarily, and beneath our armor we wear human skin, which is to say, motley. But the difference between a great man and a mere entertainer is that the former doth seek to please no audience but God, and thus he goeth against the mean instincts of humanity: the prevarications of vanity, the sentimentalizing of envy, the cowardice of greed, the slothful molesting of the weak, for all these are to celebrate nothing and to despise everything. And though man be eternally contemptible, he should not be contemptuous of that which he can achieve."

"Methinks I have achieved nothing, Gawaine!" King

Arthur cried. "For amongst our company we had every human failing, and have we been better, except in rhetoric, than these barbarians, in killing whom we die ourselves?"

"Yea!" said the ghost of Sir Gawaine. "For can we not say, without the excessive pride which is sinful, that we lived with a certain gallantry?"

Now despite the grim conditions of this interview King Arthur could not but be some amused by the obsession of Sir Gawaine even as a ghost.

"Dost mean we none of us mishandled ladies?" smiling said he to the shade of his brave nephew.

"What I meant rather," said Sir Gawaine's solemn spirit, "is that we sought no easy victories, nor won any. And perhaps for that we will be remembered."

And then his ghost did vanish, and King Arthur awakened. And he saw about him all the carnage. And he could not rise, for he was so weak, and from his bosom protruded the handle of Excalibur. And again he did swoon, and in his sleep there came to him the Lady of the Lake.

And to her he said, "Lady, surely you have come to take back your sword, the which hath killed me."

But the lady said, "Nay, King Arthur, thou art not dead yet. Thou shalt rise and use Excalibur one time more, and then thou shalt return it to me in the proper way."

"Lady," said King Arthur, "I would ask why you attended me only in the beginning of my reign and thereafter no more? And methinks you led Merlin away as well, leaving me altogether without magical counsel. Lady, I could have used some! For 'twas reality that brought me down, and I had no defense against it."

"King Arthur," said the Lady of the Lake, who was gleaming in white samite, "the passions are not real, but rather fantastic. Thou couldst not have done better than thou didst."

"Yet," said King Arthur, "was I wise to tolerate the friendship between Launcelot and Guinevere for so many years? I know that I thereby connived in a Christian sin."

"Address me not in Christian sentiments," said the Lady of the Lake, "the which I find too coarse for fine kings. Thine obligation was to maintain power in as decent a way as would be yet the most effective, and a Camelot without Guinevere, a Round Table without Launcelot, were inconceivable, as would be an Arthur who put to death his best friend and his queen. All human beings must perform according to their nature."

Now King Arthur did wonder at this speech, and he said, "Then the will is not free? And can we not choose to be either good or evil, but are selected for whichever?"

"This is the wrong question," said the Lady of the Lake, "being political and not concerned with the truth. And do not chide me for abandoning thee, my dear Arthur, for I am here now, and I urge thee to rise and to do what is necessary for the completion of thy legend." And then she vanished in a shimmer of whiteness.

And King Arthur awoke, and from his breast he pulled Excalibur, as he had in the beginning pulled the first sword from the stone, and wondrously he bled no more.

And then he went to look for Mordred.

BOOK XXII

*How Sir Galahad joined the battle and whom he
fought; and how Sir Percival fell; and how King
Arthur fought Sir Mordred; and how the king returned Excalibur to the Lady of the Lake and
then was borne away by three ladies in a barge.*

NOW THROUGH ALL THIS AWFUL BATTLE, Sir Galahad had
lain in a swoon of illness in the wood, and he was not long
for this world, and though he was the greatest knight of all
he had taken no part in this greatest battle of all time.

And there was now only a remnant left of the noble
company of the Round Table, and among them were his
father Sir Launcelot and his best friend Sir Percival, and
brave sirs Lionel and Bors, and that good man Sir
Bedivere, and gallant Sir Kay the seneschal. And all the
other gallant knights were now dead. And of the Angles
and the Saxons there remained three hundred.

Now of Arthur's remaining knights all were wounded
but sirs Launcelot and Percival, and each of these had
killed a thousand Germans without being touched. And Sir
Launcelot, who believed that all of his life had been but a
waiting for this day, was only disappointed to find so few
of the enemy yet standing, for the more fighting he did,
the stronger he grew, and after five hours he had more
prowess than that with which he had begun. And never in
the history of the world had there been such a knight as
Sir Launcelot, and many Saxons fell dead before they felt
his sword, for they could not endure his blazing eyes, and
his armor streamed with the bright blood of his enemies,

and his sword was white-hot and charred the flesh which it cut.

But no one could have seen in what Sir Percival was his inferior, and sometimes Percival would hack one German in twain with his sword whilst seizing another around the neck-armor and breaking off his head in the crook of his mighty arm. And Sir Percival, who was a naïve knight, did take no pleasure nor pain from this fight, but he did merely what he believed he ought to do as a knight of the Round Table. And withal he found time to worry about his sick friend Sir Galahad, and oft, having cleared his portion of the field of Saxons, he went within Stonehenge where Galahad lay and he bathed his friend's head with cool water and he cleansed his chin and breast of the blood he had coughed out. And having done this Sir Percival would return to the fray.

Now at length Sir Launcelot had been so invigorated by the fighting as marvelously to cure the grievous wounds of his right arm, the which he had received from Mordred and then again in the fight with Sir Gawaine, and he was quite whole. And some of the Saxons raised some horses which had fallen, and they remounted and they charged upon the remnant of the knights of the Round Table. And Sir Launcelot from the ground killed one of these mounted Germans, and he took his steed and his lance, the which had a trimming of fur beneath its steel head, and with it he soon slew all of the riders.

Now at just that time Sir Galahad did awaken from his swoon and he heard the din of battle, and though he was grievous weak he knew his duty and therefore he put on his armor, the which was clear and shining, for it had never been used, and he took up his shield, which was pure white and with a red cross upon it, and his horse had been tethered behind the stones, and he mounted it.

And then he rode onto the field, on which there was, far off, but one mounted man amidst a waste of fallen bodies of men and horses, and in the middle distance were a few of King Arthur's knights and they were fighting an horde of Saxons on foot. And Sir Galahad rode his horse carefully through the corses until he found a clear place, and he could see that the other rider was a German from his round shield and his fur-tipped lance, and when he was two hundred yards from him he put his lance in fewter and he spurred his horse and he charged upon him.

Now Sir Launcelot was amazed to see a mounted knight come from nowhere wearing shining armor, for all here, friend or foe, if yet standing were covered with red gore and their armor was all hacked and broken. And soon he came to believe that this knight was the vile Sir Mordred, who had cowardly hidden himself after starting this battle, for he had looked everywhere for him, to kill him so that he could do no more harm to King Arthur. And as if he did not hate him enough, Sir Launcelot was incensed that such a felon would display upon his shield an Holy Cross.

Therefore he put his own lance in the rest and he spurred his beast, and thus the two greatest knights in the history of the world did charge each other, and they were father and son, though neither knew it.

And never did Sir Launcelot have more prowess than at that moment, and never was Sir Galahad weaker, and he had barely the strength to hold himself in the saddle while supporting the lance, yet he persisted in his duty to fight this vicious enemy of virtue (as he mistakenly supposed him).

Now when they met there was such a tremendous shock as to shake the earth so that it cracked open for an instant and the smoke and fumes of Hell poured reeking forth and a near-by river turned to steam and for ten leagues about the trees lost all their bark and their leaves and all the birds were hurled lifeless to the earth, and the giants in the distant mountains were shaken by such a violent tremor that they were transformed into dwarfs (and never afterward was a giant seen in all of Britain). And so far away as at London shooting stars were seen in broad daylight and horses screamed like peacocks and cats did kill and eat dogs.

And Sir Launcelot's lance brake against the red cross of Sir Galahad's shield, but Sir Galahad's steel point went through the ironbound Saxon shield as though it were made of straw, and then it penetrated his father's breast-plate and the chain mail beneath, and through his skin and flesh and bones, and then through his stout heart and tore it from his body.

And Sir Launcelot plunged dead to the earth.

And with this effort Sir Galahad had exhausted all the strength he would ever have, and he fell beside his father and he could not get up.

Now from where he fought afoot, Sir Percival saw this charge and he recognized both knights (for no one sat a horse like the great Launcelot, despite his foreign shield and lance), but Percival was too far away for them to hear his cry of anguish. And therefore he watched Sir Galahad slay his father unwittingly, and then he saw him fall himself. And then Sir Percival went to that place.

"Well, Percival my friend," said Sir Galahad, "I have been of little use here today, God wot!"

"Do not speak so," said Sir Percival. "Thou hast felled thy man! I knew this Saxon, Galahad, when I traveled in Germany, and there was no fiercer knight in all the world. Till now he was invincible."

"Ah, Percival, thou must not tell kind lies to thy dear friend when he is dying," said Galahad.

And Sir Percival did have great grief in his heart, and he cursed himself for his naïveté which made him a poor dissembler.

But then what Sir Galahad said was this. "Nay, Percival, he was not much of a knight, methinks, even for a Saxon, and he put but the tiniest scratch on my shield, whereas I slew him with a lance the which I could hardly keep steady! Nay, my friend, I have done nothing which I should be proud to have my father know of."

And then Sir Galahad coughed terribly and he could hardly breathe thereafter. And then feebly he said, "My dear friend, I had hoped to see my father once before I died. Is he upon the field?"

And striving to keep back his tears Sir Percival held his friend in his arms, and he said, "Yea, Galahad, Sir Launcelot doth live! For where could he ever meet his match on the entire earth! Rest here awhile, for he must deal with the remaining felons, and I must go to join him. Then I shall fetch him to thee."

And Sir Galahad smiled, and he said, "Tell him I could not tarry, and one day I shall kiss him in Heaven." And then he died.

Now Sir Percival knelt between the bodies of his friends and he wept hot tears, and whilst he knelt there in his grief a Saxon came upon him unawares, and he raised his great iron battle-ax as high as he could reach and he brought it down upon the unguarded back of Sir Percival, and he struck him so hard with it that the edge of the blade came out of his breastplate.

And Sir Percival was so sore hurt that he could not rise nor lift his sword, and lying on the ground he seized the ankle of that Saxon, and he squeezed it so hard as to crush the iron greave and then the flesh and the bones therein, and a blackness climbed the German's leg and it went through his entire body and reached his brain, and he rotted throughout his person and he gave up the ghost.

And in his dying moments Sir Percival had so great a strength. And then he went to Heaven to join all of his brave friends.

And soon he was joined by all the remainder of the noble company of the Round Table, for in killing the last Saxons they all but one met death themselves, and that remaining one was Sir Bedivere. And Sir Kay lost his life after becoming the great hero he had always yearned to be, and he was a great seneschal and an incomparable warrior as well!

Now Sir Bedivere, who was wounded in six places but could still walk, did survey the field of blood and he found no one standing to oppose him, and therefore he at last dropped his sword, which from use had been worn down to a little stub. And then he went to look for the body of King Arthur, whom he had seen struck down by Mordred at the beginning of the day, and everywhere he went he saw his dead friends, and each was surrounded by scores of dead barbarians, and where sirs Launcelot and Percival had fought there were thousands of Saxon corses.

But King Arthur was not amongst these dead, for he had arisen after seeing the vision of the Lady of the Lake during his swoon, and he had gone to seek Mordred.

Now seeing his father rise Sir Mordred in great fear had run over an hill and into a valley, and he could flee no farther for this valley was a cul-de-sac the which ended at a sheer precipice which climbed to the sky.

And there he cowered as his father the king came over the hill, and to him King Arthur seemed eight feet high. And in his fear Sir Mordred took off his sword and he flung it far away from him, so that he would be unarmed.

And when King Arthur reached him Mordred cried out that he was defenseless. And to be even more piteous he tore off his helmet and his breastplate, and he bared his bosom.

And he cried, "Father! Shall you kill your only son?"

And King Arthur said, "Mordred, I must."

Then Mordred howled and he wept in great gasps and he fell upon his knees. And raising his clasped hands he implored his father to spare the life which he had created from his loins, and he chided him for the injustice he would do.

"Nay," said King Arthur, "do not speak further of justice, Mordred, for thou hast had thine! Didst thou not get the first stroke, and with mine own sword?"

And now Mordred thought he heard some faint hope in these words and he believed that he might detain his father's hand by clouding his reason.

"Yea, Father," said he, "but was my intention not, by wounding you slightly, to preserve you from this battle in which all others were killed?"

"Nay," said King Arthur. "Thy blow was too fierce."

"Well then," said Mordred, "was it not to prove your immortality?"

"Then thou hast failed," said King Arthur, "for I am dying." And even as he spoke he began to bleed copiously from his bosom.

And then Mordred said smiling, "Yea, Father, I did it so that you might join God and His Son in Heaven, and take the Round Table there with all of your noble knights, for you have done your duty on earth."

And King Arthur lowered his sword that he had raised, and he thought about this, and at length he turned away from Mordred. And seeing this Mordred believed he had convinced him not to kill him, and began to rise from his knees.

But he got only a little way up, for King Arthur had turned only to make a greater swing with Excalibur, and he cut through Mordred's neck so swiftly that his head stayed in place thereafter and his smile did not fade until he opened his lips to thank his father for sparing his life, and only then did the head first tremble slightly, then a great deal, and it wobbled violently and finally it fell from his shoulders and onto the earth.

And then King Arthur climbed the hill and he left that place. And at the top of the hill he met Sir Bedivere, who was the sole survivor of all of his company.

Now King Arthur had gone almost blind, for his death was upon him, and he asked Sir Bedivere to lead him to the lake that was near by. And from him Sir Bedivere concealed his own wounds, which were mortal as well, and he pretended to be hale.

"Yea, Sire," said he, "I shall wash your hurt with the cool water, and doubtless you shall soon be cured."

"Thine arm, Bedivere," said King Arthur, "and spare me thy physic. Nothing is sanguine now, when all is sanguinary."

But Sir Bedivere, who could accept his own mortality, could not believe that his king was dying. Nor did he believe that there was a lake near by, but very soon they reached a height, below which he saw a lake of some magnitude, and he asked King Arthur to rest whilst he went and fetched some water. But King Arthur, who had not sheathed Excalibur again after killing Mordred, now gave that great sword to his only surviving knight, and to him he said, "Fling this, with all thy strength, into the center of the lake."

Now to humor his sick king Bedivere took Excalibur from him, but he then laid it quietly in the grass, and he took up a stone that was there and he threw this into the water below.

And King Arthur could not see him, and when he heard the splash he said to Bedivere, "Tell me what hath happened."

And Sir Bedivere said, "The sword hath fallen to the bottom of the lake."

"O egregious liar!" exclaimed King Arthur. "Hast thou not obeyed thy king?"

And Sir Bedivere hung his head, and he said, "Your pardon, Sire." And picking up another stone, much larger than the other, he threw it into the water. "Now 'tis done, and Excalibur hath gone down amongst the slimy fishes."

And King Arthur had never been so wroth. "O contumacious wretch!" said he. "Twice hast thou disobeyed me criminally!"

Now Sir Bedivere was the most loyal knight who had ever lived, and he was attending his king though so badly hurt he should have died long since.

And he protested, "Great Arthur, abuse me if you will, but I can never discard your Excalibur!"

" 'Twas never mine own," said King Arthur, "but rather it was lent to me for a while, and now I must return it, and then I must return my life, which was on loan as well. Now, Bedivere, thou must do that for which thou shalt be remembered forever."

And with his remaining strength Sir Bedivere picked up Excalibur from the ground and he flung it out over the center of the lake. And as it fell through the air a hand did arise from the water, and its forearm was clothed in gleaming white samite, and it caught the sword, and then it brandished it once as if in triumph, and then hand and sword disappeared beneath the surface of the water and all was as it had been before.

And when Sir Bedivere told King Arthur what had happened the king was satisfied at last.

And he said, "Dear Bedivere, thou hast done the first part of thy last duty. Now it only remaineth that thou conduct me to the shore."

And King Arthur had become so weak that he could no longer walk, and therefore Sir Bedivere, who was himself grievously wounded, must needs take King Arthur upon his back. And so he carried him down to the lake.

And when they reached the shore Sir Bedivere saw marveling that a barge was waiting there, and in this barge were three ladies, and they were veiled in black.

And King Arthur commanded Sir Bedivere to take him on board and to lay him down there, and this he did. And one of these ladies took the king's head into her lap, and another his back, and the third, his legs.

"Loyal Bedivere," then said King Arthur, "forgive me for speaking harshly to thee on the matter of Excalibur, for I know that thou wert no disobedient wretch and that thy reluctance to dispose of the sword was with the best intent. But we are done now with what we did, and I must go away."

And Sir Bedivere made much grief, and he said weeping, "Sire, can it be? We have won the field and our enemies are all vanquished. True, there are but you and me remaining, and I am not much. But you, great Arthur, can collect more knights and fill the Table once more!"

"Nay, Bedivere, not in this phase of the world," said King Arthur, "for there now hath come an end to Britain as we knew it, and in the darkening epoch to come, we should with our chivalrous principles be seen but as a quaint curiosity. The time of the caitiff be upon the world, and who can say when it will end? Dost suppose a Launcelot will come soon again? A Tristram, or a Gawaine? Or a Kay, that great man who by force of will alone made himself a knight of the greatest prowess? Or for that matter, my dear friend, a Bedivere, who dying himself can carry his king down a precipitous slope? When will the world ever again know such a company as that of my incomparable knights?"

And King Arthur stretched out his hand to Sir Bedivere, and he said, "Do not weep, my friend." For though he could not see him he could hear the falling of his tears. "Rather thank God in joy that for a little while we were able to make an interregnum in the human cycle of barbarism and decadence."

And Sir Bedivere clasped King Arthur's hand and then he went back to the shore, and he watched the barge move slowly away, and the lake seemed to stretch into a sea, and a fog came towards the barge and obscured it and the shrouded figures thereupon.

Then Sir Bedivere laid down and died a happy death, for he did not feel that he had lived in futility.

BOOK XXIII

*Of the opinion of some men as to the where-
abouts of King Arthur.*

Now WHERE THE VEILED LADIES took King Arthur was to
the Isle of Avalon, and that isle hath never been found,
and whether he died and was buried or liveth yet, no man
knoweth, though some say he will return when the world
is ready once more to celebrate honor and bravery and nobility, but methinks that is a long time yet.

And some say he is buried and on his tomb doth appear
this legend,

HIC IACET ARTHURUS REX QUONDAM

REXQUE FUTURUS.

And this is hopeful. But as a great knight hath written,
"Yet I woll nat say that hit shall be so, but rather I wolde
sey: here in thys worlde he chaunged hys lyff."

And it can be said that no one, however mean or base,
hath forgotten him, and even amongst the Angles and the
Saxons he is remembered as the greatest king who ever
lived, and to all men he remaineth the virile model.

BOOK XXIV

Of the ladies who carried King Arthur away, and who survived him; and of the moral of this story.

Now TO ALL THE LADIES OF the world Guinevere and Morgan la Fey and the Lady of the Lake are exemplary, and these were the three who took King Arthur away in the barge, the not-so-wicked, the not-so-virtuous, and the supernatural. And as for Queen Guinevere it hath been said that she enclosed herself in the convent of the Little Sisters of Poverty and Pain, where her sister-in-law was the mother superior, but I do not know if this be true, for others say she did become Britomart, who was a female knight of great prowess.

But in these fair laps we must leave King Arthur, who was never historical, but everything he did was true.

Dell Bestsellers